A Vampire Love Story

BroadLit

August 2012

Published by

BroadLit ®
14011 Ventura Blvd.
Suite 206 E
Sherman Oaks, CA 91423

ISBN 978-0-9859596-1-6

Produced in the United States of America.

Visit us online at www.TruLOVEstories.com

To my beloved parents, Inez and Harold Morgan
In this life, and the next.

This book could not have been completed without the recognition and patience of my publishers and mentors, Barbara Weller and Nancy Cushing-Jones. Their insight and expertise brought Aris and friends from a spark of my imagination to a reality with every jot and tittle in place. For all their late night reading and slashing with a red pen, I thank them profusely.

Thanks as well to Ayalla Dollinger and Sheri and Jake Faller for the hours spent in conversation about my vampire world. Their insightful questions and suggestions helped enormously to bring my characters to life.

Thank you to the entire Berman family for their love and support. Larry, you opened the door to Wonderland for me and I am eternally grateful.

I wish to acknowledge my dear, belated friend Teri Kahan who has supported me in everything I have done for the last twenty five years. Without her inspiration and insight, this might just be another unfinished manuscript going to dust on a shelf in the library.

And a most sincere thank you to all my readers who have made the journey into the Catacombs with me and discovered a whole new world of vampires.

Aris Returns

A Vampire Love Story

by Devin Morgan

AN
INFINITY DIARIES
NOVEL

The first novel in a new series.

A BROADLIT BOOK

CHAPTER 1

Sarah yawned, stretching her neck and shoulders. Her muscles felt tight, tense from sitting too long at her computer. It was almost midnight, the witching hour. Her business day was filled with back-to-back sixty minute sessions, but the hard work didn't begin until her last client left her office. The analysis of each session consumed the rest of Sarah's time; the task of transposing her notes and deciphering the code each subconscious mind spoke. She was exhausted at the end of each day but never bored. Every client brought something unique and absorbing to their sessions. They allowed her into the deepest, darkest part of their minds.

Her gaze drifted to the pile of newly printed books stacked neatly on the corner of her desk. The graphics on the cover were stark and clean. "Psychosis and Past Life Regression" by Sarah Hagan. She was proud of her work. Relentless hours of research led her to develop her theory of practice, taking copious notes and reading volume after volume on psychology, psychiatry, hypnotherapy and past life regression. Some regression texts were useless, written by charlatans or people who were looking for escapes and reasons for their unfulfilled lives. But some . . . some were written by scientists and from them and her own client experience, she formulated her particular hypothesis. And there it sat in book form right in front of her eyes.

As she finished stretching, she reached to shut down her computer. She closed the lid to her lap top, unplugged it and slipped it into her brief case. Smiling, she gave in to her own minor obsessive compulsive tendencies, clearing her desk of paper and pens, squaring the book stack perfectly on the corner before she reached to turn off the small bright reading lamp.

Sarah scooted her chair away from her desk, swiveling around to look out the window at the night skyline. She was amazed and grateful for her new found success as author. Just last year her office was one small cramped room, part of a therapy group that occupied a small storefront in a respectable part of town. Now her eyes swept the bright lights of the Chicago night skyline from her office on the fortieth floor of a building with a posh address. The soft burgundy leather furniture and dark, rich mahogany desk and tables were so new they still smelled of the showroom.

Rising from her chair, she crossed to the window. Snowflakes danced in a light wind coming off the lake. The air would be cold as she walked the two blocks to the subway. She was glad she wore boots even though the weather report said no snow for two days. Growing up in Chicago, she learned not to pay too much attention to the weather people. She left the shades open. She placed her brief case and shoulder bag on her desk as she slipped her arms into her black faux fur coat. She buttoned it, tying her cream colored muffler around her neck. She twisted her shoulder length blond curls into a bun, tucking her head inside a cozy black knitted cap. It fit snuggly over her ears.

Gathering her belongings, she stepped into the hallway. Once she locked the door, she tucked her small hands into her lined black leather gloves.

She reached the elevator and just as she pressed the down button, her cell phone rang. It jolted her. Her heart began to race.

Who would call at this late hour? Reaching into the pocket of her purse lining to retrieve it, she was surprised not to find it in its designated place. Her hand dived into the bottom of her bag and just as she touched it, the elevator chimed, the door opened and the ringing stopped.

The elevator was empty. As she stepped in, she recognized some classical version of an old Beatles song playing through the intercom. She opened the phone to read the display. "Colleen Stevens. What in the world is she doing calling me at this time of night?" She tried to get into her voice mail but the elevator and lobby of the building were two places where she received only sporadic cell service.

She was concerned, waiting impatiently, watching each floor number register in a bright digital green. When the elevator reached the lobby, the doors silently opened. She hurried across the large room toward the main revolving door to the street. Snow fell in huge, wet flakes and the wind whistled through the glass panes of the door. A shiver ran through her body at the thought of the walk to the subway.

"Good night Miss Hagan." The security guard gave her a smile that was overtaken by a huge yawn.

"Night Tony. Looks cold out there."

"It sure does. Glad I'm on inside duty tonight."

Stepping close to the entry way, Sarah did her best to access her voice mail while still holding her bag and brief case. With a soft sigh she gave up, placing them on one of the bright patterned chairs arranged in an informal conversation group for visitors. She stripped her gloves from her hands as she sat down.

"Sarah, this is Colleen. I'm at the police station trying to save the butt of one of my parolees. I need your help so please call me as soon as you get this."

Sarah groaned. She wanted to go straight home, but she couldn't ignore the call. Colleen was not only one of her first clients but also one of her closest friends. As she unwrapped her muffler and unbuttoned her coat, she hit the recall button.

After five long, loud rings, Colleen's phone cut to voice mail. "Leave a message and I'll call you back." Short and sweet. Exactly like Colleen.

"It's Sarah. I'm just off work and going to the subway. If it isn't an emergency, call me in the morning. If it is, call me now." She tapped the end button; made sure the phone found its proper resting place in her purse then wrapped up preparing for the cold wind that always whistled down Adams Street.

#

The subway platform was empty except for a young couple locked in a sweet embrace. Sarah smiled as she stepped on the train. It had been a long time since she shared such a tender, loving moment. After her divorce she threw herself into her work. Thinking about other people saved her from falling into the dismal but relatively common roll of "woman close to forty loses husband to woman hardly twenty." Her study and work not only saved her, but opened a door to a new realm of a rare and non-perfect science. Past life regression possessed her. All her waking hours and dreams revolved around times long gone. The subconscious mind amazed her. It often spoke in pictures of the past. It was a thrill when her clients related those pictures to their present lives, when they found the answers they were seeking.

The train rattled as it pulled above ground. Her stop was next. She gathered her bags, buttoning her top button, girding against the wind she knew would be whipping across the platform. The bright lights reflected on the huge snowflakes and the gusts stirred them until it appeared they were falling sideways. The cold air took her breath away. She hurried down the stairs and through the turnstile into the street. Feeling the chill on her face, Sarah quickened her pace driven by the unrelenting Chicago cold. Her toes began to feel frozen despite her boots. She was glad when she reached the entrance to her building.

"Good evening Miss Hagan."

"Hi Ralph." She shivered as she stepped from the winter air into the warmth of the lobby.

"Working late tonight, aren't you Miss?"

"Not nearly as late as you are." She smiled, patting his shoulder as she passed him.

"Have a good sleep," he called as she stepped into the elevator.

She pressed the fourteenth floor, raising her hand in a wave as the doors slid closed.

Once inside her apartment, she kicked off her boots, took off her gloves and unwrapped her muffler. Flipping on the light, she yawned. She hung her coat in the hall closet and as she crossed the living room to the kitchen, the thick pile of the beige carpet felt welcoming to her cold feet. Seeing her breakfast dishes still in the drying rack reminded her she hadn't eaten lunch and as she opened the white cabinet above the sink to put them away, her stomach growled. She rubbed it in a little circle.

"Okay, okay, let's see what we have here." Opening the refrigerator, she peeked in. "What a sad, sad situation."

The all but empty shelves held a couple of old carrots, some cottage cheese and a pint of yogurt. In the back of the top shelf she found some old take-out Chinese that was growing a science project. Her stomach rumbled again. "Hush! You're just going to have to wait 'till morning. I'll take you out to breakfast." A long plaintive protesting grumble was the only answer.

#

Sarah sat in the restaurant savoring the huge plate of scrambled eggs and potatoes in front of her. She took her first sip of the strong black coffee in her cup. The deli was her usual breakfast place.

Many days breakfast was the only meal she had time to eat so she always ate heartily. The food at Saul's was simple, delicious. There was plenty of it and it was close to her office. Today Ruth was her waitress. All of the women working at Saul's had been there since the restaurant opened. Several of them had the pinkish hair that happens when red dye goes over snow white strands. Their uniforms were harvest gold with brown bib aprons and they all had their name tags pinned to the lacy handkerchiefs they wore on their lapels.

She lifted her fork to attack the eggs when her cell phone rang. She fully intended to ignore it until after breakfast but she made the mistake of looking at the caller ID.

"Colleen. Damn!" She put her fork down then answered the phone. "What's up?"

"Are you at Saul's deli?"

"Yes, why?"

"I'll be there in ten minutes. I need your help."

"What's up Colleen?"

"I'll tell you when I get there." Suddenly, there was silence.

Sarah replaced the phone on the table. She hurried to finish her breakfast before Colleen descended on her with more energy than she was ready to deal with on an empty stomach.

#

"It's colder than a well digger's butt in Alaska." Colleen slid into the booth opposite Sarah, shaking the melted snow off of her spiky black hair. "In December." Her dark rimmed glasses fogged when she came in from the cold. She removed them to clean them with a napkin lying on the table.

"Maybe if you wore a hat . . . "

"In a snowstorm."

Sarah laughed, signaling Ruth to bring her friend a cup of coffee.

"Okay Colleen, what's up? What was the phone call at midnight last night?"

"It's a whole story. Are you in a hurry?" Still cold from her walk to the restaurant, Colleen rubbed her hands together then looked at her watch. She saw her own brown, bloodshot eyes reflected in the crystal. The sight reminded her why she was already on her tenth cup of coffee of the morning. And it was only eight o'clock. "I'll never sleep again," she said as she pulled the mug closer to her, wrapping her cold hands around the warm ceramic surface.

"What are you talking about? You're not making any sense."

"I know; I've been up all night. Okay." Colleen unzipped her jacket. She slipped it behind her, tucking it around her shoulders as she realized the deli was not as warm as it normally was. "Are they conserving on energy here or what?" She waved at Ruth to warm her coffee and gave her a tight lipped smile as the waitress filled her cup to the very brim.

She muttered under her breath. "Thank you, thank you. Now I'll burn myself for sure. And I won't ask you to fill my cup again." She looked at Ruth to see if she had been listening. "Like that wasn't the plan."

"C, quit complaining or complain loud enough for Ruth to hear, not just me. Okay?"

"Sorry, just really tired." Her grin was sheepish. She stirred her coffee for a very long time before she raised her eyes. She laughed out loud when she saw the scowl on Ruth's face.

"Will you please concentrate?" Sarah exhaled loudly in mock exasperation. Colleen was highly fragmented. Her personality resembled the spikes in her hair. Extremely intelligent, she was able to handle being all over the place just fine. It was those around her who might have a bit of trouble.

"Oh. Okay. Well, I wanted to talk to you about this young guy who is one of my parolees." She sipped her coffee, made a face then poured more cream into the cup. "This guy is a special case. He's been in and out of trouble since he was in juvenile hall. Now he's twenty five and on parole for grand theft auto." She stirred the coffee, tapped her spoon against the side of the mug, then put it back on the table. "I caught him carrying a blade. If I report it, it's a violation."

"So?"

"Good coffee here." Colleen tipped her head toward the mug as she placed it next to the spoon, pausing only a moment before continuing her original thought. "He's been clean for a year, I know that. And he's really smart. I mean smart, Sarah." She played with her napkin for a moment in silence then raised her gaze to meet the eyes of her friend. "I don't know what else to do for him." Her voice had a pleading tone. "I just can't reach him. It's as if he doesn't care what happens to him." The look on her face was one of honest concern.

Sarah knew what Colleen was intimating, but she wasn't sure she wanted to work with an ex-con. She hesitated a moment, then spoke. "This is a little out of my line of expertise if you're suggesting what I think you are, C."

Colleen scooted to the edge of the bench seat, "Look Sarah, I've read your book and I think it's brilliant. I think that maybe if we hit this guy from a different angle, we may be able to figure out what's going on with him. I can't get anything out of him; he just keeps it all inside." She drained her cup as she signaled for the waitress corps to come do their duty. Ruth balked at having to return to the table once again, but thought better of it. "You get into people's heads; you know what to say. Maybe he'll talk to you." She smiled. "So, how about a little pro bono work?"

Sarah looked at the check the waitress placed under her mug, pulled her wallet out of her purse, then slipped her credit card under the bill. "I don't know Colleen. I've never worked on a case like this one."

"Why don't you just meet him? After that, decide what you think. It's worth a try, isn't it? Come on, Sarah."

"Well, I'm really not sure but I guess there's no harm in a consultation. Have him call to make an appointment and we'll see how it goes. I'm not promising anything."

Colleen smiled, "Thanks for the coffee." Sarah nodded returning the grin, glad to make her friend happy so early in the morning. "And thanks for helping Carlos. His name is Carlos Havarro."

"Carlos Havarro, huh? Nice name. I'll let you know what happens."

Sarah toyed with her cup a moment before she spoke again. "I had that dream again last night."

Colleen leaned forward. "You mean the one where you wake up with the guy standing in your bedroom?"

"Yeah, except this time he was right next to the bed and he didn't have a shirt on. It's really disconcerting to wake up in a dream in your own bed and still be dreaming."

"I've done that a couple of times. I know what you mean."

"That's all. He was just standing there. I just think it's kind of strange, that's all, C."

"Could you make out who it was this time?"

"No, it's too dark but I could see an athlete's torso outlined against the light from the window. Whoever it is, he's something to look at."

Colleen chuckled then spoke. "Sarah, have you and Steve done the deed yet?"

Her friend's cheeks turned pink as she replied. "No, not yet."

"For God's sake, what are you saving it for? You've been dating a few months already. I mean I don't particularly like the guy but obviously you do."

"That's just it. I like him okay but in all the time we've been seeing each other, we're hardly alone. We're either on a business dinner or he's exhausted from work." She sipped her coffee. "I just don't feel I really know him well enough to sleep with him."

"Hon, you're thirty seven years old. You've been married and divorced. What in the hell is wrong with just getting laid?"

"I know I'm a bit provincial."

Colleen laughed out loud. "A bit?"

"Okay, a lot. I'm just not ready to be vulnerable like that again."

"Yeah, well Steve reminds me of that narcissistic ex-husband of yours. Knocking boots with Jeff wasn't so great and I doubt it'd be any better with Steve." She slipped her arms into her jacket sleeves. "Maybe you should just carry on with your dream man for a while until a hunk with some real blood in his veins comes along"

CHAPTER 2

Sarah walked to the door of her office. Her three-times-a-week assistant, Maggie, was sitting just outside at her desk with her computer tuned to a shopping site. "Maggie, do I have a one o'clock or can I go for lunch today?"

Maggie put the roll of oatmeal cookies aside then pulled up the client schedule for the day. "Sorry Sarah, you do have a one o'clock. It's Colleen's little pal, Carlos."

"That's right. Did she email his information to us this morning? I left her three messages yesterday."

"Yeah, it just came through."

Sarah looked at her watch. "Great, now I've got a whole half hour to read up on him." She sighed. "Just put the phone on voice mail and go ahead to lunch. I've got the fort."

"Thanks." Maggie shut down her computer, grabbed her purse from her desk drawer, then headed into the hall.

"Maggie, bring me a salad." Sarah called after her, hoping she would be heard above the ding of the elevator. "Okay. Carlos here I come." She closed the door going back to her office and her computer.

Sitting at her desk, she kicked off her shoes. She brought the file onto the screen. "Ah, Carlos Havarro. Okay, twenty five. In trouble most of his life." She read in silence for several minutes then leaned back in her chair. She gazed at the ceiling thinking how different his case was from any she had worked on before. Would she be able to help him? Would he open up to her? She understood anger management, but his wasn't the usual textbook case.

Suddenly Maggie stepped though her door wearing a huge smile. "Sarah, I just got back and there's a young guy outside. He's the infamous Carlos and he is gorgeous."

"Maggie, don't worry about his gorgeousness. Just ask him to come in." She slipped her feet back into her high heels.

When Carlos walked through the door, Sarah was surprised. He didn't look like a convict. In fact, he was indeed gorgeous. Tall with black silky hair. Eyes so dark they had a purple cast to them, eyelashes so long and thick they looked like brushes. His cheekbones were strong and high, his skin, golden. His lips were indescribable, thick, shapely and smooth with a perfect cupid's bow. How could the face of a Botticelli angel be in so much trouble?

"Hi Carlos. I'm Sarah. Come in and have a seat." Appearing more confident than she felt, she shook his hand then directed him to sit in the consultation area. The seating space was designed to feel like a living room. A few chairs, a coffee table and small sofa created a comfortable, homelike atmosphere. Her clients opened up more readily when there wasn't a desk separating them from her.

He moved to one of the wing back chairs. He sat slumped down with his legs straddled, his hands folded in his lap. He wore torn baggy jeans and a black leather jacket over a hooded black sweatshirt. He rested his elbows on the arms of the chair He looked Sarah directly in the eye. "So what do we do now?"

Sarah crossed her legs feeling uncomfortable at his direct stare. "Carlos, you and I are going to see if we can work together to get some control of your life. Colleen says that interests you. Does it?"

Carlos looked at Sarah. His thoughts were completely out of

context. "Good lookin' woman. Nice legs."

"Carlos, does it interest you?"

"Uh huh, yeah. I'm interested."

"Do you mind if I record this session?"

"No, go ahead. Record away."

"Alright." As she pressed the button on the little hand held recorder she used for sessions, she cleared her throat. "First of all, I'd like to tell you a little bit about clinical hypnosis."

#

"How did it go?"

"Good grief C, he just left my office five minutes ago. Can I have a few minutes to reflect?" Sarah tucked the phone between her chin and her shoulder. She needed both her hands free to staple several papers she meticulously stacked together. "It went fine. It was just our first session."

"Yeah but what did you find out?"

"I just told you, it was our first session. What do you expect? I explained the process and took him into a hypnotic state." She placed the papers in a file folder, opened her desk drawer then tucked the folder between two others. She shut the drawer. Holding the receiver in her hand again, she spoke. "I still don't know about this but it looks like he could be a great subject. And you're right; it appears he's very bright. He asked some very thoughtful, pointed questions while I was explaining the science behind the state of hypnosis."

"Yeah but do you think you're going to be able to help him?"

"From the looks of the information you emailed me, he needs all the help he can get." Sarah checked her calendar. She was finished with work for the day. "Do you want to meet for a glass of wine? We could talk then."

"Sure, I'm right around the corner from The Bistro. Is that alright?"

"Okay, it'll take me a few minutes to shut down but I'll be there as soon as I'm able to get out of here. I have to call Steve before I leave."

Sarah could imagine the look on her friend's face as she heard Colleen sigh. Steve was always polite when the three of them had been together, but Colleen still didn't like him.

"Fine, I'll order you a merlot. See you there." Once again, silence on the other end of the line as Colleen hit the end button on her cell.

Sarah stood, smoothing the soft wrinkles in her skirt created by sitting at a desk all day. As she looked out her window, she saw the sky was still light outside even though it was late afternoon. A pale winter setting sun peeked through the dirty gray clouds. She was glad to see a little sunshine after such a cold, gloomy few weeks. She slipped into her suit jacket as she picked up the phone. Hitting speed dial, she waited as the phone on the other end rang and rang. Finally it was answered. A deep male voice spoke, "Hi babe. I'm on the other line. Got to cancel dinner tonight. Let me call you back." He shut down his phone before she had a chance to answer.

Making plans to be with Steve had been difficult from their first date. His work as a prosecuting attorney kept him busy; too busy for them to see each other very often. "Just as well he can't make it," she thought. "That'll make C happy."

Packing her brief case and bundling up against the cold outdoor temperature delayed her just long enough for him to return her call.

"Sarah, sorry. I was trapped on a conference call. I apologize about tonight. I'm just buried in paper."

"That's okay. I'm meeting Colleen for a glass of wine at The Bistro. We'll just make it into an early dinner as well." She had expected him to be too busy. He cancelled more times than not. Oddly, she found herself relieved. As much as she wished for a great relationship, she knew Steve was not the man of her dreams.

"Have fun. I'll make it up to you soon." She could tell he covered the mouth piece on the phone but she still heard him speak to his secretary. "Tess, get Zack on the phone and cancel your plans for this evening. We're working late." He spoke to Sarah, "Sorry but I have to go. Talk to you soon."

He hung up the phone again before she could say goodbye. She picked up her things then walked out the door of her office.

"Maggie, we're through for the day. Pack it in and go home."

#

The noise in the bar was deafening. The Bulls were playing and every basketball fan in Chicago seemed to be clustered around the big screen television rooting for the home team.

"Let's get a table and have dinner. I can't hear myself think here much less talk." Sarah grabbed her belongings and Colleen's arm. She pushed her way through a mass of men juggling for a closer position to the TV. Unlike the bar, the restaurant was only marginally busy. The hostess was able to seat them immediately.

Colleen looked at the menu but Sarah already knew what she wanted to eat. "Want to split a large skinny pizza?"

Colleen shrugged. "Sure, sounds good." She made a funny face, "But no anchovies."

"Okay, no anchovies." Sarah raised her arm to get the attention of the waitress. When she came to their table, they placed their order.

"Spill it Sarah. How was the session?"

"I guess you won't let it rest until we talk it out. It went fine. Considering."

"Why are you making me ask this stupid question? Considering what?" Colleen shifted in her chair. Turning, she spoke to the man seated at the table behind her. "Could you scoot in a little pal? You're practically sitting in my lap." The man rolled his eyes but moved his chair closer to his table. It was a rare person that didn't pay attention to Colleen. Even though she was petite, her friend could be a little scary looking sometimes with her multiple ear piercings and a few obvious tattoos. And her attitude, which could be considered quite abrasive most of the time if you didn't know her, was always directly to the point.

"Must be her job," Sarah thought.

She said, "Considering his background. It looks to me like he has been battling with his fists since he was a pre-teenager." She took a sip of her wine. "I guess that's probably true with a lot of your parolees."

"You got that right. Most of these guys don't know how to communicate with anything other than their fists. It starts when they're real young and just gets worse. Carlos' father, and I use the word loosely, more like a sperm donor, was a real case. He beat up his wife and Carlos' little brother all the time. Drink and batter. That was his M.O. Anyway, he pounded them once too often and even though Carlos was a little kid, he fought back. You can imagine the brutality that brought out from a drunk. Strange thing though, his family wasn't from the hood. The father worked a full time job and did well financially. It was just his after-hours activities that condemned anyone in his line of fire."

The pizza arrived. They both asked for another glass of wine.

"Go on. He didn't tell me anything about his childhood. There wasn't anything about it in his file. I didn't want to get into it the first session. I want to build some trust first."

"Sorry hon, but that isn't going to be easy. He's been screwed over by just about everybody that has come in contact with him. While he was still a teenager his mother took him to a therapist. She pronounced him bi-polar. That was real great for his self-esteem. All it did was give him an excuse to just cut loose and go nuts. This guy is no more bi-polar than I am. He's just pissed off at the world. Wouldn't you be if you were a human punching bag for a drunk from the time you started to walk?"

Sarah thought of her own father. He had been difficult but it was only because he truly thought he knew best. He had been controlling but it wasn't from anger or ill will. He shouted at her but had never raised his hand to her. He even met with the father of her best friend in high school when he found out she was being beaten at home. Sarah's desire to help was what inspired her to pursue psychology as her life's work. What a long time ago that seemed.

"Are you in there?" Colleen leaned in toward her friend and cocked her head to one side. "Hey!"

"Sorry, anyway, the abuse thing wasn't in the file you sent me."

"Naw, the court doesn't care if a parolee was abused or not." She looked down at her napkin. "But I do. This guy could be something and have a real life. Not just living in the gutter."

Sarah knew Colleen was thinking about her own damaged childhood. She wasn't sure that regression therapy would help Carlos. She still questioned if she wanted to work with someone with a police record; even though there was no violence involved, the situation frightened her. But, she overcame her trepidation to support her friend. "Well C, we'll see if we can't help him do just that." She winked and smiled putting her personal concerns behind her. "It couldn't help that he's absolutely beautiful, could it?"

"I won't lie. It makes me cringe to think of a face like that behind bars." They both laughed and took a bite of pizza. Colleen put on a solid show, appearing hard as nails on the surface but Sarah knew her very well. Her unyielding, harsh attitude built a solid wall to protect her sensitive, soft hearted nature from the world where she worked and lived.

"Anyway, what do you think little Miss Deep Sleep? Will you be able to help him?"

"I won't know for a while but we'll see. Like I said, he's a good subject." She finished her wine, wondering where his subconscious would take them on the journey into his past life.

CHAPTER 3

"The only client you have this afternoon is Gorgeous Havarro." Maggie smiled and winked.

"Don't you mean Carlos? And anyway, aren't you a little too old to be panting after some guy in his mid-twenties?"

"I just bought a tee shirt that says 'Cougar Airlines. Fly me'."

Sarah laughed, "Some cougar you are. Close the door and just leave me alone."

Maggie placed her hand on her ample bosom right over her heart. She shook her head. "How can you break an old lady's heart like that? He may like a more vintage woman."

"You're all of thirty six. Close the door and let me get back to work." She loved Maggie's over-the-moon sense of humor. There was always a lot of laughter in the office on the three days her assistant was at work.

Sarah heard the door click shut as the phone rang.

"Hi babe, got a minute?"

"Sure Steve. What's up?"

"How about dinner next week. Do you have some time? I owe you one at The Bistro."

Sarah thought it over. One more try, it was worth at least that much. "Sure. Sounds good."

"I have to work all weekend but I'll call you on Monday as soon as I see what will work for me." She heard a phone ring in the background.

"Fine. Talk to you then." She heard his good bye faintly as he picked up the other phone. Staring out the window, she wondered why she always picked unavailable men. "Do I do it just to keep me safe? What am I afraid of?"

The door of the office opened. Maggie leaned into the room, a huge smile spread over her face. She winked at Sarah. "Mr. Havarro is here to see you."

Sarah shook her head glad Maggie didn't know all the hard facts about Carlos. She grinned at her assistant wondering if she would be so smitten if she did. "Just send him in Maggie." Sarah appeared much more confident than she felt at dealing with a convict. He appeared peaceful enough however his police record proved that untrue.

Maggie disappeared. In her place stood her six-foot-two inch client. His hair was tidy. His jeans weren't torn and didn't hang down below the band on his underwear. He looked as if he cleaned up a bit before their appointment. "Or maybe he's just back from court," she thought.

"Hi Carlos. Come in."

"Where do you want me? At the table or in the sleep chair?" He motioned to the recliner that rested across the room.

Sarah noticed a slight Spanish accent when he spoke. She hadn't recognized it in his first visit but it was quite clear this time. "Let's begin at the table."

They sat across from one another. "Would you like some water?"

"No, I'm good."

"Alright" She glanced at the folder in her lap. "I've been reading the file sent to me by the court. You're quite a fighter, aren't you?"

"Maybe." He frowned at her question. "When I have to be." He leaned forward in his chair. His voice was soft, intimidating. "And what the hell does that matter to somebody like you?"

Her stomach tightened. Thoughts flew through her head faster than light. Why was she doing this? She was so out of her own element with him. But she was a trained professional. She couldn't let Colleen down. This time she couldn't give up. She must move forward.

Ignoring his angry answer, she took a deep breath. She continued. "It seems you have been pushed to it quite a few times. Want to talk about it?"

He was silent for a moment. When he answered his tone was blatantly hostile, his words clipped. "Nope. Why don't you just knock me out and do your thing."

Sarah was disconcerted by the surly attitude Carlos was presenting even though it was more in tune with his parole profile. He had been polite and agreeable during his first visit. His initial reaction to her and the therapy program she suggested was positive. She had been confident their sessions would continue in the same vein, however, his mood today proved different. Not wanting any kind of interaction he could misconstrue as confrontation she decided to go along with him.

"Fine." She rose to move across the room. Sitting in the straight back chair resting near the leather recliner, she gestured toward him. "You'll need to move over here."

Carlos sat down. He leaned back in the recliner, closing his eyes. "It felt good when you put me out last time. I felt real calm and I like that."

"Good" she crossed her legs. "Now, begin to focus on your breath."

#

"Fully relaxed, you begin to move down the stairs and with each step, you become even more relaxed. More at peace. More calm. As you step off the last step, there is a door in front of you. It's a huge wooden door that has large brass hinges and an ancient latch. This door will lead us back through time to a different place; a place where you were a different person with a different life. In a moment when you are ready, you will step through that door and it will be revealed to you."

Sarah stared at the face of the handsome young man watching for the physical signs of his hypnotic state. He appeared to be deeply responsive to all her suggestions.

"If you are ready to move forward, nod your head yes for me." Very slowly his head moved up and down. "In your imagination, you step to the door. You open it. It is very heavy and swings open slowly. On the other side is a forest. It is a wild forest. Tall trees with enormous thick trunks and dense, dark green leaves shield the vine covered ground from the sun. Brambles and bushes surround you. A thick, gray mist hovers over the soft earth making the air cool and moist."

A strange smile played with the corners of his lips as she continued. "In the distance you see a path through the trees and you walk to it, beginning to follow it. The light grows dimmer yet you feel very safe and secure. The deeper you move into the forest, the more relaxed and calm you feel, the deeper your hypnotic sleep.

"There are sounds in the forest and they are calming and peaceful. You move forward hearing the muffled shuffle of your own feet on the path. And the deeper you travel into the forest, the deeper the sleep."

Leaning forward, she watched the movement of his eyes behind his eyelids in order to gauge the depth of his trance. She couldn't help noticing the shadows of his eyelashes on his cheeks, the faint circles beneath his eyes.

"As you travel forward you see the forest thinning and in the distance, a faint light, then a clearing. As you near the clearing, you see a structure. Can you see it? If you can, nod your head for me."

Again, the faint movement of his head as he answered her request.

"Can you tell me what you see?"

He was silent for a moment as if he were remembering how to speak. "*Yes, I see a castle.*" His voice was the same yet different. Deeper. More resonant. His accent had changed. There was a distinctly British ring to his words. "*It is Hever Castle.*"

"Where are you?"

"*I am in England.*"

"What is the year?"

"*It is 1529.*"

Her eyes opened wider in wonder. "And what are you doing in England?"

"*I have been summoned to Kent by Anne Boleyn, the mistress of King Henry VIII.*"

Tudor England. How strange that this young man from the city would see Tudor England.

"Why has she summoned you?"

"*I know not. I have yet to speak with her.*"

"Are you walking?"

"*No, I am seated on my horse.*"

"Who are you?"

"*I am one of the King's knights. A warrior. A hero. One of the undead.*"

Sarah hesitated, bewildered. "Undead? Tell me more."

"*I shall speak no more this day.*"

"Who are you?" The room was silent except for his slow, gentle breathing. "What is your name?"

"I'm Carlos Havarro." His words were slow, his speech stilted.

"Tell me more of your time in England?"

"I've never been to England." His Spanish accent returned.

It was obvious to her he was back to present day. She glanced at her watch, realizing the regression had been short yet quite clearly successful. After a thoughtful moment, she decided to bring him out of hypnosis to continue talk therapy.

"I will count from zero to five. When I reach the number five you will open your eyes, wide awake and feeling fine. One, coming up, feeling your breath move in and out of your body. Two, being more aware of the recliner beneath you. Three, experiencing the movement of the air currents in the room. Four, completely focused inside your body. Five. Eyes open, wide awake."

Slowly his eyes opened as he turned his head to look at her. There was a strange, puzzled look on his face as he sat up in the chair. Then he grinned.

#

It was past eight o'clock when Sarah glanced at her watch. After taking a sip of the cold Earl Grey tea sitting on her desk, she completed her notes in everyone else's file before she opened his. He intrigued her as much as he made her nervous. His incredible masculine beauty. His childhood. His emotional battles. His past life regression. What had he meant by undead? She heard the term in old vampire movies and she knew that present day movies about them were all the rage. The media was bombarded with films, television programs and one book series after another. Had he really been under or was he just playing with her?

"No, he had all the signs of a deep hypnotic state," she spoke quietly to herself. "What in the world is his subconscious telling me?"

Reading over her notes from their talk therapy session a third time, she was still unable to make a logical connection that would link him with England.

His parents were both born in Mexico and even though his

paternal grandparents were incredibly wealthy, it was in no way similar to a royal court. Besides, his mother was of peasant stock and they left Mexico long before Carlo's birth so he wasn't exposed to the affluence of the family. She was lured forward by the mystery of his regression.

She closed the file, shutting down for the day. As she turned out the light and locked the door she was glad it was Friday. At the same time, she wished she didn't have to wait another week to see him. His past police record made her uneasy working with him yet she didn't really feel he was physically dangerous and the story he was telling was more than unique. She couldn't forget the odd look he had given her when she brought him back to real time. Bewildered and strangely compelling.

#

Shutting off the light, Sarah pulled the covers over her shoulders and nestled into her pillow. She was tired but couldn't sleep. The session with Carlos played over and over in her mind. She was still wondering at his reference to the "undead" when her mind finally quieted and she drifted off.

A sound close by roused her. Her dream vision was with her once more. Standing next to her bed, his broad shoulders were outlined by the moonlight coming through her window. She sighed, giving herself over to the enchanted fantasy.

His large hands reached to slide the comforter to the foot of the bed. She was amazed at their gentleness as he leaned toward her to stroke her hair. Shadow obscured his features but she could see the soft thick hair that barely touched his shoulders was light in color. His fragrance was overpowering, a scent warm and mysterious, woody and primeval, an aroma that wrapped around her as he sat beside her. She prayed she would not awaken.

They were in silence as his hands caressed her face, her neck. She shivered with pleasure. Slowly, he lowered his lips to press them to the hollow at the base of her throat. Gentle kisses traced her chin to find their way to the corner of her mouth. His was lush, his breath warm and sweet. She felt her heart quicken.

Tender hands massaged her shoulders then leisurely began to unbutton the top of her pajamas. Sliding his arm behind her, he lifted her until she was sitting in bed. He slid the soft fabric from her body then dropped it to the floor. He laid her down into her soft pillows. Her breasts were round and inviting. The pounding of her heart was answered by a deeper pulsing that began in a dark place inside of her.

His hands cupped her breasts and his lips found the deep valley between them.

The shrill sound of the alarm brought her wide awake, her heart exploding in her chest. As she reached to turn it off, she halted in mid-move. There, lying on the floor next to her bed was the top to her pajamas. She gasped as her hand hit the alarm button and the room became silent except for her panting breath.

CHAPTER 4

Sunday morning was her favorite. Her weekly ritual was to laze around her apartment, drinking coffee while she read the paper. Sitting on the beige living room sofa facing the sliding glass door, she was cozy and warm as she watched the snow accumulate on the patio. The cold wind blew it into a small drift against the window glass. She propped her feet on the light oak coffee table, picked up the paper and began to skim the weekend segments. Avoiding the headlines, she went straight to the calendar section. The cover showed a photo of a handsome young couple at a movie premier. "More vampire stuff. I can't get away from it, even in the paper."

Carlos had been on her mind since their session and here it was again. Vampire. She turned to the review of the film. On a whim she decided to spend the cold, dreary afternoon in the dark of a movie theatre seeing just what the fascination with the Goth world was. She didn't want to wait until evening to be surrounded with teenage girls swooning over the sexy young actor. Checking the film schedule, she found there was plenty of time before the matinee.

After folding the paper carefully making sure she didn't create any new creases, she placed it on the coffee table, then picked up her cup and carried it to the kitchen. Sarah washed and dried her dishes, carefully placing them in the cupboard so all the cup handles faced in the same direction. She smiled as she looked around her. There were baskets hanging from the ceiling and fresh basil and dill hung drying from the handles on the blond wood cupboards. She loved her new home but the kitchen was one of her favorite rooms. She turned off the light then went to her bedroom.

Tilting her blinds to give privacy, she prepared for her shower. Stripping out of her blue and white stripped flannel pajamas, she folded them neatly, tucking them under her fluffy white pillow keeping her life and world in neat order.

The skylight in the bathroom opened to the dull gray early afternoon clouds, casting shadows on her face as she looked into the mirror. She leaned closer to examine the fine lines around her blue eyes. "Not too bad for a vintage woman," she repeated Maggie's words to herself then opened the shower door to turn on the hot water. As she glanced at her body in the full length mirror on the wall, she was quite happy with her reflection. "Working out is miserable but it pays off." She smiled at her newfound vanity. The gym was one of the many new facets to her life after her divorce.

Working out helped her lose the fifteen pounds she added during her marriage, and her therapy with Bonnie helped bring back the balance that had been missing in her life for such a long time. During her marriage, her husband was always a priority to her. The unfortunate issue was that Jeff was also the priority to himself. For many years, he came first to both of them.

Accepting their marriage was one sided, she determined to stick it out; to make the best of it. She actually thought they were doing well. When he asked for a divorce telling her he loved someone else, she was sincerely shocked. Questioning her ability to see the truth about Jeff when it was right in front of her all the time, she began to question her ability as a therapist. Bonnie's insight and therapeutic expertise put her on a journey to finding her confidence once again. It had been a difficult process.

At last, the success of her book and the recognition by her peers was a rite of passage, a symbol of her own personal success in finding herself again. Once again she saw her work affect her client's lives, changing them for the better. Now, working with Carlos was another step. His situation was one she had never experienced; it frightened and intrigued her at the same time.

Sighing, she stepped into the shower. The water was steaming as she scrubbed her skin with a soft brush. She rinsed the soap then lathered her hair. Sunday was a day when she just went natural. No hair dryer. No makeup. No heels. Just jeans, warm boots and a roomy, soft sweater. She loved it. After she used a squeegee on the glass walls of the shower stall, she stepped onto the white bath mat. She dried herself, shook her towel then folded it neatly. Her hair curled around her ears in soft, damp ringlets.

She finished dressing with plenty of time for a cup of tea before the movie. The steam rising from the cup carried the smell of apples and cinnamon to her nose as she curled up on the sofa. Reaching for the paper, she opened it to the health section.

#

The line for the show trailed around the corner as Sarah stamped her feet to keep warm. She was glad when it began to move slowly. Finally able to enter the building, she stopped at the counter to buy a small box of popcorn and a bottle of water. She was surrounded by a novel excitement emanating from all the young girls and women standing in line with her. Surprised at the number of women past their youth waiting along with all the high school girls, she couldn't help but wonder what it was about a teenage vampire movie that could interest such a broad spectrum of females.

After paying the young man behind the counter, she grabbed napkins. As she opened the door to the darkened theatre, loud music from the advertising trailers blasted her ears. She climbed the stairs, easing past a group of girls to a single empty seat in the center of the row.

Just as she settled down, took off her coat and popped the top off the water bottle, she recognized Carlos taking a seat in the row two up from hers. He was alone looking a bit uncomfortable being surrounded by nothing but young females. Smiling to herself, she wondered what he was doing there on a Sunday afternoon. It didn't seem to be the type of film that would interest him. He appeared to her to be more of an action/adventure type than a teen vampire falls for a teen human type. But, there he was, his handsome face reflected in the flickering of the refreshment counter advertisement. Slowly the dim overhead lights were extinguished and the theatre grew very dark. She found a comfortable position in her seat letting Carlos slip from her mind as the movie began.

#

The sky was dark. Ominous clouds covered the city signaling more snow on the way. Sarah reflected on the plot of the movie as she bundled her blue muffler close around her throat. As she hurried from the theatre, street lights came on.

"Miss Hagan? Sarah?"

She stopped suddenly, startled to hear someone call her name. She turned quickly and there, right behind her stood Carlos. Her body stiffened, her heart raced. Forcing herself to relax, she took a deep breath. The neighborhood was well lit and their last meeting ended on a much more friendly note than when it began. Besides, Colleen had assured her he wasn't dangerous, just a very troubled young man who needed some guidance.

"Hey, what're you doin' at this movie? It isn't what I'd think a shrink would like?"

"I could say the same thing to you, Carlos?"

He laughed, "I guess you could, couldn't you." His teeth were white against his golden skin; his eyes sparkled as he grasped her elbow to help her off the curb. His gesture shocked her. She wasn't quite sure she appreciated his familiarity. But when he held her in a gentle hand to guide her carefully across an icy patch of concrete, she realized she was seeing another unexpected side of him. "You in a hurry? Want to grab a coffee?" He motioned toward a diner just across the street.

She knew he was an ex-con but, for some strange reason, she wasn't afraid of him. She experienced a brief confusion at the warmth she felt having him by her side. "Sure, I mean, I'm not in a hurry. Coffee sounds great."

He held onto her arm as they crossed the street but as soon as they reached the opposite curb, he released her. The spot where his fingers had been felt suddenly cold. "What the hell is that," she thought. He held the door for her and his eyes met hers. Feeling embarrassed by her thoughts, she stared at the ground in front of her as she walked into the restaurant.

They passed the counter moving toward the back of the diner. Only a few tables were occupied. She was glad it was quiet so they could talk easily. Sarah took off her coat, hanging it on a single hook coat rack attached to the bench seat of their booth. He wore his jacket but unzipped it. He leaned back in the seat. Sarah was still stuffed from the popcorn and he said he wasn't hungry so when the waitress came, they only ordered two coffees.

"I'm glad I ran into you Carlos. I'd like to get to know a little more about you before our next meeting. You left rather suddenly after our last discussion."

"Yeah, I needed some fresh air."

"Do you remember the session?"

"Sure. The thing I liked was the calm way I felt when it was over. I stayed like that for a few days and that's cool. Everybody thinks I get off on my anger but I don't. It's just something that takes me over and once it starts, I can't control it. At least, not until now. It's been easier to stay mellow since I've been seeing you."

"So Carlos, do you remember what happened in your regression?" The waitress brought the cups. She filled them with steaming hot liquid.

"Sort of. You took me down some stairs and through a door. I remember a forest or something like that. Then it gets kind of fuzzy. I think I was walking or riding through the woods, but I'm not sure. It was kind of freaky but okay. At least I think it was okay."

"You said you like the calm way it makes you feel. What didn't you like about it?"

"I felt kind of weird after I came back to, what'd you call it? Real time?" She nodded her head yes. "Well, I can't really explain it." He looked puzzled and was silent for a moment. "No, I can't explain the feeling. Just weird." His eyes met hers. Then a broad, cocky smile spread across his face, his eyes narrowed as he laughed out loud.

Sarah had been staring at Carlos with an intent expression and when he laughed, she looked down at her coffee cup. Blushing, she hoped her admiration for his dark, bad boy good looks hadn't shown on her face. She brushed her hair off her forehead as she sipped her coffee.

"So what about you? You know all about me. I don't know nothin' about you."

"Well, I've been doing therapy for ten years. Amazing. It doesn't seem that long. I graduated from . . . "

"No, I don't mean the business stuff. What about you? What do you like to do for fun? Is there a real you or just the shrink?" He genuinely wanted to know and he wondered what possessed him to have any interest in a woman so different from him.

Sarah glanced up to see him staring at her, his head to one side. The sincerity in his voice made her uncomfortable again.

"Carlos, I think you're reversing the roles here just a bit."

"Yeah, so what?"

"Well," she stammered as she felt her face color pink. "I don't think it's appropriate for the client to interrogate the therapist." She smiled tentatively. "Do you?"

"Sarah," he leaned forward, locking his black eyes to hers, "have you ever noticed that if you separate the word 'therapist' into two words, they are 'the rapist'?"

She gasped and he laughed.

#

As she settled in her bed, she thought about her quiet afternoon at the movies. It certainly had taken an unexpected turn. Instead of figuring out if he had been messing with her mind, she had found herself even more immersed in his case.

As she pulled the down comforter over her and turned out the light, she could see his intense dark eyes, hear his laughter in her mind.

"What the hell is this?" was her last thought as she drifted off to sleep.

CHAPTER 5

"Can't you find out any more information about him?" Sarah spoke loudly so her friend could hear her over the sounds of traffic.

"I sent you everything we have from here." Colleen cursed at the driver ahead of her. "Listen, I'm late to a meeting. If I can find anything else on him, I'll let you know." Sarah heard the car horn blow several times. "Why don't you just ask him?"

"He's evasive with me." Sarah leaned back in her desk chair. "I can't seem to get a straight answer from him other than he likes his sessions. And he's due here in half an hour. Is there anywhere else I can go for information on him?"

"Nope, you got it all. Listen, got to go. I'm at the court house and I have to park. Later." And the sounds of the street coming through the receiver suddenly came to a halt.

"Hey Maggie," Sarah called to her assistant, "will you call Steve and find out if there's any way I can get more information on a parolee than what the parole officer has to offer?"

"Sure." Her plump face peeked around the door. "It isn't about Gorgeous Havarro is it?"

"Maggie, you can be replaced, you know." Sarah waved Maggie out of the room.

"Never happen. Nobody has my sense of humor or my robust

good looks." She laughed as she left the room, closing Sarah's door behind her.

Sarah pulled his file from her drawer. She had a half an hour to think about him before the session. She planned to regress him to England once again. She wasn't sure what was going on in his subconscious mind but it was certainly interesting. She wondered at herself. She spent a great deal of her time thinking about his case without really understanding why. So far, it had been nothing too much out of the ordinary except for his comment about the undead. That could have meant anything. She needed to control her thoughts to help him to heal. That was her purpose, nothing more. Strange she felt the need to keep telling herself he was nothing more than a client.

A soft knock on the door made her look up. It couldn't be Maggie. She never knocked; she just barged in whenever she wanted as long as Sarah wasn't in a session.

"Come on in."

"Hey." He came into the room. He hung his jacket on the coat tree then sat in the chair across from her. "So, did you get home okay the other night?"

"I did. How about you?"

"Yeah. It was kind of cool running into you. I still can't figure out why you were at a flick like that."

"I feel the same about you." She smiled as she opened the file resting on her desk. "I'd like to ask you a few questions if that's alright."

He coughed, stretching out his legs. "Not today, why don't we just get going with the sleep stuff. I'm ready to be calmed down." He rose and crossed to the recliner. He sat, turning to look at her. "Are you coming?" His voice held a touch of insolence.

She hesitated. Deciding not to provoke him, she stood, crossing to the chair facing him. "All right, close your eyes. Now, begin to concentrate on your breath."

She used the same induction she had used the previous sessions and soon they were in the English forest once again.

"I am nearing the castle." He paused. *"I hear a rider approaching."*

"Can you tell me who the rider is?" She leaned closer to him to be sure the recorder picked up all his words.

"It is a woman. Wait, I see the King's mistress and she rides alone."

\#

CARLOS HAVARRO, transcript, session 3, February 26

I jumped from my horse and bowed a courtier's bow as she approached. "My lady."

"Rise, she commanded."She was small and her gloved hands were tiny. She wore an emerald green riding costume with a golden plume in her green hat. A gold letter B was suspended from a strand of lustrous pearls strung around her neck. "Aris, you have been the champion in the last three jousts at the palace, have you not?"

"I have." My eyes searched her face, surprised at what I saw. She was not as beautiful as I thought now that I stood close enough to truly see her. She had small, hard eyes and a thin mouth. "How can I serve you, my lady?"

"First you may assist me from this horse and we shall walk." I held the horse steady as she dismounted. When she stood next to me, I saw she was even smaller than she appeared at court. And when she spoke, it was a demand, not a question. "What kind of a name is yours? From where do you travel?"

"I came to England many years ago. I brought the name with me. I am now the subject of the King, however my name remains the same."

"And how did you come to be a champion?" We walked slowly down the path, our horses trailing behind in our tracks.

"I am a warrior. Being a champion was my reward for excellence in all that I do, my lady." I tipped my head in deference to her, delighted to have responded without answering any of her questions.

"I see." Silence fell between us and all that could be heard was the sound of the horses' hooves on the soft earth. "And so, you are loyal to your King?"

"Yes, my lady."

"And are you loyal to me and to my personal court as well?"

"Yes, my lady."

"I have a very private," she paused, "a very important matter to be solved. It entails my family and the honor of the Boleyn name. Are you a man who can be trusted?"

"I am loyal to the King and so to you without rewards or penalties. What is the task?"

"It is my brother, George."

"Yes, my lady." Rumors of George Boleyn and his escapades abounded throughout the palace. He was a rowdy and raucous young man with a disposition to much drink and a violent temper.

"I wish you to keep a watchful eye then report to me. His reputation is sour and he must not stand in the way of the advancement of my family at court. I have seen you in his company and I see he favors you. He acts freely when he is with you. Stay him, Aris, from ill rumors and you will win my favor."

"It will be an honor, my lady, to stand for the Boleyn name."

"And if you perform my bidding to my satisfaction, I have another intrigue, far more important and deeply dangerous."

"My lady?"

"No, not now. I will summon you again when I am ready, but I will tell you this, it involves a man high at court, some say closest to the throne."

Could it be Wolsey? The cardinal? I could feel the rise in my eyebrows at the import of the man of whom she spoke, the man who was second to only the King and who some said was the true ruler of England.

"Are you still loyal?" She laughed as she spoke.

"Yes my lady, I am always loyal." I nodded my head in agreement.

"Go then Aris. Fulfill the first task, only then will you earn my trust

for the second."

I bowed and assisted her onto her horse. She turned to look at me once more before she rode away. She heeled the animal and it jumped into a gallop.

I felt a cold chill and spoke to no one but the trees. "It is obvious by her eyes that someone in this realm should be very afraid." I mounted my horse then rode from the clearing.

#

"One, two, three, four, five. Eyes open. Wide awake." His eyes fluttered a few times then stayed open.

"Astounding! It's like watching a film. Except I am in it. I can almost taste the air and feel the earth beneath my feet."

Sarah watched him. She noticed his voice remained deeper and his words were a bit strange for a Latin American from the twenty-first century.

He was silent for a moment before he spoke again. "Man, let's go back there. I want to know what that broad wants from me."

Sarah smiled as her client returned to his full current self. "No, enough for today. We'll revisit England next session. How do you feel?"

"Kind a weird, same as last time. But calm. I feel really calm right now." He stretched his arms over his head and yawned. "Why is that?"

"It's a product of the hypnosis. Your body relaxes and your heart beat slows. Your blood pressure lowers. It's as if your body is sleeping yet your mind is alert."

"Yeah? Well, I like it so far." He straightened the chair back to a sitting position. "Want to go get some coffee?"

Sarah stopped herself from saying yes. She needed to keep a safe distance from him. She didn't understand all her feelings about him but one thing was for certain, she didn't want to explore them any further. "No, sorry. It really isn't protocol to have coffee with my clients."

"How about the other night?"

"That was an accident. And it was only once. Now, I'd like to discuss . . . "

He lifted his hand to stop her comment. "Why don't you just think that over, the coffee I mean? See if you can't change your mind next time." He stood. He walked to the coat tree, grabbing his jacket. "See you next week Sarah." His smile was sure and cocky as he opened the door to leave.

CHAPTER 6

"So what's so important about this Carlos Havarro? You've never come to me for help before." Steve placed the menu on the table as he waved for the waiter.

"This is my first parolee, Steve." She couldn't answer his question, even to herself. Why did Carlos continue to occupy her thoughts? She met other handsome young men who showed her interest. She never responded to any of them before and none of them had been ex-cons. Why this one? It was an enigma she didn't seem able to solve. He even popped into her mind when she first woke up in the morning. She wondered for just a moment if she wasn't obsessing about him to keep her mind off her stagnant love life.

Steve intruded into her thoughts. "Anyway, I couldn't find out anything more than the information in the file you sent over. He's just some small time hood who isn't worth much to society. Just like the rest of them."

"Yeah, well this one is intelligent. That and he never had a chance."

"Sarah, I honestly don't know why you're even getting involved with this guy. This isn't your usual middle class housewife with low self-esteem whose poor miserable husband pays you a hundred bucks an hour to tell her she's okay."

"Thanks Steve. It's really great to know what you think of my profession."

"Come on babe." He could see she was irritated by his attitude, yet he didn't even try to alter his condescending tone. "It's just I don't know why your friend even got you involved with this guy. This is way out of your league. And from what I read, he's pretty dangerous, really nothing but a big time loser."

"First of all," she gathered her coat and bag, "my friend has respect for what I do. She actually thinks I can help him. Second of all, go to hell." She stood, walking quickly to the door. He watched her without emotion, sure she would think better of her reaction and come back to the table to finish dinner.

Slipping her arms into her coat, she pushed the door open, stepped out into the cold evening air and checked both directions of traffic for an empty taxi. Seeing one on her side of the street, she stuck her fingers in her mouth, whistled and the cab pulled to the curb. Settling into the back seat, she gave the driver her address. As the driver pulled away, she didn't even turn to see Steve who had finally moved to the doorway, amazed that she actually left.

The lights of the city reflected in the windows of the tall buildings as the cab drove slowly through the rush hour traffic. Sarah smiled to herself. She would have to tell Bonnie how well their therapy sessions had paid off.

#

"How could I have wasted three months on that jerk?" She was bundled up in her blue and white flannel pajamas with a glass of merlot in one hand while she held the phone in the other.

"I hate to say it but I will anyway. I told you so. He was an ego on feet from the first to the last. I honestly don't know how you can be surprised." Colleen's voice had a laugh in it as she answered. "I never liked the schmuck."

"Okay, okay. So you were right. Next time I'll pay attention to you. I need all the help I can get when it comes to picking men. Not everybody can find a guy like Bob."

"Yeah, well Bob wasn't like Bob when I met him. It took a lot of work to make him human, let me tell you. A cop isn't the most sensitive guy in the world."

"Sure. Sure. Take all the credit for him. He was great right from the start."

"A lot you know. And hon, I wish you'd just realize you don't need a man in your life to make you a whole person. You're doing fine on your own."

"I know that C, it's just sometimes I feel driven to find my soul mate." She laughed. "Now I sound like one of those drippy women in soap operas."

"No, you don't. It's easy for me now that I have Bob. It wasn't always like that, remember all the losers I dated?"

"Yeah, remember Thom-ass?" They both burst out laughing.

When they were able to breathe again, Colleen spoke. "So, how are things going with Carlos? I saw him yesterday and he said he likes coming to you. I think it's making a difference in him. He can sit still for more than a minute and now, he even makes eye contact."

"He didn't make eye contact before?" Sarah sat up, placing her wine glass on the coffee table.

"No, I've never seen him look anyone in the eye. Why?"

"No reason." She adjusted the cushions then leaned back once again remembering his dark eyes locking onto hers during talk therapy. "It must be a trust thing. I use the usual suggestions for relaxation and he says they work."

"What about the past life stuff? Have you tried any of that yet?"

"A little. We're just getting into it. He seems very receptive."

"Well, he's done a lot of drugs in the past. It should be easy to make him see things that aren't there?" Colleen laughed an ironic laugh.

"He's not still doing them, is he?"

"No, he went into rehab last year. It was hell for him but he's stayed clean since then. I honestly think he wants to straighten out. He thinks a lot of you."

Sarah sat up again. "Yes?"

"Yeah. He talks about you a lot when I see him. He's always thanking me for sending him to you. I think he believes in what you're doing with him." The call waiting signal could be heard from Colleen's cell phone. "Gotta go hon. Got another bird on the line. Talk to you soon." Suddenly, dead silence. Conversations with Colleen always seemed to end abruptly without warning.

Sarah picked up her wine from the table and settled into the cushions when her cell rang again. She didn't want to answer it. She wanted to think about her conversation with her friend but, in her business, her time wasn't her own. She checked the caller I.D. It was an unfamiliar number so she opened the phone to speak. "Hello?"

"Sarah, it's Carlos. Want to have a cup of coffee?"

"Carlos, I told you before. I can't have a relationship with a client outside of the office."

"Then what if I stop being a client?"

"Don't be ridiculous. We're in this together to help to heal you."

"I like the 'together' part." Suddenly, the phone went dead.

"Doesn't anyone ever say goodbye?" She sighed as she took a sip of her wine.

#

The line at the bar was long so the two women decided to go back to their seats in the theatre and wait for the second act without the ritual glass of wine. Sarah loved going to the opera. It wasn't only the music and costumes but the whole evening. People dressed in lovely clothes, all the women smelling wonderful and wearing exquisite jewelry. The festivity reminded her of Christmas and the winter holidays were her favorite time of year.

Her mind wandered to the Christmases when she was married to Jeff. He had always acted as if the span from Thanksgiving to New Year was an enormous waste of time. How different they were. Why in the world had she married him?

"Bonnie, do you think I choose unavailable men because I'm really afraid of love?" Sarah almost laughed as she watched Bonnie put on her mental therapist's cap.

"Sarah, we've talked about this in session. I don't think you're afraid to love. I just don't think you know what it is. You sure weren't in love with Jeff. He was so crazy about himself that there was no room for anyone else to really care about him. He didn't need it. Or you."

"So, am I afraid to be needed?"

"I don't think that's it either. Your clients need you."

"Yeah but that's different. There's no two-way intimacy. There's a professional wall that protects me from that."

"Look, you've spent most of your life trying to please other people. Your mother, for instance. Anything she wanted, you did. Ballet. Gymnastics. Anything she asked you to do whether you liked it or not, you did without ever saying a word. And then we have your father. A good provider but I wouldn't say he was the most loving man in the world. Little girls need their father's love, their assurance. All he did was tell you everything you did wrong. If you got an A he wanted to know why it wasn't an A+"

"Not really . . . "

"Come on, I'm not saying he didn't care for you. I'm sure he did but he didn't instill you with a whole lot of self-confidence. You've built that all by yourself and you should be proud. When you married Jeff, you just married your father in another body. Many, many women do that, just like men marry the embodiment of their mothers. It's just what humans do.

"What I'm saying is you have never really felt love. To be loved and to give love in an adult relationship is something that is foreign to you."

Sarah began to speak but Bonnie raised her hand to silence her companion. "I know you love your friends but it isn't the same. So the answer to your question is no, I don't think you're afraid of love. I simply don't think you've found it yet."

The chimes rang and the lights of the theatre flickered to announce the beginning of Act II.

Bonnie leaned closer to Sarah and whispered, "Don't worry, you just have to find the right man and love will come to get you."

CHAPTER 7

"Where are you?" She flipped on the recorder. She forgot to turn it on at the beginning of the session and she didn't want to miss a word.

#

CARLOS HAVARRO, transcript, session 4, March 5

I am in a tavern in a poor part of London with George Boleyn. His drunken friends left us to stagger back to court but he was not about to leave while there was still ale in the cups. I stayed his companion to watch him as I was bid by Lady Anne. The fire burned low and all of the tables were empty save for the two of us and a few laughing men in the back of the room.

He spoke to me. "So Aris, it seems you are intrigued by the cousin of Thomas Wyatt. Is that so?"

I toyed with my cup of ale resting on the battered table before I answered. "She is lovely." Unable to tell the truth of my affection for her, I hoped to evade any further questions.

"Is that all, you just find her lovely? I see you staring at her at court. And," he chuckled, "she seems quite taken with you."

"I find her wit as well as her face appealing, nothing more." I downed the amber liquid in one large gulp.

George raised his eyebrows and leaned forward to speak. The door of the tavern opened and banged against the wall, caught by a gust of wind. We turned to see who entered. I was surprised to see a pretty young woman of common stock with an infant in her arms step from the cold night into the dim room. It was very late and unsafe in that part of London, quite unusual for a woman to be in the streets alone.

She stood still as her eyes adjusted to the light. She seemed to recognize George who abruptly stood as she began to move toward our table. In his drunken stupor, he knocked the bench on which he was seated to the floor.

His voice was soft and vicious. "Remove her. I do not wish to speak with her."

She moved to stand in front of him. "Your child, your son." She held the babe to him.

"Not my child, you whore." He pushed her and reeling from too much drink, made his way from the tavern.

The woman sat, holding the babe close in her arms; her gentle sobs were muffled as she buried her face in the blankets. Her clothes were tattered yet clean and her hair combed. As I approached her, I noticed her fingernails were trimmed and her hands were scrubbed.

"Madam?"

She stifled her tears and as she looked up at me I could see the moisture on her cheeks shimmering in the light of the single candle resting on the table. She was very young and fragile.

"What is your plight, madam?" My question was driven by my promise to Mistress Anne to protect the name of Boleyn but as the maid told her story, my heart opened with compassion for her ordeal.

She was silent for just a moment. When she spoke, it was in a whisper. "I was a serving maid in a tavern much like this one. Master Boleyn and his friends came into the tavern often and were always generous with those of us who served them.

"And then," she paused as if in physical pain, "there came a night when they lingered until almost dawn drinking much more than usual.

They were hardly able to stand to walk when the proprietor finally bade them leave. Laughing loudly, they staggered to the door and made their way into the earliest light of daybreak. I cleared their table and began to scrub the dark stains of the spilled wine as the barkeep bid me goodnight. He left the tavern and I was alone." Her eyes became frightened as she recalled the memory.

"Go on," I gently placed my hand on her arm as I spoke.

"The door slammed open and Master Boleyn stood in a silhouette, the rising sun behind him. His laughter was frightening as he lurched across the room toward me." She clasped the child closer to her breast and hid her face in its blanket. "He ripped my bodice. I tried to cover my bosom with the tattered cloth but he pulled it away from me. His laugh was cruel as he jerked me to him, his rancid breath vile on my face. A horrifying awareness came over me as I knew his intention. He was blind to my struggles and my strength was no weapon against his assault. He cursed as he struck me then tore my skirt to bare my thighs. His weight was heavy on me. He... he violated me." Sobs overtook her and her small shoulders trembled as she fought for control. When she had silenced her weeping, she raised her eyes to meet mine.

"This child is his. My beautiful son is the descendent of Master Boleyn."

"And what do you want of Master Boleyn, madam?" I realized that this woman and this babe were of no import to the Boleyn family yet my heart was sore at her trouble, little more than a child herself.

"I cannot return to work in the tavern. I feel terror in the presence of men who are loose with drink." Again, a moment of silence, she inhaled a deep breath as she gathered her courage. At last, she spoke. "I ask for nothing more of Master Boleyn than assistance in finding a position so that I am able to feed and clothe my child, yet he shuns me." She spoke through her grief, "I must find a way to care for my child."

I felt revulsion at the actions of the young lord and vowed to assist the pitiful mother. "No longer fear for the safety of your child. I will find a position for you. The royal kitchen is always in need of scullery workers. You will have food and shelter and a small wage. You will have a post for as long as you choose."

Her eyes shone with gratitude. "Thank you sir." She looked at her baby then met my eye. "I am forever indebted to you."

I assured her she owed me no debt. I asked where she lodged. She answered she had no permanent refuge but moved from place to place, working for a night's shelter.

"No more," I said. "You will return with me to court tonight. We will find a place for you and the child to sleep and on the morrow, I will speak with one who will assure you a position." *I would call on the Lady Anne to make it so. She would do anything to keep the Boleyn name safe from Cardinal Wolsey. He despised the Boleyns and vowed their ruin using any means he could find.*

And so, the mother and child were made safe and I stepped up in the estimation of the Lady Anne. I enjoyed her recognition and the elevation of my station in her eyes. So unlike the rest of my kind, I relished the life and notoriety of a courtier. I surmise it was a fancy brought from my life as a human.

My human family was prominent, holding vast lands and a fleet of merchant ships. I was a boy raised without want. All I desired was mine. Riches and finery were the only life I knew. Is it any wonder that the royal court was a place of comfort for me?

He ceased speaking. The afternoon light grew dim and a gentle rain began to fall outside the office window. "Please, go on."

The court housed many beautiful women and many of them presented themselves to me yet I saw only one. Time and again I wondered how much George Boleyn really knew of my affection for Thomas Wyatt's cousin. It was at a royal banquet I first cast eyes on her.

That night, at the end of the meal, the King rose from the royal table. He laughed loudly as he ordered the musicians to play a pavane. Those who wished to dance took their places as the music began.

It was there I saw her. Her hair was without decoration or hood. She needed neither. Thick, blond curls shimmered in the candle light shaming all those who resorted to jewels for their sparkle. Her eyes were the color of molten gold surrounded by the clearest blue sapphire. Her neck was long and graceful. She tilted her chin in such a way that I longed to hold her, to protect her from any harm.

A thousand thoughts ravaged my mind. Who was this beauty? Why had I not seen her before? How could I possess her, make her my own?

Suddenly, I remembered and for the first time in my living death, I hated what I was. A beast. A savage. If she knew my true self, she would flee. I hurried away from the music into the cool dark of the palace rose garden.

The pleasant evening air was a respite after the heat of the dance. I breathed more slowly, more deeply. Although I have no need to breathe, it seems to soothe the body which I inhabit. The sound of laughter reached me as I sat among the blossoms. I heard voices. I recognized Thomas Wyatt but I had never previously heard the voice of the maid.

I stood to move from the shadows to greet them when I saw her hair radiant in the moonlight. I stopped still. It was the angel. I watched as they walked and chatted amiably much as a brother and sister would. I vowed I would give Thomas no rest until he told me the name of the love of my existence, which I had found at last.

I hurried to his rooms and there, outside, I waited for him. The sun was rising when he returned. His dark hair was disheveled, his doublet thrown carelessly over his shoulder. His sleepless, red-rimmed eyes opened wide at the sight of me. He yawned.

"What are you doing here?"

"Where have you been?" I did not wait for him to answer. "The maid in the garden with you last night, who is she?"

Thomas stopped walking. He stared at me, then broke into laughter. "There is no need for accusation, sir. You speak of Bess, Elizabeth Wyatt, my cousin."

"Your cousin? Why have I not seen her here before last night?"

"She is new to court. Do you wish to meet her?"

"No. No." I paused. I lied. "I thought I knew her, but I was mistaken."

We entered his rooms. He poured sweet wine and chose a piece of hard cheese from the plate on the table. "I worked up quite an appetite with one of the Queen's ladies last night." Again he yawned. He bit into the cheese. As he chewed, he stretched his arms over his head then flopped in a chair by the fire, his muscular legs sprawling out before him.

"Here, sit." He motioned me to join him. The crackling flames caused our shadows to dance on the stone walls. We sat quietly, listening to the sounds of burning apple wood, two men lost in their own thoughts.

At last he spoke. "Aris, Bess serves Queen Katherine." He rose from his slouch and leaned forward toward me. "What is your interest in her?"

"Thomas, I cannot lie to you further. I saw her and I loved her. I see her face before me even now." I rose and paced in front of him. "I must meet her." I turned to meet his eyes. "You must make it so."

"All right." He laughed, then became serious. "I will introduce you to my cousin but never forget, she is my family. I am sworn to protect our name."

"Never fear, Thomas. My intentions are only honorable."

Later that night as I sat quietly in my rooms, I questioned just how honorable could the intentions of a vampire be.

#

Sarah sat in silence wondering at his words. There it was again, the reference to being a beast, a vampire. Not needing to breathe. What could it mean? Slowly she brought him out of the hypnotic state. She waited patiently until he was ready to speak.

"Wow. What was that all about?"

"What do you think it was about, Carlos?"

"Aren't you the one who is supposed to have all the answers?"

"Carlos, we are just beginning this journey. We'll have to define the pictures you are being shown in your sessions, what the images mean to you. Then we'll be able to relate them to your present life."

"I don't know what the hell you're talking about." He sat up quickly. "All this psycho mumbo jumbo doesn't make any sense to me and I don't get how this bullshit history lesson has anything to do with my life anyhow." His eyes narrowed as he stood looking down at her. "How is all this fairy tale crap going to help me stay out of trouble, you want to tell me that?"

Her heart raced at the anger in his expression. She smoothed her skirt, taking a moment to regain her composure. Forcing a smile she didn't feel, she rose from the chair to stand facing him. He was tall, muscular and intimidating.

"Each session will lead us closer to the answers that you are looking for. It's one step at a time. I won't tell you I have any idea right now what this sixteenth century vampire regression is about, but I do believe that it is important that we continue to pursue this." She turned, moving to sit in the chair behind her desk, putting space between them before she continued. She spoke as she made a note in his file. "Unless you would rather stop right here." She looked at him. "What do you want to do, Carlos?"

He stared at her a moment, then shrugged his shoulders. "I don't know, you're the expert. If you say we need to keep this crap up, then we'll do it. I just don't want to end up in trouble with the law again." He sat across from her, leaning forward as he spoke. "I want a better life for me and I've got a kid brother. I don't want him doing what I've done. He deserves better than that. I guess I'm willing to do whatever it takes to protect him."

"Alright. What can you tell me about your brother?"

"I'm done talking for the day. My hour is up." He grinned and stood. "I'll see you next Friday at the same time."

Sarah stood to walk with him to the door. His palms were cold and clammy as she shook his hand. She closed the door behind him wondering if he was really as confident as he appeared or if he was as nervous about their work together as she was.

CHAPTER 8

The music was blasting and the four televisions on the wall in front of her were all on different stations as she plodded along on the treadmill. In the summer she did cardio in the park but it was still far too cold. She hoped all the noise and energy of the gym would take her mind off Carlos but so far, no such luck.

"What is it about this guy?" Her thoughts just wouldn't leave the question alone. "I've met men just as handsome, a lot more mature. Not so troubled. And never have I experienced this kind of obsession with anyone. What is it about this particular guy?"

"Hey Sarah." Bonnie stepped onto the empty elliptical next to her. She was dressed in baggy gray sweats and a white T-shirt with a gray Tai Chi symbol on the front. A few light brown stray hairs sneaked out of the rubber band holding her pony tail in place and gathered around her face. "How you doing today?" She made adjustments to the machine before beginning to walk slowly. "You look a little stressed."

"No, just thinking about work." Sarah honestly enjoyed her new office space however she still missed the daily contact with Bonnie and the rest of the therapists from her old co-op. Their weekly meetings to discuss issues had always been a great aid in diagnosing her clients. She wondered just what they would think about Carlos.

She laughed. "Isn't that what we are always thinking about?"

"Yeah, I guess you're right." Bonnie picked up her pace as her legs warmed up. "How have you been? I haven't seen you since the opera. Have you had any insights about our intermission conversation?"

"Not really but otherwise, I've actually been feeling a lot better. I honestly haven't had one of those deep waves of self-doubt since the last regression you did on me. I know we didn't get past infancy but somehow, I feel more settled. And I've been so busy since the opera I haven't had much time to think about love and romance, but I do want to find some answers about that for myself."

"Honey, I didn't think it would take more than a couple of sessions to give you some resolutions on the self-doubt thing. The romance thing?" She laughed. "That might just take a little bit longer." Her legs stopped their perpetual elliptical motion as she spoke seriously to her friend. "I know you dealt with Jeff and your divorce in therapy a long time ago, but it took you until recently to really deal with yourself. How long have I been saying physician, heal thyself."

"I know. I knew it then but I didn't want to confront it. Sometimes I think therapists are the worst ones for dealing with their own issues. The divorce just made me question myself and my decisions. I hadn't questioned myself like that since I was a teenager living with my parents and it was frightening. Anyway, I've felt so much more confident lately. It's as if I'm finding that assured part of myself that's been buried for so long. I owe it to the work you're doing with me."

Bonnie looked embarrassed. She interned under Sarah and it felt a bit strange to have their roles somewhat reversed. She changed the subject, "what's new with you? Anything going on?"

"A new client, a parolee Colleen referred to me. Actually he's my first case like this and it's really interesting."

The word 'parolee' captured Bonnie's interest fully. "Sounds like it could be a really different type of case than either of us has had before. Can you tell me anything?"

Sarah would have liked to discuss it but thought better of sharing anything about Carlos. The two women were no longer colleagues and she didn't feel it was appropriate to be discussing his sessions. "No, not really." Seeing her friend's disappointment, Sarah asked, "You tell me now, what's going on with you?"

"Work is pretty much the same. Oh, I saw that new vampire movie last night. Have you seen it?"

Not again! She just couldn't get away from it. Sarah didn't want to admit that she had seen the movie so she evaded the question. "Did you like it?"

"The guy who plays the lead is amazing! He's a really young guy, but 1 couldn't believe how many older women were in the theatre."

Sarah decided this was a good time to ask some questions. "Bon, what is it that attracts women to vampires? I don't get it."

Bonnie moved a lever forward, upping the resistance on the machine while she thought about it. "I don't know really. I guess they're something that's so forbidden, so alien. And they are tortured. They don't have a choice to kill or not. They just have to do it, kind of the original bad boys." She laughed. "I guess it's the difference between a vegetarian and a meat eater. You eat what you have to in order to survive, whether you like it or not."

Sarah looked at her watch. "Wow. I've got to speed it up. If I don't, I'm not going to get the miles in and I don't want to be late for my next client."

"No worries." Bonnie nodded to Sarah, then plugged in her headphones and closed her eyes.

#

CARLOS HAVARRO, transcript, Session 5, March 12

It was gray and cold as the court prepared to ride out to the hunt.

Being one of the undead, I was neither helped nor hindered by the frigid air. I simply did not feel it however those courtiers standing, waiting to mount, stomped their feet and blew warm breath into their chilly hands; frost gathered in the warm gusts from their breath. Gratefully they shared a stirrup cup to cut the early morning chill.

At last, Elizabeth and Thomas joined us. The silver feather in his hat shimmered in the early morning sunlight; his proud black hunter neighed as they drew close. Her white horse pranced, throwing his head and great mane showing impatience to be off.

I reached for their bridles. I held them securely in my hand. "Mistress Elizabeth." I bowed. "Thomas."

"Aris, my friend."

And that is how I met her. My Elizabeth. My only love.

Sarah waited patiently for him to continue.

Fear possessed me as I courted the maid. What would become of us? I felt her affection for me grow stronger. Mine could be no more than it already was. She occupied my every thought. When I was not with her, I felt in a suspended state; simply existing for the moment I would see her again. Her touch was more to me than blood.

I no longer visited the Catacombs where the others of my kind resided. I wished there to be no chance that she know what I was. I rejected my own kind, willing myself to be human once more. Pretending. Hoping. Weeks passed in a blur of banquets and masques, hunts and chilling walks along the Thames, mulled wine and blazing fires.

I could stand our separation no longer. I made my decision, I would ask her to be my wife.I searched for her and found her in the gardens where I pledged my undying love. I opened my heart. To my joy, she accepted me. Openly. Wholeheartedly, she returned my devotion. We vowed to marry.

It was then I truly began to fear. How could I husband such a delicate human? I sought out Sebastian. When he learned of my plight he gave me courage to tell Elizabeth what my life truly was. It was not allowed to reveal ourselves to humans without a purpose and the council's permission. I petitioned to meet with the high council to beg leave to explain myself to my Bess and to take her as my life's mate. I awaited their response. My plan was to plead my case with such eloquence, all would agree. Thankfully, my plea was accepted. I was placed on the docket for the next gathering.

I knew that as a maid of the court, Elizabeth would need consent from the crown to marry so I approached Wolsey to petition Queen Katherine. He was her majesty's champion at court. His hatred of the Boleyns gave them a common cause. He stood as her friend. I knew she would listen to him. I was but a knight yet Elizabeth was simply a maid-in-waiting to the Queen, a match even the crown could smile upon. He bade me have patience, it would take time yet he would approach her Grace.

While we waited for compliance from the crown, I made false excuses to my lady and to the royal court to take my leave for a time. I went below, into the Catacombs, to the court of the undead, the seat of law for my kind. I tarried for one week. Two. I was put off while those of more importance to the council were granted audience. I was surrounded by fear the council would not grant my desire, fear that when I told Elizabeth the truth, she would either think me mad or scream and run from me forever. Or perhaps, both. My patience wore thin. Three weeks. Four.

At last I was called before the oldest ones of all, the King and Queen of the underworld from whom we are all descended, Khansu and Akira. At first, I was told by no means. But I held fast. I used all my wits to plead my case; I told all my reasons for requesting such a rare dispensation. My great age. Never finding love. This human, the first to touch my depths after centuries of being alone.

After days more of deliberation, I was granted permission to introduce her to the life we lead. To bring her below. No words could express my joy.

I rushed to the palace seeking Elizabeth to tell her all there was about me, about my kind. I knew our great love would overcome any obstacles, *even life and death.*

I came upon Thomas Wyatt as I left the stables. He was glad to see me after my long absence. He slapped me on the back as we made our way to the palace and his rooms. He left me no room to speak, he was alive with all the news of the court. He barely took a breath in between words.

We entered his chambers and as he poured wine, I asked for Elizabeth. He became a changed man. He no longer met my eye. His shoulders slumped. He became suddenly silent.

"Where is Elizabeth, Thomas." Fear was clear in my voice. "What has happened while I was away?"

He paused a moment before he spoke, "Aris, Elizabeth is gone. Wolsey sent her to the court of the Emperor where she was to be married to a man of high status. Queen Katherine petitioned the King and he agreed. She set sail on a merchant ship." He faced me. "One week out, the ship was wrecked in a storm and all were lost. Another merchant found the debris floating with all hands dead."

My legs disappeared beneath me, I fell to my knees. Thomas grabbed me by the shoulders and lifted me to my feet. My body stiffened. I raised my eyes to heaven and roared. "No. It cannot be. I will kill Wolsey with my bare hands."

My friend guided me toward a chair by the fire. As I sat, he placed a wine filled goblet in my hand. "Drink this. It will help calm you."

I knew complete despair. "Nothing will ever calm me. I have lost the only woman I will ever love. Oh Thomas, what will I do?" My voice was a whisper. "What will I do?"

We spent the long night sitting silently, gazing into the fire. At first light, I stood and walked to the window. As the sun rose, I relinquished my dream of ever having love in my empty eternity. I vowed that Wolsey would forever be my enemy. I pledged I would one day find a way to repay his treachery.

#

"Carlos, Carlos." He hadn't moved since she broke the trance.

"Where are you?"

"I'm right here Sarah. At least I think I'm right here." He stirred on the leather chair. "It's hard to lift my arms right now. Is that normal?" There was a sound of distrust in his voice.

"Yes, yes. It's perfectly normal. You were very deep in the state and it takes a few moments to recover completely. There, see? You're wiggling your fingers now."

"Whew. That was so freaky. I was really there. What's this all about, Sarah." He raised his arms over his head to stretch as he turned to look at her. "Am I nuts?"

"No Carlos. You're not crazy." She reached toward him, taking hold of his hands. His touch was ice cold exactly as it had been at the end of their last session. She let go of him quickly. "Here, come and sit up. Let's sit in the sun by the window."

As they settled in he winced. "Man, I have a rotten headache. What's that about?"

"That sometimes happens after a deep session. It will pass in just a few minutes."

"Okay, so what is all this crap?"

"Carlos, I honestly don't know. I know that your subconscious is talking to us through your session. If you believe in past lives, it can be a past life that is surfacing. If you don't, it's just pictures from your subconscious. Either way, it's a step toward your healing. If we can just find where your anger stems from, we can make it so much easier for you to calm it."

"Stems from? Hell, it stems from my old man beating the crap out of me and my whole family. Haven't you read the file that follows me everywhere I go?" His eyes were angry as he answered her.

"Yes, I read the file. It's more than that." Her voice had a soothing effect on him. "In past life regression work we find the place where the intense emotion originates and we work on it from that place. If we can change the outcome of that experience in your subconscious mind with hypnosis, then the uncontrollable emotion will be released. You will no longer be driven by it." She leaned in to him. "What do you experience when you begin to lose control?"

He sat quietly, his dark eyes staring down at his boots. Finally, he spoke. "Like I need to kill something to just keep breathing." He whispered the words so softly she almost missed their meaning.

"Kill something? Do you mean someone?"

"Yes."

"Does it frighten you to feel like that?"

It took him more than a minute to answer. "No, it makes me feel powerful." He raised his head, looking straight into her eyes. "It makes me feel strong." He smiled a long, slow smile. "When I feel like that, I am invincible."

CHAPTER 9

"Look Colleen, I just can't see him anymore. I don't think this is what he needs."

"What the hell are you talking about Sarah? You told me you thought it was a good thing. Now you want to dump him just like everyone else. What the hell happened?"

"I can't discuss it." She chewed on the end of her pen while she talked. His file was lying on her desk. She kept opening it and closing it. "It's client, therapist stuff. I wish I could talk about it, but I just can't.

"What the hell? Is he a murderer or something?" Colleen's voice became anxious.

"I don't know." She heard her friend gasp on the other end of the line. "No, no. Not in this life anyway. I honestly don't know what he is. Or what he was. I just think I'm way out of my element here."

Colleen tried to ease the tension with a sigh and a little laugh. "Well, if he hasn't committed murder in this life, what are you so worried about?"

"Look C, I don't want to dump him. I just don't want to damage him anymore. He's had just about all he can take and I don't want to push him." She closed the file a final time. She put it in her drawer. "I just cannot see him anymore."

"I swear to God Sarah, what the hell is the matter with you?" Her harsh words matched her tone of voice. "You always said you wanted to do more than work on weight issues and self-esteem and claustrophobia. I bring you someone you can really help, you start, then back off. Just what the hell do you expect me to tell him, that he's just too scary for your lily white hands?"

Sarah was stunned. She never expected her friend to come down on her with such force. She had never seen Colleen angry before.

"Well, say something. What should I tell him?"

Sarah felt ashamed of her cowardice. It was a step backward. She was in control of their sessions and she didn't need Bonnie to tell her she had the ability to help Carlos. She gave a long sigh, "You're right, C. Don't tell him anything. I'll see him as planned on Friday. And calm down. You didn't have to ream me out."

"Hon, if you think that was me reaming you out, you haven't seen anything yet. I'll tell him you're on for Friday."

#

The afternoon sunlight shined in the window creating long shadows on the floor. Carlos relaxed as he sat in the recliner, a smile on his face.

Sarah used the peaceful moment to broach the subject of Carlos' family. "Before we begin hypnosis today, I'd like to ask you a few more questions about your upbringing. Would that work for you?"

"You really crack me up." He laughed. "You think I'm relaxed this afternoon so you can hit me up about my home life."

"It's important that I know everything you feel safe enough to tell me. Unless I do, I'm working in the dark and all the regression work doesn't mean a thing. What happened in the past is dead history without a present anchor. Does that make any sense at all?"

"Yeah, you always make sense whether I like it or not." He leaned back into the chair, closed his eyes and folded his hands on his chest. "What do you want to know?"

"You said your parents came here from Mexico. Your father was from a wealthy family and your mother was peasant stock. Do you know anything about their history?"

"Sure. It starts out romantic but turns to crap. They met in a farmer's market. My mother was beautiful and my father fell for her. His family was dead against them being together because she was poor so they eloped.

"After they were married, my grandparents said they forgave him so, being old school, my father took my mother home to live with his family. My grandmother hated my mother. She treated her well when the family was together but like a dog when they were alone.

"My mother got pregnant and lost the baby. My grandmother got meaner and meaner. After a while, she began to poison my father's mind against my mother.

"My mother told him about my grandmother's rotten treatment but my father was a macho business man and didn't want to get involved in women's bull crap. He said it was up to them to get along. Well, it didn't happen. It just got worse.

"Then my mother got pregnant a second time and lost that baby too. She had just come out of surgery when my father walked into the hospital room unannounced. My grandmother was screaming at my mother. He finally saw the truth.

"That's when they moved to the states. They settled in California. Because my father had been successful in Mexico, he didn't see any reason he couldn't be successful here. So he was. And still is if you measure success by how much money a guy makes.

"Anyway, his father disowned him but his mother kept in touch. She wrote letters and called him all the time. Soon after they moved here, my mother got pregnant again.

"About the same time, my grandfather got really sick. My

grandmother kept calling and telling my father that it was his fault his father was wasting away, that his marriage to my mother was killing the old man.

"As it got closer to the time for my mother's delivery, my grandfather went downhill and fast. My father left for Mexico. While he was gone, I was born. Then, my grandfather died. Man, my grandmother worked my old man over. He came back to us not even sure I was his son.

"He started drinking, then the fights started. He accused my mother of messing around on him and using him to get out of the poverty she grew up in. I don't know what all came down, just that he was always shouting at her and she was always crying. It just kept getting worse."

There was no sound in the room except for the wind whistling around the corner of the building. Sarah sat quietly. She was grateful for the information Carlos had given her about his past. It still didn't make a great deal of sense to her but it was another step on the journey.

"You know Sarah, I've never told that story to anyone. It feels good just to get it off my chest."

"That's what this is all about, Carlos; coming to an understanding of your actions and motives. Once we know why you respond the way you do we can change the way you respond. If you want to change it."

"If I didn't want to make it all different, I wouldn't be here right now. I'd be out with my old home boys. I really do want a better life. Knowing Colleen and now you has proved that there really are good people in the world, people who care what happens to guys like me. I've never felt like that before." He caught her eyes and smiled. "Why do I always feel better when I'm here? I guess it really doesn't matter why. It's just that I do." He took a deep breath, relaxing into the comfortable chair. "Okay, take me down."

She used the usual induction to take him into state, then called on Aris.

The voice and accent that answered her were of his older, wiser vampire self.

"I am here."

Carlos lay peacefully in the recliner, his eyes closed and his breath even and smooth.

"I find a certain solace here that I have not known for centuries, a peace that is without description."

"Aris, will you tell me how you came to being, how you were born?"

"Yes, I will tell you." His voice became so soft she was forced to lean into him to understand his words. *"I am from the time of Alexander, the Great."*

Sarah gasped. "But Alexander was B.C."

"Why does that shock you more than there is such a thing as I am?" He was silent a moment, then continued his story.

"I was a young soldier in his army. I was brave and bold and did exceptional things to bring myself to the attention of my commander. Alexander was pleased by my heroics and my strange beauty."

Carlos turned his head toward her but his eyes stayed closed, his breath keeping the even cadence of hypnosis.

"He took me as his dresser. Soon, I became someone he trusted and called upon for council. I was young but bright with a talent for battle. We became more than servant and master. And then, we became friends."

Sarah was mesmerized as the vampire told his ancient story through the voice of the twenty first century man.

#

CARLOS HAVARRO, transcript, session 6, March 19

It was during the Balkan campaign while a battle raged that I was changed.

Alexander called the battle at first light. There was a raging storm and the black, ominous clouds spouted lightening, the lightening created a thunder that stopped the beating of the heart. We fought near the top of Mount Haemus and located there was a shrine to the god, Dionysus. We battled our way toward the shrine. As the soil turned to mud mixed with blood and rain water, we slid and slipped as we wielded our swords yet we were victorious. Alexander commanded that all survivors were to be killed so we worked our way to the top of the mountain, our swords spreading death to anything that moved.

As I neared the top of the mountain, I was drawn into a forest of strange, tall trees with their roots above ground, twisted into enormous knots. Trees did not flourish at this great height and I wondered at them. Moving through the unusual setting marveling at the sounds and smells, I came to a clearing. There, in the center was a unique, beautiful temple. I surmised from camp stories that it was the shrine of Dionysus. It glowed in the flashes of lightening looking as if it were appearing and disappearing at will.

A huge bolt struck and the sky lit as if it were day. In amazement I saw the clearing was surrounded by women who were tall and beautiful with muscles of warriors. They wore wreaths of flowers in their hair. Living snakes wound around their arms. I knew from the campfire talks these women must be the maenads who protected the shrine and who fed those elite worshipers belonging to the cult of the souls.

The stories told these women of incredible physical power searched out animals and even humans tearing them limb from limb. It was their task to find the blood used as a sacrament by the elite followers of Dionysus who came to them to worship their god.

As I approached, I was stunned by their great beauty. A soft sound, the murmur of a woman in ecstasy, moaned from each throat. I was drawn forward without thought or fear. I stood at the edge of the clearing just beneath the trees, listening to their beckoning call.

Suddenly, one with hair like fire licking to her waist in swirling tendrils *reached her hands toward me. Mesmerized, I moved toward her. I felt I couldn't breathe if I did not touch her and feel her flesh. If I could not smell her fragrance, I would die of sorrow. Slowly I moved through the storm as in a dream.*

The moments stood still until, at last, I stood before her. Her long fingers reached to grasp my shoulders then one hand slid behind my head. The other moved to stroke my throat. I remember so clearly, I shuddered in anticipation of a magical embrace.

At once, she plunged her teeth into my throat. The pain was inhuman, exquisite. It was agony yet filled me with pleasure unlike any I had ever known. I could feel my body growing more and more cold, my strength ebbed with each draw she made on my vein.

The rain poured down upon us, her arms holding me tight as I began to sink to the ground. A crash so loud it deafened my dying ears came just to one side. One of the trees was struck by lightning and flames somehow leaped to life through the deluge of water. I saw them devour the thick trunk of the tree out of the corner of my eyes as my sight dimmed and the world grew dark.

By legend, the maenads are terrified by fire, the only thing that could do them harm. The red haired demon dropped me. To my fading eyes she appeared to float just above the ground as she moved quickly to the cover of the shrine. I fell to the wet earth. There was just enough strength left in my body to claw my way from the clearing and through the trees. I found a spot that was well hidden. I dug myself into a shallow grave and there I lay.

For three days I was overcome with pain and pleasure. Just when I knew I could not take another moment of the one, the other would possess me and somehow create balance so I did not lose my mind. I heard soldiers pass nearby but I could not call out. I thought I saw the beautiful devil come in and out of my consciousness biting and nibbling me over and over again. There was so much sensation in my body, my voice would not respond to my mind. I was on fire. I was ice. I was in agony. I was in passionate ecstasy. I was in a nether world.

At the end of the nightmare vigil, all sensation ceased and I lay there yet somehow still alive.

By the campfires, the old warriors told the tales of the cult of souls and now I knew them to be true. I had joined them without guile or will. I had become one of the undead.

Afraid and not knowing what to do, I made my way back to camp. It was night and the sentries were snoring around the campfires. I knew only one man who could help me. I moved silently through the dark to find him.

Stumbling upon the tent of Alexander through the night mist, I hurried toward the opening. The guard recognized me, greeting me with surprise. He told me they all thought I was killed in battle. He said Alexander and his retinue would be overjoyed to know I lived.

Murmuring a brief thanks, I moved aside the entrance flap, stepping though the opening into the warm, dry shelter of my commander.

He sat on the edge of the pallet he used for sleeping, looking up as he heard me enter. His surprise and delight showed on his face as he stood to embrace me. As he wrapped his arms around me, he stiffened. He knew I was changed. He, too, had heard the campfire stories. He stepped back from me as if I were poison. He wrapped his arms around himself as protection from what I had become.

I waited in the light of the candles. It seemed an eternity before he finally lifted his eyes. They were caring, without fear. He moved toward me once again. He embraced me and led me to his pallet. He said I looked tired, I needed to rest. He laid me down, enveloping me with his own covers. I fell into a swoon almost as soon as my head touched the soft cushions beneath me. I was naive and I trusted him.

I don't know what happened in the night. I don't know what he thought or with whom he consulted. I only felt the result of those hours.

As dawn was breaking, I heard, as if in a distance, rapid movement around me. Before I was awake and could move, a pain greater than *any I felt buried in the leaves of the forest floor exploded in my chest. I screamed in agony as I looked down to see a wooden stake driven into my heart and my commander standing above me with tears in his eyes. That was the last I saw with physical eyes for five hundred years.*

The captains carried my body out of the tent and into a rocky cave. They left it resting on an outcrop of cold rock, covered it with leather hides then piled rocks on top of it. They vacated the cave in silence.

I wondered at being able to observe what was happening to my body. How could it be that I was dead yet I was able to see and understand what ensued about my lifeless self? Unable to tear myself away from a carcass that had turned to stone, I waited, I knew not for what.

In the place I dwelled, there was no such thing as time and so it seemed as days but truly was centuries before I realized I was a dismembered being, conscious yet without a physical self. Thinking yet without a mind. In anguish yet without a heart to break. Lost for an eternity."

It was silent in her office for what seemed like several minutes.

"And that, Sarah, is how I came into being." His voice was soft, peaceful as he spoke.

#

Sarah gazed at the face of the man who lay in her recliner as her mind raced with questions. How had this unspeakable experience happened? What had brought this strange being into her life? Why was she the one to take this journey in the subconscious of a vampire? Was there even such a thing as a vampire? And if there was what in the hell was she doing making friends with him instead of running in the opposite direction? "What am I thinking, of course there is no such thing as vampires."

The sky began to darken outside her window as Carlos stirred in the recliner. She knew she must bring him back. She wondered how much she should allow him to remember. Her final decision was he had a right to know everything she knew whether it was truth or fantasy.

"Carlos, in a moment you will come back to real time. One. Two. Three….."

#

When he opened his eyes, he lay quietly without speaking for a very long time. She moved to the desk, lighting the lamp as twilight took over the late afternoon sky.

"Sarah." His voice was soft, tentative.

She moved back and sat in the chair next to him. "Yes Carlos. I'm here."

"What's happening here?" He looked at her with puzzled eyes. "Have I lost it completely?"

She smiled and reached to put her hand on his arm. "Carlos, I can only tell you what I think is going on. It's your subconscious talking to us, telling us a story to help us along our journey. I have researched past life regression until I'm cross eyed and I can't find anything that relates to your particular experience." She shook her head from side to side. "I'm as clueless about this as you are."

He turned to gaze at the patterns of lamp light cast on the ceiling. "What do we do now?"

"You have the same two choices you always have. Stop right here and don't do another regression or go forward and see what happens." She stood and crossed to the window. She looked out at the night sky for a few moments then turned to face him. "It's up to you. Whatever you want to do, I'm with you."

"Can we really learn anything doing this?" He asked her a question for which she had no honest answer.

"I don't know for sure, Carlos. I can tell you we're accessing some deeper truths about you, information I hope will give you more tools to manage your present life."

He stood up stretching his long arms over his head. He smiled as he crossed the room to stand in front of her. "Well, as long as we're in it together, it can't be all bad. So, I'll see you next week for my session." He captured her eyes with the intensity of his, "And don't be afraid. No matter what, I would never hurt you."

He turned and walked to the door of her office. By the time she turned around, he was gone.

CHAPTER 10

She left the city early on Saturday morning. It was an easy drive to her mother's home if she started before the traffic. She looked forward to visiting her mother and grandmother in spite of their constant comments about her single life, about her being alone. She told them repeatedly that she was fine but she was beginning to question herself. "Am I just fooling myself? Am I really simply lonely and that's why I work so much?" She pushed the thought to the back of her mind and concentrated on driving and the soft music coming from her CD player.

The house the two women lived in was so cozy and comfortable. It had been difficult for her mother when Sarah's father died. She stayed in their large home for almost two years but it was a burden for her to care alone and most of the rooms were closed, unused anyway. Then when Sarah's grandfather passed away, the two matriarchs of the family joined forces to buy a small home in one of the many quaint towns on the Fox River.

There was an unseasonal light blanket of snow on the ground when she pulled into the driveway. Sarah phoned as she left the toll way so her mother was watching for her from the front window. As she opened the trunk to remove her weekend travel bag, her mother opened the front door, calling to her.

"Hi honey. You're just in time for breakfast. Gran is making pancakes." She wrapped her pink cardigan more closely around her then stepped onto the porch to welcome her only child. "You're too thin. Don't you ever eat?" Taking the light bag from her hand, Sarah's mother bundled her into the warm front hall. "Take off your coat and go into the kitchen. Everything's waiting for you."

Sarah appreciated all of the familiar furniture her mother had managed to fit into the small house. It made her feel safe and at home to see some of the pieces she had known as a child. She made her way to the kitchen.

"Gran." She wrapped her arms around her petite grandmother then gave her a big kiss on the cheek. "It sure smells great in here. I'm starving. I didn't eat before I left and breakfast is my best meal."

"Sit down honey. Here come the pancakes." The griddle on the stove was already heated. She poured the batter into perfect little silver dollar circles. Her mother took the syrup out of the microwave. She placed it on the table. A pot of coffee sat on the warmer and there was a bowl of ripe, red strawberries just waiting to be eaten.

"I remember when we could only get strawberries in the summer. This is great!" She accepted the pancakes being offered her, poured syrup then covered them with berries.

"I love to see you eat like this, honey. You need to put on a little weight."

Sarah smiled to herself. What a change from her early years. Her life had been a constant battle for food when the two older women pushed her to be a professional ballerina. Now, being too thin was all they talked about. Life was certainly strange. And so was past life.

"So, I have this new client. Remember Colleen Stevens?" They both nodded yes. Colleen had spent one Christmas with the

Hagan's and once someone met her, it was unlikely they would ever forget her. "Well, she set me up to work with one of her parolees." Her mother stopped still. "You're working with a gangster, Sarah?" Her look of concern made Sarah chuckle.

"No, he's not a gangster, just a troubled young man. His name is Carlos and he's the most interesting past lifer I've ever treated."

"Tell us all about it." They all settled in for a cozy breakfast as Sarah recounted what little she was able to share of the Carlos story, everything that is except that he had been a vampire in a previous life.

#

She was sound asleep in the guest bedroom when her cell phone rang. She glanced at the clock by the bed. It was two thirty in the morning.

"Sarah, I need you. It's Carlos. Weird crap is happening in my head." His voice sounded strange, frightened. "I don't get it. I'm not hypnotized and I still hear that vamp character in my mind."

"Carlos. Just a minute. Let me wake up." She turned on the light and took a sip of water from the glass on the bedside table. "What are you talking about?"

"See, I'm hanging with my brother. Suddenly I'm talking all this weird crap like I'm in session and back in England. He thought I was high again. Sarah, I haven't touched anything since rehab. I don't know what the hell is going on."

"Where are you Carlos?"

"I'm sitting in an all-night diner. I don't want to go home. And I sure as hell don't want to go to sleep. I feel pretty strange."

She sat up, throwing the covers off her legs. "I can be back in the city in about an hour. Stay put and I'll call you when I get close. Where are you? I'll come and pick you up."

When he gave her the cross streets, she was surprised he was only a few blocks from her apartment. Her office was downtown and several miles away. She wondered if she would be safe taking him to her home. She decided she would be.

Sarah threw her things into her bag and started to dress. "Don't worry. I'm on my way. It's all going to be fine. It's just a residual thing that has happened. I'll fix it as soon as I get there. Exactly what were you doing when this feeling came over you?"

"Playing some stupid video game about knights and the round table. I don't know if that's what did it or not. I just sounded like somebody else and it freaked me out."

"Just hang in there. I'm on my way. I'll call you soon and if you feel too strange before I get in touch with you, call me back. I'll have my cell close all the time. See you before too long."

She closed her phone then tiptoed into her mother's room. She touched her parent on the shoulder. Her mother opened her eyes, sitting up immediately. "What's wrong honey?"

"Mom, I'm sorry but one of my clients is having an emergency. I have to get back to the city tonight. I'll call you in the morning." Her mother rose from her bed, slipping into her warm robe against the chill of the house. "Honey, call me when you get home. I'm concerned with you driving alone this late at night." She walked Sarah to the door. Wrapping her robe more closely around her, she waved to her daughter as she went down the steps to get into her car. "Call me," she mouthed without sound so as not to wake her neighbors.

"I will." She mouthed back. "Love you." Sarah shut the car door, turned the key in the ignition then backed down the driveway.

#

She opened the door of her apartment. Carlos followed her as they walked into the living room. She turned on a light then turned up the heat. She always turned it down when she was away from home.

"Can I get you something from the kitchen?"

"No. I drank enough coffee at the diner to float a boat. Look, I'm sorry I called you. It really is okay. It just freaked me out for a minute."

"Don't worry about it. It's fine." She motioned him to sit down in the big brown chair by the fireplace. "I'll light a fire and we can talk." She picked up the remote, clicked the switch and the gas fireplace sprang to life. "Modern miracles."

"Yeah. Sure is better than a cave." He smiled, trying to make light of his earlier fear.

"I think what's happened is your state was so deep on Friday and you were under for a long time. Then the video game set you off. It's nothing to worry about. Before you leave, we'll do a little session to make sure you feel comfortable." She moved to place the remote on the table next to him.

"You don't have to do that. I feel like an idiot calling you in the middle of the night. I just didn't know what was going on."

"Don't worry about waking me up. It's my job to make sure you feel safe all the time." Without thinking, she reached to touch his hand. He wrapped his other arm around her, forcing her to sit on the arm of the chair. "Sarah." His voice was hoarse and his eyes locked onto hers.

Shocked at his aggressive embrace, she pulled away from him, putting space between them. He flirted with her sometimes but he had always showed the utmost respect for her position as his psychologist until this moment.

He reached for her again, holding his arms wide. "Sarah, please. Just let me hold you." Carlos felt out of control in his desire to draw her to him, the need to hold her in his arms. He was moved by an emotion alien to his nature, as if someone else had crawled inside his skin.

"Carlos, this is impossible." Her heart pounded in fear of him and something else she wasn't sure she could name. "I am your therapist."

"Don't tell me you don't feel anything. I know you do."

"Do. Don't. It doesn't matter." She crossed to the other side of the room. "I am your therapist. I am here to help you to heal. And please, don't do that again. It's impossible."

He looked at the gas fire. "Alright. I'm sorry. I'm really sorry." Carlos leaned forward in the chair, rested his elbows on his knees and clasped his hands. He hung his head. "I don't know what came over me." He looked up at her. "Brother does that sound lame." He hoped she didn't see the apprehension in his eyes; his fear of these strange, overpowering emotions.

"It's fine. It didn't happen, okay?" She fumbled with the remote to adjust the fire. She didn't want him to see how nervous she was in his presence. She was astonished by her desire to fall into his arms. "Am I really that empty," she thought. She took the moment to recover her self-control. "Let's do a mini-session here for you so you can go home and get some sleep." She placed the remote on the coffee table, turning to face him once again. "Where are you living now? Are you back with your family?"

"No. I'm still in the halfway house. I don't want to go back to those crazy people. I'm gonna stay straight if it's the last thing I do. My father hates me. If I go back there, he'll drive me nuts." He was getting agitated just speaking about his family.

"I understand." She smoothed her jeans with her hands and sat on the coffee table so she could be close to him while she put him in a hypnotic state yet not close enough to get comfortable. She motioned him to lie on the sofa. "Here, lie down. Let's hypnotize you. It will calm you down so you can go to the halfway house tonight and we both can get a little rest."

CHAPTER 11

Sarah finished her last bite of salad just as Maggie stepped inside her office door. "He's here."

"Fine, send him in." She tossed the empty container into the trash can under her desk, then moved to the chair by the recliner.

"Hi." He closed the door behind him. Embarrassed, he looked at the ground when he spoke.

"Hi." Her first thought was to make him more comfortable. "Why don't you lie down and we'll start today with a session with Aris."

"Sounds good to me." Relieved, he flopped into the recliner and closed his eyes.

#

CARLOS HAVARRO, transcript, session 7, March 26

Now, of course, I know I could have left the cave. Then, I knew nothing of what I was capable. I did not know if time passed or stood still. I could not see my body beneath the hides and so I had no knowledge if it was still whole or had returned to dust. As I told you, there is no such thing as time to a disembodied spirit. I did not exist so neither did the passing of days or months. The cave was dark, dry and didn't change with seasons so I was unaware if it was winter or summer. If centuries had passed. Or a millennium."

His words were soft, difficult to hear. Sarah leaned in toward him to make sure she was able to capture every word on her recorder.

At last, I sensed something or someone outside the cave. Then I sensed sounds, human rustling and murmuring nearby. I waited anxiously to see if someone might enter.

The noises continued then became intermittent and finally ceased. They were gone. I had no idea how long it had been since I had seen another soul. I ached for the sight of just one mortal being. I felt alone, desolate on the earth.

After a time, I know not how long, the silence was broken. Different this time than the last. First horses, then several·humans. There was shouting, scuffling and the clanging of swords. A sudden hush then the horses galloped away and all was still for a moment. Then I heard the groan of someone in terrible pain, a shuffling of feet. A man staggered into the cave. He was covered in blood, his hands grasped a gaping wound in his side. He fell to the ground where he lay silent, barely breathing.

My bodyless self was drawn toward the dying man, an uncontrollable vacuum sucking my soulless soul closer and closer to him. I felt his death throes were a part of my emptiness and a way out of my sorrows. My essence was swallowed by his grisly, flowing wound. The blood surrounded me and burned me, filling me with ecstasy. Just as his spirit left his body, mine claimed it. I was again an animated man with arms and legs and human senses. And I felt my new body was on fire.

The pain of the affliction almost overcame my consciousness but, not knowing how long I would survive, I refused to lose a moment of this new life. I writhed in agony. Lifting my head, I stared into my belly and before my eyes, the wound began to close. Each movement I made created a greater horror of pain yet the gash continued to seal. I laid my head back on the dirt holding the screams inside my throat, afraid, lest the killers would return. Slowly and I know not how long I lay there, the pain grew less and less. After a time, it became bearable and until at last, it ceased. My new body slept, exhausted yet alive. Yes, somehow, I was alive.

I do not know how long I slept and when I woke, my legs were unsteady as I stood. To have a body made of flesh. I almost swooned. I was overcome with sensation. I moved my wrists. I bent my fingers. I turned my hands to look at the palms. I touched my face. My fingers slid over my cheeks then down to my jaw. The flesh felt soft to my hands. I had form. I had human form. Then slowly, one tentative step at a time, I advanced. My eyes ached as I drew near the entrance of the cavern. The daylight was molten gold. Its glow revealed my new, youthful, strong male body and stoked an unfamiliar fire in my belly.

I staggered as the brilliance met my eyes. It caused a greater pain than the burning in my gut. I fell to my knees and crawled to the shelter of a rock over hang. Curling into a fetal ball, I wrapped one arm over my eyes for protection against the sun not seen for five hundred years and the other around my abdomen, a shield against the driving hunger.

I lay there in the shadow until the sun disappeared from the horizon. The night birds began their song and only then was I able to lift my eyes towards the heavens. It was glorious. Deep, black space. Cool night air. I stood and stretched my arms to the full moon that rose in the east and breathed in the scent of the night. The darkness saturated the very bones of my precious new body.

My mind raced with questions. Where was I? How much time had passed? What was the year?

As I gazed at the stars, my thirst grew stronger and lashed out as a raging beast. A beast driven by a savage hunger. A hunger for blood.

Silence filled the room. Sarah took a deep breath, and then spoke. "Human blood?"

Yes I could smell it in the air. I crept toward what was left of a camp. Did it belong to the poor unfortunate whose body I now inhabited? The smells told me it did. And my need to drink enveloped me. I burned in agony. The pain blinded my eyes and my soul, yet through it, my tracking sense was more acute than that of a stalking wolf.

I knelt to examine deep gouges in the earth made by horses' hooves.

Yes, men and their mounts. I rose and saw signs of a scuffle near his bloodied and torn sleeping pallet. Suddenly, it was clear. Bandits. This body that now was mine had been besieged by bandits in the night; they pilfered his purse then took his life. I could smell the stench of them throughout the meager camp.

Rage erupted within me fueled by a frenzied desire for human blood that heretofore I never knew existed.

My senses were a hundred fold strong. A thousand. More strong than the number of stars in the sky. I turned to follow their trail. I would kill to feed and to avenge the departed soul whose body I inhabited.

I tracked the criminals without hindrance. I stalked them the next night as they sat by their campfire and drank wine from a filthy animal skin. I watched from the darkness as they became sodden with drink and their minds and their songs turned into discordant melodies. At last, the light of the flames burned low. One by one, they ended their night in their own personal stupor. I waited patiently, quietly, watching as each one of the half dozen men fell into his own final sleep.

Just before dawn, at the deepest time of their slumber, I crept into the camp. The fire was mere embers and cast no more than a ghostly golden glow on those sleeping closest to it.

Unable to control the monster that drove my ungodly thirst, I feasted. One after another, I drained them. Silently. Deadly. Joyfully. I took their lives as I drained their warm, red blood and left their dead bodies to the elements. I fed quietly, with deadly speed until, at last, none was left alive. The blood lust left me. Satiated at last, I stood quietly, surveying my work. I grimaced at the grisly sight before me, then crept through the trees finding a sheltered spot off any path. There I rested in silence and considered my lot.

I did not choose my new life. It was forced upon me without consent. I shuddered at what I had become. As I looked at the red stains on my hands and covering my clothes, I understood my true future for the first time. I was driven to drink blood. It was primal. There was no alternative. I was a savage and would be for all eternity. I was alone, without country or family or friends. It was a desolate truth I faced on that morning and I felt I could not endure it. I know not how long I sat in solitary meditation.

At last, the forlorn stillness was broken by the sounds of bird song. I looked around me at the morning light shining on the dew soaked leaves and grass; the scent of fresh, black earth filled my nostrils. A ray of sun came through the deep green leaves of the oak trees and warmed me.

I was alive. I had consciousness, a presence, flesh and blood. The body I inhabited was young and strong. I recalled my life as a warrior in the army of Alexander. Overcome with blood lust in every battle, I slaughtered without remorse, killing on command. For those actions, I was acclaimed and exalted. How was that murder any more just than that of the slain bandits? Dead is dead. The only difference was consuming their blood and that I must do to continue my existence.

I sat without moving until the sun disappeared from above the trees. The soft light of evening settled over the forest and the air grew cool. A day of profound contemplation behind me, I was at last at peace. There was no changing my fate. I was exactly what I was, no more and no less. I was a cold one. A blood drinker. A vampire.

#

There was only the sound of her breathing as the tip of the waning moon peeked over the skyline. She couldn't speak. Plagued by the same questions over and over, was it true or just imagination? What was the purpose of his story? When her eyes were able to focus on Carlos through the thick dark of the room, she saw his perfect, white teeth as his peaceful smile reflected in the moonlight.

"*Sarah, you have been without a question for a very long time.*" He broke the long, shadowed silence. "*Have I frightened you with my story?*" The deep voice showed concern. "*I don't want to frighten you.*" He paused then spoke again, "*Yes. Yes I do.*"

The lights from the office windows that filled the tall buildings surrounding them were the only lights that illuminated the room. Carlos lay still as a corpse.

Her voice shook as she answered. "You want to frighten me?"

"*I want to frighten you so badly that you never call me again. That you turn this man out of your office and out of your life.*"

"But why? I'm certainly not a threat to you."

"*No, yet I pose an enormous threat to you.*"

"What kind of threat could you possibly make toward me?"

"*Once you understand my past, you will know why I cling to Carlos so desperately, through him I have a channel to you. I have searched through time for you and now, I have found you.*" Then he laughed. "*But for now, I will confound you and be in your every thought.*" Again, he whispered, "*And remember this always, we will, once again, be joined.*"

#

Sarah was stunned. She couldn't move. Her breath came in short gasps. What did he mean? "Once again be joined," she whispered? She stared out the window at the darkening sky.

"Don't be a fool," she chanted softly. "Don't be a fool." She convinced herself it was just Carlos' vivid imagination and the current fascination with vampires; his subconscious playing tricks on both of them. "It's just his imagination. Don't be a fool." Soon the mantra had a soothing effect on her thoughts. She was able to breathe easy once more.

When she was fully composed, she began to bring Carlos back to real time, a time where all she had to deal with was a young gang member and her hardest task was helping him stay on parole.

#

Sarah placed the remnants of her half eaten dinner on the bottom shelf of her refrigerator then sat down at her computer. She had plenty of time to finish her latest vampire research and still get to bed early.

She was stunned when she glanced up from her work to look at the clock. "Three in the morning. Good grief." She yawned and stretched then stood up, pushing the chair back under the dining room table. "I've got to get some sleep."

Turning off the living room lights, she stepped into her bedroom. "I have to be up at six. I'm going to keel over before tomorrow is through." Crossing to the bathroom, she passed her tall mirror. Stepping in to get a closer look, she cringed at her tired reflection. "Heavens, I look like one of the undead myself." She had circles under her eyes and her skin was as dry as parchment. "Too much coffee." She brushed her teeth then pulled a hair brush through her hair.

She was already wearing her pajamas so she climbed into her bed, pulling the comforter close around her shoulders. Her intention had been to go to bed at eleven. When she checked the clock the first time, she still had twenty minutes left to research vampires. When she checked again, it was three a.m. "I am out of my mind. It has finally happened. I don't sleep. I don't eat. I am obsessed by a five-hundred-year-old vampire and a twenty-five-year-old gang banger. What the hell is the matter with me? I know I have finally lost it. There is no one I can talk to about this. No one. Not if I don't want to lose my license, be classified insane and committed to an institution. What the hell am I going to do?"

A soft voice inside her head said, "Just go to sleep Sarah." And she did.

#

Sarah was dreamless until just before dawn. As the pitch black night sky began to brighten to a timid gray, her sleeping conscious mind stepped aside, allowing her subconscious to conjure images of a time long past. She watched herself, being a part of the scene yet somehow outside of it.

The otherworldly indigo sky above her was filled with thousands of brilliant stars shimmering their enchantment. Her creamy satin slippers reflected their starlight as her feet skimmed over the lush green grass beneath them. She was floating, weightless yet with human form. Her gown was of the finest blue satin, the color of a clear summer afternoon sky. The skirt and peplum were sprinkled with hundreds of tiny, creamy pearls sown to form flawless rosettes. Tall walls of lush green foliage lined the narrow path on either side of her. A lover's labyrinth? A royal English maze perhaps?

Compelled to move forward, she glided slowly at first, then faster. She was drawn by an unseeable force so overpowering her will was ineffectual against it. The towering walls of the maze grew even higher until they obliterated all light from the heavenly bodies above. The air grew heavy, moist and dank. The unyielding bodice of her dress bound her so tightly, she felt she would suffocate. Her heart hammered in her chest. Her vision grew dull as her world began to spin. Like Alice in the fairy tale, she spiraled downward into a never ending chasm and amazingly, still like Alice, she was more questioning of her surroundings than she was fearful. The deeper down she descended, the slower she fell until, at long last, her feet touched gently on an ancient stone floor.

She found herself in a corridor reaching to infinity in either direction. Golden sconces lined the time worn walls; the beeswax candles shuddered in a draft casting unearthly dancing shadows on the floor and ceiling. Spring water seeped through a few crevices in the enormous rocks sweetening the fragrance of the air. She stood stock still, unable to move left or right.

She was startled by a faint sound behind her as, without warning, large warm strangely familiar hands gently wrapped around her shoulders. "Do not be afraid. No. No, you must not turn around, be still"

A tremor ran through her. Even though she was distressed, his voice awakened a longing in her that was new and enticingly frightening.

Her senses stirred. A feeling of deep warmth flooded through her.

"I will do you no harm." His voice was low, caressing. He stood close behind her and as he spoke, his breath stirred her thick blond curls like a tender breeze of soft warm air. His hands slowly traced her arms as they slid down to encompass her waist. His fingers moved to the front of her blue satin stomacher where they touched, forming a "v" on her soft belly. Heat began to seep through the fabric of her gown into the core of her very being. Heat and a fire that raged. She felt faint, unable to catch her breath.

"Breathe, my beauty, you must breathe." His palms, resting on her hips, gently pressed her into him, into his awakened manhood.

Her breath came then. Hot. Raspy. Again she attempted to turn to face him. He held her fast. His lips brushed the nape of her neck sending burning threads of fire into the deepest part of her. Her very being was consumed by her need. She felt the caress of his sweet gentle teeth against her flesh. She whimpered in pleasure.

"Please, please," she whispered, her heart pounding wildly in her chest.

The bites grew more and more demanding. She begged, weeping with desire. "Now. Please, now."

Long sharp fangs sank slowly, sensuously into a vessel at the nape of her neck. Glorious waves of feeling swelled inside of her each time he drew from her until her body abandoned itself, surrendering to the flame that consumed her. She cried out as a deep shudder convulsed her.

Sarah was panting as she bolted upright in her bed. Her sheets were wrapped in a corkscrew around her perspiring body. She brushed the hair from her eyes with her fingers as she looked out her window at the city at dawn. After some long, deep breaths, she sighed and smiled as she leaned her head back on her pillow. She whispered a soft moan as she reached her fingers to softly and gently massage the back of her neck.

CHAPTER 12

Sarah always enjoyed having a girl's night at her apartment. She delighted in finding new recipes to cook for her friends. Sometimes they were great and sometimes not quite edible, but she happily embraced the opportunity to experiment.

"Look Sarah, I don't know if I'm ready to get married and have kids. It's not fair the way Bob's putting the screws to me." She reached across the table to spear a piece of tomato and a slice of cucumber from Sarah's salad.

"C, if you want salad, there's a whole bowl on the kitchen counter, stay out of mine. And this marriage and baby stuff is between you and Bob. There is no way I would even think of sticking my nose in here. It's just too personal."

"Some therapist you are." Colleen rose from the dining room table, picked up her plate then walked to the kitchen. "Want some more wine?"

"Sure. Sounds good. No work tomorrow. Yeah!"

"By the way, about work, Carlos came into my office yesterday on time for our meeting and wearing a belt, if you can believe it. He's even more articulate and was talking about a book he is reading. What the hell are you doing to him?" She brought the wine bottle back to the dining room, topped each of their glasses then placed it on the table between them.

"Just the usual mumbo jumbo. He simply is a really good subject for hypnosis, the brighter someone is, the easier it is to work with them." Sarah felt a little bit uncomfortable. She wanted to tell Colleen about the whole situation including her misgivings and her concern about the vampire saga but she couldn't. Her professional code made it difficult to talk about him at all.

"I mean he's really changing. Funny thing is he wants to. He's been talking about taking some night classes, about doing something with his life." Colleen twirled her pasta into a huge roll on her fork then stuffed it in her mouth, talking the whole time she chewed. "Where's Bonnie? I thought she was coming for dinner."

"She called just before you got here. She had to finish some client notes before she left the office." As if at a signal, there was a knock at the door.

Bonnie looked frantic as she entered the apartment. She rushed across the living room and closed the drapes, speaking as she moved. "I found a parking place out front. While I was parking, a guy was standing across the street staring up toward your window." Her frightened eyes darted back and forth between Sarah and Colleen. "Sarah, he didn't move. He just stood there like a statue. He scared me so I told the doorman to keep an eye on him."

Both Sarah and Colleen jumped from their chairs. As Colleen hurried to the window, she grabbed her bag, pulling out her cell phone. Sarah was already peeking through the opening in the drapes. She saw Carlos standing in the shadow of the awning in front of the building across the street.

Colleen snatched the curtain from her and looked out. "What the hell? I'm calling Bob. I can't believe it; he looks like he's on drugs again."

Sarah grabbed the phone from her friend's hand. "No. No police. He wouldn't use. I know he wouldn't. There's something else wrong. I'm going down to see him."

"Are you out of your mind?" Bonnie blocked her way.

Ignoring their words, she pushed past them. "No guys. He wouldn't hurt me. I'm going to see what's happening." Colleen and Bonnie exchanged a look of surprise, amazed at the reaction of their normally passive friend.

She grabbed her trench coat, putting it on as she hurried down the hall. She spoke as she pressed the elevator button, "Don't call anyone. I can handle this."

Her heart was pounding in her chest as the elevator doors opened. She raced across the lobby. "It's okay Ralph, just a friend in trouble. Be right back." She tried to smile as she made for the door.

The traffic slowed. She ran across the street. As she approached Carlos, she noticed his eyes weren't blinking, he hardly appeared to be breathing.

"Carlos." He didn't move. She spoke louder. "Carlos." Still he didn't move or acknowledge her. "Might as well try to bring him back," she thought out loud. "Carlos, one. Two. Three. Four. Five. Eyes open, wide awake."

He shook his head several times. "Where the hell am I? Sarah? What are you doing here?" He shook his head again. "Where am I?" There was fear in his voice as he spoke.

"You're fine. Carlos, you're fine. You're outside my apartment."

"How did I get here? What am I doing here? Sarah, what is happening to me?" His eyes locked on hers and she could see panic just below the surface.

"I'm here and we'll figure this out together." She glanced up at her window. Bonnie and Colleen were glued to the glass. "Wait here. I'm going to clear out my company so you can come upstairs to my apartment. You can stay until you feel better."

"You're not afraid of me?" He looked at her with sad eyes.

"No, of course not. You're fine. You're just fine. Now, don't move.

I'll clear them out then come down to get you." She hugged him quickly before hurrying across the street.

"Was that Colleen Stevens I saw leaving?" He sat at the dining room table while she cleared the dishes.

"Yes. She and another friend came for dinner. Are you hungry?" She paused before she removed her plate of uneaten pasta.

"No thanks." He had his elbows on the table, his head buried in his hands.

"How about a glass of wine?"

"No thanks, I haven't had a drink since rehab." His voice was muffled.

She placed the plate on the table. She touched his shoulder gently. "Carlos, everything is alright. We're in this together." When he lifted his face, his expression was like a frightened little boy. "I won't leave you. I'm here."

He stood, wrapping his arms around her. It wasn't a romantic embrace but a necessary one. She held him for what seemed like a long time. His breathing slowly returned to normal.

Reluctantly, he pulled away from her arms. "I guess I'd better go."

"Listen, why don't you stay here tonight? I've got a guest room. The bed is comfortable. You are more than welcome." She just couldn't see him spend the night at a half-way house in his present condition. "I'll have Colleen take care of the people at the half-way house tomorrow. Don't worry about that."

"Are you sure?" His voice was soft as he spoke but the meaning was clear. "I won't bother you."

"I know you won't. It's sort of my fault that you're having these experiences anyway. Carlos, I don't want you to feel you're on your own."

He smiled.

"Come on. I'll show you the guest room. There's a shower too, so if you'd like to clean up before you go to bed, you won't bother me."

On the way down the hall, she stopped at the linen closet. She handed him a towel, one of the spare toothbrushes and the individual toothpaste tubes she kept for guests. She opened the door to the guest room and turned on the light.

Stopping at the door, she let him pass. He turned to look at her. "Thanks." That was all that he could say. "Thanks so much."

"It's fine. Sleep well." She shut the door. As she walked down the hall to her room, she whispered to herself, "What have you just done?" She shivered a little then straightened her shoulders. "What I've just done is I helped someone in need of a friend." She went into her room, tucked herself in then fell into a deep sleep.

#

The harsh ring of her phone woke her. She looked at the clock. Six o'clock in the morning. Who was the idiot to call at six o'clock on Saturday morning? She reached for the phone.

"What do you want?"

"Nice way to answer the phone." Colleen's voice was angry. "What do you think I want? Are you okay?"

"Of course I'm okay. Why are you calling me so early on my day off?"

"Because you threw us out so you could bring a crazy guy into your apartment. When did he leave?"

Sarah yawned, "He's still here."

"He's what?" The anger in her voice was replaced by shock and disbelief.

"He's still here asleep in the guest room unless this frigging phone woke him up like it did me." She was grumpy and didn't mind letting it show.

"He stayed last night?"

"I just said he's in the guest room. I couldn't send him back to that half-way house last night. He was exhausted. And miserable."

"Sarah, what's going on between you two?" The concern in her voice was clearly recognizable.

"Nothing, Colleen. Nothing is going on. He's basically a good person and I am doing my best to help him find himself. That's what you wanted me to do, isn't it?"

"Yeah, sure but I didn't mean for you to put yourself at risk. He's been in trouble so much. I'm just nervous about your safety."

"C, I'm a big girl. I've been doing this job for a long, long time. I've never been accosted by a client and I don't plan on that happening now." She sat on the edge of her bed. "Thanks for worrying about me but I'm alright. Now, let me get back to sleep. Okay?"

"I don't know about you, Sarah. This hero business is way out of character. Sometimes I think you're a little flakey."

Sarah laughed, "You're calling me flaky? You? Honey, the word wasn't invented until you were born. Now quit worrying. And good night." She put the phone down on her nightstand. She slipped into her robe and quietly opened her door.

"Might as well see if he's still sleeping." She tiptoed down the hall. She peeked into the guest room. He was gone. The bed was made and a note rested on the pillow. It read, "Thank you for everything. I'll see you at session on Friday. You really are my guardian angel. Carlos."

She was sorry they wouldn't have breakfast together. She told herself it was because she wanted to be sure he was alright. What other reason could there be? She folded the note, tucking it into the pocket of her robe. She went to her room, crawling back into her bed. It was strange but somehow the house felt empty without him. Now who was the crazy one?

CHAPTER 13

"Are you sure you want to go under today?"

He pushed back in the leather recliner. "Sure. It's the only way we're going to get to the bottom of this. Come on Sarah. Deep sleep me." Smiling, he winked at her.

She had felt a little disconcerted when he walked into her office but just a moment with him and their previous comfort returned. She watched him closely as she spoke the usual induction to place him in a hypnotic trance.

CARLOS HAVARRO, transcript, session 8, April 2

I traveled many miles and many long weeks. I was able to run with the speed of a wild animal. I did not see another human being. I was grateful the burning hunger for human life did not return. When I thirsted, I drank from forest animals and they sustained me. I did notice that my skin grew more and more white as time passed and I also grew stronger; I was able to run incredible distances at inconceivable speeds.

The clothing I wore kept me covered and warm, but it was simple, rough cloth. As I traveled it became worn and soiled. I longed for soft fabrics, rich textures. My clothes in the camp of Alexander were those of a soldier, but they were the finest cloth and leather that could be purchased. I remembered my life as a human. My soul was of an aristocrat, a warrior. None of that had changed, I still longed for the finer things. For the fight, the accolades. For blood spilled and now, for blood taken.

The days turned cold and the nights frigid, still I traveled. I knew not where I was or to where I journeyed, only that I must keep moving. Slowly, quietly, the gnawing in my belly returned.

Just as a cold, damp dawn broke through the blackness of night, I heard sounds from a great distance carried on the morning wind. A battle raged, I was sure of it; where there was battle, there were human beings and where there were humans, there was warm, pulsing blood.

As I neared the skirmish, the smell of death surrounded me. I staggered and almost fell as the burning inside my core ignited. My eyes glazed over. I could not see, did not need to see. I was propelled through the woods by my hunger. The noise became a living entity as I burst out of the forest and into the fray.

I fought like the devil I was. As I killed with my hands and my teeth, my clothes became saturated and slick with the drippings from my victims. I drank again and again and was satiated, still I fought. I killed in a frenzy. I pulled swords from dead bodies and battled on fighting my way toward a huge building on the horizon.

Separated from the fray, seated on a horse surrounded by guards, sat a commander. His ornate uniform was still clean, his sword yet dry. I swarmed his protectors, killing and moving on until there was no one between me and the great man. An arrow flew, piercing his mount in the chest. Many arrows followed and the great beast lifted onto his hind legs bellowing, pawing the air. He fell to the earth in his death throes. Seizing the moment, I grabbed the commander and twisted his arms behind his back, holding him steady with my great strength. I looked right and left, not knowing what to do with my prisoner.

"You there," a voice cut the battle cry like a knife. "Bring Francis to me." Like any good warrior, I responded to a strong command. I turned toward the voice. There, behind me, seated on a tall stallion, dressed in

strange garb, sat a man, an officer by his stature and regal saddlery. "I say, bring him to me."

I pushed my prisoner through his dead comrades toward the mounted officer.

"Are you one of my men?" We were surrounded by a cadre of men protecting the clearing where we stood. Still they fought like animals all around us, yet in the center of the circle there was calm.

I was able to understand his words. I knew that his language was not my own and not from my time. Yet his desires were clear to me. I was wary of speaking to him should he learn what I was and destroy me.

"Speak up. Who are you?"

I went down on one knee and lowered my head.

"I am Aris." My words were clear to him, I knew not how, yet questioned not.

"Rise Aris. Join my ranks. You have just captured the King of France."

He threw his great head back and roared in laughter.

Taking hold of my hand, he swung me onto the back of his horse. "The Emperor will know of your courage."

"Bring this King with you to camp," he spoke to his men. "Treat him well and do not allow his escape or all your lives will be forfeit."

He tugged the reins and his horse rose onto its hind legs then shot through the battlefield as if a devil were chasing it. And perhaps it was true as I was the one that rode on its rear haunches.

"Sarah, I will not tell you any more stories if you do not breathe." He laughed.

She gulped air. "I didn't realize I had stopped. Please go on."

"No, enough for today."

"But you must tell me, where are you? What year is it?"

"I am in Pavia and it is the year 1525. I captured Francis 1st, King of France. And I surrendered him to Charles de Lannoy of the Spanish Imperial Army."

"But..."

*"No. Enough. Carlos is becoming restless. I do not want to do him
any harm. He is my medium and as I share his mind, I perceive he is a
good man. Rather than cause him distress, I wish to aid in his healing
as he is aiding in mine. So, it is time I take my leave. Farewell sweet
Sarah."*

"Aris?"

Silence filled the room. The only sound she heard was labored
breathing. She wasn't sure if it came from Carlos or from her.

#

Stretched out in her bed, her legs were numb from the weight of
her laptop. She set it aside and wiggled her toes. It was past two in
the morning. She felt exhausted but she found out all she wanted
to know about Pavia. "Wonder how they got Italy out of the name
Pavia," she questioned silently.

Aris not only stumbled onto a battle that changed the course
of history, he also had been the one who brought the change full
course. Charles V, Holy Roman Emperor of Spain imprisoned the
French King in Madrid for a year. Francis finally signed a treaty and
was sent back to France.

"They fought three more times. Boy, Francis didn't give up." She
read out loud to herself. "Well it paid off, he finally won. Wow. He
beat Charles. And Henry VIII. That's what I call a real grudge."

She closed her laptop then set it on the bedside table. Stretching
her arms, she sighed.

"Another late night brought about by Aris. I guess he was right.
He is occupying my thoughts. All the time." She switched off the
light and lay down, bringing the covers over her shoulders. "No
more. Absolutely no more. Starting tomorrow, Aris moves out of
first place in my thoughts." As she drifted toward sleep she realized
it had been some time since she had seen her dream lover and her
fatigued mind didn't know if that was a really good thing or a really
sad thing.

CHAPTER 14

"Man, if I get one more case I'll never get to see Bob. I'm booked solid for the next week and a half. I've got paperwork coming out of my ears and there are at least a hundred million new regulations coming down or at least it seems like it." Colleen took a huge bite of her hamburger. "Saul's burgers are the best."

"There's mustard on your chin." Sarah ate the last tomato in her salad then put her fork on the plate. "What kind of regulations?"

"Nothing that's going to affect Carlos. And by the way, the last time he came in, he was wearing khakis. I mean, khakis?" She dipped her French fry into the glob of ketchup on her plate and popped it into her mouth. "He said he's looking for a job. It's kind of weird. It's like he's turning into someone else before my eyes."

Sarah shifted uncomfortably in her seat. "Oh?"

"Yeah. He had this cute accent but it's disappearing. He's combing his hair and shaving." She sipped her milk shake and drained the glass. "This hypno stuff really seems to be working." She stacked her plates then wiped her hands on her napkin. "Have you hit the anger button yet?"

"No, but we're working on it." Sarah picked up the check then reached for her bag.

"No you don't. This time it's on me." Colleen took the slip of paper out of Sarah's hand, added some bills to it and tucked it under her plate. "Come on. Let's go. I've got to get to the court house."

As they stood to walk to the door, Colleen asked, "Would you be interested in taking on another one of my parolees?"

Sarah stopped cold. "Not on your life, C. Not on your life. I've more than got my hands full!"

#

Carlos sat in the chair opposite Sarah. He slouched and rubbed his chin.

"So sometimes the session is clear and sometimes I can't remember it. What's up with that?" He shook his head in bewilderment. "And sometimes I don't even feel like myself any more. I'm reading books and the newspaper and I do it because I want to. It's starting to scare me." He sat forward on the edge of his chair, leaned his elbows on his knees and looked down at the floor. "And what's really weird is I like it."

He was silent for a moment. When he spoke, his gaze was directly into her eyes. "I do want to change. I do want to be someone you'd be proud to know. You and Colleen are the first people other than the brothers in the hood who have ever really cared what happens to me. Sarah, I'd rather die than let you down."

"I understand what you're saying. I honestly do. Please, don't think I'm not proud of what you've accomplished. I see the changes in you and they're pretty amazing." She reached across the table that was between them placing her hand on his. "You are more calm. You have so much more control in your life." She smiled a tentative smile. "I know that we don't totally understand what is happening between real time and your hypnotic self. I won't lie to you and say that it's clear to me. But don't discount the positive forward steps you have taken through this. You're looking for a job. You are sober and glad to be." Her voice was sincere as she looked into his eyes. "You have come a long way in just a few months.

Don't you see that?"

"What I see, Sarah, is you." His words came from somewhere deep in his subconscious mind, nothing logical or mundane. "Every minute of every day, I see you." He took her hands in his. "Without you, I wouldn't care about any of this. Without you, I would be alone. You've changed my life."

She pulled her hands away. "No, it isn't me. It's you. You've done the work." Her heart pounded in her chest as she felt the warm spot where he touched her skin. She stood facing the window. "You're like a little brother to me." The words caught in her throat. She felt so much more than that for this young man but could never admit it to herself or to him. She couldn't explain her feelings for Carlos but she thought they were somehow connected to the strange way she was drawn to Aris, a vampire from a distant past.

He rose and crossed the room to stand by her side. "Is that what you really feel for me?"

"Yes, you are like family to me." She met his eyes for an instant. "I care what happens to you."

He reached for her and she turned quickly, stepping away from him, putting space between them.

"Now," she looked at her watch as he took a tentative step toward her, "you had better go. It's almost time for my next appointment. I'll see you next Friday."

"And I promise I will do my best not to embarrass you again, Sarah. I'm sorry." He walked out the door, shutting it behind him.

CHAPTER 15

Cranking up the volume on her headphones, Sarah increased the incline on the treadmill and closed her eyes. After a few minutes, she disappeared into the zone. It didn't seem too long since she had last visited the gym, but she could feel a difference in her workout.

"Hey Sarah." Bonnie touched her arm to get her friend's attention.

Startled, she glanced up quickly. She smiled. "Hey Bonnie."

"Where have you been? I haven't seen you at the gym since the night of the midnight stalker." She chuckled as she climbed on the elliptical sitting beside Sarah.

"He wasn't a stalker, Bonnie, he was a client in trouble." She was a bit disgruntled at the negative description of Carlos.

"Sorry. It was just a little weird, that's all." Bonnie could feel the tension between them. Aiming to ease it, she headed for neutral ground. "How's Colleen?"

"She's doing great. She and Bob have set a date. Are you going to their engagement party?"

"Yeah, I wouldn't miss it. I can't believe she finally let go and made a definite commitment for the wedding. She's been terrified of actually getting married ever since she said yes." Bonnie took a sip from her water bottle.

"Yeah, well Bob is a good guy. He'll make a great husband." Sarah wondered if she would ever find honest, true love like theirs as she wiped her forehead with a small white towel, She glanced at her watch.

"Wow, I didn't realize it was so late. It seems I'm always rushing. I've got to get going. I've got a client in an hour." She stepped off the treadmill.

"Don't be a stranger, Sarah. We miss you around here." Bonnie's voice was sincere as she spoke.

Smiling, Sarah squeezed Bonnie's arm. "See you soon." She hurried into the locker room. Humming, she stepped into the shower. The steaming water relaxed her tense muscles. She sighed in surrender.

#

"How can I help?" Sarah asked her friend as Colleen balanced two plates of hors d 'oeuvres and a tray on her hands.

"I'm good," she pushed open the door from the kitchen heading for the kitchen and her bustling engagement party. Rock music blasted, then quieted as the door swung shut again. Sarah appreciated the charm of the old house Colleen and Bob rented. She loved the swinging door and the huge single tub sink that stood on tall ceramic legs just in front of the kitchen window. It reminded her of the old black and white movies she enjoyed watching.

"Where did all these people come from?" Sarah picked up a tray of vegetables and dip, following Colleen into the fray.

"Friends of Bob's and some people from my office." She placed the new dishes on the coffee table adding the tray to the assortment of finger foods on display. "It isn't every day a cop gets engaged." She said the words as if her fiancé was the only one involved in the engagement.

"How about a parole officer?" Sarah smiled. "Aren't you a part of this too?"

"Sarah, I'm nervous enough about this commitment stuff. Don't bring it up now, okay?"

"Don't take everything so seriously. This is a party."

"So what's not serious about 'till death we do part'? I'd like to see how you'd feel right about now if you were wearing my four inch stilettos and forced into setting the date."

"Chill, Colleen. Here comes your future husband." Sarah smiled as Bob approached.

"Sarah, great to see you." He eyed all the food. "I'm starved. This looks great." He hugged his future wife. "You do all this honey?"

"Yeah, I ordered it from the deli. All by myself."

Bob kissed her on the nose. "Good job, sweet one." He munched a tiny hotdog wrapped in cheese.

"Oh, by the way Sarah, Jeff is coming by for a minute. I hope you don't mind. I ran into him today and I let it slip about the party. I couldn't not ask him." He looked at her quizzically.

"How could I mind?" All she could think was she hoped her ex-husband didn't bring his young, gorgeous, new wife. "I haven't seen him in months." She hoped her words sounded convincing.

"He said they might be late. Susan has to work late at the magazine." He turned and walked away.

"I didn't know they were coming. Honest." Colleen spoke apologetically.

"No worries," she muttered. "No problem at all."

She hadn't seen Jeff and his Susan since before their marriage. "This should be interesting anyway." She turned back toward the kitchen. "What else can I do to help?"

"Nothing right now." The doorbell rang at the same time as the telephone. "Actually, would you mind answering the door?"

"Sure I've got it," Sarah maneuvered though several groups of laughing people.

She opened the front door. Her ex-husband and his wife were standing there, smiling. "Hi." Sarah swallowed hard. "Come in. The party's just starting." She stepped aside as they passed into the living room. Bob waved to them, gesturing them toward him. Susan greeted Sarah quickly then moved away. Jeff pecked her cheek. A sheepish look was on his face as he ushered his trophy wife across the room toward their host.

Turning to shut the door, Sarah glanced down the walk way. A tall, dark figure approached. Her heart pounded as she recognized him. Her breath caught in her throat.

"Hi Sarah. Colleen invited me to stop by. She said you would be here." Carlos was dressed in jeans and a turtle neck sweater. His leather jacket was open at the throat and his hands were in his pockets. He looked a little shy, slightly embarrassed.

"Carlos. What a surprise." She glanced over her shoulder, searching the room for her friend. "Come in. I'll find Colleen."

"Wait. I came here to see you. Get your coat. Let's take a walk. It isn't too cold tonight." The porch light cast shadows emphasizing his prominent cheek bones. "She won't mind if you disappear for a few minutes."

What could go wrong just outside the house? She had already made her boundaries clear to him. Her concern wasn't Carlos anyway. It was her confusion about her feelings regarding his subconscious self. She decided to put her worries aside, to go walking with him. "I'll just get my things."

She pulled her black coat out from under the pile on the bed. As she was leaving, she saw Colleen making her way to the kitchen. She raised her voice to be heard over the music, "C, Carlos is here."

Colleen looked around, "Great, where is he?"

"Outside on the porch. He says he wants to talk." She glanced at the door. "We're taking a walk. We'll only be gone for a few minutes."

Just as Colleen began to reply, Bob called to her from across the room. She nodded her head to Sarah as she crossed to her future husband's side.

Sarah stepped through the door to find Carlos standing on the porch with his back to her. "Okay, let's go." She pulled on her leather gloves as they moved into the chill night air of early spring. "What's on your mind?"

"I need to tell you something." He walked quickly, his hands still jammed in his pockets.

"You have all my attention."

"Well, there's some trouble with my home boys. I don't want to get involved but I don't know what to do. I can't just leave them in the dust."

She stopped walking and took hold of his elbow, turning him to face her. "What kind of trouble, Carlos?"

"I can't say but it isn't good." He stared over her right shoulder. He wouldn't meet her eyes.

"You can't become involved in anything illegal right now. You just can't. One more parole violation and you're done. You know that. You've worked too hard to blow it." Her hand stayed on his arm as they talked.

"I know, I know. But more than that, I don't want to let you down. It's just I can't turn my back on them. We've got years behind us and I can't walk away."

"What is it? What do they want you to do?"

"I can't go into it. I just want you to know that you have done more for me than anyone in my life and I'll never forget you."

"What the hell are you talking about, Carlos?"

"Nothing." The pain in his voice was clear. "Nothing. I'll see you in session on Friday." He turned then ran down the street. She watched his shadow as he passed under the streetlights.

CHAPTER 16

On Friday when he came into her office, he looked tired. He wouldn't meet her eyes.

"Sarah, I'm in kind of a hurry today. Can we skip the conversation and get down to the hypno thing?"

"Sure." She was sure his hurried attitude had something to do with their conversation at the party. "Carlos, is everything all right?"

"Yeah. Everything's fine." He walked to the recliner. "I'm just in a hurry today." He lay down, closing his eyes, putting an end to their conversation.

Deciding not to push him, she sat in the chair next to him. Looking at his handsome face, she hoped he wasn't lying to her, that things had calmed down, that he was safe.

"Now, focus on your breath."

\#

CARLOS HAVARRO, transcript, session 9, April 9

His voice was soft as he spoke, contemplative. She leaned forward with the recorder to make sure she caught all his words.

I was welcomed at the court of the Emperor and treated by him as a hero. He too had come to Spain as a foreigner so he felt compassion at my strangeness. My involvement in the capture of Francis was kept a secret by Charles and De Lannoy received the accolades. But, the inner circle knew it was my doing.

My body was young and strong and I worked long, tedious hours to renew my human, physical skills of war. My fair looks were admired and no one at court questioned my white skin and my blue eyes. There were some rare Spaniards that shared my coloring. More importantly, my high status in the eyes of the Emperor placed me above question. I was careful where I fed. While it was only the thirst and not the all-encompassing hunger that assailed me, I was content feeding on animals in the surrounding countryside and forest.

The Spanish court was a very religious Catholic court in the midst of the Inquisition. A strict eye was kept and severe judgment was imposed on those who did not render all unto the Holy See. I was made a Captain in the royal army. My mission was to keep watch over the monasteries dotting the countryside around Madrid. The monks were often accused of thievery and sexual excesses so my men and I rode from place to place, being the eyes of both the Emperor and the envoy from Rome.

I led a company of rough and ready warriors. We rode long, slow hours day after day from monastery to monastery .

The men grew bored and surly. They slept little and complained a great deal. I had not fed in some time other than on small animals and a gnawing had begun in the pit of my stomach. I worried if I did not feed soon, I would turn into a wild monster that would ravage the first human to cross my path. When I craved human blood, I walked a fine edge between civilized man and hungry animal.

It was just before sunset when we rode toward our last destination. The men were worn and the dust from the dry black dirt path filled their eyes. Their mouths were encrusted with it. As we neared the church, the fire in my belly grew stronger as I smelled a strong scent of blood in the air. Blood and fear somewhere close. I knew it came from a human. An uncontrollable sound began deep in my throat, a bestial snarl. My eyes cast about me quickly, afraid one of my troop heard but they rode on *without seeing or hearing, exhausted, their mounts stumbling in the dust as they continued forward.*

My senses turned feral. From the very depths of my being, I was driven to hunt. It took all my will power to contain my wild desire to feed.

I knew that I had to move toward the scent without company. I brought my men to a halt. I advised them to set up camp. To rest. To eat. I made sure the army was secure and told the tired men we would proceed on the morrow, that I would ride forward to be sure all was safe for our rest. They cheered and grew more light hearted. They shouted what a fine captain I was. They joked and called to one another as they tethered the horses to make ready for night. Slowly, fires appeared, dotting the horizon. I knew they would soon be fed and drawn to sleep.

I rode forward alone, driven by my now undeniable hunger. Through and around and in the center of it all was an exotic fragrance, something never before known. I rode now spurred by curiosity as well as the hunger. Which of the two was strongest, I know not.

The late afternoon was warm and dry as I rode into a setting sun. After what seemed a very long time, I reached the gate of a small monastery made of old wood and in need of much repair.

Leaping down from my horse, I let the reins trail in the tall, rich, green grass. He was a good and true steed. I knew he would not wander. I left him grazing and moved toward the building. Slowly, silently, I made my way into the small sanctuary. A cool darkness surrounded me. The altar was in shadow without any candle light. All was silent and desolate. It was clearly empty of human life yet the strange scent in the air filled my being with a sense of familiarity. The smell of blood grew stronger, firing my grisly sense of the need of human life for sustenance.

I moved into the sunset once again, creeping around the side of the building along the gray stone outer wall. The stones were broken, coated with mud and filth. I slipped as I reached the corner, grasping the slimy rock to keep from falling. The fresh scent of human blood overpowered

my very sense of self. I became nothing more than blood lust, a monster
designed to take life in order to live.

The sinking, orange sunlight was shining directly into my eyes. My
vision was hampered. As I blinked to overcome my human sight, my
vampire perception gave me a clear view. I saw the outline of two figures
in the setting sun, a man and a woman. I realized the strange scent calling
to me was coming from them, so strange yet so familiar and somehow
safe. The blood scent emanated from the two limp shapes they held in
their hands. Dropping their prey, they began to walk toward me, hands
raised in the air in peace. Instantly, I knew they were of my kind, the
first of my kind I had known in my existence. In anticipation, I stopped
still, my hunger set aside by shock. I waited as they approached.

"Who are you?" The man's words had a foreign ring yet I was able to
understand his meaning. He was tall and fair, his build lean and strong.
He was clothed in rich velvet that spoke of the court.

I moved from behind the building and spoke. "I am Aris. I come from
the Holy Roman Emperor." As the sun sank lower, I was able to better
see them. Each of them was beautiful to me in a way that was almost
too perfect to be human. "And who are you?" They stood still at my
question.

The woman spoke to me. "I am Gabriela." She too was lean and
tall. She was dark with thick deep curls that touched her waist. Her dark
blue velvet frock was torn and soiled yet she carried herself as if she were
stepping into the royal audience chamber. In my eyes at that moment, her
beauty overshadowed that of the setting sun. Nodding her head toward
the tall, fair haired man, she spoke one word, "Richard." Her native
tongue was the same as the court of Madrid. "And what is one of our
own kind doing riding in the guise of the Emperor?"

"And what kind are we?" I heard the challenge in my voice, speaking
just as the crown of the sun sank beneath the plane of the earth and a
round, full moon peeked its crest on the opposite horizon behind a distant
hill.

"Ah Aris, we are one and the same. Do you not know?" Her voice was questioning as they moved once again, drawing closer to me. They moved evenly and smoothly over the garden rows, traveling through the rough dirt as if skimming along over a smooth marble floor. The woman searched my face. The man stood quietly next to her. When she spoke her words were soft, rolling from her tongue as a wave rolls onto a distant shore. Her words etched themselves into my mind, "We are the undead." She turned and the moon illuminated her face. The silver light cast ghastly shadows. She no longer seemed beautiful. Her eyes appeared black as pitch, holes in the white, bleached skeleton of a death's head. "Do you not know what you are? Where do you come from?" She stood motionless as an alabaster statue, waiting for my answer.

"I come from a time long ago and a distant land. I have been the only one of my kind I have known since I came to being." As I answered her, I felt something akin to relief. I was not alone. There was more of my kind. Each one of us wants to know there are others out there. Each one of us searches for our mates, much as you humans do, Sarah."

She jumped at his words. Her reality had become sixteenth century. Now, suddenly, he was here, with her, in the twenty first century lying on a reclining chair in her office.

"Mates?" She thought about his question. "Yes, I suppose we all want to find our own kind and yes, I suppose we all hope to find our soulmates." Shifting in her chair, she leaned closer to him. She dismissed his return to present time, "Now, please, go on. What happened with Gabriela and Richard?"

Worried that my men would grow concerned for me and come searching, I took my leave of them with a promise to meet in the church later when all were sleeping in my camp.

I rode slowly back, fighting the hunger that ravaged my very soul. Suddenly, a deer ran across my path. I leaped from my horse to catch the creature. Its life blood quenched my thirst and, for the time being, soothed the deeper hunger for human blood. I arrived at the encampment just in time; a group of soldiers were being dispatched in search of me.

I assured them of my safety. We settled in for the night and ate a poor meal of small ale and bread. With full stomachs yet not satisfied, they stretched out in the soft dirt around the night fires. One by one, they slept.

When I was sure they would not awaken, I crept away. Leaving my horse tethered with the rest, I moved out on foot. Once away from the sleeping soldiers, I began to run. Covering ground on foot more rapidly than riding my horse, I was at the church before the moon was straight up in the sky. The bright light flooded the courtyard, shining in the small door and window of the sanctuary.

Suddenly a shadow stepped into the light, then another. Richard and Gabriela joined me and we walked together.

I was full of questions. Where had they come from? When? Were there others? As they told me their story, a strange sense of peace filled me as I learned there were many of my kind.

Richard had been a lord in charge of an envoy from the English King to meet with the Emperor. King Henry was seeking an annulment of his marriage to Katherine. Because the Spanish emperor was her nephew, Henry hoped her relative would use his influence with her to aid in convincing her to join a convent. Charles was incensed by the request and sent the envoy back to England. The court was full of rumors about the outcome.

While the English guard was in Madrid, Richard met Gabriela. They were drawn to one another and became lovers. When the envoy traveled back to England, Richard stayed behind with her. They suffered many trials but at last, he was accepted into the Spanish court.

One night when they met in the Emperor's gardens for a lovers' tryst, they were set upon by two of our kind.. Knocked unconscious, they were dragged deep into the surrounding forest. It was there they were changed. They joined their first coven and it was from that coven they *were running when I happened upon them in the monastery garden.*

'No more than beasts' was the way Richard described his first vampire family. Frightening and dull of mind, they attacked without thought of capture. Gabriela was terrified the humans would learn of their presence and destroy them all. Her fear grew until it came to fruition. The guard found one of the coven in the palace. Knowing the legends of the vampires, the captain of the guard dispensed soldiers into the forest to find them and wipe them out.

Richard was hunting when he came across the soldiers' camp and heard them speak of their mission. Frightened of discovery, he hurried to find Gabriela and take her to safety. He knew where they would go.

Several weeks before; a traveler from a distant coven stopped at their forest home. He told them of an advanced group of vampires that lived in the Catacombs under the streets of London. The couple was intrigued at the thought of a more intellectual life . They wondered if they should leave Spain to travel to the Catacombs. After hearing the soldiers, Richard made his decision. He and Gabriela would return to his home, his England, to seek the British coven and some semblance of a better life.

They were on their way to the sea to find a ship that would carry them to his home country when they stumbled onto the monastery. The monks were drunk and cavorting with a woman when the two vampires found them. They drained the woman and one of the monks, the other was half dead of fright and unable to move or speak. He rolled into a tight ball and there he lay still, shivering in the garden behind the monastery. Sensing my hunger, they offered him to me. I moved quietly, under the full moon to fulfill my blood lust.

She gasped as Carlos turned his head toward her and opened his eyes. "I will leave you now, Sarah. Leave you to this young man."

His eyes closed and his head rolled back onto the soft cushion of the chair.

When she brought him back into real time, he sat up, stretching his arms over his head. "Well, that's enough for one day."

"Wouldn't you like to discuss the session Carlos?"

"No, not today. I'm done." He zipped his sweatshirt and moved toward the door.

"Carlos, what's wrong? Is it the same thing you mentioned at Colleen and Bill's party? Your old gang?"

"I told you Sarah, nothing's wrong. Why can't you let it alone? I said I'm done. See you next Friday." He slammed the door behind him.

#

Daylight streaming through her office window awakened her. She must have fallen asleep sitting in her recliner with her laptop on her lap. The battery obviously died while she slept because the screen was dead.

"Just like I feel." She closed the computer, placing it on the chair next to her. She stretched a little. Rubbing her eyes, she spoke out loud to no one. "Is this all just one big bad dream? None of this can be real, can it?" Standing, she carried her computer to her desk and plugged it into the outlet.

She turned her chair to face the window, sat down and stared out into the bleak, cloud-filled day. "What is going on? I have to deal with both a present day parolee and a vampire from the sixteenth century. I'm not sure what to do with either of them."

She stared at the city until she heard sounds coming from the outer office. It was one of Maggie's days to work. "At least I'll get some decent coffee." She turned from the window, waiting.

The door opened and Maggie stepped into the room. "Hey boss." She stopped short. "Wow! You look awful."

"Why thank you. You sure know how to start out my day with a bang. Did you bring coffee?"

"Yeah. Right here." She handed Sarah a large steaming cardboard cup. "No milk, two sugars. Didn't you go home last night?"

Sarah took a sip of the hot black liquid. Her mouth puckered. "This tastes like battery acid."

"Maybe I forgot the sugars. Did you work all night?"

"Until I fell asleep, yeah."

"Gorgeous Havarro again."

"Back off, Maggie." Her voice was harsh, angry.

Maggie looked startled and sheepish. "I'm sorry. I didn't mean anything by it. You're just so involved in his case." She paused for just a breath. She smiled. "And he is gorgeous."

"I'm sorry too, Maggie." She touched her assistant's arm in apology. "I'm just awfully tired and this thing has got me puzzled."

"Want to talk about it?"

"No. Not right now. What I want is to go home. I need a long, hot shower. Do I have anybody this morning?"

"You're free until one thirty." She stepped closer to Sarah, looking deeply into her eyes. "Why don't you go? After your shower, take a short nap. It'll do you good. You have Mrs. Grossman this afternoon. She always wears you out even when you aren't tired."

Sarah looked at her watch. "I think I will. Hold down the fort and call me on my cell if anything important happens. Otherwise, I'll be back at one."

She took her trench coat from the coat tree by her door, picked up her bag, waved to her secretary then made her way to the elevator and her bed. "I hope to hell I don't have any daymares. I've had about all I can take for a while."

CHAPTER 17

The office phone rang once and stopped as Maggie answered. Sarah's office door opened and Maggie stepped inside, her forehead puckered, a disbelieving look on her face. "Sarah, its Jeff."

"Jeff? My ex-husband?"

"Yep. The same. Do you want to take the call?"

"Yes. It can't be good." She reached to pick up the receiver.

"Jeff, what can I do for you?" Sarah sat at her desk, her back to the door as she looked out her window. A cool, spring rain fell in gentle drops across the city. Strange, her ex hadn't contacted her personally in months. It was usually his attorneys who did all the communicating.

"It was great to see you at Bob and Colleen's party. You look happy. I'm glad to see that." His tone was light, conversational.

"Thanks Jeff. What is it that you want?"

"Will you have lunch with me this week?" His words were tentative, almost pleading, so different than his usual brusque manner. "Any day you're free?"

"What in the world for?" She answered without thinking, her voice sharp and tight.

"Look, I just want to talk to you. I'm having some personal problems and you know me better than anyone."

"Jeff, you have a wife. She should be the one helping you with your personal problems. Not me." Her tone was flat, to the point.

"Sarah, give me a break. We were partners for a long, long time. I need some advice and I don't know who else to talk to."

Sarah sighed into the phone. "Okay but there's no need to meet for lunch. You don't have to bribe me." She swung her chair around to face her desk. She picked up a pen and began doodling infinity signs on the yellow pad resting in front of her. "What's the matter?"

"Well, it's a little embarrassing."

"Okay."

"It's Susan."

"Susan? You're coming to me with problems about Susan?" She stopped doodling. She couldn't believe her ears, her shock audible. "Don't you think that's a little off the wall?"

"Maybe, but I don't know who else to talk to."

"Look Jeff, you always were insensitive, but this is unbelievable. Take your Susan problems to a shrink or a lawyer, not to your ex-wife." She didn't bother to hide her exasperation. "Are you out of your mind?"

"But you're a therapist." Again, the pleading tone.

"Sorry but this is way out of the line of my expertise." She laid her pen on the desk. "Listen, good luck and have a nice day."

Shaking her head in disbelief, she hung up the phone. "Boy, I am so grateful to be out of that one." She sighed. "Unbelievable."

#

"Carlos didn't show up for his last session and I'm worried." The restaurant was noisy. Maggie leaned closer to hear Sarah speak. "I can't figure it out."

"He has been consistent up until now. What do you think happened?" Her assistant spoke as she poured all three small cardboard containers of blue cheese dressing on the lettuce and tomato left in her plate "I hate eating rabbit food." She used her spoon to scrape the last drops of the dressing onto the remnants of her salad. "Did you ever notice the first three letters of the word diet spell die?"

Sarah smiled at her friend but her thoughts sobered quickly. "I don't know what's going on with him and that's part of what has me worried. He's been so up front with me. Now, nothing." Sarah wondered if she should tell Maggie about their conversation at Colleen's party. "I'm not sure what to do?"

"Did you contact the half-way house?"

"Yeah. He goes there to sleep at night and he hasn't missed a day on his job. I've left messages both places but he hasn't returned my calls." She moved her half eaten salad from in front of her. "I don't want to push him by showing up there and I don't want to bring Colleen into this because I don't want to cause him any trouble. But, I don't know how else to get in contact with him. I just don't know what's going on."

"We have his parents' address in his file. Maybe if you go there, you can find out something."

"I hate to intrude but I think you're right. If he doesn't come to session on Friday, I'll call them." She had never done anything remotely like this before, but she was determined not to lose Carlos and his progress back to the streets.

Maggie finished her salad and buttered the last piece of bread.

#

The neighborhood where Carlos' parents lived was quiet and full of budding spring flowers. Many trees and shrubs lined the well-kept parkway and some of the driveways had children's toys scattered in them. Sarah took her time as she parked. She got out of her car, locked the door and stood for a moment looking at the front of the house. An old fashioned swing attached by chains at one end of the wooden porch seemed inviting. She walked slowly, climbing the few steps to the door.

A lovely middle-aged woman answered. Her black hair was cut short, sprinkled with silver highlights. "Mrs. Havarro?"

"You must be Miss Hagan, please, come in." She opened the door wider, stepping back, beckoning her guest into the entrance foyer. "You may call me Isabella."

"Please, call me Sarah." She stepped inside. "Thank you for taking my phone call this morning, for seeing me on such short notice."

The tiny reception hall opened into a comfortable living room. Two large soft beige sofas sat across from one another in front of a small stone fireplace. A glass coffee table stood between them and a tea set rested in the center of it. Isabella took Sarah's jacket. She laid it carefully across a chair arm.

"Would you like a cup of peppermint tea? I just brewed it." Isabella motioned Sarah to sit across from her. She poured the tea into small china cups. "I enjoy tea in the afternoon. It gives me a moment to sit down and relax before my husband comes home from work."

"You have a lovely home." Sarah sipped the warm, refreshing liquid offered to her.

"Mrs. Havarro. Isabella. As you know I have been seeing Carlos for some months now. We have made a great deal of progress."

"I know. When I visit him I see the changes in him. He respects you very much." She had a quizzical look in her eyes, wondering why Sarah had asked to see her.

"Well, for the last few weeks, he hasn't come to his sessions. I haven't been able to reach him and I'm concerned."

"Oh? I didn't know. I have seen him. He seems fine." She placed her cup and saucer on the table. "He is working. He is more settled at the half-way house." She smiled an embarrassed smile. "I wish he would come home, but he and his father have some trouble."

"Yes, I know." She looked down at her lap then met the older woman's eyes. "My concern is that he might be drifting back to some of his old habits."

"No. I am sure he is not."

They heard the front door open. A tall, handsome, gray-haired man entered the room. He wore a dark suit and carried a briefcase.

Isabella looked frightened. "Fernando, you are home early." She gestured toward Sarah. "This is Sarah Hagan. Sarah, please meet my husband." Isabella's voice quivered slightly. "Fernando, she is here to talk about Carlos."

Violently, he slammed the briefcase into the chair by the door. "What has your miserable son done now?"

Sarah spoke quickly, "Nothing, Mr. Havarro. I just wanted to make a family visit. I'm his therapist."

"Therapist, that bum needs jail." He turned, stomping from the room.

"I'm so sorry Miss Hagan." Unshed tears glistened in her eyes. "My husband and Carlos don't get along." She stood. "It might be best if you left now. It upsets him to talk about Carlos." She crossed in front of Sarah, making her way toward the front door.

Sarah rose. She picked up her bag and jacket then followed Carlos' mother.

"I'm sorry too, Isabella. I hope I haven't caused you any trouble." She stopped. "When you hear from Carlos, please tell him to contact me." Stepping through the door onto the porch, she heard the sound of the latch behind her.

#

"Sarah, he's here." Maggie whispered as she disappeared behind the door.

Sarah rose stiffly from her chair as he entered her office. "Hello Carlos. Good of you to show up today." Her fingers rested gently on her desk, but her posture showed her displeasure.

"I'm sorry. I know I should have called but I've been thinking. I didn't want to have any outside influences." He looked down at his shoes. "Even yours."

She motioned him to the chair across from her. She sat down, crossing her arms. "You could have called, Carlos. I thought we were friends."

"Sarah, we are friends. You are more than a friend to me. You have a great deal of influence on what I do." He slouched in the chair. "I needed to make a decision on my own." He crossed his arms over his chest to match her. "And I did."

She knew he was talking about his gang. Leaning forward, she placed her elbows on her desk, looking directly into his dark eyes. "What decision?"

"It doesn't matter. I'm here. That's all that's important. I won't disappear again. I've finally truly realized that I've wasted so much of my life already. I regret it but I can't change the past. What I can change is the future. I tried to talk to my dad again. He threw me out of the house and told me I was nothing but a bum. It was right then I realized I am not a bum. Not anymore. I'm so much more than he ever saw. Than anybody ever saw. Nobody before you and Colleen have ever recognized anything good in me. In school, all the counselors did was tell me I'd never amount to more than a stupid crook. I don't blame them. I know I scared them. Hell, I wanted to scare them. But this time, Sarah, when the old man threw me out, I didn't want to go to the gang. I didn't want to get drunk. I wanted to come to you. You have shown me that there is so much more out there than what I've known. You've shown me that I can honestly find myself and when I die, I am capable of leaving something beautiful behind, not just chaos and pain.

"I won't lie. Sometimes I'm scared to death with my subconscious and what's going on, the changes in me. But because of this guy, this vamp, this figment of my weird mind, I've found strength within myself. I've found a purpose. And that purpose is to be walking that straight line. And I'm committed. If I give it a hundred and ten percent, how can I fail?" He was silent for a moment. Suddenly he stood to cross the room. As he reached the recliner, he turned to face her. "I mean it."

"I'm very proud of you. You're quite a man already." She picked up the recorder.

"Yes," he looked at her for a long moment. "Yes, and I promise you, this is only the beginning." Suddenly he grinned, flopping down on the beige leather chair once again the familiar Carlos she knew so well. "Ready to see what the vamp has in store for us today?"

Sarah felt confused but decided that she would think about it later. She was relieved and somehow nervously excited to have him back. Sitting down, she turned on the recorder.

"Okay Carlos, close your eyes and begin to focus on your breath."

#

CARLOS HAVARRO, transcript, session 10, April 30

I made my decision. When my troop returned to court, I would beg my leave of the Emperor to make my way to England. I could not forget Richard's description of a more advanced group of undead. I knew I had to go to them. I had so much to learn about my new life and in England, I would find my teachers.

When we returned to Madrid, Charles was still at odds with the English King. As I told you, King Henry called upon Charles to stand for him in his 'Great Matter', as it was called. Remember, Henry decided he and Katherine were not really married because she had been married to his brother before him. It was a long story, but the truth was that Henry needed a son to succeed him and Katherine had delivered only a daughter. Katherine was past a time when she could be delivered of another child. The King decided he needed a younger, more fertile woman. Such a woman was Ann Boleyn. Young and lively, she had a strong court background and led the man a merry chase. She would not bed him if he did not marry her. So, Henry decided to be rid of Katherine, annul their marriage, and send her to a convent. He was audacious enough to actually think Charles would step in to help him. Charles was a not only her nephew but a staunch Catholic. The Pope had refused the annulment. Charles would not stand against the Holy See.

It was Charles' decision to send an emissary to Henry to demand Henry stay his actions. When I heard of the mission, I begged to be allowed to travel with them. It was a sure way to reach London and the coven of the Catacombs. Charles, knowing I was loyal to him and would do all that he asked, granted his permission for me to go.

My decision was bittersweet. I had come to know Madrid as my home. I was accepted and honored by the Emperor and his court and I was able to walk among the humans of Spain without their recognizing what I was. I had not the insight as to my fate in England yet I was deeply aware that I must learn about my kind, about the others like me. The stories told by Richard and Gabriela had whet my appetite.

I prepared for an ocean voyage. When the weather broke, we set sail. The trip was uneventful with calm seas and quiet nights. I walked on deck staring through the black sky at the radiance of the stars. I longed to share my thoughts with one who would understand.

"You understand, do you not, dear Sarah? I am able to share my thoughts, my very being with you."

She was always stunned when he returned to the present during one of his soliloquies. She thought about his question and after a moment, answered, "Yes, of course."

"And why is that, do you think? How are you able to accept me and what I am without fear?"

She was silent again. *"Sarah?"*

"I don't know, Aris." She sighed. "Perhaps I'm not sure you are more than a figment of the imagination of a very troubled young man in the twenty first century."

"*Is that what you hope?*"

"I don't know. I honestly don't know what I hope. This is all so surreal to me."

"*Surreal? This is a word with which I am not familiar. What does it mean?*"

She thought a moment before she answered, "It means something that is outside of space and time."

"*Yes Sarah, I am something outside of space and time.*" The room was silent as she watched the face of the present day man holding the soul of one other who was not hampered by human constraints. "*And one day, dearest Sarah, you will understand.*"

"I will understand?"

"*Yes, my stories will ring true for you at last.*"

"Are they stories, Aris, or are they reality?"

"*That is for you to decide, isn't it? Now, where were we?*"

Oh yes, the sea journey was easy, without incident. We landed on a day early in the afternoon and were taken to court. There we were given our rooms and bid to rest until evening. There was to be a feast and masque. It was then we would see the King for the first time.

I waited until I was sure I could leave the palace without question, then went in search of the Catacombs. All afternoon I roamed the gardens, not knowing what I was looking for or how I would recognize it if I found it. But I knew I would never give up until I made contact with those of my kind who were able to teach me. During my wanderings, a few small animals darted close enough for me to catch them and feed. Survival was simple if all I felt was the thirst. The hunger had not consumed me for some time. I was grateful animal blood was enough for my sustenance at the moment.

As an early autumn twilight began to cover the gardens with a soft gray blanket, I hurried back to my rooms to prepare for the evening.

Such an evening. A feast was laid out on gold plate. Meat dishes by the score, game, fowl and fish. Puddings. All for the humans. What for the vampire? I looked around me at the rich silks of the women's gowns. Some wore hoods encrusted with diamonds. The diamonds sparkled in the lights of a thousand candles. I could see their pulses beating in their throats as they danced with their heads lifted high. I began to feel the hunger, the pain crept inside my belly. The fire began to burn.

Quickly I excused myself from my troop and rose to leave the great hall. Just as I stood, the King's fanfare issued from trumpets announcing the arrival of Henry VIII. I stopped where I stood and bowed. As I rose, I came face to face with Henry. Our eyes locked for a brief moment. He smiled and walked on. I recognized the greatness of the man in that singular glance.

Then, too, I had my first glimpse of Anne Boleyn. She was small, angular and had a sharp jaw and narrow, dark eyes. Yet she was graceful. She carried herself as royalty even while Katherine was still Queen. Henry whispered something to her and she laughed. She glanced over her shoulder at me. She nodded her head in agreement as she turned again to answer the King. I knew they spoke of me and it was a concern.

When the King and his mistress, as she was called by the court, were seated and the feast began, I begged an excuse to my men and left the hall, the hunger in my belly growing more and more demanding. It had been months since I needed to feed on a human. I dreaded the time when I would be driven to drink human blood. And relished it.

The time was now close to being upon me. I hurried into the darkness of the palace garden and found a deer that had wandered from the woods.

I took it down. Cleanly. Painlessly. I drained it there within earshot of the great hall. My need diminished as the animal blood gave me sustenance. I could subsist on it for a while longer until the right moment, yet I knew I would need to take human life again, soon.

I hurried through the palace to my rooms. I entered the retiring room, a lit fire warmed the chill from the stone walls. A table and chairs sat in front of the fire with small ale, bread and cheese waiting for me. I smiled when I thought of what I wish had been waiting there for me."

He was silent until she spoke, "And what was that?"

"The throat of one of those lovely ladies who had been at the King's dinner."

Sarah gasped. She took a moment to compose herself, then spoke. "Please continue, Aris."

The table was set but I did not crave the food. I turned one of the chairs to the fire and sat, stretching my long legs out before me. I was warmed and as comfortable as I could be in the circumstances. I was unable to feed on human blood until I knew it would never be found out. All eyes were upon me as a newcomer from the Spanish court. I could not leave the palace grounds at night without someone seeing. I was well aware of idle gossip from my life in Spain. The stable boy would tell a maid who would tell a cook who would tell a ladies maid who would tell her lady. And there it would be. Why would someone from the Spanish envoy ride out late at night? I knew no one in England. I knew they would think me a spy for the Emperor.

I sat watching the embers snap and glow. A soft rustle behind me alerted me someone was in the room. I turned quickly to see Richard and Gabriela standing just inside the open, mullioned window.

As I rose to greet them, they moved toward me. Their greeting was warm and I felt they were pleased to see me. I asked how they had come to find me. How they entered my rooms.

"We saw you in the garden," Richard replied. "We followed you here and waited until there was no one outside. We came in the window." He pointed behind him.

I was astonished. The window was in the tower, very high above the courtyard. "How did you manage that," I asked.

"We are able to cling to stone and climb much like a spider." Gabriela answered, her accompanying laughter, a lilting, musical sound. "You

have so much to learn."

I assured them the reason I traveled all the way to London to meet the rest of my kind was to learn all there was to know about my new un-life. Gabriela moved forward, reaching out her hand to touch my arm.

Her face softened. She told me they came to help me, to take me to the coven.

A loud rap at the door interrupted our discourse and a voice called out. It was the King's messenger. The two visitors locked eyes for less than a moment. They moved quickly to disappear out the window as I crossed the room to the door and unlatched it.

The courier handed me an envelope with a royal seal. He tipped his head respectfully as he backed from the room. I closed the door, latched it then sat in a chair by the fire.

I opened the envelope. It was the King's command to appear before the court to represent Spain in the royal joust on the following day. At first I was glad of heart until I realized the smell of human blood would be everywhere. Was I doomed? Could I withstand the temptation?

The morning came. The serving boy brought fresh cheese and bread. I would rather have had the serving boy for breakfast but I thought better of it. After a time, I called for a page to ask him to show me to the audience chamber. It was there I met many of the knights who would ride in the joust. There was laughter and banter as we prepared for our feats of prowess. By the time we walked to the jousting yard, it was as comrades at arms.

The day was bright blue with a sprinkling of white clouds floating in a perfect sky. The master of the horse chose an enormous stallion as my charger. He was magnificent, full of fire and power. He was just the horse I would have chosen for myself.

A fanfare blared from the trumpets as the King and Anne entered the arena. Her head held high, she rested her small hand on his extended arm. He was dressed in splendor, his huge athletic frame spoke volumes about the man. They mounted the steps leading to their place, sheltered under a golden canopy to protect them from the sun. They settled into their great chairs. Anne smiled at the King as he grasped her hand in his. It was easy to see that in his eyes, she was his Queen already.

The opening ceremonies completed, another fanfare and the two who were first at the joust took their places. The trumpets sounded once again; the enormous horses began their thundering race, carrying their knights on their sturdy backs. A crash as one of the men was unhorsed. He fell hard, lay in the dirt for just a moment, then rose and was helped off the field by his page. He limped and so I knew he had been hurt but there was no smell of blood about him. Time after time, man after man, one unhorsed, the other proud of his victory.

As the sun rose in the sky, my moment was at hand. I mounted and the feel of the strong beast beneath me was invigorating. I held my lance and slid my hand along the shaft, finding the perfect balance point. The trumpets blared as I heeled my horse. We raced along the wooden rail, dust flying in our wake. I lifted my lance and at the perfect moment, jammed it hard into the chest of my opponent. With a cry, he fell from his horse. Just as he touched the ground, his animal reared, forelegs beating the air. In a flurry of hooves and broken metal, the huge stallion trampled his rider. The scent of blood was everywhere. It surrounded me, filled me with wild lust and desire. I sprang from my horse, jumping over the rail. Just as I neared his broken body, he was lifted on a litter and carried away. Unable to contain my need, I followed as they transported him to the stable. He cried out in pain. He was broken, dying, It was only a matter of time before he would expire and those moments would be spent in agony.

They rested the litter in the hay and stood back to watch his death throes. Incensed, I screamed at them to leave, to allow this brave knight to die in peace. He thrashed on the makeshift bed. His movement tore his wounds even more. I was hardly able to contain myself until the last man left. Once I was alone with my opponent, I crept near to him.

"Kill me," he begged me. "Please, the pain. Please kill me."

Without thought I would be seen, overcome by bloodlust, I buried my face in his throat. The smell of him drove me to madness. I moaned as I began to drain him. Quickly I brought about his death, his final rest.

I fell back on the bed of hay to wipe my mouth on the back of my hand. A few precious drops of blood smeared across my skin. I licked the flesh of my knuckles then my lips. I was satiated at last, the need for human blood met. And no one was the wiser.

I walked from the stable and found his page. "He is dead," I spoke the words as I walked away.

CHAPTER 18

The night was cool so she pulled the blanket close around her shoulders. She loved to sleep with the window open, to hear the faint sounds of the city in the distance. From her pillow she could see the lighted windows in the buildings that shared her neighborhood. It gave her a secure feeling to know other people were still awake so very late at night.

Yet the darkness of her bedroom and comfort of her bed didn't halt the struggling of her mind. Thoughts swirled in her head making her feel dizzy. Could Aris be real? More likely, he was a subconscious desire Carlos had to feel invincible in a world where he felt so vulnerable. As a twenty-first century person, believing in the undead was almost unthinkable. What was the answer? Carlos knew nothing about Tudor England or Alexander the Great for that matter. Where did his information come from if not from Aris? She researched all the history he shared. Each and every story was based on fact. Not fact about vampires to be sure, but facts about times, places and people.

Aris was a tragic figure. His life was stolen from him when he was just a young man about the same age as Carlos. He wasn't a demon by choice, but by fate. Turning to face the window, she thought of Carlos. What was the connection between the two, the man and the vampire? Each one was a victim of circumstance. Would further regressions bring light on the association?

In a state of confusion and mental exhaustion, she fell into a fitful sleep.

#

She knew she was dreaming because she would never go to the zoo if she was awake. It pained her to even think of the animals, caged, living a life so different than the one nature had planned for them, as Aris was living a life different than he had planned. The evening sky was the shade of dusty indigo blue. There were just a few solitary stars and the walkway was illuminated with old fashioned, softly lit street lights. A fingernail moon sliced the darkness; a gentle breeze rustled her hair as she walked along.

Long necked giraffes leaned their throats over the fence to get a better look at her. A baby elephant swayed back and forth in its pen as the huge mother hid in the shadows, preparing to protect her young if need be. She passed the dimly lit lion house. The great roar of the beasts told her of their distress being locked inside. She moved in that floating space that happens only when you are dreaming.

She passed house after house, each one containing a different species of animal. The last one on the path housed the snakes. Sarah wasn't afraid of snakes. In fact, she actually enjoyed watching them slither sensuously along the ground and wrap gracefully around trees and branches. She dream walked forward toward the open door.

Everything appeared in shadow as she stepped inside. She was startled to see a familiar figure on the other side of the huge, cavernous hall. As the man walked slowly toward her, she recognized Carlos. He was wearing dark pants and a short sleeved white tee shirt, his bronze forearms covered in new tattoos.

As he came closer she saw the tattoos were of snakes, King

Cobras. They appeared alive as he moved through the dim light of the room.

He stopped just in front of her, his black eyes piercing into her very soul. She was drawn to him in a way she had been denying for months. She could no longer resist his magnetic pull.

He kissed her then, his beautiful mouth tasting sweet. His full lips soft and smooth, caressing hers with each tender touch. His kiss was long, deep. As she felt his warm breath on her face, she melted into him, releasing any hidden doubts. Her dream heart belonged to him.

He stroked her cheek, her throat. He moved a step away from her gazing lovingly, questioningly into her eyes. Without a pause, she nodded yes. A smile of gratitude and pleasure lit his face. He traced her form with his eyes mesmerized by the gentle curve of her breast, the soft cleavage peeking out of her white cotton blouse.

He scooped her in his arms. The male scent of him stirred her senses, aroused her. He carried her outside into the soft night air seeking a dark solitary place away from all eyes. Soon he settled down on a round mound of grass under a huge maple tree. Moonlight filtered through the branches, the leaves casting deep shadows on the ground beneath them. Sitting with his back against the tree, he still held her in his arms.

He moaned in torment as he buried his face in the thick soft curls of her hair. His gentle kisses sweetly showered her face, her throat. As he neared the tender rise of her breast, his breathing changed. It became shorter. More rapid. His pulse raced. Strong bronze hands reached for the buttons on her blouse. In a moment, delicate white lace was all that separated his kiss from her bare skin. She closed her eyes twisting her fingers into his thick black hair, a soft groan escaping her throat.

The cool night air caressed her fair skin as he slid her blouse down her arms and laid it on the ground beside them. With one hand, he unhooked her bra. She gasped as he kissed her warm pink flesh. As he slid his tongue over the rise of her nipple, the soft sounds she made in her throat were glorious to his ears. Heart racing in her chest, she shivered with desire. She lifted her eyes to watch him. He looked up at her under his dense black lashes. He opened his lips in a slow, languid smile. His fangs were longer and sharper than any of the living snakes now coiled around his arms. As he moved toward her throat, she screamed.

The shrill sound of her own terror woke her. She swung her legs over the edge of the bed, bolting upright. She reached to turn on the light. Fighting to catch her breath, she looked out at the night sky. All the lights in all the windows in all the buildings had gone out. Everyone was asleep. She faced the coming dawn alone.

#

"It was just a stupid dream." Her thoughts were careening through her mind as she brushed her teeth. "Just a stupid dream." She rinsed her mouth with water, shut off the bathroom light and walked to the kitchen.

She checked the kitchen clock. She had an hour before she was to meet Colleen at the museum. True to her Sunday ritual, she wore jeans, a tee shirt and sandals, no makeup and damp, curly hair. It was warm, but there were clouds and the weather person predicted a steady drizzle. Her rainslicker hung on a hook on the inside of the hall closet door. She reached in to grab it. She tied it around her waist, picked up her bag and made her way to the elevator.

Waving at the doorman, she pushed open the door, stepping into the quiet of a Sunday morning. She left her car in the garage. Parking on Sunday downtown was impossible. A bright yellow cab turned the corner. Lifting her arm, she waved the driver down.

Climbing into the back seat, she leaned forward and spoke. "The Art Institute."

"Right," was the reply made in a deep voice with an exotic

accent. "Art Institute."

The rest of the ride was silent for which Sarah was grateful. She had just about convinced herself that all of her terror of the previous night was connected to the anchovy pizza she ate just before bed. Maybe Colleen was right. Maybe anchovies were something to be eaten only before five o'clock. She smiled at herself just as the cab pulled in front of the museum. The two huge stone lions on the front steps reminded her of the dream once again. She held back a shiver.

She paid the driver and just as she stepped from the cab she heard her name called in a bright, female voice. Turning, she saw Colleen come down the steps toward her. Sarah couldn't believe what she saw. Colleen had Carlos in tow.

"Just what I need," she thought, "after the dream I just had." She waved as they approached.

"I hope it's okay Sarah. Carlos has never been to an art museum. When he called in this morning and I told him our plans for the day, he asked if he could come along." Colleen smiled. She looked very excited to be giving Carlos a day of culture. "I told him I was sure you'd be glad to have him."

Sarah rolled her eyes at thin air, controlling her true feelings. After a moment's hesitation, she replied, "Sure great. Let's go inside."

They climbed the steps, walking inside the marble reception area. "Admission is on me." Colleen got in the line where tickets were sold as Carlos and Sarah waited near a huge marble pillar.

He slid his hand across the smooth, cool surface, looking directly at her. "I hope you really mean that. I honestly haven't ever been to an art museum. I can't think of anyone better than you and Colleen to be my guides." He tilted his head and his little boy grin won her over, reminding her he really didn't have fangs.

"Okay. But if you want to leave before we're ready, you're on your own."

"You can be a hard case, Sarah." He shook his head in mock disbelief.

"I have the admission taken care of. Now, where do you two want to go first?" Colleen stepped between them, taking each one by the arm.

The trio spent the better part of the day moving from gallery to gallery. Carlos marveled at the paintings and sculptures, but even more at the structure of the building.

"I've never been inside anything like this before but even so, there's something about it that is so familiar." They were standing at the top of the stairs looking out over the open second floor gallery. "Why don't you two go on. I want to hang out here for a while." The space was open and bright, works of art lining the inner walls.

"Sure, we'll just look at the things on this balcony. Then we can all go into the outer galleries before the museum closes." Colleen grabbed Sarah by the arm, leading her away from Carlos.

"I could see you were pissed at first. Thanks so much, Sarah, for not letting him know." They stopped in front of a statue of a Greek warrior. It had a perfect face, very similar to their companion. "I want him to go to school." She shrugged. "I think he's interested."

"School?" Sarah's voice was questioning. "He's no kid. What kind of school?"

"That's the thing. He doesn't know. He hasn't been exposed to very much outside his own culture."

"Colleen, why do you have such an interest in this guy? You're married now."

Colleen swatted Sarah on the arm. "It isn't that. He reminds me of me. And right now, being able to help him, I remind me of Bob. If he hadn't pulled me out of the gutter, who knows where I'd be right now." She looked embarrassed. "I'm just paying it forward."

They moved along the upper gallery. "What about you, Sarah? Why are you so interested?" She smiled a sly grin, gently nudging her friend with her elbow. "You aren't married."

"Leave it. I'm interested because he's an incredible subject for regression. Has he told you anything about it?"

"No, and neither have you. I'd sure like to know what goes on in those sessions. I've seen a big change in him."

"If I told you, I'd have to kill you." She laughed. "You know its client/therapist information. He's the only one who can tell you anything." Sarah sighed to herself, glad the crazy tale hadn't become a part of his permanent parole record.

"And besides, I'm way too old for him." The words slipped out before she could reel them back.

Colleen stopped in her tracks. "What did you say?"

"Nothing. I didn't say anything." Sarah kept on walking.

Her friend reached for her arm, spinning her around to look her in the eye. "I've seen the way he looks at you. I'm here to tell you it isn't like you're a woman who's too old for anything."

"Yeah, well we're client and therapist. Nothing more." Sarah noticed they paused just in front of a marble statue of Cupid. She looked the other way, quickly moving on.

#

"That museum was something else. I can see why people like to go there again and again." He slouched in the chair across from her desk. "Thanks for letting me tag along. I could see you didn't want me there, but I'm really grateful."

The door to the office opened as Maggie poked her head into the room. "I'm out of here. Tommy's taking me to a play tonight. There's a little theatre in Old Town doing the original 'Dracula" and I've never seen it." She waved. "Later." She closed the door behind her.

"I guess we just can't get away from it, can we?" His words formed a question but his voice was a statement. "Do you want to knock me out now?"

She hesitated. "How about we just do talk therapy today?"

"No man, I want to do the regression. I want to know what the hell happens. This is better than any movie I've ever seen and it's all right here," he pointed to his temple. "In my head."

He stood, "Come on, knock me out and here comes Aris." Laughing, he moved to the recliner, flopping down with a deep sigh. "Come on Sarah. Don't stand in the way of my progress."

#

CARLOS HAVARRO, transcript, session 11, May 7

The King honored my prowess and Lady Anne gave me her favor. I was invited that night to a royal dinner. As I dressed for the occasion I wondered at the true miracle of my being honored in two different royal courts. In spite of what I was, I enjoyed being a royal favorite once again.

It was a feast that only King Henry could provide. Meats, more fish than Neptune himself had in the sea, fowl dressed in every way. And puddings. And sauces. Again, beautiful women with low gowns and long necks tempting me from every side.

I swallowed the disgusting human food that was as sawdust in my mouth, all the while pretending to relish every bite. I drank the bitter wine, smiling in false gratitude at the King. Before much time had passed, he leaned to speak to the Lady Anne. She glanced at me before she nodded her approval.

I saw him raise his hand beckoning me. I rose and crossed the room to bow before him. He motioned me to rise. He told me I was to join him for tennis the following morning. I thanked his majesty and backed away from him wondering just what tennis might be.

A constant maid brought ale and lit my fire every morning. I waited in the chair by the fireplace for her to shuffle noiselessly into my room at dawn. As she bent to light the logs, I asked what she knew about the King and the sport of tennis. My question was a game of chance and I was the winner. She sat on the stool at the foot of my bed and told me all. She was a follower of sport and loved to sneak into the rafters to watch the game. She and some of her fellow servitors would meet there and wager on the outcome. She said she was often the winner.

She explained the rules and told of Henry's weak and strong abilities. As I listened with my vampire mind, I knew I could beat him at his own game. I had nothing to lose by playing with him and everything to gain. I smiled at the chance to match the King.

I was first on the court in the morning, waiting for the rest of the players to arrive. Soon the King came into sight surrounded by his gentlemen of the court. There were no royal trumpets and no fanfare, simply a group of men delighted to share in active sport came tumbling into the arena.

With my vampire eyes, I watched them play the early games. I knew I would be the finest in the match and once again gain the recognition of the King. I had enjoyed the safety of the favor of the Spanish emperor and I would relish the favor of this British King. A man among men, he would only respect one who was equally as quick as he, yet no quicker. He was proud and would not take to being beaten. With my supernatural skill, I could match his every move until he would call our match a draw. As a man among men, I knew this to be fact. Lady Anne waved her favor to me as I stepped onto the court. My bow was low and flawless and I saw her smile at me as I rose.

The King hit the ball and a fast and furious match was on. Henry roared with laughter and anger. He played with the power and vigor of a much younger man. As I raced back and forth I wondered at the number of games the King must have played on this court in Windsor Castle. Even at his large size, he was a formidable opponent. The match would have been much more difficult to draw had he been younger and leaner even for my supernatural self. I was glad he was not.

At last, dripping with sweat and out of breath, Henry called a draw and came toward the net with a deep laugh, holding out his arms to *embrace me. "A fine contest, my Spanish friend."*

My bow was sincere, "I am with the Spanish envoy, however, I am not Spanish your Grace." I knew where his loyalties were rooted, in England and away from the Pope.

His coppery eyebrows raised in question. "Not Spanish?" He wiped his brow with a white towel handed him by one of his gentlemen.

"I am from a very old and distant land, your Majesty." Again, I bowed as I spoke.

"I will hear more of this land. Walk with me." He handed the towel back to his man as we turned to leave the court followed by his inner circle of friends.

Walking through the gardens, we enjoyed the warm air of mid-day. He questioned me on my country, my heritage. I told wild and improbable stories that he believed to the fullest. As a man among men, he believed all difficulties could be overcome and he respected those who overcame them. In my stories, I was such a man. Again, I was invited to dine with the court and again I attended. Soon, I was assigned a permanent place in the court and enjoyed the King's favor.

"Sarah, do you grow tired of my stories?"

Startled back into real time, Sarah swallowed, then answered, "That's hardly the word for how I feel about your stories. They fascinate me."

"I am happy to be fascinating to such a charming woman as you." His flirtatious tone and attitude surprised Sarah and she smiled despite herself.

"Let's go back to Tudor England, shall we?" With a determined tone, she regained control of the conversation. "When did you hear again from Richard and Gabriela?"

Richard and Gabriela found me one dark night in the garden. I finished drinking and was making my way back to my rooms when they stepped from behind a hedge. Gabriela came forward to embrace me while Richard stood behind her. She was glad to tell me they spoke to the council and the oldest ones of all agreed to meet with me. I was to be *shown to the council sanctuary below the city in the Catacombs. I was* *to meet the wisest of my kind. I felt exaltation at finding I would learn* *what I was capable of at last.*

"*You see, Sarah, it keeps coming back to that, doesn't it? Finding one's* *own kind. Finding one's mate.*"

"Aris, I can only imagine how it must have felt to you. My logical mind can't begin to comprehend what it must have been like to have thought you were the only one of your kind on earth. The isolation." She looked at the floor for a moment to compose her thoughts, and then back at her subject. "So, you met the oldest ones?"

"*That, dear Sarah, is for a future conversation. Our Carlos grows* *restless. I will leave you now until next time.*"

Sarah was always amazed by the change in the expression on the face of her subject when Carlos again took control of his subconscious. A different man and a different time. Which was the one who called to her? She stared at his face for a few moments before counting him into real time once again. "Which is real time?" She wondered, "And to whom?"

#

Carlos leaned back in the recliner, rubbing his eyes. "It just keeps getting better and better, doesn't it? I'm glad you're recording this whole thing. We can write a book and split the profits." He laughed as he sat up.

"If you're not in too much of a hurry today, I'd like to talk a little more about your family."

His spine stiffened as he stood, turning his back to her. "You know I don't like to do that."

"I understand but I need more information about this incarnation before I can tie anything to it from the regressions."

After a moment, he faced her. "Okay." He moved a wingback

chair close to her. He sat, facing her. "You win. Shoot."

She ruffled through the file folder she held on her lap. "We finished up just when you were born. What happened after your father came back from burying your grandfather?"

"Yeah, well, he kept drinking. Crazy as it seems, when he wasn't drunk, he treated us pretty well. They had another kid, my brother, Javier. I don't know why but as time passed, my old man drank more, the hard stuff. He got meaner and meaner. When he'd start up, I'd hide under my bed. I remember I'd cover my ears with my hands to try to make the shouting go away. As I got older, it didn't tear me up as bad when he was beating on me as when he was going after my mother or brother.

"One Saturday he started drinking at breakfast and was raving by noon. Things changed that day. My little brother spilled milk all over the table. My old man took off his belt and began to swing at him. Something tweaked in my head and I started hitting him with my fists. I was only ten but I was big for a kid my age. I got him good a couple of times. That made him nuts. He broke my nose and cracked a couple of ribs. I swore one day I would make sure he never hit any of us again.

"Time passed but things stayed pretty much the same except Javier and me, we learned to stay out of his way. I grew taller and bigger than he was. Once I started high school, he left me alone. He knew I'd stand up for Javier so he backed off from him too. And I never saw him hit my mother again."

She took notes on a yellow tablet. Bonnie teased her about her hand written notes but she thought a laptop made the session too impersonal. "What about high school?"

"We lived in a pretty good section of town but I didn't fit in with the kids from my own neighborhood. They were all from middle-class families with normal lives so I just stayed by myself most of the time. Then they started bussing kids in from the barrio. They were more my style. I guess I was a perfect recruit for the imported bangers.

"The guys were cool and friendly to me. The leader was the oldest one, Manu. He was already a petty thief but I didn't know it then. I guess he saw me as a way to get to the kids with money; I was someone he thought could help him steal from the homes in my neighborhood. He really courted me.

"And I was glad. I was tired of hanging alone all the time. He introduced me to alcohol and drugs. He made me feel like I was finally part of something. I still can't separate myself completely from the guys. They're more family to me than my blood."

"But if you knew he was using you, why did you stick it out?"

"I wanted a tribe. Manu showed me one. He took me for my first tattoo. He was like an older brother to me, I guess. He introduced me to his sister Maria. He really protected her. He said he knew I'd take care of her and respect her. And I did.

"One night I had a huge blow up at home. I slammed out of the house, found Manu and told him I was ready to make it official.

"In order to be initiated, I had to steal a car. I did and brought it to Manu. He sold it. He gave me some money from the sale. 'Easy money,' he said. 'The insurance company takes the fall, it's just a business.' I figured I could do a couple of jobs a month and maybe get my brother out of that crazy house.

"So I started my life of crime," he smiled sarcastically. "Eventually I got caught, did a little time and got paroled. When I got out, I went down to see the guys. When I found them, they were high and Manu was bragging about a drive by. Everybody was laughing and joking about this kid who was shot. After spending time in jail, hearing those guys talk woke me up. I saw what I was becoming and it scared me. I asked Colleen to help me and she got me into rehab. It's been tough but I'm still straight. I plan on staying that way."

"Carlos, what did you do after you graduated high school?"

"I didn't graduate. I ran away and lived in the streets. I lived with one or another of the guys. I wouldn't stay more than a couple of nights at any one place. If there was a job, I'd stay in a cheap motel. I know it sounds rotten but it wasn't all bad.

"The half-way house is the first permanent home I've had where I really feel safe. It means a lot, but at the same time, all my buddies think I've turned on them. I don't hang with them. I even stopped seeing Maria. I've lost the only family I ever had. Those people accepted me for who I am. No, who I was. I'm not even sure who I am right now."

"I understand Carlos. There have been so many changes in such a short time."

"Part of it has to do with the vamp. Sometimes it's like Aris is an older brother too and a lot tougher than Manu."

The spring twilight gave a glow to Sarah's blond hair. Carlos wanted to take her in his arms but he knew she wouldn't let him. He wondered why he was telling her his life story. He supposed that part of it was her obvious innocence. It made him trust her. He believed she really wanted to help him stay straight. But why was he so attracted to a woman so much older than he was? Why did he want her so much? That was a question that had no answer. He watched her as she wrote on the tablet.

"Say Sarah, you seem pretty wrapped up in Aris yourself. Sometimes I wonder if these sessions haven't just become a meeting ground for you and the vamp."

"Don't be silly Carlos. You are the vamp."

He thought about her words for a moment then smiled.

CHAPTER 19

"Jeff, I thought I told you I couldn't help you with your domestic difficulties." She took the phone off speaker and raised the handset to her ear.

"Sarah, it's more than that. I need to see you." The voice on the other end of the phone was pleading. "I need to talk to you about more than my marriage."

"Look, I'm sorry you are having trouble but I can't help you." She swiveled her desk chair toward the window, the movement she always made when she didn't want to face an issue. The city was something so much bigger than she was, a few million lives that didn't come to her for therapy. Somehow, seeing the size of the city and realizing the number of stories in it, she was able to cope with her own scenario a lot easier. "I told you, you need a therapist who isn't involved in this."

"I don't want your expertise." There was a long pause on the other end of the phone. "I need your friendship."

The flat, pensive tone to his voice made her realize he wasn't just being dramatic, he was really in need. She worked for months in therapy to make sure he would never manipulate her again and yet here it was, she couldn't help herself. "All right Jeff. Let's meet for drinks at The Bistro. Half an hour?"

The uplifted change in his tone was noticeable. "Great. Half an hour."

#

She arrived before he did. She settled on a stool at the bar. As she waited, she decided this was a meeting warranting something a little stronger than a merlot. "A green apple martini," she told the bartender as he leaned forward to hear her through the noise of happy hour.

"You got it miss." He moved away from her, grabbing a shaker. He tossed the bottle of vodka in the air, catching it behind his back. "He's seen way too many movies," she thought just as she felt a hand touch her arm.

"Sarah." Jeff sat on the stool next to her. "You look great."

"Yeah, well what is this all about?"

He cleared his throat. "Let me order a drink first." He signaled the bartender. She was surprised when he ordered scotch.

"Since when did you start drinking whiskey?"

"About two months after I married Susan." He laughed a short, ironic chuckle. "I thought she was everything I wanted, easy to be with, undemanding. I liked that she thought I was perfect." He turned to look at his ex-wife. "We got married and it all changed." When his drink was placed on the bar, he picked it up. He downed it in one swallow.

Sarah looked at him in amazement. She had never seen him so upset, so out of control.

"Look, Jeff. I really can't counsel you on your marriage." She sipped her drink carefully as she wondered what he was getting at. "Don't you think it's a little outrageous for you to come to me for advice?"

He leaned toward her and reached for her hand. "It isn't advice I want, Sarah." He looked down at the bar. He paused. When he spoke, he looked up, catching and holding her eyes with his. "It's reconciliation."

"Are you crazy?" She didn't think before the words fell from her lips. "You have trouble with Cinderella and you come back here for advice and pity?" She stood behind the bar stool. "Reconciliation? I can't even respond to that."

Turning on her heel, she grabbed her bag. She left the bar just as the home team scored and everyone cheered.

#

Lincoln Park was bursting with green. The trees finally awakened after their long winter sleep. Flowers budded along the sidewalk as the two friends looked for an empty bench to share their lunch. They were happy to find the hotdog vender back in business. Chicago dogs on soft steamed buns with pickles, onions, tomato and celery salt couldn't be beat. They both piled mustard and relish on the top, wrapped them back in the sturdy white paper they came in and searched for a place to sit.

"It's the first day we've been able to eat outside since October." Colleen shifted her huge shoulder bag to her other arm, grabbed Sarah with her free hand and guided her to a bench where a young couple and their little girl were preparing to leave. "I thought spring would never come."

They sat, spreading their lunches between them. "The sky is so blue today. After all the rain the last few weeks, this is heaven." Sarah unwrapped her hotdog and took a bite. "Yum. I sure missed these during the winter. Nobody does a dog better than Louie."

"You got that right." Colleen followed suit and the two women ate in silence, enjoying the relaxed atmosphere between them.

Sarah popped the last bite in her mouth then wiped her lips on her paper napkin. "I could go for another one. How about you?"

"Yeah, I could eat it but I've got to fit into the nightmare of a dress I bought to walk down the aisle. If I put on another pound, it won't zip." She giggled. "Maybe that wouldn't be so bad."

"Come on C, you know you're looking forward to the wedding." Sarah balled the refuse from her lunch into a little, tight ball then tossed it into the garbage can. She unscrewed the top of her water bottle. She took a long drink.

"What I'm looking forward to is it being over." Colleen shook her head from side to side. "I don't know how I ever let Bob talk me into this big wedding thing. I'd much rather just get married by a judge."

"That's just because you spend half your life in court rooms." Sarah brushed the crumbs from her lap. "Want to walk?"

"Sounds good." Colleen disposed of the remnants of her lunch in the same garbage can. Standing, she glanced down at her watch. "Let's go. I have another half an hour before I have to be anyplace."

They took their time, strolling at a comfortable pace and not talking.

After a few minutes, Colleen broke the silence. "Did Carlos tell you they gave him more hours and increased his pay at the store?"

Sarah stopped walking, turning to look directly at her friend. "No, he didn't." She stood still for a heartbeat then moved forward. "When did that happen?"

"A couple of weeks ago. He's been working hard and staying clear of trouble. It's amazing what you've done with him."

"Yeah, amazing." Sarah wondered why Carlos hadn't told her. It was certainly a reason for him to be proud. It was the first real job he ever held and he was doing well according to Colleen. Why had he kept it from her? She decided to ask him the next time he had a session.

"Sarah, look." Colleen pointed to the grass by the root of a tall tree. "It's the first robin of spring."

Her voice had a pensive tone. "Yeah C, the first robin of spring."

#

A handful of spring flowers appeared around her door, then

Carlos stepped into her office. "Here, these are for you." He appeared uncomfortable as he pushed them at her.

Sarah was surprised, delighted at the array of color and fragrance she held in her hand. "Thank you. What a great surprise."

"The store has more flowers than we can sell. I never have figured out why a grocery store sells flowers." He dropped in the chair across from her desk.

"It's just another commodity, I guess, they might as well make the money as a florist." She buzzed Maggie.

When her assistant peeked into the room, she was smiling. "Need some water for those poseys?" She crossed to take them from Sarah's waiting hand.

"Yes, just leave them on your desk. I'll get them after our session." She looked a little embarrassed as she completed her thought. "And Maggie, you might as well go home. Carlos is the last client of the day."

Maggie gave her boss a knowing wink just before she left the room. She closed the door quietly.

Sarah leaned back in her chair, staring at him. He was beginning to feel uneasy when she finally spoke. "Okay Carlos, want to tell me why I'm the last to know how well you're doing at the market?" Her tone was flat but not accusatory. "I would have thought you would be proud of it."

He wiggled in his chair. She could see her words made him uncomfortable. "Yeah, I'm still just a stock person. It's nothing to brag about."

"Well, I think it is. It's the first job you've ever held for more than a week and they must be pretty happy with you to give you a raise."

His stare was angry, his words clipped. "So what gives? You and my parole officer been talking about me? I thought that wasn't allowed."

"Carlos, we both care what happens to you. She's proud of your accomplishment, that's why we talked about it. She just assumed you told me already."

He tilted his head and smiled a slow, sideways grin. Teasing, he said, "You really do care what happens to me Sarah?"

He wouldn't drop his gaze. She began to feel uncomfortable. "Of course I do." She stood, picked up her recorder from on top of her desk and walked to the chair near the recliner. "Are you ready?"

He joined her, still grinning. "I'm so ready Sarah. You'll never know how ready I am."

#

CARLOS HAVARRO, transcript, session 12, May 14

The torchlight cast tall dancing shadows on the damp stone walls as we descended deeper and deeper under the castle. Richard led the way, I walked in the middle and Gabriela moved in silence behind me. The slippery steps seemed to spiral down without ceasing. At last we reached the bottom and were in a narrow, cold corridor. Richard held the torch high as we stepped over pieces of rock that had fallen from the rotting walls. I didn't know stone could smell so musky and old. There were puddles of water here and there to be stepped over or gone around.

We walked for what seemed a very long time, finally arriving at a huge, ornate door. The ancient wood and metal hinges and latch were encrusted with slime. Richard pushed hard; at last the door swung open.

I was stunned by what waited on the other side. We entered a great room, larger still than Henry's audience chamber. It was opulent. Torches and candles burned everywhere and the room felt warm and dry. As we moved forward I felt small bursts of fresh air coming from between some of the stones of the floor.

There were no tables or chairs in the room. All the walls were decorated with gold and rare jewels, shimmering in the candle light. I glanced at the high ceiling. I saw it, too, was encrusted with treasures.

*"This is the antechamber. We remain here until we are called." Richard
spoke quietly as if not to disturb the hundreds of flames illuminating the
room.*

*"What..?" I began to speak, but Gabriela touched my lips with her
fingers to silence my question.*

*"We just wait, that is all," she whispered close to my ear. "Do not
speak until you are requested to do so."*

*Time is very different to my kind than it is to humans so I am unable to
tell you how long we stood. During the sea voyage to England I learned
to put my mind in a suspended plane where I silenced my thoughts, felt
no sensations. A different kind of death, I suppose.*

*A door I had not noticed on the other side of the room opened. A
tall male courtly figure walked rapidly toward us causing the candles to
flicker and gutter.*

*"You may enter." His deep resonant voice suited his dark, handsome
features. He was further proof our kind was a beautiful species. He
spoke just his name, Sebastian. We passed into a smaller chamber, the
walls equally as richly decorated. This room also contained two large
golden chairs set on a dais and resting in their seats were soft cushions
of the richest, deepest blue velvet; more beautiful than any I had seen in
either the Spanish or English royal courts. On the floor just in front of
the thrones were several larger cushions of the same luxurious material.
Sebastian motioned us to kneel on the cushions, to lower our heads.*

*We obeyed and again, we waited. Despite the deathly silence, I did
not hear them enter. I felt a touch on my shoulder and raised my eyes.
They appeared to be male and female. They sat tall, lean and unmoving
on their thrones, statues of marble. Their skin was white, their waist
length hair silver, shiny as polished metal. It flowed over their shoulders
and settled in the seat of the chair surrounding their entire bodies with
a glistening halo. Their eyes were light in color. I couldn't see anything
except two dark outlined circles where the pupils should have been. They
wore long blue cloaks to match the velvet of their chairs. They were both*

frightening and incredibly beautiful. I perceived they had never been human.

"Rise new born," requested the female. "Come closer." Her voice was low and melodious, almost as if she were singing the words instead of speaking them.

I glanced at Richard and Gabriela. They both continued to kneel with their heads bowed. I rose to my feet then step by slow step, moved closer to the royal pair.

"Halt!" ordered the male. His voice was deeper, more resonant but still melodic. He rose from his chair, moving toward me with slow, measured steps. I stood frozen, waiting to see if he would come all the way to my side. As he raised his hand behind him, the female rose, following him.

"Why do you come to us?" When she reached his side, he held out his arm. She rested her long fingers on it, her claw like fingernails resembled window glass, the finger tips visible through them.

I whispered as I spoke. I told them my story, that I longed to know more about my kind, what I was capable of doing and from where the first of our species came. The female smiled a slow smile, I could see that her teeth were large and pointed.

"Alright, new born, you will learn." Turning to Sebastian, she motioned him to take us away. "Take them to the sanctuary, Sebastian. Tell him the stories." My companions stood and we were led back to the door through which we had just entered the chamber.

"Shall I go on Sarah, or would you like to rest and continue at a later time?"

She couldn't wait to hear what he learned. She leaned in to look closely at Carlos. His breath was quiet; his features relaxed and peaceful. "Please Aris, continue now."

At your pleasure. We moved down the corridor to another huge, aged door. Sebastian opened it and lit a torch from the one he carried. He moved around the room, lighting waiting torch after torch, until the enclosure blazed with light.

The floor was covered with many layers of soft, thick carpets. I saw such things in the richest rooms of the palace, but these were of colors so true and pure, they resembled jewels. The walls were covered with hieroglyphics. Sebastian led us to the far corner. He pointed to a colorful drawing of a large disc, hovering in a night sky. A beam of light shown from a port on the bottom of the disc.

He told us many millennium ago the star voyagers came to earth. They traveled from place to place through the stars examining all life that was found. On this planet, they discovered humans.

Continuing to speak, Sebastian moved to the next drawing. Earth people were drawn bowing to tall strange beings from another world. The humans were primitive and without knowledge so they worshiped the star voyagers as gods. Akira and Khansu were in the landing party that made contact with the humans. They were teachers and scientists. Because our kind translates and communicates all languages without thought or study, they were able to converse easily with all they met.

The next drawing depicted an ancient city with two of the strangers drawn standing tall over the buildings and the humans. I asked if it was Akira and Khansu who sent me to this room.

He told me it was. Khansu was the leader, being older and wiser, and Akira was the scientist, being female and more adept at learning intricate information. He told me they watched the interaction of the humans and saw they were similar to a species on their own planet, a species raised for feeding the star beings. The difference was the humans had the ability to speak.

Sebastian guided me, pictograph by pictograph, around the walls of the room. The story he told was too strange not to be true. The star people traveled from a planet that had three moons circling in constant motion. One of the moons was used as a farm where they raised a species for food, but they didn't kill them or eat them. They tapped into their veins and drank their living blood. They cared for their stock and kept them well and healthy so their blood regenerated rapidly. Each feeding from

their blood would leave them weak and ill, but stronger still once they
recovered. The older and stronger the servant, the sweeter and more
powerful the blood. They were treated well and mixed with society until
at last, the blood no longer regenerated and they expired.

"Sarah, are you there?" Once again, she stopped breathing as he
told his story and only his calling her name made her catch her
breath.

"Yes, I'm here."

"Shall I go on?"

She whispered one word, "Yes."

The star voyagers were able to feed on the earth humans but the blood
didn't satisfy them as did the stock from their home. They starved and
died one after another until Akira found a solution. She found that if they
completely drained the human at each feeding, they were able to sustain
their lives and feed much less often. Blood drinking to the death began.

Their companions felt shame at taking human life even if the beings
were primitive and dull. A decision was made to return to the planet of
the three moons. Preparations were made for their departure.

But Akira and Khansu refused to leave. They were deep in research
and cared little for human life. They stayed on alone, continuing their
work and feeding from the human species. On their new planet, they
were eternal; they neither aged, grew sick nor died. They became as
gods. They were worshipped and founded an advanced civilization
with the learning they brought with them. Akira named the civilization
Atlantis after one of the moons of their home star. There they lived for
many, many hundreds of years.

Sebastian told that they would never speak of the fate of their first
civilization. But once Khansu mentioned to him the earth opened
and destroyed all they had built, water covered most of the land. For
centuries, they traveled from island to island, desiring to build a new
Atlantis. They would spend a few hundred years to see if a civilization
could be developed. If they found it could not, they moved on. They

*came to England more than two hundred years before I was brought to
London and still they stayed on with hopes of a future.*

*We came to rest in front of the entrance door to the chamber, our
audience ended. I was filled with questions and begged Sebastian to stay
with me, to tell me more. He agreed.*

*We left the Catacombs. It was bitter cold yet Sebastian and I strolled
along the Thames as if it were mid-summer. I was grateful he agreed to
walk with me. There were so many questions that he could answer. I
asked him to tell me more about the coven. How many belonged to it?
How did it come to be?*

*He told the story of his own birth. Akira found him, wounded by a
boar in the forest. She nurtured him to a new kind of health, a perfect
vampire health. He was the first of their children and the oldest. Akira
embraced having more of her own kind near to her so she began to create
a family. Slowly, one after another were made. Akira was careful in
her choice of mortals. To give eternal life and vampire powers to any
depraved mortal would have been an unforgivable sin. To set such
an undead on an unsuspecting world could create only chaos. Those
humans she chose were of the highest morals, having great beauty, and
celebrated learning. Soon, the Catacombs were a bustling hive of the
undead. As in any family, some of the children left home, going out into
the world to find their own way. They in turn created more of our kind.
Our species thrived. And as in any family, some of the first came back
to their home and some of the new born came as well. The population in
the Catacombs varies from century to century it seems.*

I asked about the wild coven that created Richard and Gabriela.

*He shared an ancient legend. It tells the story that many hundreds
of years ago, a new born fell in love with a witch. She was young and
beautiful and evil. She tricked him into telling her of the Catacombs and
the old ones, all of their truths and legends. She told him she loved him.
She wanted to share eternity with him. She begged him until he agreed to
change her. Once changed, her first act was to stake him and burn him.*

From her, the story says, a second breed of our species sprang. The evil ones. They are few. Most are unable to control the frenzy of the blood, killing their intended victims instead of turning them. He said the Italian coven that turned Richard and Gabriela was known to the Counsel as well as others in distant places.

I was enthralled with stories of our kind. Being one of the King's men, I had little time to spend in the Catacombs. It was freeing to be able to speak the truth of who I was and what I was.

Sebastian told me one day the star voyagers would return. He waited patiently. He prayed he would be allowed to go to the home planet of our species, to find a life of normalcy for our kind. A place where he could live without the self-hate of being a murderer just to sustain his existence. His memories of his human life were very clear to him. He had been a poet and a scholar. He loved and had been loved and the thought of a vampire draining his mortal family drove him close to starvation more than once. He did his best to live from animals but there were times when the bloodlust could be answered only by taking a human life.

I was amazed at his compassion. Did a lion have pity on his dinner? I thought not, yet here was a bloodsucker with a conscience. Did I have a conscience? Did I ever have a conscience? I felt no remorse for killing when I was a warrior for Alexander. I am not sure that I am repentant even now.

He sighed.

Sarah, I can think of nothing I would rather do than give you the gift of the venom to bring you into my eternity. And it would most certainly be without apology.

"Sorry or not, it is an impossible thought." Sarah spoke to Aris but in her mind she was glad it was not a choice she would ever have to make. His world confounded her, enticed her, drew her into it. He was so much more than any man she had ever known. "And he's not real. That's why." She grabbed control of her thoughts, managing the session once again.

"Aris, it's time for Carlos to come back."

"Are you afraid of me, Sarah, or afraid of yourself."

She ignored his statement and continued on, "In just a moment, I will begin to count you back. One, two, three…"

#

"So the blood drinkers came from outer space? Honestly Sarah, I think this is a story for Hollywood. Sounds like a bunch of crap to me." He slouched in the chair and drank a soda from the can.

"Then you need to be the author. If this is your imagination, it's beyond anything I could come up with."

Carlos smiled a cocky grin and winked. "Yeah, I'm just born to write sci-fi."

CHAPTER 20

Sarah was happy to be able to open the windows in her condo and let the fresh, spring air wash away all the stale, enclosed heat of winter. She and Colleen sat on her deck, watching the twilight clouds roll by, pushed by a soft spring wind.

"What a great day." Colleen sipped her wine. She dipped a chip into the carrot and dill dip Sarah left on the table. She popped it into her mouth. Surprised, she swallowed as she reached for seconds. "Hey, this is pretty good." She scooped another helping. "Don't look so proud. I didn't have lunch today and just about anything would taste great."

"Thanks pal," Sarah laughed as she moved the dip to her side of the table. "That's what I get for trying to help you get healthy."

Colleen shuffled in her chair, "Speaking of healthy, how's the boy doing?"

"Colleen, Carlos is anything but a boy." She couldn't believe what she heard herself say. "I mean, his life has made him so much older than his years."

"Yeah? Older than his years?" She scooped such a huge amount of dip onto a chip that it broke in two pieces. She piled one half on top of the other, then tipped her head back, dropping them into her mouth. She smiled as her teeth crunched down and the flavors mixed.

"Has he ever told you about rehab?" Sarah watched as her friend demolished the plate of chips.

"Naw, rehab is rehab. What's to tell?" Colleen spoke in between mouthfuls.

"C. His rehab wasn't five star. You know it was in Mexico. And it wasn't to cater to rich addicts. The goal was to clean them up, to send them back to society with some respect for themselves and for other people." She sipped her iced tea. "They weren't waited on and they weren't analyzed. They were detoxed." She paused as she thought of the stories Carlos told her. "They grew up real fast." She sat quietly for a moment.

She stood, walking the short distance to the sliding glass door. "Ready for the soup? It's the parsnip and pear I was telling you about yesterday. It's really great."

"Parsnip and pear? I don't know hon," then Colleen decided she might as well be adventurous. "Oh, all right. Bring it on." She scraped the dip from the bottom of the saucer with the last chip. She popped it in her mouth, licking the tip of her forefinger.

Following her friend into the kitchen, she spoke. "You know Sarah, somehow you built a rapport with him that no one else has ever been able to accomplish. Do you think it's the hypnosis? Or just your super human compassion?"

"I think it's trust." Sarah gazed out the window as the sky changed colors, the crimson sunset blazing over the rooftops. "Plain and simple trust. I would never do anything to break that. It's what guarantees the truth."

The parole officer nodded yes, knowing full well that Sarah had hit it on the head. The answer to most of the problems of life was divided into two main categories, the inability to trust and the inability to be trustworthy.

#

Her cell phone rang just as the waitress placed her eggs and potatoes on the table in front of her. She nodded thank you to her server as she reached for her phone.

"Sarah, I've got to see you." His voice was determined. "Now, I'm dreaming this crap."

She responded to the urgency in his voice. "I'm at Saul's. Can you meet me for breakfast and we can talk." She wondered if his dreams were anything like hers. She certainly hoped not.

"Yeah. I'm just leaving the house. I'll be there as soon as I can." He sounded tentative. "Would you mind waiting for me?"

"I'll be here." She would have to call Maggie to postpone her first client of the day. "Hurry up. I'm booked all day."

"On my way." The phone went silent as he pressed the end button.

#

She never really noticed the power of his physique until he slid into the chair across the table from her. He always wore a sweater or jacket against the cold winds of winter and the rains of spring. It was warm this morning so his arms were exposed and golden in his short sleeved tee shirt. His muscles were defined, powerful. He had the torso of someone who was born strong and toned yet never had to do anything to maintain it.

"Hey." He smiled as he sat down.

"Hey." She responded. Their waitress came by the table with the regulation mug and coffee pot. He nodded yes.

"Thanks for meeting me." He sipped the hot, black liquid in his mug. "Not bad." He nodded toward the cup as he placed it back on the table.

"This thing is just getting way out of hand." He leaned closer, crossing his arms as he rested them on the table in front of him. "It's even taking over my dreams."

Sarah shifted her empty plate aside. She wrapped her fingers around her mug as she questioned him. "Last night?"

"Yeah, last night." Looking down, he shrugged his shoulders. "But that wasn't the first time."

"Why didn't you tell me this before?"

He looked over her left shoulder to avoid her eyes. "I didn't want to think it was important."

"And now?"

"Now, I can't get away from this Aris character awake or asleep." He began to shred his paper placemat in long shreds, piling them in front of him.

"Last night I dreamed I... No. He was watching Anne. She was talking to some old hag who had a huge leather bag over her shoulder. They were somewhere in a forest and Anne was making some sort of deal with this old woman."

"What kind of deal?" Sarah drained her cup.

"It was like Aris was hiding behind some bushes so I couldn't make it out too clearly." He leaned closer to her. "Anne gave the old woman a small leather pouch that was stuffed to the gills."

"Yes?" Sarah met his posture as she leaned closer to him.

"It looked like the old woman gave her something in return but I couldn't tell what it was."

"Then?"

"Richard, the vamp, came up behind me. He took my arm. He startled me. He scares the crap out of me anyway."

"What happened," Sarah forgot everything else except the story that was being told.

"He led me away. I felt like I had no alternative but to follow him." Carlos sat silent for a moment. "He took me down to the Catacombs again, to the chamber that he and Gabriela call their lair."

"Lair?"

"Their home. Their condo?" He smiled at the irony. "Anyway, he took me to a place where we could talk without anyone hearing us."

"What happened?" He had her complete interest.

"Richard started telling me all these weird stories about vamps being put to death for disobeying the law. It was like he was warning me, uh, Aris, not to ever do anything to piss off the high council." He leaned forward in the seat. "This Aris is a pretty tough character though. I mean, he doesn't seem to be afraid of anything. In this dream, he was way cool."

"Well Carlos," she said, "In this scenario, he's already one of the undead so I don't think there's too much that can be done to him."

"Yeah, well, here's the rub." The waitress came to clear the table of dishes. He stopped talking until she walked away. "It's like I told you before about this council, these vamps have the power and knowledge to destroy him."

Sarah's eyes grew round. "What exactly do you mean?"

"It means they can eliminate him, ending his awareness totally. Or, they can leave him just a mind without a body looking for a place to land just like he was in that cave." His expression became pained. "Like in any human that was vulnerable to receive him. Whether they wanted him around or not." His lips tightened as he spoke.

"So, what are you saying?"

"What I'm saying, Sarah, is that I'm the host to this fiend. And you know it's the truth."

She felt as if she had been punched in the stomach because she knew he was absolutely right. He carried a beast inside of his subconscious, a beast that intrigued her no end.

CHAPTER 21

"There's a Mrs. Havarro on the phone for you. " Maggie's voice was questioning. "I didn't think gorgeous was married"

"No Maggie, he's not married. It must be his mother. I'll pick it up." She wondered why his mother would be calling her. She pressed the flashing light on her phone, "Hi, this is Sarah Hagan."

"Miss Hagan, this is Isabella Havarro. I'm sorry to bother you."

"No bother Isabella." She leaned back in her chair. "What can I do for you?"

"I'm concerned about Carlos. I thought I should come to you first."

She spun her chair around to gaze out the window as she spoke. "What's the matter? From what I understand, Carlos is doing very well both at work and at the half-way house."

"It isn't about work. It's about his old group of friends." She paused.

"Yes, Isabella?"

"You see, Carlos hasn't been running with them since he came back from rehab. Not that I know anyway." Her voice grew softer, "I must speak quietly. My husband is home from work today. He is sick."

"Yes?"

"Today I received a phone call from one of them. Someone called Manu. He asked for Carlos. I told him Carlos didn't live here anymore." Again, a long pause on the other end of the phone.

Sarah turned back toward her desk, leaning forward, resting her elbows on the dark wood. "Isabella, what is it?"

"This man said that if I don't have Carlos get in touch with his friends, there will be trouble in our home." Sarah could hear the fright in her voice. "Miss Hagan, if my husband finds out, he will be crazy. He and Carlos have never been acting like father and son. Fernando has a bad temper and he wasn't always good to Carlos. He and Carlos have fought with fists. It has been very bad for a long, long time. If he finds out that we are being threatened, he will blame my son. He doesn't always think clearly and I am afraid what he will do if those people come around here"

Sarah wondered if Carlos had always been honest with her about his old life, his new habits. "I'll see what I can do, Isabella."

"Please Miss Hagan, Sarah, my Carlos is working so hard to have a better life. I know he is. Please, don't let these bad people ruin it for him." She held back her tears. "Please help him."

"He has an appointment with me this afternoon. I'll do whatever I can to see that he steers clear of them. I know he's doing his best." She only hoped that her instincts were right, that he had been telling her the truth.

There was a semblance of calm in her tone of voice as the older woman answered. "Thank you. Thank you so much. And I won't take up any more of your time." A relieved sigh escaped before she spoke again. "Good bye Miss Hagan."

"Good bye Isabella." Sarah placed the phone on the cradle. She turned once more to look out the window. "Now what? What else can happen?" She sighed, leaned back in her chair and closed her eyes.

#

"Colleen? Have you got a minute?"

"Only one. I'm in the car and the speaker on my cell won't work so I have to hold it. If I get another ticket for talking while driving, Bob's going to kill me. What's up?"

"What do you know about the guys Carlos used to run with?"

"Nothing I haven't told you. A bad bunch. Always in and out of trouble and some of it, pretty nasty. Why?" Her voice got loud and angry. "You idiot! Not you honey, this fool in front of me." Sarah heard a car horn. "Why are you asking?"

Sarah already decided not to tell Colleen about the threatening phone call to the Havarro household until she spoke to Carlos. "I'm going to see him this afternoon. I thought I'd check to see if you might have picked up any additional background on his old friends, that's all."

"Well, they're really a bunch of gang bangers. There was one drive by but nothing was ever proved. I hope to hell he hasn't tied up with them again. They're all poison." The next sound was a long honk on a horn. "Oh God, got to go. There's a cop car turning the corner."

"Will she ever learn to say the words 'good bye'?" Sarah found her shoes under her desk, put them on and walked to the door of her office. "Maggie, will you bring me a salad when you go to lunch? I'm going to be in all afternoon."

#

His step was light and he looked happy as he entered her office.

"Hey Sarah, Maggie gone for the day?" He plopped down in the chair facing her desk.

"Yes, she had a hair appointment." She stood. "So, what's going on?" Crossing to the recliner, she turned to face him. "Anything new I should hear about?"

"Okay Sarah." He stood, the smile leaving his face. "It's obvious you're playing detective here. You tell me what's going on."

"Nothing really. Just that your mother got a phone call today from someone called Manu." She watched his face change. He looked defensive.

"Maybe it's time I had a talk with Manu. So, you think I might be hanging with the home boys again?" He paced a few steps away from her then stopped, waiting for her answer.

"I won't think anything until you tell me. I'm just asking you what's up?" She chose her words carefully. She didn't want this meeting to turn into a confrontation.

"Yeah? Well, what's up is I haven't seen them since rehab." His tone was angry, "Don't you see the changes in me? Haven't you been involved in making them?" He crossed the room to stand just in front of her. "Don't you know I wouldn't do anything to disappoint you?"

She lifted the recorder from the seat of her chair, sat down and looked up at him.

"Look Sarah, I don't know why I have these feelings for you. They're coming way out of left field. I've tried to talk to you about it before but if I even get close to the subject, you stop me." He sat across from her in his usual position, his elbows on his knees, his hands folded.

"I'm stopping you now, Carlos." She paused. "It's normal for a client to feel attached to their therapist. It happens often."

"Well," He looked at the floor. "This hasn't happened to me before. I look forward to seeing you. I don't even care if the vamp takes over my body and does things from a horror movie as long as I can see you when I come back." He raised his eyes to meet hers. "Don't tell me you don't feel something, Sarah. I know you do."

She cleared her throat before she could speak. "Of course I do. I told you a long time ago, you're like family to me."

There was a long silence. "Not what I've had for a family. You are so much more than that to me. Sarah, you're warm and strong and . . ."

She interrupted him, "Don't go there." Abject determination sounded in her soft voice. "That's a place where we can never go. Not ever, and you know that." She looked down at the floor for a long moment. Her heart was pounding. She realized she wasn't breathing. Her logical mind puzzled at the way her body reacted to his words. He was her client, nothing more. Yet she knew that wasn't the absolute truth

"Carlos, please don't bring this up again."

He paused a moment. "I thought I was doing pretty well for a guy. I haven't said anything or made a move on you for a while. And I want to. All the time."

"Look Carlos, didn't you hear what I just said? Now, do you want to have a session today or not?" Her voice was stern and her eyes meant business.

He sighed and lay down on the leather recliner, grinning broadly. "Shot down again." He settled into the comfortable cushions. "But it isn't over until it's over and there's a whole lot more to the vamp's story. That means lots and lots of time for us to be together, so let's just wait and see what happens." He closed his eyes and his eyelashes laid deep, mysterious shadows on the top of his cheekbones. "Go ahead Sarah, count me out."

#

CARLOS HAVARRO, transcript, session 13, May 28

I lived in the palace and returned to the catacombs whenever I was able to sneak away. I developed a deep friendship with Sebastian and when I was allowed an audience with the vampire monarchs, Akira treated me with the kindness of a parent to a child. It was from all of them I learned about our kind.

'Vampire' is the human word for our species because we feed on blood, but we are not the evil sort who murder for pleasure. If you were to give us a true name, it would be Akirians. We are all her children but those depraved ones are the seed of the ancient witch I aforementioned.

Our kind drinks human blood often only at the beginning of our eternal journey. After a time, it is only on rare occasions that the hunger comes upon us. We subsist most of our existence on animal blood just as most humans do. We simply do not eat the meat.

Even though we remain in truly human bodies, we have alien venom running through our veins. We are the perfect combination of two completely different species. We need not breathe yet we are able if we wish. We can see with human eyes, however, we are able to switch to vampire sight at will. We need not eat. Food has very little flavor to us, however, if we wish to dine, it is possible. When we consume human food, we have human body functions. We need sleep only at the beginning of our eternal existence yet we are able to at any time if we so desire. You see, we are both alien and human in one body.

Ours is an old race with deep convictions. There is judicial procedure in our society. A strict code of ethics is called out in the Book of Laws kept in the library of the Catacombs. The constitution demands honor and integrity from each soul in the realm.

I studied the vampire laws. We of the Catacombs are not a cruel species. There are rules, regulations keeping our existence silent and respecting the humans who share the land with our kind. We kill mortals only out of desperate need when driven by the hunger, when we are without choice to take human life. We feed from the dregs of mankind, leaving untouched those of good conscience. Vengeance by venom is not allowed. Killing for sport is a death sentence. We are ruled by a strange sense of compassion for those upon whom we feed. I learned then more of those renegades who were our natural enemy. Such were the witches who changed me and the evil ones that changed Richard and Gabriela.

For centuries in your world, we were merely beings of fable not unlike fairies and dragons. We walked among your kind without notice. We lived in seclusion and peace until depraved transgressors openly took decent human life. The dead, found drained of blood, turned the ancient fable of the vampire into reality. Rapidly the stories spread from village to village. From town to town. From country to country. It was then your modern myths came into being. Garlic. Crosses. Bursting to flames in the sunlight. Oh yes, and coffins during the daylight. Creations of a frightened human mind. All false. The only truth found in all the human mythology is death comes to us with a stake in the heart and the burning of the human form until it is naught but ashes.

Sebastian taught me to use the powers I was not aware that I possessed. I could climb the outside of a building with my fingers, clinging to stone as if it were a part of me. I could run faster than any horse could carry a man. I was able to leap from a tall place without injury and I could jump over wide chasms as if stepping across a small stone.

But the most marvelous power was taught to me by Richard, the powers of the venom. You see, Sarah, vampires are venomous beings. The venom when added to human blood can be used as poison to kill slowly or it can be fed into a body little by little as it is drained to create another of our kind. To rapidly draw the blood from a human will instantly bring them to their death. So you understand, the venom can be used in different ways to different ends. To slowly drain a human and fill them with venom is eternal life while venom mixed with human blood is a slow poison that leaves no traces.

Richard told me Akira created their following with the power. Some of her offspring left the court and went out into the world and so the vile, debased vampires of Mount Haemus who created me came into being.

Time passed above ground in the court of the King and below in the counsel of the vampires. One day faded into the next. Sebastian told me of the treaty between the ancient royals and the vampires not to feed in the royal house. I wondered if Henry and his court were even aware we existed but I accepted the rules; I fed only away from the palace. I quenched my thirst on animals in the nearby forest but when the hunger overtook me, I ran long and fast, far from any who knew me.

I became one of the King's favorite courtiers and rode out with him to the hunt, drinking sour wine with him in the evenings. I relished *the warmth and intrigue of the court. I spent less and less time in the dark, underground Catacombs studying, attending the vampire counsel. Richard and Gabriela began to feel I had chosen humans over my own. They quietly avoided me when I went underground.*

I frequented Henry's court. I watched as his consort, Anne Boleyn, worked harder and harder to keep him interested. She led him a merry chase for many years, never giving in to his desires because she was not his wife. It was during that time she called on me to attend her brother. If I am a monster, she was a demon. She was without conscience. Nothing mattered to her except her family and her quest for power.

Her sister, Mary, and her brother, George, were her only true friends. I cannot truly vouchsafe for her sister but her brother was besotted with her. He trailed behind her every step. He and his friends made up a small court that waited just upon Anne. They were a wild troupe and George was the most licentious. It was his supposed affair with Lord Weston that sent her to me for my aid. I was chosen as one of the King's favorites and so it was with ease I began to run with George and his friends.

It was at a royal banquet in the company of Anne's gentlemen that I first saw her, my Elizabeth. As I told you, she was a lady in waiting to Anne, she was exquisite. Small waisted, golden haired with a smile that opposed the brilliance of the sun. Her shy, sweet ways held her always in the background but her gentle beauty outshined all of the other young maids.

If I may, I will tell you more of my love. You have been told that her cousin, Thomas Wyatt, arranged our meeting. We three rode side by side on that first early morning hunt. I remember so well. The King claimed the kill and was in a boisterous mood. Elizabeth's face was flushed from the cold air. She smiled modestly when I complimented her complexion. I asked to sit next to her at the evening banquet. She agreed.

From that day, I was hers. She was constantly in my thoughts no matter my task. Her blue eyes, her musical laughter, the slight tilt of her head when she was in earnest conversation. I loved her with a love that is beyond human understanding. For the only time since the morning in the forest when I killed the bandits and fed on my first human blood, I hated what I was. I longed for mortality yet knew it was impossible. I longed to be one with her, to have her for my good wife. I sensed her care for me. Her touch was tender and longing, her eyes bright with love.

At last, I could stand it no longer. Early one morning as we walked in the garden, I held her to me and told her of my deep feeling for her. She returned my embrace and I kissed her sweet mouth. We promised each other our eternal love. I knew the greatest joy and the deepest fear I ever experienced. How could I possess her, she, a delicate human and I, eternal and indestructible? Yet I knew I could not continue on without her.

Not knowing what to do, I approached Sebastian, telling him of my plight. He said it was impossible for a human and a vampire to mate. However, there were historical instances when a human could be made into one of our kind if it was their desire and with the permission of the counsel. He told me he, too, was in love with a human. She knew what he was and loved him still. He approached the council for permission to turn her, to marry her. He waited only for their permission to proceed.

I wondered at his fearlessness in telling his beloved he was one of the undead. Was she not afraid of him? How could she accept him, his affliction? Yet he said her affection ran so deep she was willing to give her human life to spend eternity with him. Did Elizabeth love me with such depth, such conviction? That was when I decided to approach the council.

One evening as we walked in the garden, I summoned all courage. I asked her to be my wife.

She rose from the garden bench. She pondered my request as she walked slowly toward the castle. Turning on the path, she ran into my arms. Her words ring still in my heart and my mind. "I love you Aris. I would die for you and I will live for you. I will be your wife and you will be my husband."

In that moment, I knew joy as I had never known it before and peace that I have not known since, until this moment, here with you.

Sarah's heart pounded in her chest and she wondered at the exhilaration she felt at his words.

I approached Wolsey to petition the Queen to marry my lady. I went below ground to petition my own royal house.

As you know, I waited weeks in the Catacombs for the decision of the council. Would they allow the marriage? Would they give their permission to make Elizabeth one of us? I was plagued with doubts and worries. I could not go on without her at my side. Sebastian stood a friend to me, assuring me time and again that all would be well, they would decide in my favor.

At long last, he came to me in my private chamber smiling and with the greatest of news. I was to bring Elizabeth before the council where they would question her. If they were convinced she wished it of her own will, she would be permitted to become one of us. I would be with her and love her for all eternity. My joy was boundless as I returned to the surface and the palace to plead my case with my beloved.

That was when I came upon Thomas Wyatt. When I asked for her, his face flushed and he stammered as he answered. My ears refused his words and my mind reeled at the implication. Wolsey sent her to the court of Spain with the Spanish ambassador. He traded her for a wine contract to an aging and degenerate courtier of the Emperor. It was then I learned she was lost at sea, gone from me forever. I raged. I cried out for vengeance.

Thomas settled me in his rooms and there, kept me from the rest of the court until I found my sanity once more. She was lost. The only person I had ever loved was lost to me and for nothing more than gold. Wolsey was the second richest man in the Kingdom, only the King was before him, and yet it was not enough. I seethed. I hated him. I vowed vengeance. Thomas spoke calming words and soothed me, taking pains to heal my hurt and in time, I accepted my great loss. I rejoined the court. I pledged to search forever, human lifetime after lifetime for her, for my sweet Elizabeth. And I vowed to see Wolsey dead just as my only love was dead, buried so far from me.

"Enough, Sarah. Enough for today."

Sarah sat quietly, tears flowing down her cheeks.

#

"Sometimes I feel as if I don't have a body at all, as if I don't even exist. And sometimes I feel so different, alive in a way that I've never experienced before." He sipped the water she brought to him. "Does that make any sense?"

"Yes, it does." She gazed at the carpet for more than a moment then looked up at his face. "When Aris speaks through you, it's as if you've stepped aside to let him through."

"'Stepped aside?'" He nodded, "Yeah, that's what it feels like. Like there isn't any more of me, only him. It's weird and scary and, for some strange reason I really like it sometimes."

"Like it sometimes?"

"Yeah, like I'm so much more than I have ever been or ever thought I could be." He leaned forward in his chair. "Is this guy real or am I just making him up, some kind of horror story hero in my head?"

"I don't know if he's real or not but your deepest mind is telling us quite a story." She stood and looked out her window in silence.

"Sarah," He moved to stand next to her, then took her shoulders in his hands, turning her to face him. "Sarah, I know this scares you sometimes. I know sometimes you want to stop." He released her, stuffing his hands in his jeans pockets. "Hell, sometimes I want to stop. But right now, I don't. This is the first time in my life I felt any kind of curiosity since I was a kid. I want to know what he is, if he really is some vampire from a past age or just a deeper part of me. I need to know.

"And I'm starting to understand the uncontrollable anger that grips me sometimes. I don't know if it's because I lost a love five hundred years ago or not but if the vamp can overcome his rage, so can I. I don't do drugs anymore and I don't want to lose it because I'm pissed off. I want to own my life."

"Of course we'll keep going. I think you're right about the anger. But you have to tell me if you ever feel it's getting out of hand. I've always been honest with you Carlos, I'm just along for the ride the same as you are. I have no more control over Aris than you do. And I'm not sure I like that."

He grinned. "Well, I'm glad to see you out of control over something." He pecked her cheek with a quick kiss, then turned on his heel.

As he walked to the door, he looked over his shoulder and winked, "See you next Friday."

CHAPTER 22

Sarah's mother held the blue silk dress just in front of her daughter. "This color is wonderful with your eyes."

Sarah looked skeptical as she pulled it over her head, "I know you like blue, Mother, but I think it's a little low cut for a maid of honor."

"Honey, it really compliments your figure. Don't you want to be stunning?"

"Mother," Sarah let her exasperation show in her voice, "the only one who needs to be stunning at the wedding is the bride."

"Are you taking Steve?"

"I haven't seen Steve in quite a while." She challenged her mother's response with the tone of her voice. "Our free time just didn't coincide."

"I don't understand why you have such difficulty with men, dear. You're such a pretty girl. Your grandmother and I would so like to see you settled in a comfortable marriage. You proved yourself as a career woman with your book. When will you ever be ready to settle down?"

Sarah turned to face the older woman, a determined look on her face. "Mother, I'm not trying to prove anything with my career. Why can't you just accept my work is a part of who I am?"

Mrs. Hagan's eyes grew large in surprise. "Why Sarah, I don't understand your attitude. I'm only thinking about what is best for you."

"No Mother, you are thinking about what is best for you. It's time you recognized that I am not just a clone of you. Marriage is great but I'm not ready to settle for a second rate relationship just to make you happy. I've done that before and I won't do it again." She pivoted to face the mirror once more pleased with herself to be finally taking a stand with her mother.

Smoothing her skirt as she stood, the older woman took a tentative step toward her daughter. "I didn't mean to upset you, Sarah. I only want the best for you. Let's just focus on choosing a dress for the wedding."

Sarah smiled, grateful her mother didn't push the conversation as she usually would have done, proud that she had spoken up at long last. "Yes, I think that's a great idea."

"Do you want to buy your shoes today while we're already out shopping?"

#

"Miss Hagan, I'm sorry to bother you. Carlos Havarro's down here to see you." His voice grew soft as he covered the receiver with his hand. "And he's a mess, Miss. His face is bloody. It looks like he's broken his hand."

"What?"

"I told him you didn't leave his name at the desk but I've seen him with you before and he looks like he really needs some help. What should I do?"

"Send him up. It's fine." As she stepped to the living room window to draw the sheer cream colored curtains, she thought, "What now?"

She placed the tea pot on the stove when she heard a soft, tentative knock on her door. She opened it, gasping when she saw him.

"What happened to you?" She took his arm, helping him maneuver to the couch. He was battered and blood oozed from a wound on his head. He held his hand to his forehead to stop the bleeding.

Moving his hand to look at his battered face, she winced. "Sit here and I'll get something to clean your face. What in the world happened to you?" She spoke as she lifted his chin to survey the damage.

"I tried to talk to Manu about the scare tactics. Obviously, it didn't work." As he wiped his arm across his forehead to clean the blood, he opened the wound even further. "I told him about you and what you've done for me, how my life is different now. He wouldn't listen so I talked louder. I guess the rest of his pals didn't like my tone of voice or something because before I knew it, I was on the bottom of a pile of punching fists and kicking feet. I'm sorry I came here but I couldn't go to the half-way house like this. They would have to report it." His eye was swelling as he looked up at her. "Can I have some water?"

Embarrassed that he needed to ask, she answered him as she stood, "I'm sorry. Just put your feet up on the couch and lie down. I'll get some bandages." Turning to leave the room, she added, "And for God's sake, don't get up, just rest until I get back."

Sarah turned off the boiling tea pot. She dampened a clean cloth to wipe his face. The wound in his head was smaller than she first thought. She remembered she read somewhere that head wounds bled more than other places and she was glad it wasn't a deep gash. She put a bag of frozen peas wrapped in a towel on his blackening eye then looked at his right hand. "Can you move your fingers?"

He winced as he wiggled first one then another. "Yeah, I don't think it's broken although I can't say the same thing about Manu's nose." He smiled through the bruises that were beginning to appear on his face.

"Carlos, this is it. Enough. It's time we told someone about this. I don't want you to be hurt anymore."

"This is nothing. Don't worry." She cleaned his split knuckles then wrapped a second package of frozen peas in a towel and bound it to his hand. "That feels kind a good." He laid his head back on the cushion.

"Why don't you just stay here tonight?" She reached to help him stand. "You can sleep in the guest room."

"No." He raised his hand to stop her. "I'd like to stay, but I'll just crash out here on the couch." There was gratitude in his words. "Would you mind? Just throw a blanket over me and I'll be out in a minute. I'm feeling kind a dead right now."

She picked up the throw from the arm of the sofa. She covered him then took the towel wrapped peas. "Okay, just sleep right now. We'll talk about it in the morning." Turning off the light, she looked at him one last time. She went into her bedroom shutting the door behind her. She drifted to sleep, her last thoughts confused and a bit frightened.

#

She felt the dreamtime weightlessness so she knew she was in a sleep-induced fantasy. The musicians played a lively tune as the courtiers prepared to dance. They faced one another creating two long ribbons made of the lush colored satins and silks they wore. Their jewels sparkled in the light of what seemed to be thousands of candles. They were all so beautiful, dressed for the Royal Masque in the spring court of England. They all wore disguises, false faces. Ornate and colorful, each courtier's mask representing a different animal or bird.

An owl face bedecked with pristine white feathers and a beak of burnished gold plate sat above the strong body of a man dressed in finest white satin. The short cape slung about his powerful shoulders was made of cloth of gold and glimmered in the candlelight as he led his lady through the steps of a lively galliard. His partner sported the face of a tricky red fox. Her gown of russet silk shimmered as they danced; the deep rust-colored velvet stomacher was rich with embroidered golden wheat shafts. Her brown eyes shown as he lifted her high, spinning in a tight slow circle.

Sarah stood, waiting as the musicians changed the tempo to a slow pavane. A tall man stepped in front of her, blocking her view of the dancers. His rich velvet clothing was colored in shades of gray, embellished richly with diamonds and silver. His hair was black and wild. His human face hid behind the face of a savage wolf, its canines exposed and sharp. Golden eyes peeked from the narrow slits on either side of the nose.

He reached for her hand and led her in a courtly manner. Dance after dance, he kept her with him. He whirled and spun her. Again and again, his strong arms lifted her high until she was taller than he then gently lowered her until her feet touched the floor once again. The bodice of her petal pink gown was laced so tightly she became short of breath. Still, they continued. At last, when she was spent and out of breath completely, he took her hand to lead her from the palace into the rose garden. The fragrance of the sweet flowers filled the warm night air, their colors clearly visible in the light of a full summer moon. His eyes were alive with anticipation. His arm slid around her waist as he guided her into the green bowers of a lover's maze. It was familiar. She had been in this place before. They turned corner after corner, disappearing deeper into the heart of the living puzzle.

The sound of splashing water reached their ears just as they entered an intimate, sweet smelling rose garden. In the center loomed an enormous fountain. It dwarfed the surrounding greenery and the spray bounced like tiny, living balls of light in the brilliance of the moon. He untied his mask yet his face was still in shadow and she could not see his features.

He grasped her waist to turn her toward him. His hands were familiar. She was sure she had felt them before this night. Gently, he drew her to him. She went willingly, joyfully. They came together and the touch of his lips thrilled her. He gathered her into his arms and the kisses he trailed along her jaw were as soft as the wings of a butterfly. He kissed her brows, her eyelids. His tongue brushed her eyelashes then trailed to outline her small perfect ears. His scent enveloped her and she could no longer catch her breath. Her heart embraced the sweet madness of the moment. He kissed her deeply. Her tongue toyed with the soft tuft of hair beneath his lower lip. He moaned as she pressed herself into him. She could feel him, firm and sweet, through the thick layers of her silk gown.

Her trembling fingers slid his doublet down over his sturdy shoulders then lifted his exquisitely made cambric shirt over his head. Her breath caught as she gazed at his sculpted, muscular body. He turned her away from him to loosen the tightly drawn lacing that imprisoned her breasts within her stiff bodice. He removed it then turned her to face him once more. He divested her of her kirtle and her puffed, padded sleeves. She stood before him in nothing but her chemise and petticoats. Reaching for the ribbons at the neck of her shift, he pulled them loose. Slowly, sensually, he slipped it over her head to pile it in a froth of silk and lace at her feet. He peeled away her petticoats and undergarments. Her nude form glowed like living marble in the brightness of the moonlight.

He stripped his boots and hose. His perfect body glistened like the finest bronze as he stood, ready to take her. He was a magnificent man. Arousal coursed through her veins as he lifted her soft curves into the warm water of the fountain. He raised his hand to gently touch her hair. He bent her head back and tenderly kissed the pulsing vein in her throat, his breath warm against her burning skin. His hands caressed her firm, full breasts. Her heart pounded in her chest, desire flaming out of control deep within her secret place. She was in torture. She was in bliss.

When she could bear her need no longer, she entwined her arms about his neck and lifted herself to wrap her legs around his perfect middle. He leaned over her cradling her in his own chiseled arms, sheltering her from the inquisitive eyes of the man in the moon. She wanted to weep, to cry out in uninhibited abandon as he swept her away on waves of endless bliss. The water swirled about them and when they were spent, he held her close, thigh to thigh and heart to loving heart as he softly whispered an ancient poem of love.

The bird song alarm next to Sarah's bed told her it was morning in real time. She slowly opened her eyes then reached to turn it off. She sighed as she drew her knees close to her stomach and wrapped her arms around herself in a hug. Her dreams had never been more lucid, more real, more thrilling. She wished she could go back to sleep to see what might happen next but she knew she had a guest sleeping on her couch. She wanted to make coffee and feed him breakfast before he left.

She splashed water on her face, brushed her teeth then her hair and put on some old gray sweats and a thick soft cotton tee shirt before she went to wake Carlos.

When she walked into the living room, he had once again flown the coup leaving her with an empty feeling inside and a sincere wish that he had waited to see her.

#

It had been two weeks since Carlos showed up on her doorstep battered and beaten. In their last session she tried to talk sense into him but he refused to turn to anyone for help. It escalated into an argument. He had stormed from her office. It was Friday again and she wondered if he would even show up. She called the half-way house every day leaving messages for him, but he never answered her calls and his voice mail on his cell phone was full.

She paced the floor and vowed she wouldn't mention the gang again. As his therapist she was bound to silence unless he was willing. She didn't want to push him away with any demands to bring police into it.

Her phone buzzed. Maggie's voice was almost a whisper. "He's here. Should I send him in?"

"Yes." She sat behind the desk, waiting impatiently. The door opened and a bouquet of flowers appeared before she saw his face. He grinned as he walked into the room.

"Peace?"

"Peace." She smiled, stood and crossed the room to give him a welcoming hug. His eye was almost healed and there was only a small scab on his forehead. His hand was still bandaged, but he was able to use it as he placed the flowers on her desk.

"Sorry about my temper. You're the last person in the world I should get mad at. I know you're trying to help me." He glanced at the rug then back at her. "Maybe I need a few more anger management suggestions while I'm in hypno, right?"

She sighed, "Right." Keeping her promise to herself not to bring up Manu, she took his arm to guide him to the recliner. "So I guess we might as well get started."

"Yeah." Lying down, he closed his eyes. "Let's get started."

She settled into her chair and began the induction to take him into hypnosis.

#

CARLOS HAVARRO, transcript, Session 14, June 11

It was late when she summoned me to her rooms. Smeaton, her lute player, sat in a far corner playing a sweet tune for a few of the ladies who lingered.

"Come with me." She led me to an alcove where our conversation would be private.

"Aris, you served me well in the matter of my brother. Are you ready now for a more dangerous intrigue?" She spoke softly and her black eyes danced malevolently.

"I do not fear danger, my lady."

"Good man." Then in a whisper, *"How do you feel then, about murder, Aris?"*

"Murder, my lady?"

"Yes. Murder of an old, degenerate despicable dog."

"Of which dog do you speak?"

She moved closer to me. I had to watch her mouth as she spoke; her words were too soft for even my vampire hearing.

"The King's banished dog, Wolsey."

"I am your man." I was unable to believe her request. I had fought my desire to murder the cardinal from the moment I found he sent Elizabeth to her death. When the King banished him to the north, I even began the trip to York to do away with the cad. My friends in the Catacombs reminded me of the vampire law about killing humans and my mortal friend, Thomas Wyatt, stayed my hand and kept me at court.

Yet here was the answer to my deepest desire requested of me from the second most important person in the court, second only to the King. I took it as an omen. A blessing. I would rid the Kingdom of the stench of Wolsey. And I would do it as a vampire, no human poison for him. Venom and hate would be the implement of his death.

When I set out, the road to York was wet and muddy. The thick, gray fog hung heavy all around me and I walked my horse so it wouldn't tire too quickly. I hoped to find an inn soon to get out of the damp, miserable weather and I was beginning to feel hunger. London was the last place I fed.

Suddenly there was a clearing in the mist. A thatched building rose next to the road. 'The King's Hart.' That sounded as good as any and at least I knew it would be dry. I rode to the stable behind the inn where there was a dirty little child acting as stable boy. His hands were raw *with chilblains and his nose was running. He had no shoes and his feet were wrapped in rags. He shivered in the cold yet he smiled at me, the well-dressed visitor.*

"Here lad, take the reins." The boy caught them as I let them loose. "Take care of my animal and there will be a crown for you in the morning."

The boy smiled a broken toothed smile at his luck. It was more money than he had ever seen. "Thank ye, sir." He led the huge animal inside the shelter as I turned to walk toward the inn.

The large room was dingy and dirty but the fire in the hearth was warm as I found a seat.

A great beast of a woman approached me. Her hands were filthy and her nails were broken, black dirt encrusted beneath their ragged edges. "Small ale," was all I said to her. She grinned an evil grin as she saw the fat purse I brought out to pay her.

"Bill, what ye doin' inside." Her voice was loud and harsh as she turned from my table and saw the small stable lad huddling by the fire. "Get out with the animals."

"But ma'am, I'm so cold. And I've bedded all the horses." He looked hungrily at the pot of stew bubbling over the fire. "And I haven't eaten since yesterday. I am so hungry." He held his small stomach as if it needed his hands on it to keep it inside his body. "Please ma'am."

"Get out!" She swung her huge leg toward him and kicked him in the shin so hard he fell to the ground. She grabbed him and tossed him like a sack of sugar. He howled as he bounced on the stone floor. He was limping as he hurried out the way he came.

"Woman." I spoke, anger emanating from my very core.

"Sir," She turned and her vacant, miserable gaze was now on me.

"Bring the lad inside. I will pay for his dinner." She looked at me with evil pig eyes as I demanded, "Do it now!"

She ambled toward the door and disappeared from the room. When she came back she carried the small ale to my table.

"*Let me speak with the boy.*"

"*He's busy just now. I'll feed him later.*"

"*You will feed him now or you will deal with me.*"

The look on her face was one of hate and fear. "*I'll feed him now.*"

"*After he eats, send him to me, madam, or there will be hell to pay in this house.*"

Some minutes later the child came through the door. He walked shyly to stand by my side. He grinned with gratitude in his eyes and spoke quietly. "*Thank ye. I was so hungry my eyes weren't seein' proper and now I am doing so much better. You are a kind man.*"

His words made me smile. I reached down and tousled the boy's hair.

"*Go, sit by the fire lad. She will not mistreat you again.*"

"*You're wrong sir. She beats me daily just because she can.*"

"*No boy, she will never beat you again.*"

The child moved quietly to sit on the stone hearth near the warmth of the fire.

I downed the bottom of my small ale and climbed the stairs to my room. I knew without doubt what was to come. The evil greed showed in her eyes when she laid them on my heavy purse. Closing the door to my room, I piled the dirty blankets in such a way as to look like a sleeping man. I placed my purse on the spindly table next to the bed, crossed to stand behind the door and waited.

Time passed as I stood, still as a statue. The hours moved slowly however I felt nothing of their passing. I became like the stone of the fireplace. Still. Waiting.

Just before dawn the door opened slowly. I heard the heavy step of the proprietress as she made her way into my room. She moved with stealth toward the table and my purse. Just as her hand reached to lift it, I moved more quickly than light.

I grabbed her, wrapped my arm around her greasy head and held her tight as I pulled her head back to expose her throat. She tried to call out but before she could, I sank my teeth into her fat neck. She twitched and struggled for only a moment. Then she went limp in my arms. I drained her quickly.

Before I released her, I snapped her neck so there would be no question as to how she died. I carried her dead body to the window, opened the shutters and tossed her hulk into the garbage heap behind the inn. She rested where she belonged.

Wiping my mouth on my handkerchief, I felt a smile deep within me. My body felt warm and I knew I had done the countryside a service.

As I rode from the stable at dawn, I tossed the stable boy a small sack filled with golden crowns.

"A promise well met." I hummed a sweet song as I found my way back on the road to York.

CHAPTER 23

It was a perfect early summer day, just made for a wedding. A few cotton ball clouds played tag in an otherwise clear blue sky. A soft breeze rustled the bright green leaves in the cottonwood trees surrounding the gazebo.

"I can't do this." Colleen sat on the grass with her legs crossed Indian style, her elbows on her knees and her head in her hands. "I just can't."

"Colleen, for God's sake, snap the hell out of it." Sarah squatted in front of her friend. "Of course you can do it. Look, you love him. You've known him forever. You're in the same line of work. Good Lord, the guy cooks. What the hell has come over you?"

"Nothing." Tears streamed from the bride's eyes. "Nothing. I've always known I couldn't do it. I just went along with it to shut everybody up." She sniffed, rubbing her nose on the sleeve of her shirt. "I never wanted to get married."

"C, do you love Bob?"

There was a moment of silence before she answered. "You know I do. That isn't the question." Her words were barely coherent through her sudden sobs. "It isn't about love." She cried like a child who is afraid of the dentist. "It's about marriage."

"What about marriage? You two have been living together for

over a year. What's so different about marriage?"

"My parents were married." She whispered, drying her tears, combing her fingers through the grass growing green and thick on the ground in front of her. She raised her eyes. Sarah recognized fear and something more in them. "They hated each other."

"Honey, you two are not your parents." Her voice became soft. She took Colleen's hands in hers. "Bob is a great guy. He knows the difference between right and wrong. He isn't an alcoholic. He isn't abusive. He loves you with all his heart. He's handsome as hell." She smiled. "And, like I said before, he cooks. Where else are you going to get such a bargain?"

The sob caught in Colleen's throat. She gulped down a giggle. Throwing her arms around Sarah's neck, she squeezed her tight. "What would I do without you?" Releasing her, she smiled back. "And you're right. He's a damn good cook. I guess I'll just have to go through with it."

"About time. Now, the wedding is in four hours and you look like hell. We better get to work or he's not going to say 'I do'." Sarah stood, pulling her best friend to her feet. "Now move it." They wrapped their arms around each other's waist as they walked down the sidewalk toward the hotel and the bridal gown.

#

Colleen was as radiant as a bride was supposed to be. Sitting in the place of honor at the head table, she removed her satin headpiece. She placed it on the table next to her plate of half-eaten food. Grabbing her new husband's hand, she lead him onto the dance floor. He couldn't take his eyes off her as he held her tightly to him. She laughed out loud at something he whispered in her ear.

Sarah sat watching them. She thought about her own wedding and the anticipation she had felt to be starting a new life. It seemed like so long ago. She never imagined that it would all end with a crash, that she would be sitting here alone. She realized in that moment that she had been lying to herself for a long time. Her emotions were only superficial, clean and organized as her home, but deep inside, there was a longing for something more. Passion, yes, and something even greater. She felt passion for Jeff when they were first married, but it faded in the day-to-day routine. Her desire was for something that would never fade. She wasn't sure what it was. Bonnie called it love.

She thought of Aris. He searched for his one true love though eternity. Was it he or was it Carlos who so longed to find their soulmate?

She heard a scraping noise as the chair next to her was pulled away from the table. "Hey." Carlos looked handsomely uncomfortable dressed in a dark gray suit. His white shirt was tieless and open at the collar. He unbuttoned the jacket as he sat down. "I came in late and didn't have time to see you before the ceremony." He nodded at the bride and groom. "She looks great. I hope they have a happy life. Married to a cop? I don't know about that but she's kind of strange anyway." He laughed, resting his hand on the back of Sarah's chair. "Want to dance?"

"I didn't know you danced, Carlos."

"There's a whole lot about me you don't know." His black eyes locked onto hers. He stood, holding out his hand to her.

He led her onto the dance floor, holding her close as they began to move to the music. The room was warm in spite of the French doors that were open to the patio. The fragrance of the roses in the center of all the tables permeated the heat. Slow music with a Latin flavor was being played by the band and Sarah sighed, enjoying the happiness of the moment. She was surprised by the smooth steps and strong lead of her partner.

A sudden hand on her shoulder stopped her in her tracks. "Sarah, may I cut in? I'd like to have a dance with my ex-wife."

Carlos stiffened. His hand gripped hers so hard it hurt.

"Jeff, I didn't see you." She saved her hand from her partner's crushing grip yet stood with her other one still resting on his shoulder. "Were you at the ceremony?"

"Yes, I was in the back of the church. You looked beautiful standing by the altar." His voice was almost a whisper and he gave her a very private look. "It reminded me of our wedding day."

Carlos let go of her waist, turning quickly to walk away. Sarah looked after him. She began to move toward the exit where he was heading.

"No Sarah, I must talk to you. Don't leave." He took her hand and swirled her into his arms. "Just for a moment. Just like old times."

She looked after Carlos but he had disappeared through the crowded room.

"Alright Jeff." She scanned all around but couldn't find him. "One dance for old time's sake."

#

"And then he actually started talking to me about Susan again. Right there. At your wedding." She sat on her bed in her blue and white pajamas pulling her hair brush through her hair. "Can you believe that?"

"Sure, I can believe anything about that guy." Colleen's voice was light and happy coming through the telephone. "What does he want you to do, counsel Susan on how to become a successful divorcee?" She was happy to be talking with her friend. She was enjoying her honeymoon in Hawaii but she wasn't much of a beach girl. After two days of sun and sand, she missed her work and her normal life. Home was sounding better every hour. It would be easier for her to ignore the whole marriage thing when everyone was back to the day to day of living.

"I don't know. I just threw my hands up and walked away. I looked everywhere for Carlos but I couldn't find him. By the time I came back inside from the gardens, you were throwing your bouquet and getting ready to leave." Placing her brush on her bedside table, she leaned back on the pillows. "I haven't talked to him since."

"I only saw him for a moment but he sure cleans up good. He is one good looking man."

"You are a married woman now. No more checking out the merchandise."

"Am I married or am I dead? As long as I'm breathing, I'll be checking out the produce. I'm not in the market to buy but squeezing the tomatoes isn't against the law, you know." She laughed.

Sarah reached to turn off her light. "Yeah, well I'm not telling Bob what you said. Miss you and see you soon. Good night and sleep tight Mrs. Drake."

Colleen's voice was playful when she answered. "Don't you ever 'Mrs.' me again if you plan on staying friends. Miss you too. Night."

#

She hadn't been sleeping long when her phone rang.

"Miss Hagan, that Havarro fellow is down here in the lobby. He wants to come up to see you."

She turned on the light and wiped the sleep from her eyes. The clock read twelve thirty. "Carlos? In the lobby?"

"I'm sorry to bother you, but he said it was an emergency. From the look on his face, I believe him."

"It's okay. It's fine. Send him up."

Sarah got out of bed, threw on her sweats and ran a comb through her hair. She brushed her teeth. Just as she stepped from her bedroom, she heard a knock at the door. She flicked on the lights as she crossed the room to let him in. She opened the door and he stepped across the threshold. She could see fear and anger in his eyes.

"What's wrong, Carlos?" After locking the dead bolt, she went into the kitchen to brew some coffee.

His voice was gruff as he answered. "I just finished my shift at the store when some of the guys I used to run with showed up. I don't know how they found out where I was." He paused for a breath. "Sarah, I swear, I've been straight. I've stayed off the street and away from all of them except when I confronted Manu."

"I know you have. I trust you and I know you wouldn't lie to me." The smell of the brewing coffee filled the little kitchen. She reached into the cupboard for two mugs. She kept her voice calm as she spoke, "What did they want?"

He paced the tiled floor staring at his shoes. "Same thing they were after me for last time. They want me back in the gang. I know too much for them to let me go." He stopped pacing. "Sarah, they had my little brother with them. I don't want him in the same mess I just got out of."

"Alright, just calm down." She handed him one of the mugs, then placed hers under the spigot of the coffee maker. "We'll handle this, whatever it is. You're not alone in it. I'm here. Colleen's here." They waited in silence for her cup to fill; she shut down the brewing machine, turned off the light then took him by the elbow, leading him into the living room.

Sitting side by side on the sofa, she turned to face him. "Now, who are these guys?"

"I can't tell you that, Sarah. I'm worried about my brother." His voice was low and guttural. "My little brother's had it so bad for so long. He's taken the fallout for all the crap I've gotten into. He's had enough."

He fought back tears of anger and frustration but one lone drop escaped and rolled down his cheek. She set her mug on the coffee table. She leaned toward him to brush it away. As her hand touched his skin, he reached for her, burying his head on her shoulder. Her arms wrapped around him to comfort him. She was shocked at the heated response of her body. It frightened her. She tried to separate herself from him but he clung to her tightly like a drowning man holds his rescuer. She held him, hoping he wasn't aware of the depth of feeling flooding her.

As she breathed in the sweet smell of him, his touch changed. Shyly at first, his large hands began to caress her back. His breath grew ragged. Suddenly, he grasped her shoulders. He held her at arm's length, looking into her eyes with a burning hunger. She tried to look away but he held her gaze with his longing. He drew her to him. His full, beautiful mouth covered hers in a deep, slow kiss. His lips were sweet, soft and so warm. She disappeared into the kiss and returned it, tasting the salt of his tear on his lips.

Her hand moved to his face. Her fingers caressed his strong jaw.

"No." The word exploded from him as he shoved her away. "No. Not now. Not this way." He shook his head to clear his mind, to regain control. Was it him or was it Aris who had kissed her? He wasn't sure. He stood, crossed the room and unlocked the door. He turned to look back at her.

She sat shaken, short of breath. Wrapping her arms across her chest, she leaned back into the cushions.

"I'll see you on Friday, Sarah. We'll never mention this again."

He opened the door leaving her alone in the night with nothing but her thoughts to warm her.

CHAPTER 24

The sound of the grand piano was soft in the background of the elegant restaurant as the waiter placed their plates on the table. He carried each one in a thick, white napkin and reminded Sarah and her mother that they were hot to the touch.

"Tell me, dear, how is your friend Colleen and her new husband?"

Sarah laid her napkin across her lap. She sipped her water before she spoke. "They're doing great. It was hard for Colleen at first, but she's getting used to the routine."

"I'm glad. She is such a nice girl."

"She's hardly a girl, Mother, she's thirty-five." Sarah laughed when she thought what her friend would say to being called a girl. "They really are happy. They're made for each other." She took a bite of her salad as her mother cleared her throat.

"I'll be honest. I wanted to have lunch today because I'm worried about you. You've become so involved with your work we hardly see you anymore. I can't remember the last time you came for the weekend. You're too thin and you seem nervous." Her mother leaned in as she spoke. "Sarah, what's wrong?"

"Nothing, Mother. I'm just really busy with clients and . . . well, just busy with clients."

The older woman wanted more of an answer from her only child. "That's not enough. You've been busy with clients before. You wrote that book; you published it. You still had time for your family. What is it? Are you involved with a new man?"

Sarah sat silent for a moment. "Yes, I suppose you could say that, in a way. But not the way you think." She took another bite before she answered. "It's a client. He's in trouble and I want to help him and his family. That's all." Even as she spoke, she knew she was telling a half truth. She was more involved with Carlos than she could explain, even to herself.

#

He walked into her office without looking at her. He crossed the room to the recliner and lay down, closing his eyes before his head touched the cushion. His body was tense, his forehead wrinkled as if he was in deep thought. "Let's get started, okay?"

"Carlos." She didn't know what to say to him. There was a distance between them that had never been there before. The intimacy they shared at her apartment had somehow created a wall. She didn't know how to break it down or even if she should try. "Carlos." He still didn't look at her. Not knowing what else to do, she picked the recorder up from the corner of her desk and moved to the chair next to him.

She sat, turned on the recorder and began the usual induction to take him into the hypnotic state. As she spoke, his body began to relax and his breath grew steady.

#

"As you open the door, what do you see?"

CARLOS HAVARRO, transcript, session 15, June 18

As I crept into the sleeping chamber of the Cardinal, I could hear the old man snore. Nearing the bed, I saw two figures beneath the blanket. I couldn't help but smile. It appeared the celibacy requirement of the priests of the church didn't apply to this man sleeping with his mistress. And now, instead of just one human, there were two. I knew I must be very delicate and quiet as I went to work. Silence surrounded me as I moved closer.

Wolsey slept on his back while his mistress slept as far from the snoring hulk as she could. Leaning over the bed, I was presented with the folds of his flesh lying in rings around the Cardinal's neck like necklaces made of sausages. How to find the vessel in such a hunting ground? Such a task. I remember moving closer to him and the night smells of him.

Silent as death, I watched the sleeping pair. The moonlight coming through the high window illuminated the covers and Wolsey's hand and wrist as it lay exposed in the cool, white beam of light.

"Ah, I'll begin just here." My thoughts continued in a stream as I kneeled silently next to the bed and softly placed my tongue on the Cardinal's wrist. The saliva from my mouth numbed the skin and made it insensitive to pain. Slowly, I sunk my teeth into the soft, moist flesh of the man's wrist. I was careful and only a small amount of venom entered the wound. A small bit daily would mix with his blood and no one would notice. Within hours, he would feel ill. Within days he would waste away. Soon he would be dead.

I could not help but laugh softy under my breath as I moved to the window and climbed down the outer wall of Cawood Castle.

For many nights I scaled the wall to the bedchamber of the doomed man. On my last visit, the moon was bright, illuminating the room as I crept through the window. I found only one mound in the bed. Wolsey's mistress no longer slept with the Cardinal. She was sure he had the wasting sickness and she was afraid to be close to him, awake or asleep.

The sleeping man before me was a shadow of the doomed Cardinal. He was thin; his flesh hung on his bones. He couldn't eat. He barely slept. He knew he was dying yet he didn't know why. His physicians had bled him. His servants had nursed him. His clergy had prayed over him. Still he wasted away. He tossed in his bed unable to find comfort.

Suddenly there was the sound of running feet in the corridor. An evil tiding.

The door swung open. "Your Grace," a servant boy stood at the foot of his bed. "The King's men are in the castle. They are coming for you. You must rise and dress."

I quickly stepped behind a large, ornate tapestry hanging on the wall. It was in the shadows and I was well concealed behind it.

Wolsey rose, his night clothes hanging on him like a shroud. "The King's men, you say?" He spoke with trepidation, "and who leads them?"

"Lord Henry Percy."

George Cavendish, the Cardinal's gentleman usher, rushed into the chamber. "Allow me to assist you in dressing, your Grace." The sound of stomping feet grew louder. Before Cavendish could move across the room to his master, soldiers burst through the door.

"You are under arrest, Cardinal." Percy spoke. "Come as you are. No need for your red Cardinal's robes. You are arrested for treason and for treason you will die."

The soldiers surrounded the Cardinal, marching him toward the door. He stumbled on the cold stone of the floor.

"Boots. May I not have my boots?" he pled. "At least my boots?" He was a broken, sick, old man, but that did not stay the hatred emanating from the Lord of Northumberland.

Percy snarled, "No boots. You will feel the cold on your body equal to the cold in your heart. And you will die hungry and alone like the traitor that you are." He shoved the Cardinal ahead of him. "Now move."

When the chamber was empty, I moved to the window. There were horses and a wagon waiting in the courtyard below. Wolsey would be exposed to the freezing air of winter on the road to London with nothing but straw to cover himself. He was weakened and I knew he would never survive the journey.

"But I will trail along behind just to make sure." I spoke to no one other than myself as I crawled out the window and down the steep

wall.

The Cardinal died in Leicester and was buried there. There was no pomp at his burial as there was none at the death of my dearest Elizabeth, entombed in the sea so very far from English soil. It was justice. After all his years as servant to the Pope and the King, the once wealthiest man in England died a pauper and a traitor. King Henry wept. Queen Anne cherished the day and called for a masque ball. And I, Aris the vampire, rode south to London.

When Anne was told I had arrived, she summoned me to her. I entered into the dark audience chamber. She was there, standing in front of a huge blaze in the hearth, a warm, welcome scent of burning applewood logs filling the room.

"So, you have accomplished the deed." It was a statement, not a question.

I bowed low before her, smiling as I lifted my head to look into her eyes. "Yes, my lady. I have."

"A job well done." She was dressed in a red robe lined with fur and her long dark hair reached her waist. The room was chilly in spite of the fire. Moving closer, she wrapped the robe around her legs then sat. "And was it difficult?"

"No, it was my pleasure to do your bidding. Pity he didn't live to arrive in London." I saw her black eyes glistening in the dancing light of the burning logs.

She laughed, "Yes, it is a pity." She lifted the goblet from the table and tasted the wine. "You must help yourself. I do not wish any servant to see you in my chamber."

"Thank you my lady, I do not have a thirst."

"You will be given a rich reward for your service."

Again, I bowed to her compliment. "You are most gracious."

Her laugh was harsh. "Yes, I'm sure Wolsey would feel the same way. I understand Percy was the one to bring him into Leicester. Is that true?"

"It is true."

"Circumstances can be so strange, can they not?" Replacing the goblet on the table, she rose from the chair and began to pace. "And what if I should ask you to perform another task? Would you be up to doing it?"

I tipped my head in acknowledgment. "Most certainly, my lady. I am loyal to you in all things."

"Precisely what I want to hear. You are a good man, Aris, a good man." She moved into the shadows, and then turned to stare at me. '"I will call on you again when the time comes. Until then, you are most welcome at court." She swept from the room leaving me staring after her.

After a moment, I too left the room and as I walked the darkened corridor my thoughts were of Anne, the look in her black eyes. "The undead are not the only cold ones."

#

"Man, she sure is somebody I wouldn't want to cross." Carlos laid back on the recliner after his return to present time. "She is one bad-assed broad. I've been up against some really tough people and let me tell you, she is somebody I wouldn't want to have pissed at me."

"You can't be a mouse and displace the ruling Queen of England and that's just what she did." Sarah leaned forward. "Carlos?"

To avoid any personal conversation, he spoke quickly. "And she wasn't even much to look at, except when you saw her eyes. They were almost black in this snow white face. She could have been a vamp except she still had a heart." He smiled a sardonic smile. "A heart beat anyway."

"Carlos?"

He stood immediately. Crossing the room, he lifted his hand in goodbye. "See you next week."

He quietly closed the door behind him leaving Sarah to ponder this new turn in their relationship.

CHAPTER 25

"I don't really know what happened. We just sort of lost our connection." She couldn't bring herself to tell Colleen about the kiss. She was almost certain her friend would think it was great but Sarah wasn't sure how she felt about it even now. "He shows up for session without fail, but I don't feel as if I can touch him anymore." She swiveled her desk chair to face the window as they chatted on the phone, looking at the city and hoping for a distraction.

"I don't know, hon. He seems the same to me. Well, not the same. Better than I ever thought he would be. Hold on a second, Bob's calling me. He's in the kitchen and I can't hear him. Hang on."

Sarah waited while Colleen checked with her husband. "Dinner is almost ready. I've got another minute but I haven't seen Bob in two days and he cooked for us so I've got to go." Colleen covered the mouthpiece on the phone as she spoke to her husband, then returned to her conversation with her friend. "Quit worrying. He's better than he's been since I got him. He's doing better than I thought was possible and it's all because of you. Hang in there babe." She heard Bob say something unintelligible to Colleen. "Okay, coming." Her voice called to the next room, then quietly, back into the receiver, "Hey hon, got to go. See you soon."

Silence filled Sarah's dark office as she stared out the window and contemplated how different her life was now from the normal lives of all the people who lived outside her strange reality.

#

It was late when she got off the train. Her day was long, exhausting. Her thoughts were always returning to Carlos and the kiss. She worked diligently to remove the memory from her mind but she couldn't. The thought of his warm mouth nagged her with the question of 'what if?' ringing over and over.

As she cleared the turnstile, she felt a presence in her shadow. She turned and saw a tall, Latino man a few steps behind her. He looked angry, his pockmarked face twisted in a scowl. She left the stairs moving into the street. He stayed close. As she walked under a burned out street light, he stepped in front of her, grabbing her hard by the shoulders. She opened her mouth to scream.

"Carlos will be hurt if you make a sound." His eyes looked her up and down. He smiled a crooked, yellow toothed smile. "So, you're the little shrink messing with my boy?" He held her firmly, but his hands didn't hurt her.

Her voice was stable when she spoke. "Who are you? What do you want?" She marveled at how steady her words sounded in her own ears while her body was paralyzed with fear.

"I want you to lay off. He doesn't need your help." His face moved closer to her as he whispered. "If you don't back away, somebody is gonna' get hurt real bad." The smile disappeared. His black eyes bored a hole into her blue ones. "You hear me, shrink lady?"

Sarah nodded, afraid to form words, knowing if she spoke again, she would no longer be able to control her voice.

"Now, go home. Remember, I know who you are. I know where you work and where you live. I'd hate to hurt a pretty piece like you, but I will if I have to. Stay out of his business." He released her, pushing her away from him. He moved down the street without looking back. Tears of fear and relief filled her eyes as she watched the tall shadow on the pavement change as he passed under first one lit street light, then the next.

#

The sun was hot as Sarah rode her bicycle down the path in Lincoln Park. The humidity was formidable and the blond hair at the nape of her neck curled in tendrils in defiance of the pony tail she wore. Thin rivulets of perspiration ran down her back, still she pedaled faster. No matter how hard she pedaled she was unable to outrun her thoughts.

Her emotions ran from fear to outrage to disbelief. Did it really happen to her? Could he really have meant that she would be harmed if she continued her sessions with Carlos? She prayed it was only a threat.

For the first time in Sarah's life, she was unable to formulate a plan. Telling Colleen was out of the question. Her friend would tell Bob, the police would be brought into it and Carlos would never trust her again. If the police became involved, she wasn't sure he wouldn't be implicated somehow. One thing she was sure of, Carlos had nothing to do with any of it.

Telling Carlos was impossible. He would want to protect her. God only knew what that could mean in his life. He worked so hard to stay out of trouble, she was determined to help him at any cost, to continue seeing him regardless of the threat. But why? Over and over, the question rang through her mind. Why was he so important to her? Why was her own safety secondary to his? Why was his success and freedom the most important thing in her world? And finally, was it really Carlos or was it a need to continue speaking with Aris? Questions without answers, all questions without answers.

#

"You look exhausted." Scowling as he spoke, Carlos slouched in the chair across from her desk. "What's going on with you?"

Sarah avoided his eyes, picked up the recorder and stood. "Nothing. I just haven't been able to sleep very well the last few nights. It happens sometimes." She gestured toward the recliner, "Let's get started. I'm anxious to hear the next episode in the 'Adventures of Aris'." She smiled a half smile as she sat.

"Okay, me too, I guess." He brushed her shoulder with his hand as he passed her. It was a casual movement, but it was the first time he had touched her since their kiss. It unsettled her.

He lay back in the chair. Closing his eyes, he began to breathe deeply. His face softened in relaxation as he waited for the familiar words that would raise the vampire.

#

CARLOS HAVARRO, transcript, session 16, June 25

After I returned to the palace from York and met with Anne, I sat before the fire in my retiring room wondering at what I had become. There was a sound at my window as if a branch scraped against it, but I was high in a tower, no trees nearby. I knew it was a visitor. I crossed the room and threw open the glass. Sebastian climbed over the sill. He stood before me, tall and foreboding.

He was sent by the counsel. In the service of the oldest ones of all, he came to tell me I was summoned. We left the confines of the human court and I was led to the court of the undead. We descended deep into the tunnels beneath the city. I was certain that I was called to the council to answer for the death of Wolsey.

"Don't deny anything Aris. They know." Sebastian spoke softly and still it echoed off the damp stone walls.

"There's nothing to deny". One step at a time, we continued down.

"The death of Wolsey, Aris. They know." He forced his words through clenched teeth. "Richard told you not to do it. He told you they would find out."

"No one at Henry's court is the wiser for it. It was accomplished

without any suspicion." I spoke more lightly than I felt. I knew the power of the council, the power of life and death. I heard of one such execution. During the time of my education, I was told of a woman who killed from spite. She was tried for murder, her sentence was elimination. The tale of her dismembered, burned body was a symbol of what horror was possible, even for the undead. Only through burning did the vampire cease to exist. Dismembering alone left the essence, the true being of the vampire, continuing forever, a lone entity floating through time and space. I knew dearly of that bleak existence. I feared it. And after losing my sweet Elizabeth, that was all that I feared.

Sebastian embraced me and spoke with a sad voice. "Good bye my friend." He turned and left me to my judgment.

"And so you were executed? Is that why you are without a body now?" Sarah was leaning forward in her chair so as not to miss one word that he spoke.

"No. Although murder was punishable by death, Queen Akira, stood for me.

I entered the chamber, bowed then knelt on the cushion in front of her. She sat on her throne still as a sculpture. When she finally broke the silence, she demanded I explain myself, her beautiful voice hard as stone. I felt the deepest fear at her displeasure yet my words were confident when I replied. When I finished speaking, she rose, taking all who were judges at my trial into another chamber. I was left on my knees before the thrones. There I waited while my fate was decided. My mind escaped into the timelessness of the vampire void.

A soft shuffle of fabric brought my attention to my surroundings once again. She stood unmoving in front of me, at last touching my shoulder. I raised my eyes to meet hers. She rebuked my rebellion. Her cold short words cut to the very heart of me. I recoiled at her anger. Her condemnation complete, she stood in silence. I waited for my sentence. And, to this day, I know not why, I was allowed to go free. I believe if Khansu had been present, my fate would have taken a different direction.

The truth to that, I will never know.

After a time of silence, she dismissed me from the council chamber.
Sebastian walked with me down the long corridor to the stone staircase.
I praised the devil for my fortune, promising myself I would never put
myself into jeopardy again for any one. Not even the King himself.

I returned to the palace, to my rooms, climbing the outer wall of the
tower so no one was the wiser I was gone at all.

"And now Sarah, you have knowledge of a great deal of my
existence."

"Yes, but you had a body. You had a human body that you
inhabited and now, you don't, at least not one that belongs to only
you. How did that happen?"

"And that Sarah my sweet, is another story."

And she knew the vampire had left the session. She sat quietly
for a few moments then brought Carlos back to real time.

#

Sarah now made sure she left the office long before dark. Her
run in with the frightening stranger was a warning well taken. Just
as she went through the turnstile, her cell phone rang. She was
surprised to see it was Carlos.

"Hi." She was careful not to sound too eager. They hadn't spoken
outside of session since the incident and she didn't want to make
him uncomfortable.

"Hi." She heard him take a deep breath as she crossed the
street. When he spoke, he stammered. "Look, I . . . Silence as she
waited for him to finish his sentence. "I want you to know that
what happened at your apartment will never happen again. Your
friendship means more to me than anything."

"I understand. Me too." She smiled, "God, I feel so much better
just talking to you."

"I know. Lately, since . . . well, you know, I don't even feel like
I'm at the session. It feels like it's just you and the vamp." He took

another deep breath. "And I don't like it. So, let's just be what we have been all along."

"Friends?"

"More. Family." His words were soft and sincere.

"Sounds good to me." She entered her apartment building, waving at the doorman as she crossed the lobby. "I just got home and I'm getting in the elevator. I'm going to lose you in a minute."

"You'll never lose me." She was left with empty air waves as the elevator door closed.

CHAPTER 26

"Is Miss Hagan in the office today?"

"This is Miss Hagan. Isabella?" She asked into the receiver.

"Yes, Miss Hagan." The voice on the other end sounded frightened and desperate.

"Please Isabella, do call me Sarah. What's the matter?" She controlled her anxiety when she spoke. "What's happened?"

"My son, Javier, didn't come home last night. This morning I found him drunk and drugged on my front lawn. I got him to his room while my husband was taking a shower. I shut his door and pretended he was there all night.

"After my husband left, I went to his room. He was being sick in his bathroom. I helped him to bed. He is there now, sleeping." She held in a sob. "Sarah, what can I do? I don't know what to do. I know those bad friends of Carlos had my son."

"They are no friends of Carlos, Isabella. Stay with Javier and I'll have Carlos talk to him. Everything will be just fine. We'll take care of it."

"I hope so, Sarah, I hope so."

#

"I just told him, they weren't my friends and that he should hang with guys in his class and not these older guys. We talked for a long time. I think he understands." He picked up his coffee mug, draining the cup. The new young waitress at Saul's filled it immediately with a big smile, but Carlos didn't even notice.

"Sarah, I don't know what to do. I can't go back. I just can't but I can't let my brother be hurt either." He placed his elbows on the table and rested his head in his hands. After a moment, he looked up. "What should I do?"

"I think it's time we talk to Colleen. I won't do it unless you say it's okay but she is on your side." To buy time to think, she took a bite of toast, chewed and swallowed. "So is Bob."

"That isn't the answer. The cops will just make them mad, then who knows what they'll do."

Sarah pushed her breakfast away, signaling the waitress to take her plate. "Colleen can help us. I know she can."

"No, I don't want the cops involved. Not yet. As my shrink you can't tell them anything if I don't say it's okay, right?"

"Carlos," she began to speak.

"No Sarah, it's a done deal. Are you ready?" He stood holding out his hand to help her from the booth. He picked up the check. "I got this one."

#

The drive to Starved Rock State Park was beautiful. The recent rainfall made the trees and the grasses along the road so green they were almost blue.

The car windows were down and the breeze ruffled Colleen's spiked hair, making it look like the dark fur of a forest animal. It was a perfect day for a hike, warm but with a breeze and almost no humidity. A classical song Sarah liked was playing on the radio. She tried to remember the name of the composer but she couldn't recall who it was.

As she turned her head to ask Colleen, Colleen spoke first. "So what's up with Carlos?" She kept her eyes on the road, waiting for her friend to answer.

"Nothing. And I guess everything. You know we do sessions regularly. I think we're making progress." She watched her words. She wondered how much Colleen really knew or guessed. "No, I know he's definitely making progress. He's doing everything possible to keep his life clean."

"Yeah, I know." She glanced at Sarah, then into the rear view mirror and back to the road. "If you know anything I should know, please tell me." The trees whizzed past, their trunks black against the bright green foliage. "I want to help him too."

"I don't quite know what you mean." Sarah was evasive. She knew it was obvious.

"Just don't keep things from me trying to protect him. It'll take a village to keep that guy out of trouble. And I'm a part of his tribe."

"I know you are." She turned to look out the window. "I know you are."

#

They sat comfortably across from one another, her desk between them. "Carlos, have you heard anything else from the gang?" Her voice was a lot calmer than she felt.

"Not really." He hesitated. "Well, yeah. Some of the guys came by the store the other night. They still want me to help them do a job on the market."

She stood quickly.

"Don't worry about it. I think they want me involved in another theft so they don't have to worry about me spilling my guts to the cops. I know more about them than anybody else and it scares them I might tell you or Colleen. I made sure they understood that I'm still a brother to them and I won't squeal about anything."

"A brother to them?"

"I told you, they were family to me when I didn't have one.

Nothing is going to change that, nothing is going to turn me against them. I may not be one of the gang anymore but I'm still tied to them. I always will be."

"After all this work you still don't see that you're different from them?"

"Yeah, different but no better, Sarah. I just got lucky when I met Colleen and you. I told you, you've shown me I can be something worthwhile in my life if I just keep on going forward. Nothing is going to get in the way of the promise I made to you." He smiled. "Look I haven't gone nuts once since I've been seeing you. Talk therapy and those regressions have helped me calm down and see myself more than you know."

"How have the regressions helped you? I still mostly think Aris is just a figment of your imagination stemming from all the horror movies you've seen in your life."

He downed the last drop from the can of soda he held in his hand, crushed it and placed it on the edge of her desk. "You keep saying that but I don't think I've got that kind of shock theatre in me, Sarah. I don't know where he came from or what kind of subconscious evil seed he is, but he's some kind of bad."

"You sound as if you like having him around." She leaned forward in her chair, opening his file.

"Yeah. Are you going to write this down?" Smiling at him, she picked up her pen. "Okay, yeah. I do like having him around. It's like having this really macho big brother. Nobody would mess with me if they knew about Aris." He chuckled.

He watched her make notes for a few minutes. When he spoke, the tone of his voice was very different. "You know, sometimes I think it's him that you're interested in. I mean, we spend a lot of sessions talking about him or talking to him. I thought a shrink would be more interested in their patient, not some figment of somebody's imagination as you called him."

"I don't know what you're talking about. The reason we began this therapy was for you, to help you." She laid her pen on her desk, closing the file, lifting her eyes to meet his.

He stared at her. "Yeah, well that's how it started. But I'm not so sure it's the same equation now, is it Sarah?"

"Carlos, it's impossible for you to be jealous of a two thousand year old vampire."

"Is that right, Sarah? Are you sure that's right?" He stood, reaching for the soda can. He threw it in the wastebasket. "Well, I'm not so sure." He walked to the door, turned and looked at her one final time. "I'm not so sure at all."

#

"Thank you for seeing me, Miss Hagan." Isabella sat on the edge of the chair, twisting a handkerchief in her hand. Sarah couldn't remember the last time she saw anyone carry a cloth handkerchief. There was something dignified about it.

"Please, Isabella, please call me Sarah."

The older woman looked over Sarah's shoulder at the city outside the window. Sarah saw fear and sorrow in her eyes. She stood and walked around her desk. She stooped down next to the chair where Carlos' mother sat.

"What is it? Can I help you?" Her voice was soft, filled with compassion.

"Oh Sarah, I am so afraid." She dropped the handkerchief into her lap, bursting into tears, she buried her head in her hands.

"What is it? We'll figure it out." She wrapped her arms around Isabella. Sarah held her gently until her sobs quieted.

"There was a dead dog on our front porch this morning. And a note." She handed the envelope to Sarah.

She opened it and read. "This is what will happen to your son if he doesn't come through." She folded it and put it back in the envelope. "Did your husband see this?"

"No, no." She shook her head as she spoke. "I buried the dog before he came home. I hid the note. He must not see it. He will go to the police and those bad people will kill my Carlos." Her voice broke as she spoke.

Sarah pulled several tissues out of a ceramic container. She handed them to Isabella, waiting until she was calm once again.

"Don't worry Isabella." Brushing the dark hair out of the woman's eyes, she assured her, "I'll handle this. Nothing is going to happen to Carlos. There are too many people who care about him right now." Isabella's hands were cold as Sarah took them in her own warm ones. "I promise you. Carlos is going to be alright." She smiled what she hoped was a confident smile.

"Now you just sit here while I go into the other office to get you a drink of water." Sarah stood, moving toward the door. Just before she reached for the handle, she turned. "Are you going to be okay for a minute?"

Isabella sat up straight in the chair. "Yes Sarah, with your help we will all be okay."

#

"Carlos doesn't want me to tell anybody what's going on but I don't know what to do. If I tell him about the dog, he'll confront them. Then who knows what will happen."

"Crap. Let me talk to Bob. Maybe we can work this on the outside and not bring anyone into it." A car horn honked twice just before Sarah heard Colleen curse under her breath. "Why do all the lousy drivers always get in front of me?" She honked again. "Look, don't mention it to him. Let me see what I can do before we bring him into it. Don't worry. We'll take care of it. Got to go."

"Bye," Sarah spoke to an empty line then looked at the dead phone in her hand. She sighed, put the phone down and picked up the book that lay open on the sofa next to her. A loud crash of thunder threatened rain as Sarah leaned back onto the soft cushions. She stretched her legs along the seat, crossing her ankles. "Everything is going to be okay. I'm sure of it. I just have to believe it. I will believe it. No. I do believe it. I'm not going to think about it anymore right now."

She leaned over the coffee table to grab her tea. "I might as well learn all I can about the sixteenth century since it looks like I'm going to be hanging around there for a while." She spoke out loud to no one, wrapped her hand around her warm mug, tipped it to her lips and finished drinking the amber liquid. She let the empty cup rest on the pillow next to her as she began to read. The rain commenced with a soft shower then suddenly fell in torrents. Huge drops pounded on the deck as her eyes grew heavy and she drifted into sleep.

#

She felt the power of his muscular legs as the black stallion galloped into the wind. Her long blond hair blew wild behind her and her blue velvet riding skirt flapped in the blast of warm air. It was a glorious summer day. The sun shined down on the rich green fields of the King's hunting grounds. She had left the royal hunt to feel the freedom of a ride without the eyes of the court constantly watching her. The baying of the dogs grew distant as she urged her horse to run faster and faster. She laughed as her horse jumped one gully after another.

Suddenly a boar ran just in front of the horse. Surprised and frightened, the huge animal slammed to a halt, pawing wildly in the air. She fell as he took off across the meadow at full gallop.

Standing and taking note, she found she was uninjured. A bit bruised and a great deal chagrined but without any broken bones or blood. She brushed her skirt free of weeds and grass. She sighed as she was about to begin the long walk back to the hunting lodge when the sound of hooves pounding on at a great speed reached her ears.

She turned in the direction of the clatter and saw a rider racing toward her from the thick forest to the east of her meadow. As the horseman approached, she saw he wore a mask over his eyes and was dressed all in black from his boots to the cloth that held his long, dark hair in a thick braid at the base of his neck.

He swept her onto his horse, holding her tightly against his chest and turned to race back into the forest. She fought like a demon but he held her steady. She tried to twist out of his grip but he just laughed and his laughter was carried away on the wind.

In one quick moment, they reached the forest and he slowed his mount to a steady walk. She felt the warmth of his broad chest behind her and his heavy breath against her hair. She shivered in terror. "Fear not my beautiful lady," he whispered in her ear. She wasn't sure if it was he or the wind. "No harm will come to you."

The trees parted and before them was a glade of flowers and tall grass. He dismounted, lifting her easily to the ground. She spun out of his grasp and began to run. He seized her hair and wrapping his hand in it, brought her into him. His free arm wrapped around her tiny waist as he held her close. His lips met hers in a demanding kiss. For a moment she fought him, beating against his chest with her small fists but he held her firm, his lips burning into hers. His clothes and hair carried the scent of the forest. His mouth tasted of the fresh streams that flowed through the dense greenery. Her knees buckled and still he kissed her. The fight left her and she moaned as the tip of his tongue traced the soft flesh inside her lower lip. Her body was a bed of hot coals.

He swept her into his arms and carried her to a soft hill of earth and leaves under a huge oak tree. It was there he began to undress her. When she was nude, he spread her skirt and rested her porcelain body on its soft folds. Her hair surrounded her head in a halo of spun gold. Quickly he disrobed, his manhood alert and strong. His mask still tied firmly to hide his face.

She reached to draw him to her but he held off. He plucked a blade of soft grass and began to stroke her long strong legs. She moved languidly beneath his touch. She was hardly aware when the grass became his hands. He pressed her flesh with his fingertips then slowly began to part her legs. His hand rested sweetly on her mound as he lowered his lips to her warm firm abdomen. His tongue traced lines of fire and ice.

A loud crash of thunder was followed by the crash of the tea mug as it hit the floor. Sarah jumped awake, knocking the book onto the floor. Her breath came in jagged gasps and her heart was beating as if to leave her chest. "My God, I've got to get a sex life. This is too real."

She brushed her hair from her face as she stooped to pick up the pieces of the shattered mug.

CHAPTER 27

Bob appeared a lot taller than he was standing next to Colleen. He was at least six feet, but she was so tiny he looked like a giant. His dark hair cut in a crew cut matched her spikes almost as if they planned it that way. His shirt was open at the collar and his wedding ring was his only jewelry. He was handsome in a rugged sort of way.

Colleen dished the pasta onto their plates as he filled their glasses with wine.

"I checked up on this guy, Manu. It seems he's the head honcho and one mean sucker." He wiped the lip of the bottle with a napkin then placed it on the table. "He's been nothing but trouble; a huge instigator for most of the gang related crime in his neighborhood and who knows where else."

He took a bite of his dinner. "Hey babe, this is great. Where did you order from?"

Colleen's smile was smug, "I didn't order, I cooked."

Bob grinned and Sarah was shocked, but happy Colleen was beginning to be domesticated. She wasn't sure her friend would ever settle completely into her new life as a wife, however marriage seemed to agree with both of them. Seeing them together brought back memories and kindled a desire to once again be one half of a couple. She quickly put the thought out of her mind reminding herself that she and Jeff were never like Bob and Colleen. She sipped her wine.

"Anyway, this guy has a record of petty crime. He's been under suspicion of some heavier stuff but we've never been able to prove anything to put him away. Does this woman have any way of proving it's Manu who put the dog on her porch?"

"No, there was a note but it was typed. She's scared. Her husband is a real hot head and she's worried he'll get Carlos in trouble if she tells him anything about it."

"What do they want him for? Has he mentioned it to you?" Bob spooned another helping of pasta on his plate and winked at his wife.

"He swears he doesn't respond to them. That's why this is happening to his family. He doesn't want to get involved with them again. He's working hard to change his life and so far, he's doing a good job of it. I don't want to see him in trouble again."

Colleen poured herself another glass of wine. "None of us do, hon. We're all trying to help out here to make sure he isn't dragged into something illegal."

The sound of a cell phone interrupted their conversation. Sarah stood, moving to the sofa. Her purse lay on the armrest. She pulled the phone from its compartment just as it stopped ringing. She crossed the room back to the table, laying the phone next to her plate, waiting for the voice mail signal to beep. When it did, she checked her message.

"It's Carlos. Excuse me a moment, I just want to make sure everything is okay." She dialed the code to retrieve the message. Her face was a blank mask as she listened. "He wants me to call him and his voice sounds anxious."

"Go ahead. Call him. Bob and I will clear the table. We can finish our wine in the living room." Colleen rose and began to stack the dishes. Bob shoveled the last of the ravioli into his mouth, picked up his plate then the couple carried the dishes to the kitchen giving Sarah some privacy.

She hit the recall button. She waited. His phone rang several times then went to voicemail. After she left a return message, she joined her friends.

"Strange, he didn't answer." She looked puzzled. "But he just called me."

"Maybe he's at work." Colleen spoke over the grind of the garbage disposal. "Why don't you two go in the living room? I'll be right in as soon as I rinse these dishes."

Bob took her by the arm, leading her to the couch. He sat next to her. "Sarah, what's with this guy? Why are both of you so interested in some petty crook?"

"He's not that. He's a really smart young man who hasn't had much of a chance. Colleen sees herself in him. She wants to rescue someone the way you rescued her. She says she wants to pay it forward. Does that make sense?"

He shrugged. "I guess. But what about you? Why are you so concerned?"

She stared into space for a moment, a look of serious thought on her face. After a silence she turned to look at Bob and answered. "I don't know." She shook her head as she spoke. "I honestly don't know."

#

"You still look really tired." He grinned his old grin at her as he rested his head on the recliner. He closed his eyes. "Maybe you need to see a therapist."

"Very funny." She aimed the recorder at him and began to take him into a relaxed state.

#

CARLOS HAVARRO, transcript, Session 17, July 2

The great hall was ablaze with candles, many thousands by the light, the feel of warmth. I stood to the side of the dancers, watching as the Lady Anne bewitched every man who came close to her. Her green silk gown flashed sparkles of light as the jewels sewn into the skirt shifted when she spun in the dance.

Suddenly the harsh sound of the heralds echoed throughout the cathedral-sized space, bouncing off the stone walls like the harsh crash of lightening. The music stopped. The dancers stood stock still. Their King was coming.

He was always larger than life. Tall, imposing, he entered the room with the step of an athlete. The courtiers bowed low in his honor. "Continue the festivities." He waved his jeweled hand toward the balcony that held the musicians and they immediately resumed playing.

"Ah, Anne." She crossed to his side with a perfect curtsey.

"Your Majesty." Rising, she looked into his sparkling eyes, her smile radiant.

"To the banquet." She rested her small hand on the curve of his outstretched arm, gently letting her fingers drape over his soft golden sleeve.

As they led the court into the dining hall, the heralds played the King's fanfare. They moved together to the high table. When they reached their places, they turned to face the court. Henry raised his goblet of gold, then drank it dry. The court applauded and waited for their monarch to be seated. He sat, followed by his mistress. Only then did the court take their seats at the dining tables.

Wine flowed and the gold and silver plate reflected the candlelight like fireflies in the meadows in late summer. Again, the trumpets sounded as the servers began to bring the food.

The grandest tray was carried by the server in the most magnificent livery. A peacock served with all its feathers in place and the tail fully furled, created a magnificent show of color. Inside, the bird was stuffed with other fowl, one inside the other. It was placed in the center of the high table between Henry and Anne.

Another trumpet fanfare announced the Master Carver. He carried sharp knives that glistened with a light of their own and his fingers were heavy with rings of gold. He approached the high table and performed a low bow. When he rose, the King motioned him forward.

The trumpets sounded yet another time as he began his craft. He was able to create a perfect slice for each one at the table; every slice containing every bird yet, even after carving, the beauty of the sculpture remained intact. As he raised the gold plate showing his art, the court applauded. He bowed with a flourish then continued to slice the creation. The servers carried the laden plates to each of the waiting court.

I was seated on a lower dais, watching Anne. She was animated, keeping the King delighted and laughing. She took care of his every need before he knew it existed. Before his goblet was empty, it was filled. Before he ate the last bite of any delicacy, it was replenished. I could not help but respect her ability to create an air of perfection around them. I focused all of my attention including my sensitive hearing on their conversation.

"Hal, my Hal." She poured him yet another goblet of wine then leaned close to whisper in his ear. "Do you see how the courtiers mock me?"

The King was startled at her words. "Mock you, sweeting?"

"Yes." Sadness filled her dark eyes. "Katherine still lives at court. They whisper behind my back that you do not truly love me." She lowered her eyes then gazed at Henry from beneath her eyelashes. She looked forlorn, even to my vampire eyes.

Henry sat straighter in his chair. His eyes searched the court seated below. "Who would say this? Just say their name."

Her touch on his arm brought his gaze back to her. "Too many, my lord. While Katherine still lives at court, I am ignored." She reached to clasp his hand as unshed tears filled her eyes. "You must send her away, banish her."

"Banish her?" Henry's booming voice was heard down to the lower

court whose long tables were set many steps away from them on the stone
floor of the castle.

"Yes, Henry. While she is here," Anne filled his goblet once
again, "I will never be recognized as your consort." She smiled at him
conspiratorially, "and our sons never honored as princes."

Henry's face lit like the sparklers from the East. "Our sons? And how,
Anne? Sons, when you will not share my bed?"

"I remain a virgin while Katherine remains at court, until I am truly
Queen and our marriage is fully recognized and honored." She turned
to face him and her eyes shone in the dancing light of the candles. "I will
give you strong sons once Katherine is sent away."

He drained his goblet in one long drink, and then slammed the empty
golden cup on the table. "And so, she will be banished." He stared at
Anne for a long moment in silence, and then laughed. A laugh that shook
his large body and turned his drink bloated face red. "And so we will be
married and you will give me sons."

#

"It seems you have turmoil in your life right now."

"How do you know that?" She was surprised Aris knew what was
happening in real time. He hadn't shown up in Carlos' life for quite
a while. The last was the night in front of her building when he
possessed the young man's mortal mind.

There are times when I am able to see out of his eyes and hear what
his mind thinks. I have no explanation for it other than his consciousness
has been opened in some strange way from the drugs he has taken in the
past. I have no control over it, but there are occasions when he and I are
one being.

She wondered why she always felt so much safer, more secure
when she was in the presence of Aris. "Carlos is in trouble and I'm
not sure how to help him."

"It angers me that I do not have a human body to be your champion.
This man will not relinquish his to me."

"You must never hurt Carlos." Anger rang in her words. "Never, do you hear me?"

The voice was smiling as he spoke, *"Ah Sarah. Can you be in love with him?"*

She stammered. "I'm not. But he means a great deal to me. I don't want anything to hurt him."

"To live inside his body is not to hurt him. It is to make him into something much stronger than he is. Something invincible."

"No. Promise me you will never do anything to harm him."

"Would you believe a promise from a monster such as I am?"

"I don't believe you are a monster, Aris. I don't know for sure what you are, but a monster? No."

#

The dark of her bedroom and the comfort of her bed didn't drive away the thoughts of her last session with Aris. She wondered why she thought of it as a session with Aris. Was Carlos right? Was she beginning to forget the whole ordeal was to help him, not to know more about this sixteenth century creature? Was Aris really a monster?

Thoughts swirled around in her head until she felt dizzy. Was Aris real or was it a subconscious desire Carlos had to make himself feel invincible in a world where he was so vulnerable? As a twenty-first-century person, believing in the undead was almost impossible. What was the answer? Carlos knew nothing about Tudor England or Alexander the Great for that matter. Where did all of his information come from if not from Aris? She researched everything that came out in session. Each and every story was based on historical fact. Not fact about vampires to be sure, but fact about times and places and people.

In a state of confusion and mental exhaustion, she fell into a dreamless sleep.

#

She smiled at him as she finished her notes. It had been a good talk therapy session with Carlos. She was glad she decided not to take him into hypnosis. They spoke more about his childhood, about his need for a "tribe," a place to belong. She was surprised when he spoke, once again showing confusion.

"Look Sarah, I know I said I'd stick it out 'til the end and I will, but I'm just not sure about the hypnosis part anymore." He sat slouched in his usual chair across from her desk, his hands folded in his lap and his chin on his chest. He rarely stayed in her office after a session as he used to. She wondered what was on his mind.

"I don't know what you mean, Carlos." She leaned forward as she always did to let him know she was really interested in what he was saying.

"Well, I don't see how you spending all these sessions with this Aris guy is helping me find out why I'm pissed off at the world." He sat up straight in his chair and leaned forward toward her. "Do you? I mean really, do you? Besides I don't feel so pissed off any more."

"Look Carlos, if you don't want to go into trance anymore, you don't have to." Moving to stand in front of him, she leaned on the edge of her desk. "You vacillate all the time between not wanting to move forward and being gung ho, let's go. Just what do you want to do?"

He leaned back into his signature slouch as he silently stared into her eyes. When he spoke, he smiled, "How can we stop in the middle of a scary story?" He nodded his head up and down. "I guess we have to go through to the end whether its death and destruction or here comes the bride of Dracula."

\#

The July afternoon was hot and humid. The flowers limply hung their heads. The two women sat in the shade of a big, very green maple tree and sparrows pecked a piece of a hotdog bun that had fallen on the ground. They enjoyed a late lunch in Lincoln Park whenever they found time. It was a perfect end to a hectic week and Maggie and Sarah both leaned back into the bench, stretching out after they finished eating. "I guess it's time to go back to the office," feigned disappointment showing in Sarah's voice.

Maggie looked at her watch. "It sure is. You've got an appointment in half an hour."

"Sorry Mag," she giggled. "I forgot to tell you, the two o'clock cancelled. We've got another hour's reprieve."

"I could have enjoyed my lunch a lot more if I knew that before we ate." Maggie gave her associate a fake scowl. She stood. "Want to take a walk since we've got plenty of time?"

"Sure." Sarah bundled the wrappers and containers from her lunch. She tossed them into the recycling barrel, then stood to brush the crumbs from her skirt. The birds immediately began to eat the little pieces of chips that fell to the ground. "What a perfect day." Her full skirt ruffled in the wind as they began to walk.

"Yeah, it is." Her reply didn't match her tone.

Startled, Sarah paused and looked at her friend. "What's up Maggie? I can hear it in your voice."

Maggie stopped walking, turning to face Sarah. "I didn't want to have to tell you this, but it's gotten a little weird." She looked off over Sarah's shoulder.

"What are you talking about? I don't understand." Sarah stopped walking in the middle of the sidewalk. Other pedestrians circled around the two, giving them exasperated looks for stalling the foot traffic.

"Let's sit." Motioning toward an empty bench under another big maple tree, Maggie led Sarah away from the lunch crowd getting their daily exercise. They sat in dappled shade.

"The last few nights, I've been followed home. At least I think I've been followed." She twisted her hands in her lap. "I can't really be sure. It's just a feeling. I think there's someone trailing behind

me but when I turn around, there's no one there except the usual
commuters. I start to walk again and I feel that creepy feeling
again." Her voice was soft and apologetic, "Do you think it has
something to do with Gorgeous?"

"I don't know, Maggie. Have you spoken to anyone else about
this?"

"No, I wanted to talk to you first. I know he's a special client
to you. I don't want to get him into any trouble. And I know the
whole thing could just be my imagination. I've been going to a lot
of scary movies lately."

"Let me talk to him first. We'll see what he says. We'll go from
there." She reached for her friend's hands, holding them in her
own. "Is that alright with you? The most important thing is that
you feel safe."

Maggie thought in silence. When she answered, her voice was
sure. "Yes, I think you should talk to Carlos before we do anything
at all. I trust him to tell you the truth." She smiled a nervous smile.
"And I'll stay away from fright night at the movies."

"I'm sure it's nothing to worry about." Sarah's response was
immediate and strong. It gave Maggie the confidence she needed
to relax a bit, to just wait to see what happened next.

#

Sarah left Carlos a message early in the afternoon but he didn't
return the call until evening. The tall, bright lights of the shopping
center parking lot came on as the sky darkened after sunset. Their
reflection bounced off the dark, waxed finish of her car hood. She
waited to go inside the market while she finished her conversation.
A low beep on her cell phone warned her that the battery was
almost dead. "Hang on a minute, Carlos, I've got to plug this thing
in or I'm going to lose you." She plugged the phone jack into the
cigarette lighter. "There, now we're good to go."

"I don't know why Manu would have Maggie followed. She

doesn't have anything to do with any of this crap. I don't even know how he would know she exists." Carlos sounded as puzzled as Sarah was.

"I don't know either, but she was worried about it. Is there any way you can check it out?"

"Let me make a phone call. Stay put. I'll call you right back."

The phone went silent. She placed it on the console and leaned against the leather seat. Manu was turning into a constant problem. There had to be a way to get him out of the equation. She closed her eyes to let her mind wander for a solution.

The ring of the phone brought her back to the moment. "Hi."

"Hey Sarah, I talked to one of the guys who I can still trust. He says no, none of the guys are tailing anyone. He's pretty close to Manu and I'm sure if anything like that was going on, he'd know. I'm sure she's okay. Just tell Maggie to hang tight and let me know if anything else like that happens again."

"Thanks Carlos. If you're sure it's no one related to the gang, I'll tell Maggie. I know it'll make her feel a lot better. Maybe it is just her imagination."

"Cool. Gotta' go. See you Friday."

She placed the phone in a pocket in her purse. Climbing out of the car, she walked toward the market feeling relieved for the first time since her conversation with Maggie. Her stomach growled and her mind went to shopping for her dinner.

#

Each one of the four televisions mounted on the wall in front of the treadmills showed a different channel. The volume was turned down. The words of closed caption for the hearing impaired moved across the bottom of the screens. The music blared so loud from the speakers attached to the sound system, she thought she would soon be in that category. Not only was the gym freezing cold but they blasted loud, upbeat music constantly. She pulled her ear plugs out of her pocket, fitting them into her ears.

She wondered why all gyms seemed determined to ruin the hearing of their clientele. She couldn't attend any of the classes. The instructors blasted music, shouting into microphones making static and loud screeches. If she had room for a treadmill in her apartment, she wouldn't have bothered joining a gym in the first place. "Soon," she thought, "Soon I'll have a house and a basement with my own little Zen gym. She smiled at the thought of a fountain and soft classical music while she worked out. Great idea. She laughed at herself as she wondered if she was getting old or she just needed more sleep.

As her mind drifted, Bonnie mounted the elliptical next to her. Sarah pulled the plugs out of her ears. She was attacked again by the pounding bass line. She shouted, "Hey Bon, how are you doing?"

"Great, haven't seen you in a while. How's Colleen doing?" She set the controls and started moving her legs to the beat of the tune on the speakers.

"She and Bob are doing fine. I had dinner with them last week. She thinks she might be pregnant." As soon as the words were out of her mouth, she wondered if she had made a slip by telling their friend. "Well, she doesn't really know yet. It's way too soon to tell." Sarah took the small hand towel off the console of the treadmill, wiping the perspiration from her forehead.

"I won't mention it. There's no reason to upset her if she isn't sure." Sarah thought she caught what Bonnie said through the noise.

"She's not upset, Bon. I think she's made up her mind that either way, it's okay. Colleen's finally adjusted to married life. I think she may even be ready to have a baby."

"That's so cool. She and Bob are going to have one beautiful kid. Smart too." She cranked up the resistance. She started to breathe a little bit harder. "What about you? You seeing anyone?"

Sarah thought a moment, wondering what her friend would think if she said yes, a gangbanger and a vampire. She chuckled as she shook her head, "No, no one right now. I just don't seem to have any time available for that." She increased her own resistance, grabbed the rail and began to jog in place.

CHAPTER 28

CARLOS HAVARRO, transcript, session 18, July 16

It was dawn as I made my way through the garden from the chapel. There had been but a handful of the court present at the secret ceremony. I wondered why I had been one of the chosen few to witness the wedding between Henry and Anne, no longer Lady but Queen. Christmas day was a mere few weeks away and now, the new Queen would preside over the court. Katherine was banished long ago and Anne would never again have to sit quietly in her rooms while Katherine shared the festivities with the King. Now, she could Queen it over the whole court and Queen it she did.

As Christmas day approached, the court was decorated with holly and ivy. There was mistletoe, laurel and yew branches scattered everywhere. The pungent fragrance filled the halls and great rooms of the castle, an air of excitement hovered even in the darkest corners. True to the spirit of the season, everyone fretted over the gifts they would give and wondered at the gifts they would receive.

Anne chose her gift to the King with special care. Her ladies wrapped the two beautifully decorated boar spears in the finest velvet then tied them with the most ornate ribbon that could be found. They were set aside for the first day of January, the day of gift giving.

I knew the feast of Christmas would be one I had to endure pretending to enjoy the vast choices of food prepared just for the holiday. It was the same each year. The traditional boar's head garnished with rosemary and bay as the centerpiece of each table, a feast for all after the restricted dining following Advent Sunday. It was Anne who single handedly orchestrated the celebration and all was perfection. It was said to be the grandest Christmas of Henry's reign. The King laughed and stroked her and showed his love in his every glance. She was brighter than the grandest jewel and her dark eyes returned his affection.

The King ate copious amounts of food and drank a greater quantity of wine than the strongest youth of the court. There were Christmas poems and stories and music. A lovely melody was played, composed by the King himself. Everyone cheered at Henry's genius. It was late when the royal pair rose from the dais to bid the court good night. Anne placed her small hand on his arm as he led her to their rooms. As they left the hall, Anne nodded her head to me, smiling. I wondered at her meaning.

I had not long to wonder. The very next day she called me to her. As I entered her audience chamber, she dismissed her ladies so we sat alone except for her lute player. He was seated in a far corner playing softly as if to himself. His attention was on his instrument and the sounds his fingers made as he stroked the strings.

"Aris, I have called you to me for a purpose." She sat with her hands folded on her lap and the toes of her golden satin shoes peeking out from her emerald green velvet skirts. "I know not what you are but I know you are more than a man."

I was startled but held my tongue. I waited for her to continue.

"I watch the court and I see how strange and unique you are among the other courtiers. You hold yourself above the petty small talk and court intrigue. You seem a man without ambition. At court that is rare indeed. What is your true purpose here?"

"Majesty, my purpose is to serve the monarchy and my sovereigns, nothing more."

"Yes, Aris, a rare man indeed. And serve me you did. I wish to repay *you."*

"My Queen, you have paid me over and over again by allowing me to be in your presence, by the luxury you afford me in my rooms and by the glorious horse and saddle that you made my gift. I ask for nothing more than to continue to serve you."

"And you will. Your service to your Queen is greatly valued."

I was relieved my Queen had not seen the true difference between me and the rest of the courtiers. Her summons had been for an audience of praise. She told me there would be a special present for me on New Year's Day then dismissed me.

The days were short and cold and soon New Year's Day, the day of giving of gifts at court, was upon us. I was invited to the King's chamber in the morning to attend his dressing. It was an honor to be invited and I knew Anne had a hand in it. It took a great deal of time and many servants. Just as his shoes were placed on his feet, a fanfare sounded. The door to his chamber was thrown open. A servant appeared, one of Queen Anne's ladies, she carried the gift the Queen had so carefully chosen for her husband.

He unwrapped the spears, laughing out loud with pleasure. If a gift was given and the King rejected it, the giver was known to be in deep disfavor. Each year a few were sent from court. They knew they would be sent away when the King sent their gifts back to them. If he accepted the gift, he would send something to the giver in return much more valuable than that which he received. If that was the occurrence, they knew their place at court was secure.

Servant after servant appeared before the King, each with a gift from their master. Each waited to see if the gift was well taken. They were dismissed to return with the verdict, accepted or rejected, in favor or out.

As he sat in the midst of all the gold and silver plate, the jewels and the shirts, the spears and a gilded saddle, a servant of Katherine was bid to enter. A scowl appeared on the face of the monarch as he realized *from whom the gift was sent. He unwrapped the golden cup, threw the wrapping cloth on the floor then handed the cup back to the shivering man. He refused her gift just as he had cast her out. He shouted at her servant to be gone. Before the man reached the hall, word was circulating through the court of the King's action.*

The King's man then handed me a huge trunk, telling me to make haste to Queen Anne. It was Henry's gift to her. I was grateful for my unrivaled strength as I hurried down the corridors carrying the heavy weight on my shoulder. I knocked on her door. I was bid to enter.

Her eyes were bright with excitement as she opened it. Inside rested the most beautiful bed hangings my eyes had ever seen. Cloth of gold and silver embroidered with crimson satin threads, made and fit for a Queen. She threw her head back with a triumphant laugh. Her long black hair swung to her waist as she held one of the hangings to her breast, dancing about her room.

She whispered to me as she spun close. She whispered that her greatest gift to the King was yet to be given. I wondered at what it might be but she twirled away before I could ask.

There was feasting, joy and a masque for the New Year. The twelve days of Christmas were a time when all court business was set aside. Instead there were plays with fine actors, music, dancing and romance, candle flames, roaring fires, holiday smells and thick rich velvets.

It was the very next day she called me to her rooms. I was ushered into her bedchamber. She sat before a mirror, one of her ladies brushing her luxuriant hair. She was clothed in a black satin robe lined with opulent fur. I heard her humming softly to herself.

Smiling, she spoke to me. "Ah Aris, I have watched you watch the ladies at the festivities and so as your special gift, I wish to help you find a wife."

"Wife?" The word was choked from my throat. No human wife could ever be mine. I wanted no maiden. "My lady, you are all that I adore. I see no other woman in court except your Majesty," I bowed my best

courtiers bow.

She laughed out loud. *"And how do I persuade you, my dear Aris?"*

"Your Majesty, please, do not even make the attempt. You are the sun and the moon in my heaven. I may enjoy the sight of other women but your wit and beauty far outshine all others. I am loyal to my Queen in all things."

Her eyes flirted with me as she laughed. *"You are all I expected you to be. Now you may go. Your solitary life is granted you for the time being."* Turning back to her mirror, she once again began to hum. I backed from her room, grateful to have escaped so narrowly that which would have been my uncovering and feeling that I had passed some test of hers as to my loyalty to her alone. There could be no human love in my life. All hope of that died with Elizabeth Wyatt.

Quickly, twelfth night was upon us. Westminster was ablaze with candles and jewels. The King escorted Anne to the Tower of London where she had her pick of the treasury of England. Needing refreshment, she called for the wassail bowl. As she tipped her head to sip, a ruby the size of a robin's egg, a gift the King had placed in the bottom of the bowl, caught the light and turned her face a blazing scarlet. She was beautiful, vibrant and the King had eyes only for her.

The Lord of Misrule arranged a bawdy play. Anne arranged a glorious masque with dancing and costumes. The King presented himself in disguise as he loved to do and we all feigned surprise when he unmasked. It was the finish to a Christmas season such as the court had never known.

At the end of the festivities, I saw Anne lean into the King with the look of a special secret in her eyes. She whispered into his ear. Suddenly he threw back his head in a roar of laughter, rose from his chair to pick her off the floor then spun her in circle after circle. Just as suddenly, he stopped. He placed her gently on her feet then touched her belly. He caressed it softly as he stared into her eyes. He put his arm around her protectively to escort her from the room.

The court was filled with gossip that the Queen was with child. Soon we were to find it was truth.

"I tire from all of these memories. Tell me, Sarah, what do you do for your Christmas?"

She was shocked out of her stupor. She hated to be brought back from the court of the Tudors. When he spoke through Carlos, the sixteenth century came alive to her. It all seemed so familiar. She felt she had actually been there with him, seen the candles, the royalty.

She spoke. "Yes, my Christmas. Well, I don't think it will be anything to compare with the court." She laughed at the thought of her mother's Christmas tree and traditional dinner. It was a time of year when she loved being with her family. A time when she missed her father very much.

"I would very much like to share a Christmas with you."

"I believe you would be bored." She shut off the recorder. "We do have turkey but it is nothing like your Christmas pie. Of course, we do have a Christmas tree but nothing as grand as the palace filled with winter boughs."

"Nonetheless, I would like to be there with you. Your present time is very interesting to me." His voice became very quiet, very intimate. *"You are very interesting to me."*

As always, there was silence as he waited patiently for her to speak. When she didn't respond, he continued, *"And now sweet Sarah, it is time for this young man to awaken. I bid you farewell."* She knew that he was gone until their next session.

CHAPTER 29

Sarah was excited to go camping with her girlfriends as she dragged her tent out of her storage unit to air it on her balcony. It had been packed away for almost a year. She washed her sleeping bag hoping it wouldn't be lumpy. As they packed everything in the back of Bonnie's SUV, they were all in high spirits.

The windows in the car were down, a fresh, clean breeze ruffling their hair. The three women laughed and talked as the highway took them out of town to a campground in Wisconsin. It was the third camping anniversary of a lifetime of camping anniversaries to come.

This was Colleen's first get-a-way since she and Bob were married. She was happy to have a few days with her friends yet she still missed him like crazy. Sarah lost count of the text messages she sent to him and caught her looking wistfully out the window.

"Are you kidding, C?" She teased her friend. "You haven't been gone a day and you're already homesick."

"Yeah, well I miss the guy. Sucks, doesn't it? I really do love my husband and being married to him." She laughed out loud. "Who would 'a thought?"

"Yeah, well I did." Bonnie spoke up.

"Yeah, and so did I."

"Yeah?" Colleen closed the subject as she settled back into the seat to watch the landscape change outside her window.

The drive was under three hours so by mid-afternoon, they were pulling into the Wahaname Campground.

"I swear, if you text him again, I'm going to throw your phone away." Sarah opened her door. She stepped out of the car.

"This is the last time, I promise. He wanted me to let him know when I get here. He's just more cautious because of the baby." She closed her phone before she slid it into her jeans back pocket. "See?" She held out her hands, palms up. "See? No phone. I promise, no more texts."

Sarah looked skeptical.

"I said I promise. You'll see." She began to unload their gear. "I need this time to myself. I just miss the guy, that's all. I haven't been away from him a night since we've been married." She shook her head in wonder. "Amazing. And I like it that way."

"So, I guess you did the right thing?" Sarah picked up the cooler. She carried it to the picnic bench then went back to the van to grab the sleeping bags. The three friends had the camp set, ready to take a hike long before twilight.

The late afternoon sun was warm on their backs as they climbed to the top of a small grassy hill looking for a comfortable place to have their light picnic supper. They traveled light. Sarah carried a bottle of wine, a bottle of water for Colleen and a corkscrew in her backpack. Bonnie carried three glasses and napkins. Colleen carried cheese, some apples and an army knife. They delighted in the place they found. The opposite side of the hill was covered in summer wild flowers. In the warmth of the setting sun, the fragrance filled the air.

They settled down as each one of them did their chore. Sarah opened the wine and the water. Bonnie held the glasses as she poured.Colleen sliced thin pieces of the wonderful smelling Italian cheeses and apples.

"This is perfect. Wow, I can't believe this is so close to home. It's a different world." Colleen held her glass high for a toast. "And here's to this weekend." Her friends agreed. They all touched glasses, then took a sip.

"Do you guys know where the term 'toast' came from?"

They both turned to look at her as if she was a bit crazy. "No, where?"

"Well," She tipped her glass to them again taking another sip. "Back in Tudor England, when they passed around the wassail bowl at Christmas, the most important person at the party got to eat the piece of toast that was floating around in the bottom of the wine. It was supposed to be an honor."

Colleen looked at her friend with incredulous eyes. "Where the hell did you find that out?" She paused. "And why?"

Sarah sat quietly for a moment, and then answered. "From a friend." She nodded her head, "Yes, a friend."

#

Sarah woke up to the smell of coffee perking. It was the most wonderful smell in the world. Fresh, crisp, cool, morning air and coffee. Who could ask for more than that? She snuggled down in her sleeping bag for an extra moment to enjoy the sounds and smells that surrounded her.

"Hey, you guys, get up. Times a wasting." Colleen's voice was wide awake. "Come on, I'm hungry. Get up."

Both her friends muttered they were coming. Before long, they both opened the flaps of their tents. The campfire was already lit. Two huge coffee mugs sat on the picnic table. The two late risers picked them up, filling them with the thick, black liquid that came out of the coffee pot. Colleen had a special brew she concocted for their camping trips. It was so black and so strong it could wake the dead.

"Where's the sugar?" Sarah yawned as she spoke.

"I thought you brought it."

"I thought you brought it."

"What, no sugar?"

"Sarah, you're the only one who uses it. Why didn't you bring it?"

She yawned again. "Well, I can't drink this stuff without it." She placed the mug back on the table.

Bonnie went back into her tent, returning with her car keys. "I think I've got some packets of sugar in my glove box. I'll go look."

She walked down the path toward the car.

"Colleen. Sarah. Come here quick." Anger in her voice cut the air like a steel knife.

The two women hurried to the car and found Bonnie crouched down by her rear tire. "Look, these two tires have been slashed." She pointed to the rear and front tire on the driver's side. "Who the hell would do such a thing at a campground?" She stood, brushing her dirty hands on her jeans. "I only have one spare. Crap. Now what?"

Colleen took over the situation. "First we go to the ranger and tell him. Then we call Bob to bring us a tire. I'll tell him to bring his tent. If he's here, we'll feel safer and we won't have to cut the trip short."

"This isn't funny. Somebody vandalized my car. And for no reason."

Sarah wondered silently if there, perhaps, was a reason, a very bad reason.

#

"So how was the annual girl's get away?" He sat in the chair across from her desk as she opened her drawer to retrieve her recorder.

"It was fine. We had a great time." She kept the tire episode quiet.

"Are you sure? You don't sound like you had a good time."

"Come on, lie down." She stood, crossing the room to the recliner. "Let's get going." She sat in her chair motioning him toward her.

"Okay." He sat down, leaned back and rested his head on the cushion. "You know, when I think back to where I was when we started, this has been an amazing trip."

"You have made so much progress in so many areas of your life, Carlos. You must be proud."

"It's kind of hard to admit it, but I am. Sometimes I even feel happy, like when I think I really do have some kind of a future other than being a petty convict. You and Colleen have shown me a part of life I didn't know existed. And, I like it. I'm still not sure where I'm going but what I am sure of is I'm not going down. I know I can be better than I ever thought I could be and I want that. I want whatever it is that's called a normal life. I want a place of my own, someplace I can call home. I never thought it would feel good to work and get a paycheck, but it does. Hell, I'm even going to have to pay taxes this year." He laughed. "A real law abiding citizen. Now if I can only figure out what the hell this vamp is doing in my head, I'll be home free."

"Don't worry. We'll figure it out together sooner or later. Right now relax and just begin to focus on your breath."

#

CARLOS HAVARRO, transcript, session 19, July 23

"While there was revelry above ground in the palace so were there festivities below ground in the Catacombs. Sebastian was to be mated. He chose a mortal to be his partner. She chose to become immortal to share his world. The celebration in the coven was for the joining of the two, for her changing. It is the law a human must become one of the undead in order to mate in our world. The changing ceremony had not been performed in many years. Akira and Kansu were to act as officiators of the joining. The ceremony takes three days. My transformation at the

temple of Dionysius was much the same save the ceremony. At the end of the vigil, the shift is complete.

The festival in the winter of 1532 was for Sebastian and Emily. They met in the gardens of the palace. After a court banquet, Emily ventured away from the party of strolling courtiers. She heard soft splashes of water from a fountain hidden within the tall hedges of a lover's maze. She found it, the water sparkling like diamonds in the warm summer moonlight. Standing next to the fountain was Sebastian. It was there they met.

They continued to meet quietly, out of the sight of others. He loved her. He won her love. He was honest and she was brave. She desired to be with him always, desired to become just as he was. Over and over, he petitioned the counsel never being fully refused, yet never receiving permission. He persevered until, at long last, he received their agreement to create a new member in the coven.

It is quite an ordeal for the changeling as well as the ultimate temptation for the vampire. The blood drinker takes a little blood and replaces it with venom. The exchange must be exact and there is no way to measure other than with the vampire senses. It is a time of trial for the changeling. There is immeasurable pain and also ecstasy hidden somewhere deep inside the torment. The overwrought senses beg that it stop yet plead that it go on forever. The changing ritual is performed in seclusion with no witnesses. The vampire must use all skill and discipline not to kill their chosen one. It is the most intimate of times for our kind. Do you wish to hear more?"

She nodded her head and mumbled, "Yes, oh yes."

On the day of the rite, Akira nodded to me as I entered the sanctuary. As my Queen, she was privy to the many rumors of my unusual choice of human companionship yet she held no judgement against me. I thought her simply benevolent; I know now she favored and indulged me much as a mother would her child.

The light from the candles cast moving shadows on the tapestried walls *as Sebastian stood at the foot of the dais. The lovely young woman at his side looked frightened yet ecstatic as she stared into the face of her beloved. His gaze held hers for a very long time then drifted to the beating pulse on the side of her warm throat. I saw a shiver of fear run through her body yet she steeled herself against it. She stood to meet her chosen fate, a brave smile lifting the corners of her lips.*

The low bodice of her dress enhanced her long slender neck; her shinning auburn hair was piled high on her head. She was beautiful. The singing beat of her heart called to him. The hunger lit his eyes. He swallowed as his mouth filled with desire.

Akira rose from her throne to face the two supplicants. The royal attendance chamber was large, beautifully appointed and the arena surrounding the central dais was filled with one hundred of our kind fortunate enough to be invited. All were silent as Akira stood before Emily and Sebastian, the small weak female, the strong fierce male. The young mortal was afraid yet she found great courage from somewhere. She stepped forward.

Akira had never been human. She wondered at many of the emotions of our species, questioning her courtiers at length and over millennia . She sought to understand what it meant to feel sentiment be it sorrow or joy, anger or forgiveness. She found the changelings incapable of remembering or unable to explain exactly what an emotion was. Yet on this day, as the ritual began, a palpable sense of peace surrounded us all. Akira hesitated for just a moment before continuing.

She turned to face a young vampire climbing onto the dais. He was carrying a golden chalice resting on a gilded tray. Holding the tray above his head, he knelt on a soft blue velvet cushion as he bowed. Akira relieved him of his burden. He rose then slowly backed from her sight, disappearing into the crowd as she turned to face Sebastian and Emily.

Emily knelt at Akira's feet, lowering her head in a bow. Tilting the vessel, the Queen slowly poured a soft stream of warm oil onto the bare shoulders of the kneeling girl. As she began to massage the oil into her soft white skin, she chanted softly.

"I relieve you of the burden of the sorrow of killing to live, a life for a life."

Emily slowly lifted her head. Akira poured a drop of oil onto her forehead, whispering softly, "To open your mind to the knowledge of the millennia held in the mind of your chosen one."

Emily stood, raising the hem of her skirt to her knees. Akira stooped to drop oil on her feet then massaged the warm liquid in circular motions. "That you may walk with the pride of an immortal though all eternity."

I stepped closer to the dais to see the couple more clearly. This was the first I saw a human make the choice to be a vampire. Only once have I hated myself for being what I am, only when I wanted to take Elizabeth for my wife. My changing was not my decision, not of my doing. This young woman had a choice. Her adoration for Sebastian showed in her eyes as she looked at him. When her gaze caught his, I could see something alive between them that one could almost touch, the very reason for her being here. Love. On occasion Gabriella and Richard had that mystical air about them. In those moments, I longed for my lost maid, my Bess.

Akira stood quite still. Khansu rose from his throne. He moved to her side, reaching to touch first Emily on her brow, then Sebastian. Akira did the same. The couple bowed then backed slowly from the chamber. The royal couple returned to their thrones. The attendees broke into scattered groups, the ceremony complete.

Sebastian and Emily were led to the privacy of their rooms. There they performed the secret rite; he exchanged her blood for his vampire venom a little at a time. Slowly he brought her to be his mate, his child, his only family. When they emerged from the chamber, they would be of the same kind, of the same lineage, pledged to one another as immortals.

As I made my way back to the castle, I pondered. Would any human woman ever do such a thing for me? What do you think, Sarah? Do you know of a human woman who would do such a thing for me? Hum?"

She stammered, "I don't know. I don't really know."

"*You think about that Sarah. Keep it in your mind always. Would you do such a thing for love?*"

She could tell right away that Aris had left the building. The atmosphere in the room changed immediately when his essence disappeared. She sat quietly for a moment questioning herself Would she do such a thing for love?

CHAPTER 30

The thought of seeking out Manu wouldn't leave her alone. Every time the situation came into her mind, and that was plenty, she thought of going to talk to him but it scared her to death. She remembered the evil look on his face as he stalked her when she left the subway. But she knew if she brought Colleen and Bob into it Carlos would find out what had been going on and she didn't want that. She didn't want him in another confrontation with Manu. Even though the idea of meeting with the gang leader frightened her, the episode with the tires really was the last straw. She had no proof it was his gang that flattened the tires, another car had been vandalized too, but it didn't matter. The phone calls to Mrs. Havarro. The possibility that Maggie really had been followed. She had to know. The harassment had to stop. She was the only one, it seemed, who might convince him to lay off Carlos. "Am I nuts? No, I can do this."

She carried her coffee mug to the sink in one hand, the telephone in the other. She had Isabella Havarro on speed dial. She hit the buttons to connect a call. The phone rang a hollow note for two rings. A soft woman's voice answered.

"Hello."

"Isabella?"

"Yes?"

"This is Sarah Hagan." She poured another cup of coffee, then made her way back to the comfort of her sofa. She sat in a sunbeam coming through the patio door. She waited for the other woman to respond.

There was a silence that lasted for such a long time, Sarah thought she lost the signal. She opened her mouth to ask if they were still connected when Carlos' mother spoke.

"Yes Sarah, what can I do for you?" Her voice sounded tight, unfriendly.

"Isabella, I need your help."

"I'm sorry but you will have to find help some other place. I cannot help you." It was a statement that left no room for negotiation, but Sarah refused to take no for an answer.

"What has happened, Isabella? What's wrong?" She placed her coffee cup on the table next to the sofa. She stood, pacing back and forth in front of the patio door as she continued the conversation.

"Nothing has happened. I just don't want to get involved in this anymore, that's all."

"But Isabella?"

"No Miss Hagan." She was firm. "No."

Sarah sighed. The illusive Manu had gotten hold of Isabella again. She was sure of it. Her irritation with his scare tactics began to outweigh her fear. She was even more determined to contact him to tell him to back off.

"Alright, I understand. I just need to know where Manu hangs out. I'm going to talk to him."

There was panic in the voice of the older woman. "No, you must not go to him. He will hurt you."

"Someone has to put a halt to all this and I'm going to talk to him. Now, you can make it easy by telling me where to find him or hard by not telling me but you're not going to stop me. I've had enough of Manu."

Silence surrounded her. When Isabella spoke, it was with resignation. She told Sarah where Carlos' old gang hung out. She said a quick goodbye. Sarah placed the phone on the table. She sat on the couch, wondering what happened to make Isabella so frightened she wouldn't even talk on the phone. She was attacked by momentary panic at the thought of what she planned to do but she took control.

"I'm going to see him. I'm not afraid." Even she didn't believe the whispered words that came from her lips.

#

The neighborhood was run down. Abandoned cars seemed to be on every block. Tattered curtains and blinds with missing slats were in apartment windows on both sides of the streets. She even saw a line of laundry hanging on a fire escape. The street looked like a scene from a fifties police movie.

She wondered why the street was so empty in the middle of a beautiful fall day. The only pedestrian was an elderly man in torn jeans and a tee shirt with a peace sign logo on the back. He hobbled along with the use of a cane, stopping every few feet to take a rest. A car pulled up to the curb. The old man watched as a teenaged boy jumped out of the back seat. He waved goodbye to his friends, turning to go up the steps into one of the apartment buildings. Sarah saw that the boy was dressed similar to the old man, torn jeans and a tee shirt with a peace sign logo on the back. She thought it ironic that the man dressed that way out of necessity, the boy because he chose it.

She knew the coffee shop should be in the next couple of blocks so she slowed the car. Isabella didn't know the address or the name, just the general location. It was the only coffee shop in the neighborhood. Her hands felt ice cold on the steering wheel, her mouth dry, as she saw it on the next corner.

Suddenly, a car horn blasted long and loud right behind her. She jumped, looking into the rear view mirror. Carlos stopped his car in the middle of the street. He jumped out of the door, bearing down on her, obviously furious.

"What the hell are you doing here?" He jerked her door open, leaning into the car. His face was inches from hers. His eyes flashed with anger.

"I came to talk to Manu." She didn't flinch. Her eyes held his when she spoke.

He spluttered, unable to believe his ears. His words were loud, harsh. "You what?" He stood, turning his back on her. He was silent for a moment, while he willed control of his anger. He looked at her, speaking very softly to keep from shouting. He continued, "You were going to talk to Manu? Are you out of your mind?"

"I'm just tired of all this intrigue. I don't want you hurt again."

"Sarah, I'm a big boy. I can handle myself." He closed the door, stepping away from the car. "Go back to the office. I'll meet you there. We have to talk. You can't go running around getting involved with people who could hurt you."

He turned to walk to his car, then stopped, looking at her once more. "But I'm kind a glad you care enough to put yourself on a limb for me." He smiled at her, waiting for her to make a u-turn to head back to her side of town.

#

It was two hours before Carlos walked into her office. He sat in a chair opposite her and took a long drink from the can of soda he brought with him.

"Why won't you believe me, there's nothing to tell. You know it all." He met her eyes when he spoke but Sarah didn't believe Carlos.

"Why is this guy so determined to get you back on the street? Why doesn't he just leave you alone?"

"I honestly don't know, Sarah. I was his second in command. I know about all the robberies and the drive by. Maybe he's afraid I'll turn on him. That's the only thing I can think of."

"Would you turn on him?" She leaned forward in her chair, resting her elbows on her desk.

"No. I told you. I may not want to live like that anymore but I'll never turn on a brother." He smashed the empty soda can. He tossed it into the trash. "So, I'm here, you're here. How about a session? I could use a little relaxation time with the vamp." He grinned at her as he walked to the recliner. He settled down into the comfortable cushions. "What do you say, Sarah? How about a little 'deep sleep'."

She realized that conversation about Manu was a lost cause so she sighed, picked up the recorder from her desk and moved across the room to her chair. She sat down, pushing the record button.

"All right, just begin to focus on your breath."

#

CARLOS HAVARRO, transcript, session 20, July 30

Sebastian and Emily were mated that winter as were the King and Anne. The English royals married officially the end of January of that year. Well they did because the following September, a child was born.

While Anne carried the King's child, he waited on her as her loyal servant. He was tender and loving. While in her presence, he looked at no other maid. She fulfilled his purpose, his desire, carrying the future prince, the prospective King of England. Her womb held proof of his virility, a witness to his youth and power.

When the Queen began her lying in, he visited her every day. She hated the dark room, miserable, spending every moment in bed with hangings over all the windows to keep out the light, surrounded by nothing but women. She despised the mid-wives and court ladies constantly telling her horror stories of birth and death. She wanted to scream long before the pains began. Then, scream she did. We could hear her in the outer chamber.

The King requested some of his closest friends and personal guards to stand with him as he waited for the birth. I was there along with several of his most trusted gentlemen. Henry was agitated. His heels clicked on the stones of the floor as he paced restlessly.

Suddenly, all was quiet, no sounds issued from the birthing room. Just as the door cracked open, the King grabbed it, yanking hard. The midwife stood on the other side. "It is done, my lord. The Queen is delivered."

Laughing, he rushed past her. "My son, I want to see my son. Where is my son?" The door closed behind him.

All was quiet. Suddenly, we heard the cry of a babe. In a moment the King returned , his step heavy, his face crestfallen. "I have not a son, but another daughter." He stood still in front of us all, his feet planted apart in his familiar stance, his hands on his hips, his gaze cast to the floor. In deathlike silence, Henry remained frozen to the spot. He looked at his men, one at a time. At last, he began to smile. "A healthy daughter. And if we can have a healthy daughter, we can have a healthy prince. Her name shall be Elizabeth and she is a red haired Tudor to be sure."

Henry did his best to play the part of the proud father yet all the court knew he was deeply disappointed. Anne had not presented him with a prince. That evening he and his fellows drank great amounts of wine to celebrate the birth. Soon they were all sodden and his false gayety turned to deep melancholy. He whined he was betrayed. Anne promised him a son but presented him a girl. He bellowed and cried until, at last, George Boleyn assisted him to his rooms. He staggered out the door, his huge frame resting on the lean arm of Anne's brother.

I stayed with the gentlemen of the court. They continued to drink quantities of wine. The festivities went on until, as the sky grew light, they left the chamber one by one, staggering to their rooms to sleep the morning away. Thereafter, the King spoke rarely of Elizabeth.

But it seemed it was not quite so that the King and Queen should have *a healthy son. They never had another child together and, in the end, that was the demise of their marriage and the end of her life.*

Shortly after her birth, Elizabeth was sent to her own household. Anne once again returned to court seemingly unscathed to Queen it over us all.

"And now Sarah, I will ask you a question." There was a silent pause. "What do you intend on doing with all of this information that you gather?"

"I... I am using it to help Carlos." She stammered when she answered.

"Are you? Or are you using Carlos to be closer to me? Think about it Sarah. Just take some time to honestly ask yourself the reason why."

CHAPTER 31

She raced up the steps of the hospital, pushing her way through the revolving door. The woman behind the reception desk had short gray hair with tight curls. She was wearing a pink smock. Sarah wondered at herself, noticing such inane things when she was in the middle of a crisis.

"Colleen Stevens-Drake. What room is she in?"

The woman checked the computer then, replied, "Third floor, room 316A."

"Thank you," Sarah's reply missed its mark. Her words hit thin air as she turned to hurry toward the elevator. Glancing at her watch as the door opened, she realized it hadn't been a half hour since she received Bob's phone call.

She picked up the panic in his voice when he told her Colleen was in the hospital. There had been a car accident, a hit and run. Bob was on his way to the hospital when he called Sarah. His wife was going to be okay but she was really banged up and scared. Sarah had never seen her friend frightened of anything, ever.

The elevator dinged as the doors slid opened at the third floor. Sarah stepped off, checking up and down the hall for room numbers. She hurried toward the door, barely avoiding a food cart standing in the middle of the aisle.

She stopped for a moment just outside the room to compose herself. When she felt more calm, she tapped on the closed door very lightly, waiting to hear an invitation to come in.

Colleen's voice was soft and sleepy when she answered. Sarah opened the door, not knowing what to expect. She was stunned to see her friend bandaged from head to toe, propped up on pillows in her bed. She had an oxygen tube in her nose. What little was visible of her face above the bandages was already turning black and blue.

"Hey, I'm happy to see you." She slurred her words through the medications she was given to ease the pain. "Bob's not here yet but he's on the way."

"Don't talk honey." Sarah sat next to her in one of the visitor's chairs. She held Colleen's uninjured hand. She could see tears trying to fight their way out of her bruised, swollen eyes. "It's going to be alright, C. It's going to be fine. You're hurt but you're going to be just fine."

"I lost the baby." Her words were soft, filled with tragedy.

"Baby? I thought you weren't sure."

"I just left the doctor's office when I was hit. She told me it was for certain. And now . . . " She burst into tears just as the door opened and Bob came into the room. Sarah moved aside to let him near his wife.

Colleen spoke to Bob through her tears. "I lost the baby. I lost our baby."

Sarah saw Bob's eyes fill. She knew they needed to be alone. "I'll be down in the cafeteria getting some coffee. When you're ready, I'll be waiting there."

Bob reached for her, hugging her tightly. When he let her go, she picked up her bag from the chair and left the room.

#

She saw Bob enter the large lunch room. She stood to wave

to him. He saw her, nodded and moved toward her table. Sitting across from her, he buried his head in his hands. When he looked up, his cheeks were wet with tears.

"We just hung up the phone. She was so excited when the doctor told her she was really pregnant, she couldn't wait to tell me. She called me before she got dressed to leave the office. She was so happy." He buried his face once again. "Oh Sarah, she's so banged up. Her arm's broken. She's got a fractured ankle and her shoulder is just about torn out of the socket. She's so little and so hurt."

Sarah rose from her chair. She circled the table to stoop down next to Bob. She put her hand on his shoulder as she spoke, "I know. I know. But she is okay. She'll heal. It's awful but she will heal." Her words were meant to comfort her friend but they did little to bring comfort to her. How could anyone demolish a car like that and just leave? "Did anyone see it happen?"

"Yeah, the police report showed two witnesses. They both said the same thing: someone in a dark colored two door car, no make, no year. Nothing else. They were so stunned that neither of them got the model or the license plate so we're at the starting gate without a bell. I don't even know where to go from here, but I'm going to find her and fry her."

"We've got to keep it together for Colleen right now. Are you assigned to the case?"

"No, but the detectives are all my buddies and I've got a hand in it." His voice was vicious through his tears. Sarah wrapped her arms around him, comforting him as best she could.

#

"I can't believe how bad she's beat up." Carlos shook his head side to side. "She looks like she was hit by a train, not a car."

"When did you see her?" Sarah placed the coffee mugs on her coffee table as they sat side by side on the sofa.

"Yesterday. She looks like a little kid in the middle of all those bandages. She was smiling. She told me she was glad I was there but I could see she is miserable." He sighed. "Do they have any leads at all?"

"None. How can two people see something like that and neither of them catch the car make or the license number? It doesn't make sense."

"Bob was at the hospital. He sure is crazy about her."

"Yeah." She turned to look into his eyes, afraid to ask the question that had been on her mind since morning. "You don't think this has anything to do with your old street gang, do you?"

He was silent a moment, then answered. "No, they're a bad bunch but they wouldn't go after a woman." He looked out the window when he spoke.

"Are you sure? I mean after that thing with your brother." She didn't want to tell him about her encounter with his old pal.

"Sure, they got him drunk and high and they'd steal anything, but they wouldn't hurt a woman."

She hoped he was right.

#

"I'm so glad they let you come home today. Would you like some tea or something?" Sarah brushed Colleen's hair as she sat up in her bed.

"No, I've got water here. That's all I want right now." Sarah fluffed her pillows and she settled into them, careful of her injuries. She wanted to keep the conversation light and easy. She asked, "So what's going on with the handsome one?"

"Just the usual." Sarah smiled to herself, wondering what her friend would say if she knew exactly what the usual was. "He's coming along fine."

"Any insight to the anger stuff?"

"A little. Hey, what about you? Any new info on the hit and run driver?"

"We're not really sure. One of the witnesses says she thought it was a really young woman driving, but Bob says what makes her think that now when she didn't know right after it happened. I tend to agree with him. Then the other witness said he remembered it was an elderly woman driving the car. Who knows?"

Sarah placed the hairbrush on the night stand. She sat on the side of the king-size bed. "How are you feeling about... everything?" She didn't want to mention the miscarriage but she wanted to make sure her best friend was feeling reconciled with it.

"I'm still sad. And sorry. But there's nothing I can do about it now. I'm lucky there's nothing wrong with me so we can try again. One thing I know for sure, I am finally ready to settle down and be a mother. Enough running around with gangsters." She smiled. "Except our one special one."

"Yeah, he really is a good guy. He's so frightened. Part of it is from his past and part from his present. I only hope I can help him to fight the fear, to come to the other side of it." She paused. "Colleen, do you think he would become involved with his old friends again?" Colleen looked at her with questioning eyes. "Not that I think he has or anything, I just wonder what he would do if they tried to get him to join them again."

"What do you know that I don't know? I've asked you that before and you always evade the question."

"I know a lot and I can't discuss it. But I can tell you this; nothing that I have discussed with him leads me to believe he would go back."

"Then why do you ask me over and over again if I think he would?"

Before Sarah could answer, Bob's voice called from the kitchen. "Hey Sarah, come here. I need help to carry in the food." Happy to have his wife home, he left work early to prepare dinner for her and her best friend. They planned a bedroom picnic on the king-size bed. They were going to watch a movie to celebrate.

Glad not to have to answer her friend's question, she hurried from the room. "On my way, Bob."

#

CARLOS HAVARRO, transcript, session 21, August 6

The golden sand glistened like window glass in the noonday sun. The Queen sat under the royal canopy to protect her fair skin from the heat. Her ladies sat readily near her should she need attending. It appeared there were thousands of people come for the entertainment, the pageantry of the joust. There were merchants hawking their wares and flower girls selling their poseys. The courtiers bet heavily on their favorites as the knights prepared for the challenge and their men prepared for the promenade before the royal box.

On this day, I was not a participant so I enjoyed watching the event from just behind the canopy's shadow. The Queen smiled. She tossed her head as lords and gentry approached to greet her, to introduce their ladies. As the standards flew on the flagstaffs, their colors undulated in the wind. The fabrics made sharp cracking sounds as the sudden gusts slapped them against the polished wood of the poles. There was laughter and bantering from every corner as Anne ruled - the Queen of Charm - sitting high above it all.

Suddenly, the sounding of trumpets. The knights mounted. Another fanfare as they rode into the arena at a gallop. Their armor glistened in the morning light and the saddles of their great horses were polished until even the leather gleamed like jewels. The lords and challengers reined in quickly so their horses reared, pawing the air with their front feet. I ached to mount, to ride, to once again be champion of the joust, but this was not the day for me. The Queen asked me to stay with her. I knew there was a greater purpose to her request than the pleasure of my company.

The knights and lords promenaded before beginning the tournament, some even employed bards to tell a poem or sing of their bravery. The trumpets sounded the King's fanfare as he made his way into the arena.

All rose to greet him. He bellowed a hearty laugh. The ladies of the court dressed in Tudor green and white followed in a wagon appointed to resemble a forest glen. Their dresses glistened in the sunlight as it shined down on the metallic threads and jewels bedecking their gowns.

The crowd grew silent as the King dismounted to make his way toward the Queen.

She rose and curtsied. He kissed her hand. A roar of approval went up from the crowd. The radiant King sat, merry in the morning light, motioning Anne to sit beside him. No sooner was he seated than he was handed wine and sweetmeats. The King did not ever sit for long without eating and drinking as if being seated had only the purpose of being fed.

Once more the knights circled the arena with the heralds shouting their titles. Each knight rode before the royal box presenting their arms while Anne had something personal to say to each man. Her dark eyes glistened as she tilted her head, flirting with each of the champions. The crowd was in an uproar when the last knight left the arena, ready for the jousting to begin.

The King rose, moving to his personal box across from the Queen. He chatted with the men surrounding him, his favorites, as two knights prepared for the first challenge. When all was ready, he rose. The crowd grew silent once more. He raised his great gauntlet above his head, paused a moment, then gestured toward the Queen, bestowing the honor of the calling of the joust upon her. The crowd thundered with cheers, stomping feet and clapping hands.

The two contenders waited at either end of the jousting line, their horses pawing the sand. Anne rose and with a flourish, dropped her glove. The knights spurred their horses as the huge beasts thundered toward one another. Each rider balanced his lance, preparing for the moment of contact. The sound of armor being hit echoed through the arena like thunder. One of the knights was knocked from his horse but there was no wound, no bleeding. Being one of the King's personal guards, I was constantly with the court and I had not fed for days. I worried that the

*smell of blood would incite my hunger. I stepped back on the platform as
the vanquished knight lay in the sand. I was safe for the moment. His
man helped him from the field, nothing broken, nothing cut.*

*The Queen sensed my movement. She called me close to her once again.
As the next two champions prepared for the challenge, she motioned me
nearer still so she could whisper to me. "Aris, I have another mission for
you." She caught my eye, her lips curled up in a malevolent smile. "Are
you prepared to once again be my own special champion?"*

*I lowered my head, speaking quietly, "I am always prepared to be your
champion, my Lady."*

*She touched my arm. "Very well, I will call on you soon," she turned
her attention to the joust.*

*I stepped into the shadows behind her, gazing around the arena
wondering which poor knave was the next to die.*

"Sarah." She was called back to present time at the sound of her
name. *"I am prepared to be your own champion and I swear, I will find
a way to be with you in your own time."*

Her heart pounded at the thought of being with him. She
whispered, "It seems, Aris, that all things may be possible." She
wondered what it would be like to stand in the presence of the
vampire. To be held in his arms. To be kissed by his immortal lips.
A hot flush spread over her body at the thought.

#

Carlos sat in his usual chair across from her. The lights in the
other office buildings came on one by one as the sky grew dark. She
sipped from her mug of tea. He toyed with his soda can, spinning it
mindlessly in his hand. He enjoyed the time he spent with her after
his hypnotic sessions.

"So, what's going on now?"

She was surprised at the gruff tone to his voice. She answered
quickly, "Going on?"

He placed the soda can on the corner of her desk. He leaned back in his chair, his long legs sprawled, his hands resting on his belt. "So what's up with you and this Aris character?"

"Carlos, you're talking about him as if he were someone else. He is you."

He tipped his head and stared at her. He finally spoke. "So I'm a thousand-year-old vampire, huh? Sarah, I've told you before, you need some therapy." He laughed, reaching for the soda once again.

"You know exactly what I mean. He's a part of your subconscious." She stood and paced in front of the window. "It's a deeper part of you telling us a story. But that story has a deep meaning for you today. I think we're on the brink to discover what that meaning is and how it relates to what is going on in your life right now."

"Sarah, do you honestly believe that? I mean that all this vampire crap can have something to do with why my life's so screwed up?"

"First of all, your life is getting better all the time. You have a job. You're out of trouble. Colleen told me you've even done some sketches. I didn't know you could draw."

He glanced at the floor before he met her eyes, "Yeah, well I never tried before. That day at the museum got me thinking so I started messing around with a pencil. Picked up a couple of books at the bookstore. I got a lot of tips from there." He looked embarrassed. "I'm not good or anything. It's just something to do in my spare time."

"Colleen said they were very good. Will you bring them in to show me?"

"Sure," he stood, moving toward the door.

"Carlos, what's wrong."

"Nothing Sarah, just quit trying to make me into something I'm not. I'm no artist." He turned the knob and left the room. The door clicked softly as he closed it.

CHAPTER 32

Sarah looked out her window, sipping morning coffee. Sunday's were always quiet. The newspaper was scattered around her on her bed. She tried to read but she couldn't concentrate. Her thoughts were full of Aris and Carlos and the man of her intense dreams. Carlos and Aris. How did the one fit with the other? So different, yet so alike.

It had been months and Aris continued to be a dominating force in the sessions. Sarah thought another subconscious story might surface eventually, but it didn't. She knew their work together greatly reduced Carlos' anger, his frustration. She saw definite changes in him. So did he and he appreciated them. He liked his newfound discipline, his work ethic. He was taking night classes, excelling in them. His world was expanding as his knowledge was growing.

His confidence was coming from his personal growth, his self-awareness, not his fists and his anger. He began to see himself as a man with inner strength, to understand that there were more important things than being part of a pack of petty criminals. He kept his word and his job. He read books and searched to find a deeper part of himself. Yet it seemed that in his subconscious, there was no one but Aris.

And Aris? What of this being? What about the stories he told?

How did Carlos know about things happening five hundred years ago? She never before questioned her findings with her clients. She knew their stories were from the subconscious, authenticity wasn't important, just content. But his hypnotic tales weren't just stories. She was being taught history by someone who was there. How? Why?

The harsh sound of the ringing of the phone snapped her attention to the present. Loud music blasted from the receiver as she answered.

"Hello?"

"I told you to lay off. It was tires last time, next time it will be you. I've given you way too many chances. You just used the last one." The voice was barely audible, the words bitten off. "This is your last warning hypno lady. And I mean last." The phone went dead in her hand.

Sarah caught her breath, placing the receiver on the night table. "I have to talk to Bob and Colleen." She whispered to herself, trying to calm her racing heart. "I have to tell them everything."

#

Colleen waved as Sarah crossed to her table. Sarah sat down across from her friend, an alarmed expression on her face.

"What's up, hon? What's the matter?"

"Colleen, it's about Carlos." She was careful in presenting her story. She still didn't want to involve Carlos with the police, but she needed help.

"What about Carlos?" She leaned in to hear better in the noisy restaurant. It was late Sunday brunch time and the deli was full of families eating and laughing. "What's going on?"

"I think his old gang is trying to get him involved again."

"Yeah?" Her brow puckered in concern. "How so?"

"Well." Sarah wasn't sure how much to tell. She was glad the waitress came to the table to take her order. It gave her a moment to think. She looked at the menu without seeing the words, ordering coffee and scrambled eggs out of habit. When they had privacy, she spoke. "I've gotten a few phone calls from one of them."

"Phone calls? How did they get your number?"

"I don't honestly know. All I know is that they want Carlos back and he refuses to see or talk to them."

"Do you know who it is who called you?"

"No, not for sure but I have a good idea. He contacted Carlos's mother. She knows who he is."

Irritation showed through Colleen's voice when she spoke. "When did this happen, this thing with his mother?"

Sarah looked at the coffee mug as the waitress set it on the table. She glanced at Colleen quickly, "A while back."

"A while back? Was this before or after the tire slashing? Why the hell didn't you tell me then? What's going on with you Sarah?"

"I didn't want to get the police involved. I don't want anything to stand in his way of moving forward and out of the lousy life he's led." Her tone was apologetic, "I want him to succeed."

"You think I don't? What the hell is the matter with you? I'm here to help him, not hurt him. Don't you remember who sent him to you in the first place?"

"Yeah, I know. But I don't want any of this to be official." She looked directly into her friend's eyes. "I'm coming to you as a friend. As someone who knows him and knows how different his life is becoming. God, Colleen, I want him safe and happy more than anyone knows."

Colleen leaned closer and reached across the table to take her hands in her own. "I know it." Her voice softened as she spoke, "I know it. And I'm here to help both of you. I think I know more how you feel about Carlos than you do."

Sarah jerked her hands away. "Don't start with that romantic crap. He's a client and a friend, nothing more. He's just someone who is so deserving, so basically good. He's come such a long way. I don't want him pushed back into the gutter."

Colleen took her hands again and squeezed. "I know, I know. I want to help him too. We'll take care of this, nothing official, but Sarah, I'm going to have to tell Bob. We need his help here."

The word was clipped as she spoke. "No!"

"Yes, hon, we need more information than either you or I have. Bob won't turn cop on us. He likes Carlos and more important than that, he respects how hard he is working to turn his life around. Sarah, I told you, it takes a village to raise one person up, a village, not just two hard working women. We need help and my husband will be glad to do it."

Silence reigned for a moment, then Sarah spoke quietly, "Okay, ask Bob. I'm just at a place where I don't know what to do next."

Colleen nodded her head, "So what did the guy say to you on the phone?"

Sarah sipped the hot coffee, and then began her story.

#

It was early afternoon the next day when they met. The air was hot, the high humidity made their lightweight clothes stick to them as the three friends walked through the park. Even in the heat, the sidewalk was crowded with people.

Bob motioned to a bench that was vacant. He placed Sarah between he and Colleen. She wasn't sure if it was to protect her or to make sure they both could give her equal hell for not telling them sooner.

"There's no use hashing over why you didn't trust us to come to us sooner." There was controlled anger in his tone when Bob spoke. He had demanded to meet with Colleen and Sarah as soon as his wife told him about the threats.

"It isn't about trust. Honestly." She reached to take each one of their hands. "I trust you implicitly. I just didn't want to get anyone else involved, most certainly not the police." She let go their hands, folding hers in her lap. She looked like a contrite little girl caught being naughty. But she wasn't a little girl and this wasn't a petty incident. It was serious business.

"Look Sarah, we both want to help you and we both like Carlos." Colleen touched her friend's arm. "We'll find a way, won't we Bob?" She looked at her husband for back-up.

"Sure we will." He touched her other arm. "But I'm going to report this, Sarah. We've got to put a stop to it now. I'll put a tale on Manu. We don't have any proof it's him, but he's a suspicious character and he's always in trouble. I'm sure there's a good reason to have him watched. Maybe we'll be able to get him off the street without involving either you or Carlos. Don't mention any of this to him until I tell you. I'll do my best to keep him out of it. And I'll keep you informed so you'll feel more comfortable."

"Do you think you could really do that?"

"Sure, I can do anything. I'm a cop." He laughed and stood up, "Now, come on. Let's go get a hotdog."

Sarah felt glad and relieved when she linked arms with her friends; they crossed the lawn to the hotdog vendor, the grass damp beneath their feet.

CHAPTER 33

C̲ARLOS HAVARRO, transcript, session 22, August 13

As I waited for the Queen in her private audience chamber, I gazed out the window. The clouds covered the sky in a thick blanket of grays and dark purples. The bushes in the garden hung their heads with the weight of the rain water beating down upon them, yet I was warm, satiated from my hunt of the morning.

Upon arising, my thirst turned to hunger so the early light found me riding out to find fresh blood. I rode before the storm began and as luck would have it, I happened upon prey. It was a quick and clean kill, no pain to the mortal, no soil to my clothes. I rode back to the castle just as the first drops began to fall. Dry and content, I entered my rooms to find a summons from the Queen. I wondered at her hapless victim on this occasion.

Laughter filled the outer room as Anne and her ladies entered the chamber. I bowed my finest courtier's bow. When she saw me, she turned to dismiss her court. We stood alone in her chamber. She was dressed in blue velvet trimmed in gold. Blue and green velvet seemed to be her favorites. Her headpiece was embroidered in threads of gold, laden with golden pearls. I wondered at her small neck holding such a weight.

She moved to my side, standing silently, looking at the sodden garden beneath the window. I waited for her to speak. After some time, she did.

"Aris, I have another situation for you." She continued to stare out the window. "This is more dangerous and demands a greater loyalty than the first." She turned to me. "Are you prepared?"

"As always, my lady, I am at the disposal of my sovereign."

"This will be more difficult, filled with even greater danger than the first."

"I have no fear where my Queen is concerned." I tipped my head toward her, smiling.

She moved a short distance from the window, then returned. Leaning toward me, she whispered. "It is Katharine of Aragon. It is the false Queen. She must be eliminated. While she lives, there are many who would have her on the throne instead of me. When the time is right, will you stand for me?"

I was silent. This was a woman without conscience. I felt no remorse in killing Wolsey. He was a cruel old man who deserved to die. Had he not been the death of my Elizabeth? But Katharine? She was a just Queen, still loved by the people. It was clear, the love of her loyal subjects was the cause of the death sentence from this vile woman before me.

"Your Grace,…"

"Wait, before you answer. I have proof that Katherine worked with Wolsey to send Elizabeth Wyatt to the Emperor's court. It was a relation to her that desired an English maid to breed. Katherine herself chose Elizabeth. She convinced Elizabeth you would never return. She would be left unmarried at court. She kept a secret of the ancient age and ill health of her grand uncle. It was she as well as Wolsey who caused the death of the woman you loved."

"How do you know…?"

"Thomas Wyatt informed me when the court was notified of her death. Katherine was in partnership with Wolsey. She held the sword that murdered your beloved."

I stood still. I burned. I turned to ice. I knew what I would do. I would *avenge the woman I loved even if it meant my demise. What could be offered by eternal life without my chosen mate? Everlasting emptiness, nothing more. After a moment of silence, I nodded my acceptance of the challenge, my aching, non-beating heart crying out for retribution for my lost love.*

And still, I love her. Through time and lifetimes. Sarah, can I have found her once again? Will I possess her at last?"

Sarah gasped. She was drawn to this vampire from a different age no matter how hard she fought against her desire. She longed to separate him from Carlos, to know him in real time. To feel his arms embrace her, his lips against her own. Desire that wouldn't be ignored awoke within her. Steeling herself against her own yearning, she spoke. "Please, go on with the story of Katherine."

"*If I must.*" A moment of silence, then he spoke again.

"*I was on the cold road to Kimbolton Castle on my second mission as a messenger of death. I carried no regret I would be the disease that would kill the first wife of the King, the woman who sent my only love to her grave. It was my sworn duty to uphold the monarchy and my place within it so I rode quickly to my destination, eager to put to an end the life of the second murderer of my Elizabeth.*

I entered the castle with a false letter from the King to his abandoned wife. It was, yet again, another request for a divorce. The present Queen knew Katharine would renounce the letter and the accusation of an untrue marriage, but agreement was not her purpose. Getting my person into the castle was.

As an envoy from the royal house, I was treated with great favor. I had a suite of rooms with servants to meet my every need. Katharine of Aragon hoped I would speak for her to the King so she saw to it that I was made comfortable. Angry beast that I was, I took every advantage of the hospitality given to me.

Luck would have it that the weather turned impassable. I was kept at the castle for a few desolate weeks, weeks of ebbing life and slow death.

Each night I would climb the outer wall into the false Queen's sleeping chamber, injecting her with my deadly venom. Each day she would appear a bit more weakened, more confused. The guard was doubled at her door. Yet, night by night, I executed my charge from Anne, watching the King's first wife grow weak and pale. Her physicians were called. One by one, they proclaimed the wasting sickness. Her slow death progressed as I added venom to her blood while she slept.

In months past, Katherine sent letters to Henry begging he allow their daughter, Mary, to be with her in her sorrow. Henry refused time and again. Now, in her last days, the roads were impassable for further letters. I knew it was Anne that tormented her old rival through the voice of the King. I marveled at her confidence, her control.

It was clear to all except Anne. Henry would do anything, love anyone, murder anyone he felt stood in the way of his design for a true, male heir. No one was safe from his hand. I heard in the court she lost another child. Henry's Kingly eye began to wander and it was the maid Jane Seymour who caught his attention. Her family jumped to the challenge to defeat the Boleyns, to take over as first family of the royal court. It was his interest in another woman that drove Anne to take her last measure to assure her position as undisputed Queen.

And so, Katharine of Aragon died of the wasting sickness, alone, without her only child at her side. Did I feel sorrow? In my bitterness, I felt only justification. What do you expect of the undead?

Before the body of the Spanish Queen was even cold, I was on the road back to London. As I left court, there were rumors the Queen was once again with child. I hurried to tell her of our good fortune at Kimbolton, knowing my tidings would give her courage and security.

I arrived at the palace yet was held back from seeing Anne. One of the court midwives told me the Queen knew of Katharine's death. She had been rejoicing when she felt pains. Immediately, she was retired to her rooms where, at fifteen weeks or thereabouts, the Queen gave birth to a premature boy child.

I stood outside her chamber door as the King rushed by me to her bedside. I heard her sob and scream through the open door as the Queen's women carried the soiled, bloodied sheets from her room. Over the sounds of her tears, I heard the King speak. "You have killed him." The words were quiet, full of sorrow.

"I did not. He came too early." She sobbed, hanging her head. "I did not kill him."

His reply was no longer soft, but a bellow, "You have murdered my son."

Weak with exhaustion yet feigning hope for the future, she spoke. "We will have another."

"There will be no other." The man who had turned England upside down for her stormed from her room. "I will see you no more."

I could see through the open door to her chamber. She fell back onto her great bed, her emotionless eyes staring at the royal canopy above her. She lay still as if dead.

Henry mounted his great horse. He rode far and fast from the castle, away from Anne to his new interest, the Lady Jane.

Anne cried, screaming for the King when she was told he was gone. She called for her brother. I was told George lay next to her on her bed. He stayed with her, consoling her for three days without leaving her chamber. In desolation, Anne turned her face to the stone wall refusing to respond to anyone.

Yet, the day after the still birth, a Queen's messenger arrived at my chamber. He handed me a purse filled with precious jewels. He presented me a new sword, the hilt encrusted with rubies and burnished gold. I knew all was for the life of the dead Queen. I moved the sword left and right, marveling at its perfect balance.

Do I disappoint you, Sarah? But you must see that I can be only that which I am. And yet, somehow, I know you feel compassion for me. I can sense it."

"I don't know if it's compassion for you or the absurdity of the situation that keeps me waiting for our next meeting." She spoke truthfully to the vampire.

"My joy, Sarah, is that you wait for our next meeting."

Carlos didn't sit with Sarah after their session. He rose from the recliner, leaving the office after a short good bye.

CHAPTER 34

"Why have you missed your last two sessions and what about a phone call?" She hurried down the street, trying to hear him through the noise of traffic and the weak signal on her cell phone.

"I said I'm sorry." Carlos sounded disconnected from his words. Sarah didn't know if it was the cell reception or if he was putting space between them.

"I don't get it. What's going on?"

"I honestly don't know. I just feel like I'm losing myself somewhere here and I don't like it." He sounded irritated at having to explain himself.

"You're not losing yourself, you're gaining new parts to yourself. You're seeing more of life and embracing it." She sighed. "I know it's hard to have so many changes happen in such a short time but they're all good."

She paused but he didn't answer.

"Please, don't pull away from this future you're beginning to build. I know it feels pretty weird but, that's because it's all new."

"It isn't that, I just feel so out of myself so much of the time. Work, reading, this new thing with sketching. I feel like I'm losing something I've had all my life."

"You're losing nothing, you're gaining a life." She reached the door of her office building. Her cell signal would drop when she stepped inside so she stood outside the revolving door to finish her conversation.

"Look, I'm standing in the street and it's hotter than hell. Will you just please come in on Friday?" The only sound she heard was the traffic on the street. "Carlos?"

"Okay, I'll see you Friday, same time still okay?"

"Same time is great."

#

Perspiration dotted Sarah's forehead as she and Maggie hurried down the street. A hot wind was blowing, the humid air felt like a steam bath on their faces. "If I wasn't so hungry, I would have just skipped lunch."

"Not a good idea, besides there isn't anything going on this afternoon."

They ducked into the deli and settled into a booth, both reaching for the menu. Soon their orders were placed and tall glasses of iced tea were placed on the table before them.

"When it's this hot, iced tea sure hits the spot."

Maggie grinned. "A nice frozen margarita would hit a higher spot."

Sarah laughed. "In the middle of the day?"

"Hot is hot, doesn't matter the time of day." Maggie shook her head, reaching for her straw. "Well, this will just have to do." She sipped the cold amber liquid, smiling. "Hey, it's better than I thought it would be."

The women chatted about the August weather and their predictions for an early autumn until the waitress brought their lunches.

"This salad isn't half bad. I guess you can get used to anything." Maggie poured every drop of the creamy dressing on the raw vegetables. She took a bite, added salt and smiled. "Just what the doctor ordered. And speaking of that, what have you done with Gorgeous? Have you stopped seeing him? I haven't asked you but I've wanted to for the last couple of weeks."

"He's just adjusting to his life. There have been so many changes for him in such a short period of time. It would be difficult for anyone."

"So did you tell him you didn't want to see him anymore?" Maggie's curiosity had the better of her. "What's going on? I hate being the last to know."

"Nothing Maggie. He just took a break for a few weeks. He'll be back on Friday."

Her assistant's eyes lit up. "I was afraid I would never get to look upon that face again. A fate worse than death, I tell you."

"Well, he'll be in on Friday. Same time, same place as they say." She spoke the words with a great deal more confidence than she felt. She wasn't sure of her position with Carlos any more. And that fact wasn't comfortable.

#

He came through the door and sat quietly across from her. "Look Sarah, I'm sorry about the sessions. I just needed some time away from everything to think."

She leaned forward. "And so, what do you think?"

He stared out the window at the late afternoon sun reflecting on the tall buildings for a few moments. He turned to look at her.

"I think I've become way too attached to you. You pretty much became the most important person in my life. And the vamp? The vamp became who I wanted to become, not who I am. I know I've acted like a kid sometimes, but I'm feeling things I've never felt before, thinking about things I didn't even know existed in my world. It's just been a little too much and a little too fast. That's all."

"If I've pushed you or misled you in any way, Carlos, I'm so sorry.

It's been confusing for me as well. And I know that's no excuse but it's a reason." She rose and moved from behind the desk to stand just in front of him. "You are the most unusual client I have ever had, it's been fascinating and bewildering." She sat on the corner of her desk facing him, her red toenails peeking out from the cut out at the front of her shoes. "I can't deny how much you mean to me personally. I would be lying and you would know it. I want only the best for you."

"I really thought about it after you called me and I've made a final decision. No more changing my mind. Sarah, we are so close to the end of this story, I just can't quit. I decided that I want to know what happened to Aris, why he is here now and how he got here. I don't want to be away from you anymore. I'll take what I can get."

He stood and took her hands in his. "So I'm back. And I'm staying until the end. Again." He smiled. He released her hands, stepping toward the recliner. "'I'm a better man for knowing you'. Isn't that what the leading man says to the heroine in movies?" He laid down resting his head on the cushions of the chair. "Okay, let's keep up the good work. One step at a time."

Sarah's head was whirling. He was here one day, gone the next, then back again. She was confused but refused to worry about it while he was in her office. As always, she allowed herself to fall easily into their past pattern. She picked up the recorder and moved to her chair. It was the most natural thing in the world to begin the familiar induction, "Focus on your breathing."

CARLOS HAVARRO, transcript, Session 23. September 3

After Anne lost the child, the King literally disappeared from the palace and her life. Each day he would ride to the hunt with his gentlemen, the Seymours were always among the first chosen, those who rode closest to him. George Boleyn lost his high rank in the King's company just as

Anne lost her position in his heart.

History has been unkind to Henry. Yes, he was selfish beyond redemption, however, many of his darkest decisions were seeded from his desire for an heir. I do not make excuses for the King, yet Anne promised him a son. She did not deliver. Henry, no more than a spoiled child himself, saw her failure to produce an heir as betrayal. He loved Anne as he had never before loved nor would ever again. But he loved England more. And his vanity, his public display of virility more even than England, so he was left with what he saw as no other choice. To rid himself of yet another Queen; to find a new one who would give him a son. He presented Cromwell with the puzzle of ridding him of Anne.

Cromwell hated her. It was with joy he received Henry's request. And find a way, he did.

The King knew he could not use the same excuse to marry a new Queen as he used with Katharine so a new tactic must be found.

Cromwell trumped charges of the Queen's adultery with members of her court and under torture, her musician, Smeaton, admitted to the charges. He gave the judges names of others the Queen supposedly used to betray the King, including her own brother.

As if knowing what was to come, her ladies and her gentlemen began to drift away from her rooms to find their way into the apartments of Jane Seymour. It was with a light heart they left her. Anne had never been an easy friend and her title made her even more petulant and spoiled. She alienated any who would have stood for her with her evil tongue. Her uncle was glad to have her lose her power and, in time, even her sister left her side.

It was alone, without a friend she faced her judges, so eloquently defending herself. Yet it was too late. The die had been cast. Anne was proclaimed guilty of treason. She was sentenced to death along with the men who were also unjustly accused.

Her brother and his friends were held in the tower awaiting their execution. Anne was placed in a room with a window looking down on tower green. She watched as the scaffold was built where they would all die. The men were executed in May. Two days later, Anne met the headsman. She proclaimed her loyalty to the King and died well.

On the day she died, Henry proclaimed his love for Jane Seymour, his next wife.

I waited quietly to find my own fate. Richard visited me often in my rooms. He told me the counsel knew of my action with Katharine. He stood for me, he said. Akira had not made a final decision as to what would be my punishment. Khansu was determined that I should be eliminated for my misdeed yet she still cared for me as a son. She strove to bring her mate to her way of thinking.

Richard told of counsel meetings again and again debating my execution. Akira was the only one who wanted to allow me to continue. All the elders saw my actions as disobedience to the ancient law, disobedience performed not once but twice. It was against their judgement that I was pardoned at my first indiscretion. Their fear was for the coven, their own authority as leaders over the members. If I were allowed to continue, what would stop others from doing the same thing, killing because they desired to kill and nothing more? They spoke of the danger I brought to the coven with my actions, my disregard for the kindness of the counsel after the Wolsey affair. Akira's determination to keep me began to lessen as the arguments for my destruction were repeatedly spoken. Finally, even Sebastian was against me.

So I waited. There was no escape from their judgment. There was no place to go where they would not find me, nothing I could do to prevent my execution if they chose that as my end. The days were interminable, the nights, longer than the days.

It was with deep sorrow that he continued to speak. *"I waited much as you wait, Sarah, for the outcome of our story."* There was silence and when he spoke again, his voice was once more powerful and in command.

At last, the day came of my sentencing. I faced the dais on my knees.

The soft velvet cushions were no longer there for my comfort. The hard, cold marble floor matched the look of ice in the eyes of the vampire King and Queen, sitting on their thrones above me.

"Aris, you were forgiven when none before you has ever been forgiven." Khansu leaned forward, speaking softly, yet his words were full of anger and recrimination. "You ignored your great fortune at being allowed to continue without punishment for your first transgression." He stood, facing his mate, "And you, Akira, were paramount in his forgiveness."

She rose from her seat, standing, motionless before him, unable to deny the accusation.

"This time there will be no forgiveness." He turned back to lock eyes with me as he spoke of my judgment. "This time, you will pay with your existence for your selfish crime. You were manipulated once again by the vixen, Anne. Yet this second time, she spoke false about her rival. You murdered an innocent, one without blood on her hands. And so, for that and that alone, you will be eliminated."

Akira caught my eyes for an instant, then turned her back to me. I saw compassion in her glance yet I knew my fate was sealed.

"Sebastian, take this traitor to the law to the executioner." It was finished, the royal couple walked from the room leaving me to my fate.

I rose from my knees as Sebastian stepped beside me. "Come with me foolish one." He gripped my elbow, guiding me through the few members of the elite counsel invited to my trial. They were silent, casting their eyes down as I passed by.

"Why did you do it?"

I did it to avenge my lost sweetheart. I did it because I could, nothing more and nothing less. I did not answer him. My unbeating heart broke at my transgression. I felt no sorrow when I thought she was the second hand that murdered my Elizabeth. Now I knew the truth. She had been faultless. I ached for my crime, if I could have wept, I would have.

The halls were dark, lit only by the candle held in Sebastian's hand.

We walked slowly. After a time, he asked the question once again. Still I gave no answer. We continued in strained silence until the light of the candle displayed a huge, wooden door at the end of the passage. Sebastian slowed his steps; he spoke softly.

"I cannot let them end you yet you must be punished." He was torn between our close fellowship and his loyalty to the coven. " You have betrayed the law. You are a convicted traitor yet you are still my friend." We stood in silence for an eternity . He spoke again. "You must face the executioner and end the life of this body, but I will not burn you. I will not end your existence. I will carry your body to a deeper pit to leave it there. No one will know you have not been fully destroyed. You must take your essence from the Catacombs never to return. Go far from this place, disappear forever from your kind. "

Gratitude filled me as I reached for his hand. "I will do so."

"Do I have your word?"

I gave him my truest word. He embraced me quickly. We crossed the few remaining steps to the entrance of the chamber of execution. We passed over the threshold.

A large stone slab rested in the center of the room; a vampire in a black cloak with a heavy hood stood next to it. What little of his face that was visible was covered in a black mask with slits for his eyes. Resting on a small stone table next to the slab were a long polished wooden stake and a huge mallet, the tools of my destruction. .

Resolutely I moved to the slab, standing silently, observing my final resting place as this man that I was. I heard the door close as Sebastian stepped outside the room. I was grateful that all vampire tradition called for privacy for any ritual be it joining of mates or execution. Had there been other witnesses, I would not be here with you in this moment.

I lay down, closing my eyes, waiting for the pain of the stake. Sarah, I will not take you into that horror. Just know it was swift, the body was empty of my essence from the first blow. From that moment, I seemed to be floating just above it all exactly as it had been during the time of Alexander yet very different. Now, I knew what I was. I knew a disembodied spirit is free to move about unfettered. I still was conscious. I could once again inhabit a human body.

I watched as Sebastian re-entered the room. He spoke quietly with the executioner. I watched as the black clad man left the chamber. Sebastian stood, looking at the dead remains before him. He whispered, "Remember your promise. You must never break it."

He lifted the dead carcass in his powerful arms, carrying it from the room. I paused only a moment then left the chamber, the Catacombs and the palace. I left the world that I had come to know as mine. I floated, an essence in search of a host, a home for my spirit. I vowed then that my formless eternity would be spent in aiding mankind in whatever way possible as small restitution for the blameless life I took without true reason.

"And so Sarah, here we are at the end of yet another tale. It seems all of my stories are sad and of death. For that I am sorry. My deepest hope is you can forgive me for taking an unblemished life. I am not evil. I do not rejoice in death. I was manipulated by a vile malevolent woman. She used my grief and despair to her own ends. All horror is now placed behind me. I seek a fresh existence. Your pardon will give me hope I can be at the beginning of a new story filled with joy and life."

"Of course, I forgive you. You were used as a tool of execution. I understand your feelings of retribution for the death of your loved one. Anyway, all of that happened in the very distant past. But, Aris, how did you get here, in the twenty first century?" She hoped to draw him on; she was not ready to end their conversation.

"That is for another time, Sarah. If I answer all of your curiosity, you will have no further need of me. And so, I bid you farewell for today."

She sighed knowing that once he said goodbye, the session was closed. Emptiness pervaded the space without him, an unexplainable void. She sat in silence for a moment as she always did when Aris left, then began to count Carlos into real time.

CHAPTER 35

Bob saw his wife and her friend as he walked in the door to the theatre. He joined the two women in line as they stood to buy tickets for the movie.

"Hey ladies, would you like an escort for the evening?" He hugged his wife and kissed Sarah on the cheek. "It sure is hot tonight. I hoped the temperature might cool down when the sun set but it looks like it's a no go on that."

Colleen snuggled under his arm and grinned. "It's not too bad besides, we'll be inside in a minute where it's nice and cool."

Bob wrapped his free arm around Sarah, looking over her head at the line. "Is this line moving at all? I knew we should have gotten tickets ahead of time."

"Relax husband. It's slow but it's moving."

"Sarah, I was going to call you today, but when Colleen said we were all going to the movie tonight, I decided to wait to talk to you."

Sarah knew it must be something related to the Carlos/Manu saga so she just nodded.

"I think Manu must know we're tailing him. There's been no activity between him and the rest of his gang in a few weeks. The group hasn't been together or at least not in a way that my people have seen. I can keep on it for another week or so but if there's no action, I have to back off. I won't pull everybody off it, but I've got a limit as to what I can do. I'm trying to keep this whole thing quiet so Carlos isn't implicated but without anything else to go on, I can't justify the men on the punk's tail."

"I don't get it." Colleen nudged him to move forward as the line began to snake closer to the door.

"There's nothing to get. There's no activity. Maybe he figured he was being tracked so he's laying low or maybe he's given up on the Carlos thing. I don't know, but it's quiet with that bunch right now."

"I'm glad." Sarah spoke with more conviction than she felt. "I hope it all just disappears and everybody can get on with their lives."

Bob turned to walk down the hall to their movie but Colleen grabbed him by the back of his shirt. "Oh no you don't, dude. I want popcorn."

He groaned as he turned to look at the refreshment stand. "Not another line."

She took his hand and maneuvered her way to stand at the end of the shortest queue of people. "What's a movie without popcorn?"

"How about a better seat in the theatre."

"You knew I was a popcorn kind of girl when you married me."

He ruffled her spiked hair with one hand while he rested his other arm on her shoulder as he settled in for the wait.

Sarah enjoyed the Colleen and Bob show every time the three of them were together. This time was no different. Their relationship was so comfortable and caring, best friends and lovers, husband and wife.

#

Her bed linen felt cool to the touch after the warm ride home from the theatre. She slid her arm beneath the pillow and cradled her head in the crook of her elbow. Sarah smiled as she thought of her two friends and the easy way they loved one other. As she wondered if she would ever find that kind of complete relationship, her thoughts drifted to Aris and Carlos. Soon she floated into a sweet sleep.

Her dream began where the movie ended except it was she and not the female lead that walked down the forest path with the tall, well-built man. He carried a picnic basket in one hand and a rolled blanket under his free arm. And, this time the man who walked beside her was clearly Carlos. He wore jeans and a light tee shirt. She was dressed in denim shorts and a loose tank top. It was a perfect day as the sun filtered down through the trees and a gentle breeze ruffled their hair.

They stepped from the path, crossing over a felled tree. Before long the dense forest opened into a perfectly circular clearing. Tall meadow grass and the remnants of late blooming spring flowers covered the ground inviting them to share their lunch in the sweet smelling glade.

Carlos spread the blanket and beckoned her to sit next to him. She took off her shoes and socks then settled in for lunch. The picnic basket was full of wonderful things; hard cheese and crisp French bread, sweet purple grapes and a bottle of rich, red wine. There were napkins and crystal glasses nestled in the bottom of the basket along with a corkscrew and a small tablecloth.

He spread the cloth then popped a grape into his mouth. He grinned as he plucked another one from the bunch and touched it against Sarah's lips. She drew it in and smiled as she bit into it, anticipating the sweet flavor of warm juice teasing her tongue. But the taste was bland as if it had been picked too soon.

He broke off a piece of the golden cheese and fed it to her. It smelled wonderful but again, as she chewed, it tasted like sawdust in her mouth. She sighed and lay down with her head in his lap. He stroked her hair softly. His demeanor was a bit odd, off somehow. Just not quite Carlos but the look in his eye as he bent to kiss her was of pure love. His breath was warm and its fragrance burned into her senses. She tasted the sweet flavor of his lips as the tip of her tongue gently pressed them open. Her hand trembled just slightly as it rested against his cool smooth cheek. She caught her breath as he kissed her throat, nuzzled her ear.

Without knowing quite how, she found herself lying nude wrapped in his arms. He stroked her soft back then he turned her to rain gentle restrained kisses along her spine. His lips came to rest just below her waist and traced small circles in the shallow hollows on either side of her lower back. As desire awakened in her, she longed to feel his weight on her, to feel the power of his manhood. She rolled to face him.

He stroked her neck, her bosom. His kisses grew more demanding, more intimate. Gasping for breath and drunk with lust, she yearned for more of him. His skin was smooth as carved marble and her hands traced his perfect muscles as she pressed him into her. He entered her, velvet into silk. They moved together as in a wild dance until her raging passion made her labor for breath. A deep shudder convulsed her and she floated on waves of what seemed endless bliss. He moaned deeply as he found his release then gently wrapped his arms around her, drawing her tight against him. They lay like that for minutes or hours; dreamtime is without watches or clocks.

When, at last, he moved, he kissed her neck then nuzzled her ear. She smiled as he sat up to open the wine. He poured two glasses and the ruby liquid glistened in the late afternoon sun. It had a strange fragrance for wine. The scent of salt and rust filled her nostrils. As she lifted her glass to drink, she understood why. It wasn't wine in the glass. It was blood. Without a second thought, she tipped the rim to her lips and drank deeply.

Sarah was startled awake by a sharp pain on the corner of her lower lip. She had bitten it hard as she slept and the warm taste of her own blood flooded her tongue. She hurried to the bathroom to rinse her mouth and when she spit the water into her white sink, it swirled in red spirals down the drain. She wondered if she should talk to Bonnie about her nighttime adventures then decided against it. They were too intimate and carried too much meaning to share.

#

"Carlos was my only appointment for today and he just called. They asked him to work so he won't be coming in. How about we close up shop?" Sarah stood in the door of her office as she spoke to Maggie.

"Sounds great to me. Want to go to lunch?" Her assistant turned off her computer. Happily, she began gathering her belongings.

"Thanks Maggie, I think I'll stay here and just go over a few case histories. I really need to catch up on a couple of clients before next week. We're super busy on Tuesday after not working on Labor Day."

"It gets that way after any holiday. It's like people look for any excuse to get stressed out, don't they?" She turned off her desk lamp. "Glad I'm not like that." Her smile was smug as she lifted her hand to wave goodbye. "See you on Tuesday boss."

Sarah laughed as she crossed the office, locking the door behind her friend.

The light outside the window was soft and golden. Sarah settled down in the recliner with the Havarro file on her lap. She began to read from the first page. So much and so little had happened. Nothing and everything. Her life was changed. Carlos was intertwined with her and so was his alter-ego. As she read page after page, story after story, she wondered where the tale would end.

The last few months, she was torn between fear and intrigue.

The possibility that there really might be such a thing as vampires terrified her. She methodically ignored the thought because, somehow, Aris had managed to captivate her. She had no fear of him. There was substance and honor in his words. He was more than a man, more than any man she had ever known. And, real or not, when he spoke through Carlos, he spoke with a deep desire for her. Could she be falling in love with him, with someone who was either a figment of Carlos' vivid imagination who didn't truly exist or a real being who was the lead in some bizarrely real horror story? She had no answers to any of the questions that plagued her and the questions just wouldn't go away. The only thing she knew for sure was when she considered never again being in his presence, she felt interminably sad, empty, and alone — somehow more vulnerable than she had ever felt before. Was this what it felt like to slowly lose one's mind, or was it the first time she truly understood how love and passion defy all logic?

#

A sudden gentle breeze broke the intense heat as they approached the front porch of her mother's house. The smells of bar-b-que coming from the backyard were wonderful. Sarah was sorry Bob and Colleen couldn't make the traditional Labor Day picnic the Hagan's hosted every year but she was glad Carlos agreed to still be her guest. The half-way house was no place for anyone to spend a holiday.

The late afternoon sun reflected off the few white clouds, turning them intensely pink and mauve. She always looked forward to twilight. It was sad and beautiful all at the same time. Standing on the porch, she turned to watch the sunset behind the trees. It was such a bittersweet time of day, that place that was neither light nor dark. She opened the door.

They heard laughter coming from the back yard. Sarah took Carlos' hand, leading him through the house, following the good smells.

"Mom? Gran? We're here."

"In the kitchen honey."

She felt Carlos stiffen at the sound of her mother's voice. "What's the matter?"

He stopped, "I don't know Sarah. Maybe this isn't such a good idea."

She grabbed his elbow with her free hand and pushed him forward. "Come on. It's free food and my family is looking forward to meeting you."

"That isn't the question. The question is why I am here in the first place?"

#

"So how did it go?"

"What do you mean, go?" Sarah held the phone between her ear and her shoulder as she buttered her toast placing it on a blue and white saucer.

"You know, your mother and Carlos."

"Good grief, Colleen. It's not like I took a boyfriend home with me. It was Carlos." Her frustration was plain in her voice.

"I'm sorry hon. It's just he's not the normal guy you would bring home for dinner. Hang on a minute, I have to order."

Sarah heard her friend order into a loud speaker at a fast food restaurant, then talk to the window person as she claimed her food.

"Sorry hon, I just hate to be on the phone and treat the people helping me like they don't exist." The sound of bags rustling interfered with their conversation for a moment.

"There, I parked. Now I can have lunch with you." More sounds of paper then a question, mumbled over a mouthful of hamburger. "So, how'd it go?"

Giving up, Sarah answered with a sigh. "It went fine. Just fine."

"Yeah? I'm really glad." Sound of a soda being sucked up a straw was another brief interruption in their conversation. "You've really helped him come a long way."

"He's been doing it himself. It isn't me. I just believe in him. He's doing all the work." She carried her plate and coffee mug to her living room, placed them on the end table and sat down. Taking the phone into her hand, she swung her legs onto the sofa, leaning back into the cushions.

"So, what did your mother think of him?"

"Honestly, Colleen. Give it up, please."

#

CARLOS HAVARRO, transcript, session 24, September 10

My aching soul returned to the netherworld. There I floated without form or voice, only thought. It was the same disjointed otherworldly state I occupied so many human years before yet very different. I knew I was unfettered, free to move, to study, to learn.

Being no more than thought, I imagined the forest and I was there. This was new. This was exquisite. For the first time in my existence, I knew what complete freedom meant. I was unhampered by the bonds of time and space, a consciousness without weight and matter. I was able to travel great distances within split seconds, I could hear without ears, see without eyes. I was a silent witness to the unfolding life that surrounded me.

I felt time pass only in the changing from dark to light and light to dark. I watched Queens and Kings play a human chess game with the people in their charge. I watched governments change and governing bodies remain the same. All was new, time and again and yet, all remained the same. How can I express this to you who are bound so tightly by the encumbrance of a physical body?

I left England; I visited distant lands. Understanding all language made knowledge easily accessible to me. I studied humans as a species. I learned things all men share regardless of where they live or how they live or what they worship. Yes, Sarah, there are many common denominators in all people. The same emotions are felt by all. There are needs that are universal. I found as I traveled that there are more similarities than there are differences in the human race. And I found ignorance in every culture; ignorance and intolerance. Sadly, those have not changed through the centuries.

I found all men have courage and determination. All beings have a need for companionship. These things remain true regardless of time or place. And I found that I too have need of companionship, I too have need of love.

The past brings us to this moment. I am here with you because I willed it. For centuries I lived isolated from all creation and I thrived. I studied. I traveled. I was free. And even though I found some sort of other worldly peace, I began to crave communication, real discourse. I craved relating to a human, speaking with a human voice to answer human questions. I craved touch. I felt neither the thirst nor the hunger as I was without a vampire body to nourish. It was a yearning deeper than either of those two. A desire for companionship that was greater even than the desire to possess a human body, a longing connected to the essence of every being, animal, man or vampire.

I searched all the great documents to find answers to questions of the soul. Does it end? Where does it go? Was there an end to my Elizabeth or did her spirit somehow continue. Through my search, I came to believe there is no end. The substance of a person is captured time and again in one embodiment after another. One life after another. One century after another.

So I sought my beloved. Time and again I thought I found my Elizabeth. Then I would discern that I was mistaken. My search was never ending. At long last, I found you. For months I hovered near you, bodiless, without a voice to speak. I determined to find a way to communicate, to declare myself. My essence cannot invade a living human though in my resolution I tried and failed many times. So, I waited, praying to find a way to make myself known.

Your work with the human mind, the conscious and the subconscious, intrigued me. I believed it could be an avenue to express my presence. I tried innumerable times to reach you through your hypnotic patients but I was unable to find a way to control their thoughts. Then came Carlos. His conscious mind slept so deeply, his subconscious so confused by his past use of opiates, it was with ease I utilized his voice for my words. I was able to introduce you to my world.

In the beginning, I was tormented that you would fear me and I know you did. But, after a time, as you began to understand me, I could feel you reach out to me, to anticipate our time together. I no longer felt adrift and without companionship. Alone and without hope. I had you.

And it is through you Sarah, that my need is fulfilled. You see, my beloved, you are my Elizabeth reborn. Alive here and now. You are my companion, my chosen companion for all eternity. And with that thought as the last of our meeting, I leave you. Farewell, Sarah."

#

"I said I don't feel like discussing the session. I just don't see any reason to hash over the vamp's story again. Besides, what's the crap about you being some dead broad from the sixteenth century?"

"I don't know what he meant about Elizabeth, but it appears the story has ended, Carlos. We are now here in present time. Where else can it go?"

"I don't want to think about it." He stood. "I'm finished for the day."

"We may be finished with Aris but we have a lot more to learn about you." She moved to his side. "Come on, I'll walk you to the elevator.

CHAPTER 36

The evening breeze coming from the open patio door was still warm but it carried the fragrance of autumn. Sarah curled in the corner of her sofa comfortable in her pajamas. The sun was setting earlier each day and stars were already visible in the twilight sky.

Her unread book lay by her side as she stared at the surrounding buildings. Her mind was full of the same questions and some very powerful new ones. What if Aris never returned to a session? Whatever could he mean, she was "his Elizabeth?" What would happen to her relationship with Carlos?

She had no answers to the puzzles. Standing, she crossed the room to step onto the patio. Leaning on the rail, she searched out the brightest star. Smiling, she repeated the old poem, "Star bright, star light." Still, she wasn't sure just what it was she should wish.

\#

Bonnie took her friend by the arm and led her off the sidewalk into the vestibule of a bistro that wasn't standing room only. "Let's have lunch, okay?"

"Sounds good to me." Sarah was tired and not just a little bit hungry. The smells of the restaurant made her stomach growl. She was glad they didn't have to wait for a table.

The two women listened respectfully to the specials then turned to the menus. They chose their lunches, ordered, then settled back to chat.

"Colleen is acting a little remote lately. Have you noticed anything strange about her?" Bonnie questioned, sipping her wine as she waited for her friend to answer.

"I can't say I have. What do you mean, Bon?"

"I don't know exactly. She just seems different. I know she's happy with Bob but there seems to be something on her mind that she doesn't want to talk about."

The waiter placed their lunches on the table then filled their water glasses.

"But maybe I'm just imagining things. Everybody is so busy lately, it's hard to find time to really sit down and talk. Maybe that's what I'm feeling, just no quality time with her."

"I know. This is the first opportunity we've had to get together and she couldn't make it. I'm sorry she isn't here now. It's been so long since we've had any girl time."

"So, let's not waste this." She took a bite of her pasta, chewed, then spoke. "So, anything happening in your love life?"

"Not a thing," Sarah shook her head. "Not a damned thing."

"Except in my dreams," she thought.

#

CARLOS HAVARRO, session 25, October 1

#

"Wonder why the vamp didn't show today. This is the first time since he came on the scene that he didn't show."

"I honestly don't know, Carlos. I can't figure it out."

"Maybe the story is finished."

"Yes, maybe the story is over." She sat silently, staring out the window.

#

CARLOS HAVARRO, session 26, October 8

#

"No more vamp, huh?"

"It appears that's the case, Carlos."

"Okay, let's go get some coffee. I think we're finished here." He stood and moved toward his jacket draped on the chair by the door.

"Don't you want to have a session anyway, Aris or not?"

"Sarah, the vamp has nothing to do with me. He never did. It was just some sort of crazy story from somewhere in my subconscious mind. That's what you said, right? I'm calmer now. I have you in my life and that is the best thing that's happened to me so far. I have a job. I'm off drugs and booze. It seems my life is on track for the first time and I don't see any reason to keep doing this client/therapist thing any longer.

"You said as long as I was your client, we couldn't go any further in our personal life. Well, I am telling you I am no longer your client. I am now just Carlos Havarro, your friend and admirer. So, what do you say, want to go for some coffee?"

Sarah decided not to argue with him. She sighed, "Alright, let's go." She would let him win the battle but the war was far from over. She felt she might never meet with Aris again but she knew that Carlos still had the need for the regularity of his sessions with her. She was determined not to let him struggle with his new life without the help of therapy. She put thoughts of Aris from her mind, ignoring the empty feeling she had in her chest as she locked the door behind her.

#

The drive back to the city was uneventful. Sunday evening was a quiet time for traffic. Sarah was happy and content. She had a wonderful day with her family and looked forward to the party Colleen and her husband were having later in the evening. She finally noticed the changes to her friend Bonnie mentioned at lunch. From the way her best friend had been looking and acting, Sarah thought there might be a happy announcement this evening. She hoped it was so.

As she drove, her mind drifted to the story of Anne Boleyn and King Henry. Sarah had never been interested in history except in relationship to her work involving past life regressions, but now, it all had a new meaning. She wondered about Aris. What had he looked like? Was he tall? Was he handsome? To be chosen by Alexander, he must have been beautiful. And why was her mind full of him even after his disappearance? It seemed she thought of him most of the time. Her other clients had become only cases to fill the spaces between her conversations with him. Now, he was no more. There were times when she wasn't able to differentiate between he and Carlos, when she melded them into one being, one person, one human.

"This is ridiculous." Her frustration with herself showed in her angry whisper as she parked her car in front of her friend's house. Cars lined the curb and music could be heard even outside the house. The door was unlocked and as she entered the room, Elvis belted a song on the CD player.

Bob was carrying a tray of drinks when she walked in and he moved to her side to kiss her cheek. "Glad you're here, kiddo. Have a drink."

Sarah laughed, "Sounds good."

He held the tray in front of her and she reached out to take a glass of the bubbling champagne. He winked at her as he walked away.

"Sarah." She heard her name. She turned to face Carlos. "I thought you'd never get here."

"Hi." Placing his hand on the bend of her elbow, he ushered her into the party.

"I want to say hi to Colleen." She eased her arm from his grasp.

"She's probably in the kitchen." As she made her way across the crowded living room, she enjoyed the sounds of friends chatting and laughing.

She peeked her head around the door only to find her friend standing stock still in the middle of the kitchen, a spatula in her hand, a far off look in her eyes. "Colleen, what is it? What's the matter?"

Colleen burst into tears. "Nothing is the matter. I'm just so happy I could explode. I heard from the doctor yesterday and I'm going to have a baby."

Sarah hugged her and kissed her cheek. "I'm so happy for you. Did you tell Bob?"

"I wanted to wait until today but I just couldn't. I told him last night and Sarah, he cried. I would never have thought a big, tough lout like Bob would shed a tear, but he cried." She was laughing as Sarah wiped the tears from her friend's cheek with a napkin she found on the cutting board.

"Well, little momma, you've got mascara all over you right now. Go fix your face." Taking the spatula from her hand, she spun her friend toward the door. "Go on. I'll man the kitchen for now."

The microwave beeped. She turned to open the door to remove the little hot dogs wrapped in pastry. She placed them methodically, one by one, on a serving dish. Hearing the sound of the door behind her, she turned quickly, expecting to see Colleen, clean faced and ready to reclaim the kitchen. She was not surprised though to see Carlos.

He looked strange as he crossed to stand just in front of her. "What's the matter?"

"There is nothing that is the matter now." His voice was deep, unlike his own.

She gasped and dropped the plate. "Aris?"

He nodded.

"But how, how?"

"How is not important, this is." He wrapped his arm around her waist. Bending to kiss her, his lips neared hers. Her heart raced. Was she mad? Was this possible? Then there was no thought, just the feel of his warm mouth on hers, the scent of his sweet breath, the feel of his arms around her.

"Whoa!" The sound of Colleen's voice brought her back to her senses. She pushed him gently from her, quickly bending to pick up the broken pieces of the plate and the ruined little hot dogs. "Sorry I barged in like that." She sounded embarrassed and tickled at her intrusion.

"It's fine." Sarah kept her head down so her red cheeks were visible only to the floor. "It's fine."

"Yeah," Carlos stooped to help her, "its fine. Not a problem, just a little friendly welcome smooch."

And that was how Sarah found Aris had not gone forever, that he still lived and breathed within this young man who had just taken her breath away with a kiss.

#

She hadn't slept very well the previous night and she was already on her second cup of coffee. She yawned loudly as she reached for her phone.

"Sarah, there's a woman on your line. She says she's a friend of Carlos but she won't tell me her name." Maggie's voice had an edge to it. "What should I do with her?"

"Put her through."

#

She knew she had to get away from her office, from thoughts of the strange phone call she received that morning. She said goodbye to Maggie and headed for her car. Sarah was grateful that the receptionist at the hair salon was able to fit her in among her hairdresser's already scheduled clients of the day.

The sound of the scissors and the feel of Nina's hands shaping Sarah's hair made her feel more calm, almost relaxed. The buzzing of the salon was comforting. She chose the sisterhood of the salon hands down over the gym as a place to hide out. She needed some time to think.

Her eyes closed as the blow dryer puffed warm air onto her forehead. The wonderful tingling feel of the hairbrush against her scalp was familiar, reassuring.

Inside the steady hum of the blow dryer, she remembered the feminine accented voice on the telephone warning her that Manu meant business. She said she didn't want to see Carlos get in any more trouble. Her Latino accent was thick as she told Sarah Manu would kill her or Carlos without a second thought to keep Carlos from giving evidence against him.

"Who are you?" Her only answer was a dial tone.

She phoned both Colleen and Bob. Neither one of them was available. She waited impatiently to hear from them.

She leaned back in the chair. It took all her effort but she was able to move her focus to the music in the background, the sound of the dryer and Nina humming along with both.

#

Reluctantly she returned to her office for her four-thirty appointment. It was an easy session and when she was finished with her client, she walked her to the door and said goodbye just as her phone rang. Reaching across the desk, she snatched it from the cradle before it stopped ringing.

"Sarah?" Bob's voice was excited as he spoke. "We just picked up Manu."

She sat down. A welcome sense of calm settled over her at his words. "What happened?"

We found evidence that he was involved in a drive by, pretty strong evidence, so we picked him up. He had a gun in his car and it's the gun that was used."

"What's next?"

"He says it's not his, of course. He said he found it. There are no prints on it and it's not registered but we're working on it. Sarah, I need you to help me find Carlos. Manu is using him as an alibi on the night of the shooting."

"Bob. I don't know where he is any more than you do. Have you tried the half-way house or his job?"

"I checked both places. He hasn't been around the house and he took a week off work. I've got to find him. We need someone who will tell the truth about this guy or we have to let him go."

The office was silent. "I'll try to find him but you realize the position this will put him and his family in, don't you? It isn't just Manu, it's his whole gang."

"Sarah, we need help with this from someone who has been involved and no one else is going to witness."

"Bob, I said I'd talk to him and I will. I've got to go."

"Are we seeing you on Saturday for dinner?"

"Yeah, I'll be there." They said their goodbyes and she returned the phone to its cradle.

She spun her chair to face the window and for the first time, she found no solace in the city. Her thoughts skimmed the last few months of her life. So many changes, so much drama. Part of her longed for the calm, quiet of her existence before Carlos entered it, yet she also knew a perverse excitement at the life she now shared with him.

She sat staring out the window until heavy clouds moved in and covered the sun.

#

"I thought Saturday would never get here." Colleen slid open her kitchen window to let out the heat from the oven. "This whole week was one big blur." She chopped vegetables for the salad while Sarah sat in one of the tall chairs on the opposite side of the breakfast bar. "So what's up with Carlos? How did you find him? What did he say?"

"He said he'd think about it. He said he'd call me soon. It's not just about him, Colleen; it's about his whole family. He's worried about what they might do to his brother."

"It's a hard situation but Manu used Carlos for an alibi. Manu's prints weren't on the gun. We can't prove it's his. Without Carlos, we're going to lose and the scum will walk." She tossed the salad then placed the utensils in the sink. "Sarah, I hate to tell you this, but they had to let him go. He made bail and until Carlos tells the truth, he's walking around outside again."

Sarah stood and paced the floor. "That's bad news, really bad news."

#

The ringing of the phone roused her from a restless sleep. She sat up, snatching it from its cradle.

"Sarah?" Colleen spoke with a measured calm. "Sarah, I need you to wake up." She waited for an answer.

"Colleen, I am awake. What is it?" Her heart was racing as she reached to turn on the light. "What's going on?"

"Carlos has been shot."

"How bad is it?" She had to remind herself to breathe as she stood. She hit the speaker button on the phone. "Where is he?" She grabbed her jeans from the chair next to her bed.

"It's pretty bad. We're at St. John's Hospital." Her voice broke as she continued, "you'd better get here right away."

"I'm on my way." Sarah fought panic as she finished dressing then hurried to the parking garage. She glanced at her watch. It was just past three in the morning and she was grateful there wouldn't be much traffic at that hour

As she opened her car door, a sob tore from her throat. He

couldn't be that bad, he couldn't die. He could not die.

\#

Colleen was pacing the floor of the lobby when Sarah stepped through the automatic door.

"How is he?" Sarah gripped her friend's arm.

"He's out of surgery." Colleen evaded Sarah's eyes as she guided her to the elevator.

"Colleen," she stopped walking. "Tell me the truth. How is he?"

Tears poured down the parole officer's cheeks. "Honey, they don't think he's going to make it." Her shoulders shook in silent sobs.

Sarah stepped inside as the elevator doors opened. They rode up the three floors without speaking. When the doors opened again, Colleen took her hand as they hurried down the hall.

"He's awake but he's really groggy. He's loaded with pain meds. His insides were pretty torn up." A nurse left the room as they entered.

His eyes were closed and his breathing was labored as she stood silently at the foot of his bed. "Carlos?"

At the sound of her voice, he turned to look at her. He was deathly pale, his golden beauty torn from him. His belly was wrapped in bandages and tubes were in his arms and nose. He looked like a frightened injured boy as he lay in the hospital bed.

"Sarah?" He smiled a slow, drugged smile at her.

She went to him, carefully taking his hand in hers. "I'm here and I'm staying here with you until you're well."

He tried to laugh but it sounded like a gurgle. She fought tears, forcing a smile.

Even through the medication, he grimaced in pain. "I give up. I'm through fighting. It's all been just too much of a battle."

"You can't give up. Your life is worth the fight."

"I'm not going to get well." His voice was soft and the words were slow in coming. "It's going to be over soon, I can feel it." His eyes closed and he willed them to open so he could see her.

"No, no, you can't think that way."

"Sarah, this is the only way out for me and for my family and to keep you safe. I'm going to take it."

She was silent, unable to speak without crying.

He tried to talk but his voice was so low, she had to lean her ear close to his mouth. He struggled to make himself heard. "Now, maybe you will let me tell you how much I love you. How grateful I am. You are the first good thing that ever came into my life."

"Carlos, please." She bit her lip to help hold back her sobs.

He grimaced as another wave of pain swept through him. "Sarah, will you hypnotize me one last time? Count backwards for me . . ."

A nurse and doctor hurried into the room. The doctor lifted his patients closed eyelids then released them. They looked at the displays of the machines that surrounded him and hopelessly shook their heads at her.

"Yes." And she began the familiar induction. As she counted backwards, taking him into a final calm and peaceful state, all of the sounds of the life-monitoring equipment in the room ceased.

"No. No. No." She shook her head as sobs tore from her throat. Colleen gathered her into her arms to comfort her. The nurse moved to draw the sheet over him when suddenly the heart monitor began to beep, softly, slowly at first, then growing stronger with every electronic sound.

Everyone in the room stood still, unable to move, unable to believe their ears. The doctor moved to the bedside.

"He's breathing. His heart beat is getting stronger." He turned to face her, an incredulous look in his eyes. "I don't know what just happened but if this miracle continues, he just might have a chance."

Sarah sank down into the chair by the bed and cried thankful tears of hope.

CHAPTER 37

She was awakened by a soft groan. Disoriented for a moment, she glanced around the room. Carlos was awake, watching her. He smiled as she stood to move closer to him. She reached to take his hand in hers.

"Sarah, my Sarah, I touch you at last."

She gasped. She dropped his hand.

"Aris?" she whispered.

He didn't answer. He didn't have to. Her eyes closed as she moaned, sliding to the floor in a cold faint.

"Sarah." He raised himself from the pillows and pressed the button to summon the nurse.

#

The nurse stood by as the doctor checked his pupils and his vital signs. "This is uncanny. I don't understand it." He opened the dressings that circled the abdomen of the injured man. He stopped, unable to move or speak.

"Doctor, what is it?" Sarah stepped closer to the bed.

"This man's wounds are healing, rapidly." He whispered the words in disbelief. "What happened here?" He turned to the nurse. "Get him to radiology immediately."

#

Bob and Colleen sat on either side of her as they waited for Carlos to return. The stunned doctor had no explanation for the smooth, wound free abdomen of the man who, the night before, had a bullet hole in him.

"Don't worry, Sarah. We'll get him. I know Manu is the bastard who orchestrated the shooting."

"But he didn't die. I thought he was dead, but he didn't die." She rested her elbows on the cafeteria table and leaned her forehead into the palms of her hands. "He was dead, I know he was dead." She refused to accept the only conclusion that was obvious to her. Aris. Somehow Aris had entered the dying body, taken possession of it. It could not be and yet, what else?

"Honey," Colleen wrapped her arm around her friend's shoulder. "You're in shock. It's okay. Everything is okay." She brushed Sarah's hair from her face, lifting her chin to check her pupils. Her eyes were glassy from lack of sleep, dilated even though the lights in the cafeteria were bright. "You're in shock, we're all in shock. They obviously made a mistake about the severity of his wounds."

Even as she spoke, Colleen knew he should be dead this morning. Her eyes met the eyes of her husband. Neither had an explanation for the miraculous healing of the dying man, yet both were grateful for his life. Both were grateful he would recover.

Sarah spoke quietly. "Please, let's go back to his room. I want to be there when he wakes up." They rose, pushing their chairs under the long table and the three friends left the room together.

#

"We've got him for attempted murder and this time, it's going to stick. Carlos just left the office and he's going to testify." Bob smiled as he gave his friend the news.

"I'm glad that animal is off the street, but I can't help worrying about Carlos." Sarah switched the phone receiver to her left hand, picked up her pen with her right and began to doodle infinity signs on the yellow pad that rested on her desk.

"Strange, but he doesn't seem the least bit afraid. Almost dying has made him so different but I suppose it would do that to anyone. He even walks differently and his mannerisms have altered. Have you noticed?"

Sarah paused before she answered. Had she noticed? Of course she did but she chose to ignore it. She had seen him only once since his release from the hospital and only in Colleen's office. He was avoiding her and she was almost glad. She was frightened that being in his presence would verify her theory. "I really haven't seen him much, Bob, but a near death experience and a miracle healing would change anyone, wouldn't it."

He chuckled. "I guess you're right. He's a good guy and it seems he has a second chance to act on it." She heard him sigh into the receiver. "I'll never understand it though."

"I don't think anyone will. The doctor's didn't believe their own eyes but he's walking around, alive and well, thank God."

"Are you doing okay now?" His voice softened as he questioned her. He and Colleen had been worried about her. She, too, appeared different after their hospital experience. She seemed withdrawn from the world. She hadn't accepted any of their dinner invitations of the last few weeks.

"Yes, I'm fine." She didn't want a conversation about her emotional state; she wasn't even sure what it was at the moment. "Just fine. Things are settling back into their normal routine. But thanks for asking."

"Hey, how about dinner with us on Friday?"

"I'll get back to you on that if that's okay."

"Sure." He silently questioned her being 'fine' but accepted her answer. "Sure, just let us know."

"Bob, I've got a client coming in a few minutes. Thanks for keeping me updated."

They said their goodbyes. She sat quietly. Thoughts of Aris filled her mind. Refusing to accept them, she stood, crossed to the door and opened it.

"Maggie, let's go to lunch."

#

The sound of men snoring echoed through the concrete cell block. Carlos entered unseen and unheard, his newly acquired otherworldly powers silencing the minds and closing the eyes of any who might have stopped him. He made his way down the long corridor until he reached his destination. Gazing at the sleeping man behind the bars, he smiled.

"Manu." His voice was clear yet soft spoken so as not to wake those sleeping around him. "Manu."

Sleepy eyed, the man inside the cell swung his legs over the side of the cot and sat up. In the dim light of night, he didn't recognize the figure outside the bars. Suddenly his eyes grew wide as he made out the features of his visitor. He leaped to his feet as if to move toward the bars, then held back. "Carlos?"

"Yes, Manu, it's Carlos."

The prisoner's eyes darted furtively from side to side. "What are you doing here, man? I thought you were, I mean, how'd you get in here?"

"I found a way in and I'm going to get you out of here for good."

A smile spread over the convict's face. "Yeah?" He moved slowly toward the wall made of bars that separated the two men. "Brothers to the end." He stopped inches away from the bars peering through at his would be savior.

"Brothers to the end." Carlos grinned. Just as their eyes locked, his arm darted between the bars, his fingers locking around Manu's throat. Manu struggled for only a moment, then hung limply from the hand of his killer. "And this, my brother, is the end."

He laughed softly as he tossed the dead man on the floor. Turning, he walked away.

#

"I honestly don't know how it happened." The three friends sat around the dinner table as Bob refreshed Sarah's glass of wine. "It's uncanny. They found him dead in his cell with his neck broken. There's no explanation for it. No one heard or saw anything. At least that's what they're all saying.

"The same night, Manu's two seconds in command were found dead, side by side, next to a dumpster in back of a bar. Same thing, both with broken necks. It must have scared the gang because they're all scattered. We can't find any of them."

Sarah shivered, "I can't say I'm sorry. At least now Carlos and his family are safe."

"Yeah, well, at first we thought someone in prison got to Manu and maybe that's how it went down. But, the two outside? It couldn't have been the same person. Weird, in all three cases, there was no sign of struggle. It's as if someone just walked up to them, said hello and snapped their necks. It's the damnedest thing."

Colleen began to clear the table. "Carlos came into the office yesterday. He didn't seem too surprised, but he's been acting removed from everything ever since he got out of the hospital. He didn't even mention you, Sarah, and that's pretty strange."

Sarah avoided her friend's eyes as she stood to help with the clean-up. "I've only heard from him once, but he's been through more than any human should go through. I'm sure he just needs time to adjust to his new life.

#

Her last thought as she fell asleep was of Carlos. His avoidance of her only made her more sure of her theory. The single time he had seen her since his release from the hospital had been unfulfilling. He wouldn't meet her eyes. He hadn't been friendly to either

Colleen or to her, just answering the questions that needed to be answered to maintain his parole. Would they ever be able to speak openly with one another again? She wasn't sure it was possible. With her mind full of turmoil, she fell into a troubled sleep.

Just before dawn, a shadow covered the window to her bedroom. The screen was lifted silently and placed on the floor beneath the casing as the figure climbed soundlessly into her room. He moved to stand next to her bed. As he watched her, she stirred softly, then settled beneath the covers into a deep and timeless sleep. He had been by her bed every night for months. He had watched her sleep, invaded her dreams, longed for her so deeply he could barely control his desire. He licked his soft, full lips and moaned. At long last, he had found his beloved, but would she want to be his?

THE END